first

Kiss

WITHDRAWN WITHDRAWN

GRACE
BURROWES

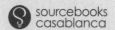

sourcebooks
casablanca

Published by Sourcebooks Casablanca, an imprint of Sourcebooks, Inc.
P.O. Box 4410, Naperville, Illinois 60567-4410
(630) 961-3900
Fax: (630) 961-2168
www.sourcebooks.com

Printed and bound in Canada.
MBP 10 9 8 7 6 5 4 3 2 1

To Karoline Louise Miller Rossi, who taught me how to play the piano, and so much more.

Chapter 1

A YEAR IN DIVORCE PURGATORY HAD TAUGHT VERA Waltham two lessons.

First lesson: when her ex acted like an idiot, she was allowed to be angry—she was getting good at it, in fact.

Second lesson: Vera could rely, absolutely and without hesitation, on her attorney's word. If Trent Knightley said somebody would soon be on her doorstep with a copy of the restraining order, that somebody was already headed her way.

Vera's emergency automotive repair service was a shakier bet.

"Ma'am, if this is the number where you can be reached," the dispatcher said, "we'll call you call you back when we've located a mechanic in your immediate area."

"In my immediate area," Vera replied, "you'll find cows, chickens, and the occasional fat groundhog. The truck is sitting in my garage."

"Then this isn't a *roadside* emergency?" The dispatcher clearly had raised small children, for she'd hit the balance between dismay and shaming smack on the nose.

"I'm stranded without wheels, nothing but open fields, bad weather, and my lawyer's phone number to comfort me. Please get somebody out to fix that tire, ASAP."

Vera was stranded in her own toasty kitchen, but what if Twy came home from school with a sore throat? Long walk to the urgent care in freezing temperatures, that's what, because bucolic Damson County boasted no rural taxi service.

"We'll do the best we can, ma'am. Please stay near your phone until a mechanic calls you back."

"Thanks. I'll do that."

The line went dead, which meant the next step was locating the truck's owner's manual. Vera was still nose down in a description of something called the spare brace assembly when wheels crunched on the crushed gravel of her driveway.

An SUV pulled up at the foot of her steps, and a man in a sheepskin jacket and cowboy hat got out.

Could be a mechanic. He was broad-shouldered, he drove a motorhead's sort of vehicle, and he wasn't wearing gloves.

A pianist noticed hands. His were holding a signature Hartman and Whitney navy blue folder. When he rapped on Vera's door, she undid all three dead bolts and opened it.

Not Trent Knightley, but a close resemblance suggested Vera beheld one of the brothers with whom he shared a law practice. Same blue, blue eyes; same lean, muscular height; same wavy hair, though this guy was blond rather than brunette.

"Hello," she said, opening the door wider. "You're either from Hartman and Whitney, or you're the best dressed truck mechanic I've ever seen."

"James Knightley. Pleased to meet you." He stepped over the threshold, removed his hat, and hung it on the brass coatrack. "Trent asked me to bring you a copy of a restraining order. He said it was urgent."

"My thanks, Mr. Knightley." Vera closed the door

behind him and shot the dead bolts, then extended her hand in anticipation of gaining possession of a copy of the court order.

Instead, Vera's hand was enveloped by a big male paw, one graced with calluses she would not have expected to find on a lawyer.

James Knightley had manners—also warm hands. When he'd tended to the civilities—firm grip, not out to prove anything—he passed her the blue folder.

Vera flipped it open, needing to see with her own eyes that he'd brought her the right court order.

"Was there a reason to get it certified?" she asked.

"The courthouse was on my way here. If you needed a certified copy, then nothing less would do."

Consideration and an eye for details were delightful qualities in any man.

As were warm hands and a mellow baritone voice.

"May I offer you a cup of tea, some hot chocolate? It's cold out, and this errand has brought you several miles from town." Vera offered out of basic good manners, but also because anger eventually burned itself out, while a front tire on her only serviceable vehicle was still slashed, and the intricacies of the spare brace assembly thingy had yet to reveal themselves to her.

Then too, James Knightley had something of his brother's reassuring air. Maybe lawyers took classes in how to be reassuring, the way a pianist took a master class in Brahms or Rachmaninoff.

As he unbuttoned his jacket, James glanced around at the foyer's twelve-foot ceilings, the crown molding, the beveled glass in the windows on either side of the foyer. Vera had the sense he did this not with a mercenary eye—not pricing property in anticipation of litigation—but rather with the slow, thorough appraisal of the craftsman. Pine dowels in the cross beam, handmade stained glass insets for the oriel window—he inspected these, the way Vera had to stop and listen for a moment to any piano playing in any venue, however faintly.

"A cup of hot chocolate would hit the spot," he said, shrugging out of his jacket. "Trent said you had a lovely old house, and he did not lie."

That smile.

Good heavens, that smile. Trent Knightley was tall, dark, and handsome, a charming and very intelligent man whom Vera had happily flaunted in Donal's face, but this James...

He left a subtly more masculine impression. Donal would hate him on sight.

James's gaze held a warmth Trent's had lacked, at least when aimed at Vera. His smile reached his eyes, eyes a peculiarly dark shade of blue fringed with long lashes.

Vera had no business admiring a man's eyelashes, for the love of St. Peter. Or his hands, or his voice.

"To the kitchen, then," she said, leading James through the music room and into the back of the house. "My favorite room in the house."

"I'd guess this place predates the Civil War. Did you have a lot of work done?"

"I intend to raise my daughter here, so I had the house fitted out exactly as I wanted it." Right down to the security system, which had done her absolutely no good earlier that very afternoon.

"I have a renovated farmhouse of my own," James said. "Every night when I tool up my driveway, and she's sitting under the oaks waiting for me in all her drafty splendor, I am glad to call her mine."

A poet lawyer, who composed odes to his farmhouse. Different, indeed.

"But we're not so glad to pay the heating bills," Vera said as they reached the kitchen. The room was blessedly cozy because of the pellet stove sitting in one corner of the fireplace.

"Good Lord, this must be original." James ran a hand over the gray fieldstones of the hearth. "Five feet square at least, and these look like genuine buggy axles."

He fingered the pot swings on either side of the enormous fireplace, then draped his jacket over the back of a chair.

"I don't know what they are," Vera said. "An old Mennonite gentleman came to point and parge, and he ended up doing a great deal more than that. I love that fireplace, but I also love the exposed chestnut logs and the flagstone floor. This time of year, I wear two pairs of wool socks twenty-four-seven. Have a seat."

James wandered around the kitchen a while longer, a man who apparently enjoyed touching things—the mantel, the cabinets, the marble counters, the drawer pulls of the antique breakfront that stored her mother's china. He caressed wood and stone as if he'd coax secrets from Vera's counters and chimney, while she wondered where he'd acquired his calluses.

"Whipped cream, Mr. Knightley?"

"Please, and a little nutmeg, if you have it."

"A connoisseur." And lo, lurking next to the oregano in Vera's spice rack was a canister of nutmeg, probably leftover from holiday baking. A connoisseur would appreciate fresh, homemade cookies, so she got down her cookie tin and peered inside. "We're in luck. My daughter has left us a few cookies."

Half a batch of homemade chocolate-chip pecan turtles remained, and they'd be scrumptious with hot chocolate.

"Don't bother putting them on a plate," James said. "I can dip into the tin, same as any other civilian. How long have you lived here?"

He could probably finish the rest of the batch without gaining an ounce, too, and keep up the small talk the entire time.

Which was…charming? A lifetime spent in practice rooms and concert halls didn't equip a woman with a ready ability to analyze men.

Sobering thought.

"I moved here with my daughter a little over a year ago," Vera said, putting a plain white mug of whole milk into the microwave. "Twyla will get off the school bus in about fifteen minutes, and if I'm going to walk to the foot of the lane, I'd better not linger over my hot chocolate."

A bit rude, offering the man a drink one minute and hustling him along the next. Anger could leave a woman that rattled, but Vera's guest didn't seem offended.

"Your lane has to be half a mile long," James said, "and it's not quite thirty degrees out with a mighty brisk breeze. Are you sure you want to walk that distance?"

"I'm sure I do not," she said, giving his hot chocolate a final stir. "But somebody has broken into my garage. Today, I don't expect an eight-year-old to trudge that distance by herself." Though Twyla did, on the days when her mother wasn't feeling paranoid.

Angry, not paranoid. Rattled, anyway.

And mildly charmed.

Something in James's expression changed, became more focused. "Your garage was broken into? You mentioned a mechanic."

"One of my tires is flat," Vera replied. "I've called the road service, but I'm off the beaten path, and finding somebody to put on the spare will take a while. I'm pretty sure I can figure it out. I've changed a tire or two."

Half a lifetime ago, on a vintage Bug, while one of her brothers had alternately coached her and laughed uproariously.

Now would be a good time for a guy with broad shoulders and competent hands to tell her that tires went flat for no reason all the time. Even brand-new tires that had cost a bundle to have put on and balanced.

When Vera had squirted whipped cream onto James's hot chocolate, he appropriated the nutmeg from her and did the honors, then spun the lazy Susan that held her spices and added a dash of cinnamon.

They worked in the same assembly line fashion on Vera's drink, the spices contributing a soothing note to the kitchen fragrances.

"Ladies first," James said, saluting with his mug.

Because James looked like he'd wait all winter, Vera took a sip of her hot chocolate.

Rich, interesting, sweet, and nourishing—an altogether lovely concoction in the middle of a dreadful day. A small increment of Vera's upset slid away, or at least from her immediate grasp.

"Your vehicle was vandalized while your car sat in a garage that I'll presume you keep locked," James said, staring at his mug. "You suspect your ex is behind this?"

Lawyers, even hot chocolate–swilling lawyers with interesting blue eyes, were good at putting together facts.

Right now, that was a helpful quality.

"I'm fairly certain my ex is carrying a grudge," Vera said, "and fairly certain he stole my copy of the restraining order. Without it, if I call the cops, they might show up, but they won't do anything if they find Donal here. If I can wave the order at them, they might lock him up."

James helped himself to a paper towel and passed one to Vera, folding his up to use as a coaster on her butcher-block counter. He wasn't shy about sharing personal space, and he smelled good—piney, outdoorsy, and—best of all—not like Donal.

"Domestic relations law hasn't been my area for several years," he said, "but I think you have the gist of it. If you like, I can reach Trent on his cell and verify that."

"Please don't. I already feel like a ninny for calling him. He's newly married, isn't he?"

"Very, and he chose well this time."

James's tone suggested the first Mrs. Knightley had not enjoyed her brother-in-law's wholehearted approval, though her successor apparently did.

"I chose reasonably well the first time," Vera said, "not so well on the rebound."

"Whereas I have yet to choose. You make a mean hot chocolate, Mrs. Waltham." James touched his mug to Vera's, probably signaling an end to the self-disclosure session.

"Call me Vera, and have some cookies."

He took a bite of cookie, catching the crumbs in his hand. "What time did you say the bus came?"

"Any minute. Why?"

He put a set of keys on the counter. "We can take my car."

"That's not necessary." In truth, as charming as he was, as handsome as he was, the idea of getting into a vehicle with James left Vera uneasy. Donal was handsome and occasionally gruffly charming. He could also be a damned conniving snake with a bad temper.

"You take the car then." James slid the keys toward her. "It's colder than a well digger's…boots out there, and I have a niece who's seven—a pair of them, actually. This isn't weather a lady should have to face alone at the end of a long day."

Twyla bounced up the lane on colder days than this, and James had to know that—the Knightley family was local, after all. He'd passed Vera his keys for another reason, one having to do with her near panic at having no wheels, and ladies facing bad weather all on their own.

"I can put your spare on, and you can wait for the bus," he said, while the keys sat three inches from Vera's hand.

Until fifteen months ago, Vera had never lived on her own, ever. She'd given up leaning on a man, and so far, the results had been wonderful—when they weren't scary.

"I can't let you do that, James. It's too much trouble."

"It's no trouble at all to a guy who was tearing down engines from little up. I like the smell of axle grease, and I haven't had homemade cookies since I don't know when. Scat," he said, taking her hand and slapping the keys into her palm. "If you leave now, you can have the seats nice and toasty by the time your daughter gets off the bus."

He brought his mug to the sink and rinsed it out, leaving it in the drain rack. The line of his back was long and lean in the vest of what looked like a very expensive three-piece suit.

What was Vera *doing*, ogling the man's back?

James Knightley washed his dishes, and for some reason, that reassured Vera he could be trusted to change a tire. Even so, she had to wonder what Trent Knightley had told his brother of her divorce. Attorney-client privilege was one thing, but James was both brother and law partner to Trent.

Men gossiped. Alexander had assured her they gossiped as much as women did, and Vera's first husband had not lied to her…all that often.

"The garage is this way," she said, leaving her hot chocolate unfinished. "You can take the cookies with you."

"They're good." James took one more and set the tin back up on top of the fridge with the casual ease of a tall man. "Trent recalls your cookies fondly."

Not a hint of innuendo in that line—not that innuendo would have been welcome.

"I'll drop a batch off the next time I'm in town," Vera said, turning on the garage lights. "Call it a wedding present. I think the temperature has fallen as the day has gone on."

"We're supposed to get a dump of snow later this week and—Vera Waltham, I am in love. You own a 1964 Ford Falcon, and this blue is probably the original paint color. My, my, my. Does she run?"

Cars and houses were female to James Knightley. Would he also consider pianos female?

"Not at the moment. The Faithful Falcon needs a

battery, among other things, but some fine day, I want to see my daughter behind that wheel. The car belonged to Alexander's grandmother, and he wanted Twyla to have it."

James left off perusing the old car and scowled at Vera's other vehicle, a late-model bright red Tundra, listing slightly.

"That's why nobody wants to come change your tire."

"What's why?"

"These pickups have the spare up under the bed," he said, opening the truck's driver's side door.

His movements and his voice were brisk, all male-in-anticipation-of-using-tools-and-getting-his-hands-dirty. "The mechanism for holding the spare in its brace always gets rusted, and to get the tire down, you have to thread this puppy here"—he rummaged under her backseat—"through a little doodad over the tag, and into a slot about"—he emerged holding the jack and a long metal rod—"the size of a pea, and then get it to work, despite the corrosion. I love me a sturdy truck, but the design of the spare brace assembly leaves something to be desired. Why are you looking at me like that?"

Like Vera had heard no sweeter music that day than a man recounting the pleasures of intimate association with a truck? James cradled the jack assembly the way some violinists held their concert instruments.

"You reminded me of my oldest brother," she said. "I forget not all men are like Donal."

Some men dropped their afternoon plans, took time to get a court order certified, minded their manners, and rinsed out their dishes. Some men changed tires without being asked. Vera would never be in love again—Olga had an entire lecture about the pitfalls of romantic attraction—but Vera could appreciate a nice guy when one came to her door.

"I couldn't stop you from changing that tire if I tried, could I?"

"No. You could not. Trucks and I go way back, and I don't like this Donal character very much." James's gold cuff links had gone into a pocket, and he was already turning back his sleeves. "Don't you have a school bus to catch?"

He said it with a smile, with one of those charming, endearing smiles. Could he know that for Vera to even drive down the lane alone would take a bit of courage?

Fortunately, nobody embarked on a solo career at age seventeen without saving up some stores of courage.

"You're right. I have a bus to catch," Vera said. "You're sure this is OK?"

"Shoo," he replied, positioning the jack under the axle with his foot. "I may not be done by the time you get back, but I will put the hurt to the rest of those cookies before I go, if your daughter doesn't beat me to it."

Vera left him in her garage, cheerfully popping loose lug nuts. If she'd had to do that, she'd probably have been jumping up and down on the tire iron while calling on St. Jude, and still the blasted bolts would not have budged.

*

"My brother, my very own brother, an officer of the court admitted to practice law in the great State of Maryland, has lied to me," James informed the Tundra as he rotated the rod that lowered the spare from its brace. "He led me to believe that Mrs. Waltham was a lonely old fussbudget whose Mr. Waltham was more annoying than dangerous."

That last part might be true—annoying and cowardly.

The spare was properly inflated—praise be—and James rolled it around to lean against the driver's side door.

"You've been slashed, my dear," James said, eyeing the front tire. "I was hoping for a leaky valve or winter pothole wreaking predictable havoc. This is not good."

Contrary to television drama, driving a knife into a truck tire—a new truck tire especially—took significant strength. Vera Waltham's attribution of vandalism to her ex wasn't as outlandish as James wanted it to be.

He raised the truck, wrestled the damaged tire off, and fitted the spare onto the axle.

"A real spare," James observed, spinning the five lug nuts onto the bolts. "Not one of those sissy temporary tires, which any rutted country lane will reduce to ribbons before you can say, 'Which way to the feed store?'"

Vera was isolated here, a single lady with a little girl, her house set back from the winding country road by a good half mile. Woods stood between the house and the road, assuring the property had privacy.

James liked his privacy too, liked it a lot, but sometimes privacy didn't equate to safety.

"Trent also neglected to tell me his former client is a very attractive woman," James groused to the truck. "She has good taste in vehicles, I might add."

Vera Waltham stood about five foot six, and she packed a lot of curves into a frame substantially shorter than James's own six feet and three inches. She had sable hair worn in a tidy bun at her nape, and big, dark eyes that revealed a deep brown upon close inspection.

"Nobody wears their hair in a bun anymore," James said as he lowered the truck off the jack. "I like it—gives a lady a classic look, though a tidy bun wants undoing."

James, unlike his brothers, was one to closely inspect the women in whose kitchens he found himself.

But then, Mac was a monk, and Trent was such a damned saint he was constitutionally incapable of noticing a client was pretty. James noticed, and occasionally did more than that.

At least until lately.

By the time James had re-stowed the equipment, voices came from the kitchen adjoining the garage.

A second pair of big brown eyes studied James as he crossed the kitchen to wash his hands at the double sink. These eyes were set in a heart-shaped little face and regarded him with frank curiosity.

"Is that the man who lent you his car?" the child asked.

"Twy, say hello to Mr. Knightley," Vera instructed. "And, yes, he was kind enough to lend me his car."

"Hullo, Mr. Knightley. You look like the other Mr. Knightley. He was Mom's lawyer. You ate some of my cookies."

"I'll eat every last one of your cookies, they're so good," James said, sliding onto the stool beside the child's, same as he would have with either of his nieces. "I'm James. How was school?"

"School is boring," she said, much as Grace or Merle might have. "You really look like my mom's lawyer."

"Trent's my older brother, and I think he's kind

of handsome." One should always be honest with the ladies. James reached for a cookie. "What do you think?"

The girl smiled, clearly understanding that James had set himself up to be complimented. "I think my mom said he's a damned fine lawyer."

"Language, Twy," Vera murmured.

Was that a blush? Vera was making quite the production out of choosing a mug from the colorful assortment in the cupboard.

"Well, you did say it, Mom."

"What kind of name is Twy?" James propped his chin on his fist, because of all things, *Vera Waltham was shy*. "I don't think I've ever met a Twy before."

"Short for Twyla. I'm the only Twyla in the whole school."

"And you like that." James liked this kid too. "Always had lots of Jameses and Jims and Jimmys in my classes."

"Was it horrible?"

"Bad enough." Other parts of his upbringing had been horrible. "What's your favorite subject?"

The child prattled on happily about her favorite, her least favorite, and some juvenile reprobate named Joey Hinlicky, who'd learned from his older brother how to snap the bras of the fifth-grade girls daring enough to sport such apparel.

Over at the stove, Vera stifled a snort of laughter, suggesting despite her bun and tidy kitchen, she might be the sort of woman who could be teased, or even tickled.

Or not. The house was spotless, a showplace, and the garage floor had been clean enough to eat off of. Other than the kitchen, which was inviting, the rest of the dwelling had a posed quality, like a movie set, not a home. The big black grand piano in the front room actually gleamed.

Did anybody ever play it? Such a fine instrument ought not to be simply for show.

"I can pick you up a battery for your Falcon," James heard himself say around a mouthful of excellent cookie. "It wouldn't be any trouble."

"That's very kind of you," Vera replied.

She stirred something at the stove in such a manner that surely, her thank-you was about to turn into a no-thank-you.

"I've imposed on you enough, though," she said. "Twy, what's in the homework notebook?"

"Vocabulary, fractions, and social studies."

"Busy night," James said. "You need any help?"

The child's brow's rose, while Vera's stirring slowed. "No thanks, but thank you for offering. School isn't hard for me, except for the boys."

"Boys take a while, but they'll grow on you eventually."

"They blow the best arm farts."

"That's enough out of you, Twy," Vera said, but she was again trying not to laugh. "If you've demolished your cookies, you can start on that homework, and do the fractions first."

"Yes, Mother." She swiped one last cookie and flounced out of the kitchen with the long-suffering air of a child who knows where the limits are.

"What a neat kid," James said, helping himself to the last sip of Twyla's milk. "Is school truly easy for her?"

"She's small for her grade, but, yes, it's easy, except for the math."

Homemade turtle cookies and milk had to be one of the best combinations ever.

"I never had any trouble with math," James mused. "I'm a CPA, though I keep that under my hat."

"A CPA *and* a lawyer?" Vera laid out two place mats on the butcher-block island where James had pulled up his bar stool.

Flowers, pumpkins, and roosters in green, red, and orange.

"I don't advertise the CPA part, as it hardly impresses the ladies, but it's handy when the accountants start throwing around the tax code like it was handed down on Mt. Sinai. My clients are businesses or people setting up businesses."

"A third brother is in practice with you, if I recall correctly?"

She'd set out napkins in the same autumn barnyard motif—Laura Ashley need not apply—and an orange pepper grinder, all on a weeknight for a kitchen meal with her only child.

"MacKenzie is the criminal defense expert," James said. "Trent's wife, Hannah, will soon handle all the alternative dispute resolution services for us, so her expertise will cut across disciplines."

Vera next set a matching red salt shaker beside the pepper grinder. "My first husband was a lawyer, though he never sat for the bar exam."

"The guy you chose well?"

She arranged silverware next, each utensil carefully lined up with the others. She'd loved the Husband Who Got Away, maybe still loved him, which had probably irked old Donal the Tire Slasher.

It might irk any guy lining up to provide post-divorce rebound services too.

"Women divorcing second spouses often go back and revisit their first love," James said. "It isn't anything to worry about." Nor was that something passed along in law school.

Vera snatched a third napkin from the center of the island.

"Alexander was killed by a drunk driver five years ago. I'm damned lucky he'd made a will, leaving everything to me, or we'd still be wrangling with probate."

She turned the napkin into cloth origami, so it resembled a half-open rosebud. Vera Waltham had beautiful hands—also a broken heart.

"When you said you married Donal on the rebound, I concluded you were bouncing back from a divorce. I'm sorry."

"And I didn't correct you." She shook out the rose and started folding again. "Don't ever bury a spouse, Mr. Knightley. Divorce them all day long, provided you don't have children with them, but don't say that final good-bye."

A moment later, a napkin-peacock sat in the middle of the island. Vera crossed to the cupboards, took down two crystal water glasses, and kept her back to James for a moment longer.

James liked women; they were interesting, dear, sweet, and lovely. Also fun to take to bed, but they could be complicated as well, which he did not enjoy. Nor did he enjoy being called *Mr. Knightley* by a pretty woman whose bun had slipped a tad off center.

"What makes you think your ex slashed your tire?" James asked.

"He left me a phone message. Not the first, and probably not the last."

When Vera faced James, her expression was mildly pissed, an improvement over mooning after Saint Alexander.

"You recognized his voice?"

"It's disguised, whispery, but, yes, it sounds like him. Would you like to stay for dinner?"

James was in the habit of accepting invitations from the ladies; he was not in the habit of accepting invitations to dinner. Vera's house was too tidy, she was still entangled in a nasty divorce, was a client of his brother's, and was pining for a man who'd been gone for years.

Nope, nope, nope.

"Dinner would be nice," he said, "provided you let me find you that battery."

Chapter 2

VERA REGARDED JAMES CURIOUSLY OVER THE CLOTH peacock. "Negotiation is probably second nature to you, isn't it?"

More of a survival skill, when both older brothers were attorneys. "Why would you say that?"

"You're a corporate lawyer. You wheel and deal for a living."

"I don't think of it as wheeling and dealing," he said, putting the cookies back on top of the fridge. "I think of it as collaborative problem solving. I want to hear Donal's message, and you should consider reporting it to the authorities."

"I'll report it to the sheriff's office, but they'll just make one more note in my extensive file and wish I'd leave the county."

No. They'd wish her ex would leave the county—as did James. "Let's listen to the message before Twyla comes down to spy on us."

Vera moved the cookie tin—more splashy, autumnal flowers—so it was dead center on top of the fridge. "Do you have younger sisters?"

"I have nieces. Not quite the same species, but in the same genus."

Vera hit a few buttons on an old-fashioned answering machine on the counter, then stood staring at the little piece of equipment like it had eight legs and stank.

James prepared to listen to some sour grapes ranting from a spurned husband, though, Vera couldn't have been married to the guy for long if she'd been in this house for more than a year, and dear Alexander had gone to his reward only five years ago.

"Don't think I'll forgive you, Vera," said a raspy voice. "Don't think you're safe. Don't think you'll ever be safe."

Not very original, but the hair on the back of James's neck stood up. "Play it again."

She did, twice, while James tried to absorb not only the words, but also the emotions. That voice and that threat, whispering across this cheery, colorful kitchen, were obscene.

"He leaves you frequent messages like that?" James asked.

"No. He lets me believe he'll go away and abide by the protective order, and just when I think I'm about to put him and his miserable tricks behind me, he starts up again. I honestly never thought Donal would stoop to this level. He hates messiness and whining, and in its way, this is a lot of messy whining."

James hoped that was all it was. "Can you trace the calls?"

"He knows my schedule, apparently, because he never calls when I'm home."

James was beginning to sound like Mac with a witness in a criminal trial. "Do you get hang-up calls?"

Vera moved away from the answering machine and its malevolent little red number one on the message counter. "He's cunning, Donal is. It's part of what made him a good agent."

"Agent for whom?"

"For me. How do you like your hamburgers?"

"Medium," James said, stifling an urge to unplug that answering machine and toss it in the trash.

Vera set about making hamburgers, mashing a whole egg, some spices, salt and pepper, and a few bread crumbs into extra-lean ground beef, then using her hands to form the patties.

For a woman tormented by her ex, she was calm, but when she managed to meet James's gaze, anger and exasperation lurked behind her basic cordiality. Her movements were quick, a touch brittle, and when Twyla had been with them, Vera had watched the girl a tad too closely.

Trenton Knightley, Esquire, needed to follow up with his client.

"I'll make you two," Vera said. "Unless you're a three-burger man?"

"Two will be plenty. What can I do to help?" Help— with dinner, only with dinner, because the trouble Vera faced was best handled by cops and court orders.

"Can you make mashed potatoes?" Vera asked.

"I'm a bachelor. If I didn't learn to cook, I'd soon lose my boyish figure." James foraged in the fridge for butter, sour cream, and ranch dressing. The potatoes, still in their skins, were boiling away on the stove.

He and Vera worked in companionable silence, she tending the meat while he drained the potatoes and used an old-fashioned masher on them until they were relatively smooth.

"What are you doing to those potatoes?" Vera asked.

"Old family recipe," James replied. "I guarantee

Twyla will love them. Are we going to heat some green beans?" Every farm boy knew that the bliss of burgers and mashed potatoes had to be balanced by the penance of some green vegetables.

"Green beans sound good," Vera said. "And I have a tossed salad in the fridge. Beans would be in the freezer."

He found a pack, put them in a pot with some water, tossed in a bouillon cube, and started opening cupboards.

"What are you looking for, James?"

"Slivered almonds."

She gave him a skeptical look, but produced nuts in a bag rolled up and sealed with a rubber band.

James couldn't exactly ask Vera about the Ravens latest televised game, now could he? Beside, the Ravens had sucked goose farts on national television, and James was, to his surprise, out of practice with the predinner chitchat.

"Does Donal have visitation with Twyla?" Really out of practice.

"He does not. I was adamant about that, and Trent backed me up. Stepfathers have no basis in law to assert a right to visitation, not yet."

James turned down the heat under the beans. "I take it Donal lacks paternal inclinations."

"He has children of his own," Vera said, "and he does love them, though he's incapable of showing affection for them. They're older than Twy, and he has his hands full with them. I try to keep in touch with the kids, but when there's a restraining order, that's tricky. I don't want to send a mixed message to anybody. The buns are in the bread box."

James wasn't picking up a hint of a whiff of a frisson

of a mixed message—unless the lack of a third place setting was significant.

Vera slid the cooked burgers into a bright red ceramic dish with a clear glass lid, then called up the stairs, "Twy! Dinner's ready!"

Next she tended to that third place setting, arranging a place mat, cutlery complete with two forks, folded linen napkin, and crystal water goblet just so.

Was a woman neurotic if she used linen napkins to eat hamburgers in the kitchen with her kid?

But even as James considered the question, he mentally played back the message her ex had left her. Linen napkins and matching place mats could be a defense against feeling chronically victimized and objectified.

A lousy defense.

Twyla came down the stairs, her expression pleased.

"We never have company anymore. Is Mr. Knightley going to have dinner with us?"

"He is," Vera replied. "Wash your hands, Twy, and think up some grace."

"Company grace," Twyla said, twirling around on one stocking foot. "I haven't had to do a company grace forever. I'm good at it, though. If I have enough time, I can make it rhyme."

As James pulled up a bar stool and bowed his head on cue, he felt Twyla's hand slipping into his. On his other side, Vera was holding her hand out to him, palm up.

"Mine are clean," Twyla said. "Mom's hands are always clean."

A family ritual, then. James had almost forgotten such things existed. He took Vera's hand, and to his surprise, her fingers gripped his; they didn't merely rest in his hand.

A sincere family ritual, then.

"For what we are about to receive," Twyla said, "we are grateful. I'm also grateful I'm not in the same class as Joey Hinlicky. Amen. Are there *nuts* in the beans?"

"Almonds," James said, putting half a spoonful on her plate. "Vera?"

"Please." She served her daughter a hamburger, and James two. Twyla's did not sport cheese.

"You don't like cheese?" James asked the child. "It's good for you."

"I like cheese raw, not melted so it sticks to the bun and the meat both. These beans are good, but they taste different, and they crunch."

"Textural variety," James said. "Makes the meal almost as interesting as the company. Did you get your homework done?"

"Nah."

The kid knew enough to put her napkin on her lap and keep her elbows off the table. She also didn't talk with her mouth full. Were females born knowing these things?

"Fractions got you stumped?"

Twyla pushed the green beans around with her fork. "I don't get the denominator thing. It's complicated."

"You just have to learn your way around them. Did you bring your math book home?"

"Too heavy," Twyla said, taking a bite of mashed potatoes. "Man, these are good. We should have company more often, Mom."

James did not gloat, but he did offer Vera another helping of mashed potatoes, because she'd taken about a teaspoon the first time around, and James would finish off the batch when she'd enjoyed a proper portion.

"They are good," Vera said. "Can you write the recipe down?"

"You cook with recipes, then?"

"She does," Twyla volunteered, "but Mom says you have to improvise sometimes too, like with the cookies."

"I learned the cookie recipe thoroughly first," Vera said. "And you will not be improvising your way past learning fractions, Twy. I can help you with them when we get the dishes done."

"Or I can," James said. "But then, I'm certified competent to do dishes as well. Who's your math teacher, Twy?"

"Mrs. Corner. She's old."

"I think my niece has her for a few subjects too. My nieces."

"Who are your nieces?"

"Grace Stark and Merle Knightley. They're in second grade."

"I know them," Twyla said, pausing with a forkful of potatoes halfway to her mouth. "That's so cool. Grace is really good at drawing horses, and Merle *has* horses."

Vera shot him a "now you've done it" look as James put the rest of the mashed potatoes on his plate.

"I take it you like horses?" James plainly loved them, always had.

"I adore them, but I like all animals. Mom says we might get a cat, because the mice like our house a lot when it gets cold. She says when the cornfields come down, the mice think moving to the house is like going to Florida for the sunshine. What's for dessert, Mom?"

"Fractions, and maybe a brownie."

"Mom makes the best brownies. We have them with ice cream sometimes, but mostly I like them plain. I do not like fractions."

"Fractions aren't so bad," James said between bites of very good potatoes, if he did say so himself. "You just have to show 'em who's boss."

"How will you do that when she brought only her worksheet home and not her math book?" Vera asked, repositioning the napkin-peacock in the middle of the table.

"Fractions and I go way back," James said, swiping a neglected crust of bun from Vera's plate. "Show me a work sheet, and I go to town."

"Like you and axle grease?"

"Not quite that close a bond, but almost. You have a little piece of green bean…" James extended his pinkie finger to brush the offending morsel off Vera's lip, but she flinched back.

Well, damn it to hell.

She used her napkin.

"You got it," he said, determined not to make her feel self-conscious—her, too. "You want my green bean recipe too?"

"We do," Twyla said. "You probably want our brownie recipe."

"Then we'll trade, but let's not make your mom do the dishes."

"We can all clean up," Vera said, "and that way, Twy will get to her fractions that much sooner."

"Can't wait to get to those fractions," James said over Twyla's theatrical groan. They made short work of the dishes, though without the extra forks and table linen and all the trimmings, the job might have been done much sooner.

But then, James was bachelor, and a cold hamburger occasionally sounded like breakfast to him—lately.

"Come on, sport," he said, running a hand over Twyla's dark hair. "Let's wrassle some fractions."

She looked pleased at the prospect, which was inordinately flattering. James didn't exactly have trouble inspiring females to spend time with him, but the lure had never been fractions.

James sat beside the child in the big warm kitchen, and walked her through the business of numerators and denominators. She caught on fairly quickly, though her attack was marked by impulsivity rather than a methodical approach.

"This is a slow and steady wins the race kind of thing," he said to her. "Your teacher doesn't want to just see you know the steps, she wants you to get the math right too."

"It's boring, but at least it's done. Thank you, Mr. Knightley."

"I think, seeing as we've conquered fractions together, you might call me James. With your mother's permission?"

Vera had been wiping counters for the past ten minutes—they were the cleanest counters in the county by now.

"He who spares the mom the Battle of the Fractions can choose his own moniker," Vera said. "Who wants a brownie?"

They were good brownies, damned good, in fact, but

James limited himself to one the same size as Twyla's. "I do want the recipe."

"I'll write it down," Twyla said.

"You need to pick out your clothes for tomorrow, pack your lunch, and get into your jammies," Vera countered. "Then we can have some princess time. Say good night to Mr. Knightley."

Twyla's lower lip firmed as if she were preparing to stage a post-fractions rebellion, so James stuck out his hand.

"Pleased to have made your acquaintance, Miss Twyla. I never in my whole, entire, long, and illustrious-nearly-to-the-point-of-being-famous life met another Twyla, and I will never forget you."

She grinned at him, mutiny forgotten. "Never?"

"Never one time," he said, "and I would not lie to a lady."

She shook his hand and scampered up the stairs, yelling good nights over her shoulder.

"A good kid, Vera. I hope you're proud of her."

"Very, but I'm also anxious. I'll blink, and she'll be a teenager."

This prospect appeared to daunt Vera, while Donal the Slasher had merely pissed her off. Had her priorities straight, did Vera Waltham.

"Nobody likes teenagers," James said, indulging a need to speak up for his younger self, "but I think they're wonderful. They can mow grass, do laundry, keep an eye on the little ones, make dinner, run the vacuum cleaner, and work on engines. I can't wait until my nieces are teenagers."

"When they are, their parents will gladly hand them off to their favorite uncle James. Thank you for showing

Twy the math, though. She and I do not operate on the same wavelength when it comes to schoolwork."

"Parents and their offspring never do," James said, considering a second brownie now that the kitchen was adults only. "If it weren't for my brothers, I'd probably have flunked out of high school."

No probably about it.

Vera worked the controls on some high-tech coffeemaker thing, her movements as efficient as a short-order cook's.

"You're a lawyer and an accountant," she observed. "How could school have been hard for you?"

"I was a boy, that's how." A boy whose brothers had simply expected him to make good grades. They'd made good grades—how hard could it be?

"Time I was heading out," James said, though he'd watched a few princess movies in the line of uncle duty. "You should get your tire repaired, or at least buy a functional spare. I can take care of that if you like, but for now, the damaged tire is sitting in the truck bed."

"Thank you, James. I'll get to it tomorrow."

James had known Vera would refuse his help, but had felt compelled to offer anyway. "You'll tell Trent about the messages Donal is leaving?"

"I don't see what Trent can do," she said, crossing her arms and leaning back against the counter. The coffeemaker gurgled and steamed behind her as a beguiling caramel aroma filled the kitchen.

"Trent can put the state's attorney on notice," James said. "He can send a threatening letter to Donal's lawyer, he can rattle swords like nobody's business, and create a paper trail that will incriminate the daylights out of

Donal when you do catch him violating the order. You should tell Trent."

"If I don't, you will?"

Vera remained braced against the counter, arms crossed, her expression carefully neutral. From upstairs, Twyla started bellowing the lyrics to "Can You Feel the Love Tonight."

Vera turned to the coffeemaker, but James would have bet his best set of jumper cables she was smothering a smile.

"Wanting to keep a woman safe doesn't make a man a bully, Vera Waltham. If you can't see your way to calling Trent for yourself, do it for Twyla."

She nodded, though James knew it was no guarantee she'd call Trent; but then, he hadn't promised to keep his mouth shut either. He was about to yell a final good night up the stairs to Elton John's latest competition when Vera half turned, her gaze straying to the window and to the darkness beyond.

And instead of "good night, thanks for a wonderful meal," what came out of his mouth?

"I live less than two miles away." James scrawled his house phone number on a notepad beside the phone. "That's my number. We're neighbors, Vera, and you owe me a brownie recipe, while I owe you a battery for your Ford."

"You don't owe me anything, and even a CPA lawyer needs his beauty sleep. Good night, James, and thanks for wrangling those fractions."

Good night, James? Wrangling fractions? No, James did not want to become entangled with this lady, but neither would he accept a brush-off. A guy had standards to uphold. He'd made his signature mashed potatoes for her, after all, and tamed the dreaded, fire-breathing least common denominator.

"If you asked me to stay," he said, as upstairs, Simba and Nala caterwauled their way toward a litter of lion cubs, "I would. You and Twyla are isolated here. It's pitch dark out, there's no moon tonight, and that fool man means to upset you."

Vera tore off the page that had James's phone number on it—a phone number he'd stopped giving out months ago.

"Of course Donal's out to rattle me. You think I don't know that, James?"

"I think you don't know what to do about it," he said gently.

Vera affixed James's phone number to the fridge with a rooster magnet. "I'll call your brother tomorrow."

Her promise relieved James more than it should have. "I'm your neighbor," he said. "Around here, that still means something. You can call me too."

Except Vera wouldn't, which was probably all that allowed James to make the offer.

Vera put the kettle on as James Knightley's SUV rumbled off into the night—the coffee would have been for him, had he stayed. Olga had disparaging things to say about caffeine in anything more than moderation—Olga had disparaging things to say about much of life—so Vera got out the chamomile tea.

The phone rang as Vera turned the coffeemaker off.

Her first reaction was to stick her tongue out at the machine, but the caller ID assured her Donal wasn't making a further nuisance of himself.

"Hello, Olga. I was just thinking of you."

"You think of me," came the accented reply—tink uff me, "but you do not call. You are a bad girl, my Vera, making a lonely old woman wait by the phone for you to call."

A shameless old woman, also ferocious and endlessly dear. "I'm sorry. Twyla has just now finished her homework, and I did mean to call you."

Soon, not tonight.

"Homework, bah. You should find a man to flirt with you and take you dancing." The way Olga said "dancing" suggested even a ninety-four-year-old veteran of four marriages might relish an occasional flirtation.

"We had company for dinner tonight. My lawyer's brother brought me some paperwork and then joined us for hamburgers."

A considering silence from the other end. Vera could picture the older woman having a sip of chocolate from a translucent porcelain service that probably cost as much as Vera's useless security system.

"He's nice," Vera added, because Olga would not pry, but she'd wield a silence more effectively than some conductors wielded their batons.

"The nice ones are often overlooked," Olga said. "What did the child think of him?"

Insightful question, which from Olga was to be expected. Olga Strausser was a living legend among classical musicians. As a girl, she'd been introduced to Rachmaninoff, whom she'd referred to forever after as, "that poor, dear man." She'd taken tea with Serkin, and given a private four-hands impromptu recital with Rubinstein that was still talked about.

She'd traded licks with Eubie Blake, and known Brubeck as a young man, "before he could read music, much."

Vera had been sixteen when she'd snagged a slot in one of Olga's rare master classes, and so nervous she'd barely been able to eat for a week prior. Once the class had begun, Olga had become a fairy godmother to the music, the auditors had fallen away, the nerves had fallen away, and Vera had learned as she'd never learned before.

How to be present to nothing but the music.

How to listen *and* play.

How to make judgment calls as a piece unfolded, crafting the music as it wanted to be performed on that instrument, in that hall, on that day by the person Vera was on that occasion.

Olga had continued as a benign presence in Vera's musical development, gently steering her toward her first international competitions, when the professors at the conservatory had suggested Vera wait another year, or two, or three.

"They are old men," Olga had said. "They think if you don't win, they lose. We know better. We know you are ready, and you can still gain experience worth having if you come in last. But you play what I tell you, the way I tell you, not what those old men have been teaching for the past fifty years."

Vera had won, and won again.

Olga had steered Vera into Alexander's hands as a manager.

"He's a good man. Look how patient he is with the wife, and her such a child. He will pace your career, so you can still perform at one hundred, like me."

About Donal MacKay, Olga had been mostly silent, but her distaste for Vera's agent had come through.

"That *Scot*. To him, all is pennies and nickels and bright, shiny dimes. When did coin ever soothe the soul?"

Hot chocolate and cookies soothed the soul, and watching James tutor Twyla through the intricacies of third-grade math had also gratified some need Vera couldn't describe to herself, much less to her friend.

"Twyla got on well with James," Vera said, recovering the thread of the conversation. "He's patient, he has a good sense of humor, and he's bright."

Brilliant, probably—a CPA and an attorney, for pity's sake. Why hadn't some equally brilliant lady lawyer snatched him up?

"Children know whom they can trust," Olga observed. "When will you bring my Twyla to visit?"

"Not this week," Vera said, pouring the boiling water into her mug. "We're supposed to get snow by the weekend." Thank heavens, because Olga would expect Vera to play for her, and that she could not do—yet.

"You have that great, noisy beast of a truck," Olga scoffed. "In Russia, we had mountains of snow, and managed it with mere horses and a nip of vodka. You must not be afraid, Vera. You can no longer play like a young girl, and that's good. The music will sort itself out."

Vera took a sip of tea and scalded her tongue.

"I'm practicing." Practicing hour after hour, with a single-minded concentration she'd not had as a younger musician.

"Better that you invite that young man over for more

than hamburgers. Play him the Chopin. If he can listen to Chopin, that will tell you much."

"You have a naughty mind, Olga. Twyla is summoning me to Pride Rock."

"Pride, something you could use more of. Sweet dreams, my Vera, and come see me."

Click.

Olga was a force of nature, but a mostly kind one. She'd made her points—stop hiding, book more concerts, dip a toe in the waters of flirtation and frolic—then retreated with a verbal hug and encouraging wink.

The idea of playing Chopin for James had an intriguing appeal. He'd looked *sexy*, patiently explaining one simple concept after another to the child, until an entire process had been made clear.

His patience, his generosity, his kindness to somebody else's little girl, they'd been *sexy*.

Not his smile, his broad shoulders, or his big, competent hands—those had been a little unnerving.

But his kindness, that had been sexy. Vera added a dash of honey to her tea and ventured another sip, the temperature now perfect for a chilly night.

She hadn't found anybody or anything sexy in years, but James Knightley in her kitchen with a pencil behind his ear…

Interesting.

～～～

"How's my niece?" James asked.

"She's asleep," Trent said into the phone. James had known Trent left the office to heed a summons from the school nurse, so Trent had been expecting this call. "We hit the urgent care on the way home from school, and Merle's on antibiotics. Grace brought home all Merle's homework, and life is good."

Trent had just finished giving the same report to Mac. Hannah's parents would probably call next.

"Grace holding up OK?" James asked.

"She had a similar bug a couple of weeks ago, so I expect she's safe for now. You got that order to Vera Waltham?"

"I did," James said, his reply holding a touch of evasion only a brother would have sensed.

"But?"

A pause, and Trent could hear James rearranging word choices, polishing the facts to a higher shine— preparing his proffer for the court.

"I ended up staying for dinner," James said.

"It's a nice old house." Owned by a lovely, and possibly lonely, woman. James liked old houses. He liked women between the ages of five minutes and ninety-five years too. "I suppose you met the daughter?"

"Twyla. A neat kid, and she knows Grace and Merle. She'd be a good candidate for a playdate."

"Three little girls in my house? If anything happens to me or Hannah, you and Mac are named co-guardians in our will, by the way. Be mindful of what you sow, little brother."

Trent had meant the words in jest, but they reaped a small silence.

"You really mean that? We get the girls if anything happens to you?"

"Who else would we entrust them to? Hannah's folks are not young, and she has no siblings."

"I just… I mean… Thanks."

A double load of responsibility and expense, and James said thanks.

"You're welcome. I'll tell Merle you did a wellness check."

"Ah, Trent?"

"Hm?"

"Vera Waltham is having trouble with her ex."

Wasn't that what exes were for? "She told you this? In my experience, she's jealous of her privacy."

"She apparently let *you* into her kitchen."

"But only into her kitchen," Trent said. "Unlike you, the sight of me doesn't make most women's clothes fall off, with the happy exception of my wife. What sort of trouble is Vera having?"

"Her ex is leaving her threatening messages, but is clever enough to disguise his voice and make the threats vague. Somebody slashed the tire of her truck while it sat in a locked garage, and she suspects him."

Why was Veracity Waltham confiding these things in James rather than telling them to the attorney who'd spent a long, hard year battling on her behalf?

"I can't do anything about it until she tells me to, James."

"She said she'd call you tomorrow, but if she doesn't call you, I might nose around, see what I can find."

Like most younger siblings, James was a first-class noser-arounder, second only to the private investigators the firm kept on retainer.

"You're not her lawyer," Trent said, not sure if he was being protective of Vera or of James. The guy had a soft spot for damsels in distress, and all the swashbuckling and mighty swordsmanship in the world didn't disguise that from his own brother.

"I'm not *her* lawyer," James retorted, "which means I can discreetly discuss her business with my brother, and I can drive past her place on my way to and from work, and I can get a damned battery for her 1964 Ford Falcon."

"Her what?"

"Never mind. Tell Merle to get well soon, and give Hannah my love."

James hung up before Trent could ask what he'd thought of that lovely old house—or if, in his raptures over an antique car, he'd even noticed the house.

Chapter 3

THE THIRD SATURDAY OF EVERY MONTH WAS JAMES'S one inviolable standing date. He ran riot the rest of the month, or had until recently, sometimes doing drinks with one woman, dinner with another, and—when he was particularly restless—the final round of the evening with yet another. The third Saturday of the month he was up early, in his jeans, and headed out by 8:00 a.m. without fail.

"Hi, Uncle James!" Merle clambered off the hay bale she'd been using for a grooming stool. "I told Grace you're never late, didn't I, Grace?"

"You did," Grace said. "Hello, Merle's uncle."

They were two dark-haired little peas in a pod, stepsisters by virtue of Grace's mom having married Merle's dad, and friends by virtue of divine providence.

James swung Grace off her hay bale and perched her on his hip. "None of that. I'm *your* uncle James now too." He did not glance at Merle, because he'd already had this talk with her, and she'd given her blessing.

"You're not related to me."

"Your mom married my brother," James said, poking Grace gently in the tummy. "That means I get uncle privileges where you're concerned. Mac does too."

"Are you sure?"

"Ask your mom if you don't believe me, but I'm right, aren't I, Merle?"

"Yes, Uncle James. Grace is my sister now too."

"Stepsister," Grace said, gaze on the barn's dirt floor.

"Details." James set Grace on her feet and kept her hand in his. "Step, schmep. Are these your stephorses now?"

"Merle's…Dad explained we're a family, and the horses belong to the family. But Pasha is Merle's personal horse."

So careful, like her mother. Grace and Hannah both liked order and predictability, and given what they'd known prior to joining the Knightley family, James didn't blame them.

"Well, I'm special," James said, "I get more than one personal niece. We're going out for breakfast as soon as I tell your parents you've been kidnapped."

Merle caught his other hand, and he let them drag him into the house.

"Anybody home?" he bellowed.

"James, welcome." Hannah, James's newly acquired sister-in-law, came out of the kitchen, wearing sweats, a dish towel over her shoulder, and a T-shirt that said "Lawyers do it in their briefs."

Also a smile.

"Greetings, Hannah." He kissed her cheek, enjoying the flowery, female scent of her. "Prepare to repel boarders. I've come to kidnap these beautiful damsels, but first you have to assure Grace I'm a properly certified uncle with all the privileges and immunities attendant thereto."

"He's talking like a lawyer," Merle said to Grace. "He does it to be silly."

"My secret is revealed. We must ask Merle why it is

her uncle Mac talks like a lawyer, because he's never silly."

"Is too," Trent said, emerging from the hallway to his study. "Mac's silliness is subtle and coincides with full moons. You have to watch for it. Good morning, Brother. Have you come to steal our treasures?"

"At least until this afternoon. Come along, treasures."

James bundled the girls into the backseat of his SUV and headed out to the county's only mall. The weather was too brisk to spend much time outside, particularly with Merle getting over a cold, and James needed to make a stop at a certain car parts store.

After the girls finished a course of Belgian waffles, they ran James from one store to another. Grace found a stuffed unicorn, a silly, fluffy little thing with a pink horn, and insisted James buy it for himself.

"Everybody needs one," Grace explained. "She can be your personal unicorn too, Uncle James."

"You have to give her a name," Merle said.

What came out of James's mouth would matter to his nieces, and they mattered very much to him. What should he call the first stuffed animal he'd acquired in nearly thirty years?

"Justice?" he suggested. "No. She'd have to be blind then, and these big blue eyes don't look blind to me. I don't know. I'll have to think on it."

"Take your time," Grace said. "My first bear was named Aloysius, but I couldn't say that when I was little. I called him All The Wishes, and then he said he wanted his name to be Wishes, and that's what it is."

"Pasha is really AM Appomattox," Merle chimed in. "We call him Pasha for short."

"I'm really Lucy Grace," Grace added…and the girls were off into a conversation regarding names of classmates, stuffed animals, Disney characters, and entire universes that uncles—even doting uncles—were excluded from.

James suffered a pang, to know he'd been nudged down a hair in Merle's pantheon of grown-ups. With Grace as a friend and sister—nothing "step" about her— Merle didn't need James's avuncular companionship quite so much.

The word for that realization was *lowering*. Maybe Mac would admit to the same observation, that Merle was growing up, but Mac would never in a million years admit to feeling nonplussed about it.

"We having ice cream cones for lunch?" James asked.

"Mom says you have to take us to the park for ten minutes if we get ice cream for lunch," Merle said.

Mom would be her stepmother, Hannah, but Merle had been without a maternal figure for so long, she didn't dither over what to call the woman her father had recently married.

"Then it's ice cream cones and a walk to the park, but only for ten minutes, Merle Knightley. It's cold out, and I'm a tired, skinny old uncle who might blow away on the first stiff breeze."

"You're not skinny," Grace said. "You're just right."

Ten minutes at the park turned into twenty, of course, but James called a halt to the festivities before anybody was truly cold. The girls kept moving the whole time, and James was dragooned into underdoggies at the swings, and twirling the merry-go-round, so even he stayed comfortable.

"I'll make a place in the backseat for Uncle James's unicorn," Merle said, tearing off for the car. By rights, Grace should have followed, making suggestions at the top of her lungs, but James was learning that little girls often did not act the same as little boys.

"Uncle…James?" Grace kicked the dirt, then stared off in the direction of the SUV. "You're a lawyer, right?"

"I am."

"Can you do things at court like Merle's…like my dad?"

"I can. I do different things from Trent because my clients are businesses usually, not individual people, but I use the same courthouse, the same judges."

"I think I need a lawyer."

Her expression was resolute, and she was one smart little girl. "Do you have any money in your fanny pack, Grace?"

"Sure."

"Give me a dime. If I'm going to be your lawyer, you have to pay me, and then all your business with me stays private."

James didn't know what prompted him to insist on this ritual, but it seemed to make sense to Grace.

"My mom says there's a word for it."

"Attorney-client privilege," James said, taking a dime from Grace's small hand. "Now before your sister is here listening to our every confidential word, tell me what's on your mind."

James led her to a bench, and while Merle waited patiently in the backseat of James's SUV, James listened to his client. When Grace had finished a few minutes later, he agreed that she did indeed need a lawyer, and he'd be only too happy to take her case.

"I need a riding instructor," Trent said. "In your vast social network, can you point me to any?"

James looked up from the subcontract he was reviewing—one without a merger clause or a conflict of laws clause, which always signaled weak draftsmanship.

"You know how to ride," James said. "Has marriage addled your wits?"

"The instructor isn't for me." Trent took a chair, as if subcontracts were never urgent matters. "It's for Grace, and possibly Hannah."

"Hannah doesn't have a suitable mount," James said, setting the document aside. "Pasha's too old and too little to do lessons for Grace and Hannah both, as well as pack Merle around, Zeus is too damned big, and Bishop has a dirty spook."

Though the gelding was a former steeplechaser, and nobody should hold the spook against him.

"He has an honest spook, not a dirty spook," Trent said, picking up an old Rubik's cube. "I don't suppose you'd be interested in doing some horse shopping?"

Instead of teaching some Washington, DC, shyster-meister how to write a fair subcontract?

"Sure I would, but why me?" James asked.

Trent start flipping the cube around, lining up the greens first. "I ride," he said, "but when it comes to horses, you know what you're doing. I'd ask Mac, but no horse on earth would be good enough in his eyes for Hannah, much less for Grace."

True enough. "So we're looking for *two* horses?"

More flipping, which suggested James ought to retire the damned toy to a desk drawer.

"Maybe. Start with one for Grace."

"You is doomed, Brother," James said, taking the Rubik's cube from Trent before he had it all organized. "That will bring you up to five, and five horses is a lot of horses when viewed from the business end of a muck fork. I'm telling you this for your own good. You have to feed them, worm them, look after their teeth, get the farrier after them regularly, buy the bedding, the tack, the fall inoculations, the spring inoculations, foot the vet bills when they do stupid horse things like run smack into trees... You're smiling."

"You sound like Mac."

"Cripes, that's low, Trent." James tossed the Rubik's cube into a drawer and tucked the lousy sub-contract back into its file. "I'm only trying to give you some perspective."

James also considered giving his brother a hand with the herd—keeping a couple of the mighty steeds in his own backyard, for example—and discarded the notion.

Horses were beautiful and first-rate company, but way too much work.

Trent fished a pile of colorful paper clips out of the glass bowl on James's desk and started stringing them into a chain.

"Riding will be a family pastime," Trent said. "I've already resigned myself to that. We all need recreation, and the girls won't outgrow the horse crazies until they're at least teenagers."

When they'd graduate to boys, as James could attest.

"Adelia Schofield is a good instructor," James said.

"She's fun but safety conscious, and she said hanging out with horses growing up added two years to her virginity." She hadn't been wearing a stitch when she'd shared this with James.

"The things women tell you."

"Under the circumstances, it wasn't that much of an admission," James said, though God above, riding did great things for a woman's thighs. "She has a point. Not too many young swains are afflicted with the horse crazies, at least compared to the number of girls who have them. I was the exception, but then, I realized early on that the odds at the horse barn favored a guy, provided he was straight."

One of the paper clips broke, and James held out his hand for the resulting casualties.

"Is that why you took to riding so enthusiastically?"

"I like horses; I like women better." James had loved the horses, loved the smell of the barn, loved the sense that in the saddle, none of the problems at home could catch him.

"You need a hobby though," Trent said, rising. "You can't work and chase women all the time, James."

"Can too." Maybe he'd get a dog, though.

"Except you're not." Trent scanned James's office, which was neither as cushy as Mac's nor as cozy as Trent's. "You're putting in brutal hours because you're in such demand, but you've hardly kept up with your usual social whirl. I might worry, except I've concluded you're making a strategic retreat."

Dogs were a lot of trouble too, and they stank and rolled in dead groundhogs.

"A strategic retreat?"

"So the ladies will be that much more appreciative when you're riding circuit again," Trent said.

"Quite honestly, if the ladies were much more appreciative, I'd be…"

"You'd be what?"

James would be dead. Worn out from sexual excesses and the accompanying disillusionment.

"I think there's something wrong with most men," James said, leaning back in his chair and feeling a twinge at the base of his spine. "All the ladies want is a little consideration, some affection, someone to take genuine pleasure in their company. Am I the only guy who understands that?"

"I have dated a few women," Trent said, holding up the paper clips in a rainbow-colored loop and letting it coil into the bowl. "I am more inclined to think you underestimate yourself, James, than to conclude most men are too dumb to treat their womenfolk decently. You have Adelia's phone number?"

"Hold on." James popped open a directory on his computer. "Write this down." He gave Trent the number. "If she can't take you on, try Amory Bennington at this number."

"Thanks."

Trent left, while James sat frowning at his screen for long moments.

Trent hadn't asked him to teach the ladies how to ride, though James had put himself through two years of college as a riding instructor. Maybe Trent did not want to impose, or Hannah was self-conscious at the thought of James teaching her to ride.

James scanned down the list of names on his screen,

dozens of them, recalling the women he could, trying to remember those whose faces eluded him.

He was nearly thirty years old, and what he had to show for himself was a long list of lonely women and a pile of business documents that, quite frankly, bored him to tears.

Maybe Trent was right. Pets were a lot of bother, but maybe it was time for a hobby. A *real* hobby.

"Is James coming to dinner again?"

Vera should have seen that question coming, because Twy had been loudly hinting every night for a week.

"He might some day, but I haven't invited him back. How was school?"

"We had a quiz in math, and I nailed it," Twyla said, grinning, and executing one of her signature kitchen pirouettes. "I showed those fractions who was boss."

"Mr. Knightley was helpful, wasn't he?" Mr. Knightley had been a godsend.

"He said I could call him James," Twyla replied, reaching blindly above her head for the cookie tin. "He's tall enough to reach the cookies. I think you should invite him back."

"I think you should wash your hands before you have your snack."

"Are we having mashed potatoes again?" Twyla asked. "They were de-licious."

"They were good, but no, we're having lasagna with salad and garlic toast."

"Yum." Twyla went to the sink and let the hot water

run until steam rose. "I bet James knows how to make lasagna, though. You should ask him."

At dinner, Vera endured more of the same. James this, Mr. Knightley that, until Vera wanted to scream.

She hadn't called Trent Knightley, but she had made the requisite report to the sheriff's office. They'd taken down her statement, the same as they always did, and told her they'd keep it on file.

The phone rang as Vera put away the dinner dishes, and on principle, she picked it up without glancing at the number.

"Hello, Waltham's."

"Hello, Vera. James Knightley here. I hope I didn't interrupt dinner or fractions or vocabulary?"

Good God, he had a sexy voice, like a concert grand Bösendorfer she'd performed on in Berlin. Silky, resonant, and so very, very male.

"Dinner is over, the fractions are cowering in complete subjugation, and Twy has been singing the praises of your mashed potatoes for days." While Vera had just about convinced herself she'd never hear from James Knightley again.

"A guy likes to know he's made a good first impression, or his mom's mashed-potato recipe has. I picked up a battery for your Ford."

Who knew an antique Ford could be a guy-magnet? "The Falcon is Twy's, technically. You didn't have to do that."

"Yeah, I did. You might need backup wheels if Donal decides to slash more than one tire next time."

"Cheer me up, why don't you, counselor?"

"It's been nearly a week, Vera, and I suspect you

haven't called Trent, so when can I bring over this battery?"

James glossed over his accusation like so many grace notes, but Vera still heard the reproach.

Also a genuine offer to be helpful. "I'm free this Saturday, James. Twy likes to sleep in Saturdays, though, so let's make it about eleven."

"Saturday at eleven, then."

He hung up before Vera could ask him what the battery had cost, or remind him to bring his mashed-potato recipe.

Twy would ask, after all.

"Who was that?" Twyla came down the kitchen steps on her backside, bumping down one step at a time.

"Doesn't that hurt your back?"

"No. I heard the phone ring."

"It was your friend, James. He's bringing over a battery for the Faithful Falcon on Saturday."

"Cool." She was on her feet and scampering back up the stairs.

"Where are you going?"

"To look for some more recipes for him!"

That was why Vera should have shooed James off, or told him to return the battery. Twyla missed the influence of an adult male in her life and would get ideas about James, and about James and Vera. Vera should have told him to leave the battery with his brother Trent, whom she'd been meaning to call.

But calling Trent meant admitting Donal was not going away, not going to behave according to the court order, and Vera labored under the stupid, stubborn hope that if she just ignored Donal long enough, he'd sprout some of the common sense the Scots were supposed to be famed for and leave her in peace.

Maybe she should get a dog—a big, noisy dog with lots of teeth.

"Mom?" Twyla called down the stairs. "For the turtle cookies, do you put the vanilla in before or after the melted chocolate?"

"After."

"What time is James coming over?"

"Around eleven, but if you want to carry on a conversation, stop bellowing and come down here."

Silence. Vera finished wiping off the counters, telling herself the whole time that accepting a man's offer to put a battery in her car did not obligate her to anything more. She'd be pleasant to Trent Knightley's brother on Saturday, wangle his mashed-potato recipe from him, and ply him with a few fresh, warm, sinfully good brownies.

Then send him on his merry, practical, sexy way.

———

Harper Nash was a scrumptious woman, on the tall side with big green eyes and masses of red hair that she tried to subdue into a French braid. Best of all, she was smart enough to listen to her lawyer, though James was having a hard time remaining focused on their conversation.

"You want a clause in the subcontract that gives you control over the lower-tier subcontractors your vendor gets in bed with," James said, though he might have chosen his words more wisely.

"Why do I want my nose in their business?" Harper

asked, tapping lacquered red nails on James's conference table. "I'm hiring them to do a job, I'll inspect their work, and if it's not to spec, I'll withhold payment."

"Damned right you will," James said, though two years ago, when Harper had first inherited her dad's business, she'd written checks simply because invoices came in. "You don't want a subcontractor who's just skimming a percentage. You want to hire a driller, say, because he has the equipment and know-how to take all the samples you need, on time and within budget. If you don't keep control of the subcontract-consent language, then your subs can give a piece of your business to your direct competitors."

She wrinkled her pretty nose. "Hardly in my best interests."

"Hardly," James agreed, tidying up the papers spread before him. "Then too, you don't want just anybody on your work site, watching how you go about a project, talking your best people into jumping ship. You want to be the gatekeeper."

While James wanted this appointment to be over.

"I don't want my subcontractors colluding to jack the bid prices up," Harper said. "Tell me again why I don't sell this business?"

James fished an orange paper clip out of a small bowl only to find it was attached to about thirty others.

"Because then," he said, twisting the orange clip free, "I wouldn't get to see you from time to time, and my dreary life toiling among the fine print is made bearable if I have at least a few clients whose company I enjoy."

Not quite a lie. James liked Harper. He liked homemade turtle cookies more.

Harper crossed long, shapely legs. "Do they teach you that kind of flattery in law school?"

"It's not flattery," James said, unhooking more paper clips. "It's the God's honest truth. My small-business clients do a much better job of considering my advice than the big boys do, and I can feel some pride when the little guys prosper as a result."

"You give advice I can understand," Harper said, coming to her feet. "What are you doing for lunch, James? My stomach is reminding me that breakfast was hours and a spin class ago."

"I have a few errands to run," he said, rising as well. "I also want to finish marking up this draft subcontract for your contract administrator before close of business. The construction season will begin sooner than we think."

"We live in that hope. Thanks again." She leaned in and kissed his cheek, lingering near for a mere, telltale instant.

In that instant, James's body heard the invitation in places low and friendly. Harper was quite, quite single, up to her ears in keeping the family business together, and likely as much in need of comfort and affection as any lady in her position. She trusted James, she liked him, and she found him attractive.

So why not?

She left his office, treating James to the lovely sight of her retreating backside. Harper knew how to dress, and she knew how to walk away from a man so he might harbor a few regrets.

Except James…didn't. What he felt, watching her walk away, leaving him in peace for the afternoon, was an odd kind of relief. When he sat down at his computer, he opened his address book to the particular directory that held the most names.

He had a printout of the list somewhere in his hard-copy files, and it likely lurked in his email too, because emailing files to himself was a cheesy way to make a backup.

Why keep such a list? The women invariably called him, though the only number he gave out was the office number. They slipped him their numbers, and he dutifully cataloged each one, but he was the one they called when they were between boyfriends, at loose ends, trying to get back on the horse after a bad breakup, or just plain horny. If Damson County had an award for booty call of the year, James would have won the past three years at least, hands down.

Because when the ladies called, he answered.

He stared at the screen for a long time, then, in a few deft keystrokes, deleted the entire file.

———

"He's here! He's here!" Twyla went tearing to the front door, sliding at the corners on the hardwood floors. "James is here!" She threw open the front door and would probably have run right down the steps, except she was in stocking feet.

"Hullo, James! Is that my battery?"

"Hello, only-Twyla-I've-ever-met, and yes, this battery is for your Ford."

Twyla hugged him around his middle, squeezing tight, while he stood holding the battery and smiling over the child's head at Vera.

"If I'd known what bringing a battery did for my reception, I'd take one with me everywhere. Good morning, Vera. Sorry I'm a few minutes late, but I stopped at the hardware store."

Even his version of sheepish qualified as low-grade sexy.

"You're male," Vera said. "If you were loose without supervision in a hardware store, we're lucky to see you before sundown. Come on back to the kitchen. Twyla made you a fresh batch of brownies."

As greetings went, that wasn't exactly gracious, but the sight of her daughter being so openly affectionate with James unsettled Vera. Twyla had never hugged Donal like that. Had never hugged Donal at all. She barely tolerated the offhand affection Darren, Donal's son, showed her.

"The best part about baking," James was saying, "is the whole house smells good. They ought to make candles scented like brownies."

"They do," Twyla said. "Mom won't let me have candles in my room, or I'd have one. Do you want ice cream with your brownie?"

"I want to get this battery into that car, and then we can talk about brownies. How's that?"

Twyla looked a little nonplussed at this example of male single-mindedness when in Fix-It mode.

"I'll need some help with the battery," James added, "and if we cut the brownies too soon, we'll get a mess. You think you can be my assistant?"

"Sure!" Twyla trailed after him through the kitchen and into the garage like a puppy with a new canine buddy at the dog park.

"You have the key to this old sweetheart, Vera?"

James patted the hood of the Falcon, his hand smoothing over the metal as if it were warm and alive.

"Here," she said, taking the keys off a pegboard near the door and tossing them at him. "I have some laundry to fold, but holler if you need anything."

He caught the keys one-handed, then reached under the grill and popped the hood. "Twy will keep me out of trouble, won't you, Twy? The first thing I'm going to ask you to do is get a stool from the kitchen, so you can see what we're doing."

What did it say about Vera that she resented James, simply for showing polite consideration to Twy, who'd had far too little to do with considerate men?

It said Vera was insecure and selfish, and not as healed from her divorce as she wished she were.

She folded the towels—did anything smell as good on a winter morning as clean laundry?—and had most of them put away when James and Twyla came back into the kitchen, James toting the borrowed stool.

"You look pleased with yourselves," Vera said. "Mission accomplished?"

"James showed me how to check the tire pressure and where the oil pan is and what a valve-stem cover is."

His automotive genius-ship set the stool down near the sink, and Twyla climbed up on it to wash her hands, as she had as a much younger child.

How had he known to do that?

"Somebody takes care of that car," James said as he lathered his hands. "The timing is close to perfect, but you should take it out for a spin every so often."

"We do," Twyla said. "We go for road trips and take a picnic basket. It's lots of fun."

"Be a little breezy picnicking in this weather." James appropriated a towel, dried his hands, and then draped the towel over Twyla's shoulder, which had the girl positively beaming. "I heard a rumor some brownies in this kitchen might be looking for a good home."

"Mom, can we get the brownies now?"

James was so easy with the child, so relaxed and charming. Vera wanted to order him from the house, though he hadn't done anything wrong.

She also wanted him to show her what a valve-stem thingy was.

"Brownies for lunch, then," Vera said, going to the refrigerator. "We'd best have ice cream if we're to make a meal of it. Chocolate or vanilla?"

"Some of both," James said. "I like variety in my pleasures."

Vera wasn't looking at him, so she couldn't tell if he'd meant that as lasciviously as she'd heard it. "Twy, what about you?"

"Some of both," she said, beaming at James.

The child was well and truly smitten, and by a guy whose greatest accomplishment so far was that he was a motorhead who could explain fractions, for the love of Saint Elizabeth.

"Whereas I will have neither," Vera said, aiming a look at James, "because I like my pleasures simple and uncomplicated."

He reached for the chocolate ice cream, dipped a spoon into the middle, and took a bite, sliding the spoon out of his mouth s-l-o-w-l-y.

"*Vive la différence*," he said in a perfect French

accent, lowering his lashes. "I guess I'll need another spoon, lest I get my wrist slapped for double-dipping. Where are the spoons, Twy?"

She showed him which drawer, and he kept the used spoon for his own bowl, but served himself and Twyla with a clean spoon while Vera cut the warm brownies.

"I like brownies for lunch," Twy declared, hopping up onto a stool. James took the stool from near the sink, and planted it right next to where Vera stood at the island.

"I wonder if brownies for breakfast would be as good," he mused, settling onto the stool. "Might have to do a direct comparison, have brownies for breakfast, lunch, and dinner." He took a bite, and again, Vera had the sense he'd made some almost-flirtatious remark.

Why did he have to smell so good? Not like a grease monkey, but like a jeans commercial made sniffable.

"Could we, Mom? Breakfast, lunch, and dinner?"

"We'll ask James how his experiment goes instead," Vera said, breaking off a corner of her brownie. "That will save on our dentist bills."

"I hate the dentist," Twy said, sculpting ice cream with her spoon. "We go during summer break, and it's the worst thing about summer."

"What's the best thing?" James asked.

Point to James for diversionary skills.

"I had riding lessons last summer, and that was the best," Twyla said. "We go swimming when Mom doesn't have to work, and we go on picnics, and sometimes make a trip to see the ponies at Chincoteague and hike on the Appalachian Trail or the C & O towpath, and all over. What's your favorite thing to do in the summer?"

James studied his empty spoon, holding it at mouth level.

"I like to do nothing. To put a book over my face and hang out in the hammock for an hour or two. I built my niece a tree house last summer, but my brothers had to help, which was sorta fun, and sorta not, because they're my older brothers. I take the occasional walk in the same places you do, but I think I should get a dog to go walking with me. I also like to sit on the porch swing at night and listen to the crickets and cicadas, and enjoy some of my favorite music as it gets dark."

Quite a speech for him, and his low, lovely voice brought sleepy, sultry summer nights to mind as if conjured by magic. What would he listen to? Country? Blues?

What would it be like, to lie in that hammock with him and do "nothing"?

Chapter 4

Vera was rescued from further inappropriate musings—about hammocks, summer evenings, and James Knightley—by Twyla's chatter.

"I want a dog too," Twyla said. "We have lots of room for a dog, and I'd take real good care of it."

"Dogs take a lot work, Twy," Vera said. "They're a commitment for life. Even a hamster costs money and requires constant care."

"This would be a perfect property for a dog," James said—the dolt. "I'm sure when the time comes, you'll pick out the very best dog in the whole world for it, but right now, I need to get up and move around, or I'll sit here and help myself to another brownie."

"He can have seconds, can't he, Mom?"

"I cannot have seconds," James said, which spared Vera the next step in the argument: If James could have seconds, why couldn't Twy? "I'll become a fixture in this kitchen if I take another bite, like Winnie the Pooh when he ate too much honey. I noticed something about your garage door, though."

"What did you notice?" Twy just had to take the bait.

"Your garage door locks down nice and tight, but the service door doesn't have a dead bolt."

"What's a dead bolt?"

"Come here, I'll show you." He led Twyla to the kitchen door, and showed her how the mechanism on the dead-bolt lock worked. Twyla had used the lock herself many times—locking doors was a house rule—but now she was fascinated with it.

"When I was at the hardware store, I picked up a dead-bolt assembly, and I would be happy to install it on that garage door," he said, and now he was watching Vera, no hint of teasing or flirtation in his blue eyes.

"I can't believe that door has no dead bolt," Vera said, abandoning her last bite of brownie. "I'm certain I ordered dead bolts installed on every outside door, but now that you bring it up, I can't recall *throwing* the bolt on that door. Show me."

She followed James and Twyla out to the garage, and sure enough, no additional lock had been installed on the service door.

"This solves a mystery, in any case," she said. "A credit card ought to be sufficient to slip this open."

"Not for long," James said. "Let me get the hardware out of my car, and we'll take care of this before I've digested my brownie."

Vera wanted to tell him no, that he wasn't allowed to get anything from his car, he wasn't allowed to correct this troubling oversight, but she kept her mouth shut. She could install a damned lock, but not until she'd bought a power drill and some other tools and figured out how to use them.

Besides, she was too relieved at the realization that Donal hadn't somehow managed to get his hands on a key.

"Twy, didn't you have a recipe written down for James?"

"It's up in my room. I'll go get it, and maybe write down

the one for raccoon droppings too." She scampered off, leaving Vera alone in the garage with James Knightley.

"Raccoon droppings?"

"Chocolate peanut butter oatmeal no-bake cookies. Some people call them school-lunch cookies. Alexander said they looked like raccoon droppings."

"I have seen raccoon spore," James said, one corner of his mouth tipping up. "The man was mistaken."

Well, of course James Knightley had seen raccoon droppings, and he could probably describe them in French too, while building palaces with his bare hands and arguing arcane law before the World Court at The Hague.

Men. "Weren't you going to get some hardware from your car?"

The second corner of his mouth tipped up. "Be right back," he said, going through the unlocked door.

Minutes later, he was drilling and squinting and muttering to himself, a man transported by the mysterious task of installing a lock, while Vera wrestled with an uneasy mix of gratitude and resentment.

"Don't take this the wrong way," Vera said, talking to his long, muscular back, "but I'd appreciate it if we didn't see much of you after today."

The power drill went silent. "Hand me that rag, would you?"

He didn't turn, but instead inspected the doorknob, turning it this way and that, then turning the knob that controlled the dead bolt.

Vera passed him a rag. "I said we're grateful, but I'm concerned Twyla will get attached to you, and that wouldn't be good for her."

Concerned Twy's mother—who hadn't noticed the

lack of dead bolt on her own garage door—might be tempted to call on James for something other than handyman skills she ought to have acquired herself by now.

"I think that about does it." James closed the door and shot the bolt, then packed up his tools in a metal box Vera could probably not have lifted to save herself. When he straightened, he seemed taller to Vera, more imposing.

"Now what are you going on about, chasing me off the property like I'm some stray dog you don't want getting into your garbage?"

"It isn't that," Vera said, for stray dogs never made a pair of worn jeans look half so good. "It's that Twyla lost her father, then she lost her stepfather, and I'm protective of her. She'll get ideas about you."

James set the toolbox down with a solid thunk, all the tools rattling about the way Vera's insides rattled when she had to manage a confrontation with anything other than classical repertoire.

"Twyla is about as well adjusted as a kid can be, Vera, and that is thanks to you. I could tell you we're neighbors, and you'd be within your rights to occasionally ask me over to see to something like a lock, or a squeaky hinge, or a dead battery. I'd gladly accept some homemade cookies in return, but you wouldn't believe I could be that kind of neighbor."

Was that how it was supposed to work? "You live two miles away."

"By the road. As the crow flies, one farm and some woods are all that separate us. That makes us neighbors out here in the country. The problem isn't Twyla. The problem is you, and whatever that damned Donal or sainted Alexander did to annihilate your confidence."

"He didn't annihilate my confidence," Vera said, except he had, and that wasn't the worst of it. "Maybe the problem is you, James, and the fact that I'm not interested in being neighbors, as you put it."

Unfair. Vera knew the words were unfair. She used to be a fair woman who could control her own mouth, one who didn't feel like crying for no reason at the worst possible times.

James stared at the newly installed dead bolt, then hefted the toolbox. "Please ask Twyla to get me those recipes, because her feelings will be hurt if I don't take them with me. But, Vera…"

The expression he turned on her was somber to the point of sadness, as solemn as the key of B-flat minor.

"You're snakebit and gun-shy. I understand that because maybe I am a little too, but I am not who and what you need to be afraid of. I'll go—I've worn out my welcome, clearly—but I want a promise from you. Two promises."

She nodded, because he was leaving. He'd said he was going, and that was what she wanted. Sort of.

"First, call my brother. He's a damned fine family-law attorney, and if anybody can spike Donal's guns, it's Trent."

"I will call him. I've been meaning to, but I've been busy."

"Stop thinking you have to take on an idiot like Donal by yourself. Trent can make him go away, and stay away, and you deserve at least that."

"What was the second promise?"

"Second, keep my number, and show Twyla where it is. You're isolated here. If you're concerned about

Donal coming on the property in broad daylight, you really ought to get the place posted, and put a damned gate across the foot of your driveway. Failing that, keep my number."

Was it controlling behavior to ask woman to keep a phone number? To steer her back to the attorney who'd done such a good job for her in the past?

No. It was not. Not by any sane lights.

"I tossed your number out, James. I didn't mean to. I was tidying up. I don't have your number."

Even his smile was solemn. "I'll give it to you again," he said, taking out a pen and a scrap of paper, "and again, and as many times as it takes. The whole world is not your enemy, Vera."

"I know," she said, but when the man she'd married turned into an enemy, the man she'd entrusted her entire career to, she'd stopped relying on her ability to gauge who was a friend and who wasn't.

James waited in the garage for Vera to fetch Twyla and the recipe card. He made a fuss about how to halve the recipe—"How 'bout that? Fractions everywhere!"—before stuffing it into his jacket pocket.

"When you're in school on Monday, bossing around those fractions," he said to Twyla, "you take a minute to spot Merle and Grace on the playground, and tell them you helped me install a battery and a lock. They'll be no end of impressed that you have your own car already. Might even want to come over and see it, assuming your mom's willing for you to have some company of your own."

As closing arguments went, James's suggestion was dead-on, because nothing would do but he had to write down a phone number for his nieces, and suffer another hug from Twyla before he left.

Vera walked him to his car, wishing this morning, like many parts of her life, had come equipped with a do-over button.

James scanned the wintry landscape of her property, set the toolbox in the back of his vehicle, then leaned in close, close enough that Vera could catch a whiff of expensive, spicy aftershave.

"You know," he said, speaking almost into her ear, "if you were any other female who'd treated me to a brownie and some company on a Saturday morning, I'd be kissing your cheek when we parted, maybe sneaking in a friendly, innocuous hug. It wouldn't mean much, just a gesture of casual affection, but you might have enjoyed it. I know I would have."

He drew back, his expression still very much in B-flat minor.

"Thank you for installing the lock, James, and the battery, and for being so nice to Twyla." *And to me*, which was the real problem.

"Call Trent, Vera. Please."

Because she was an idiot, a cold, lonely idiot who felt a lot safer thanks to the man she was about to run off, Vera balanced with a hand to James's shoulder and planted a swift kiss on his cheek.

Before she could thank him again, or apologize, or make some other kind of fool of herself, he was gone.

His SUV had disappeared down the lane and into the trees, and Vera was still standing in the chilly breeze, her fingers tracing the cold curve of her unkissed cheek.

Why, why in the name of all that was sensible, sweet,

and lovely, did the first kiss she'd given a man in years
have to be a kiss of parting?

—◊—

"I do believe this is a historic moment." Mac plopped
his briefcase down on the conference table and settled
into a chair catty-corner from James. "You are in the
courthouse archives, doing research, and no delectable
clerks are fluttering about, stepping and fetching. You
have no patience for research."

James had no patience for fluttering.

"I don't dislike research," he said, though he disliked
the file in front of him very much. "I'd lose my edge
as a litigator if I didn't occasionally read an appellate
opinion, but this isn't quite research."

He tossed a glossy color photo across the table,
then another.

"Well, shit." Mac didn't pick them up, but he studied
them where they lay in all their appalling and dubious
glory. "Somebody done somebody wrong."

"Vera Waltham's second husband," James said.
"She's lucky she didn't lose an eye or suffer permanent
scarring. He didn't land a lot of blows, but the one she
took counted."

"She's one of Trent's clients? The cookie lady, right?"

"Was one of Trent's clients." Vera still baked a mean
batch of cookies. "The decree is final, and a restraining
order is in place."

"I expect this kind of evidence when I'm defending
an assault and battery, or assault with intent to maim, but
in a domestic…" Mac passed the photo back, handling
it by one corner, as if it were contaminated with some

nasty virus. "I cannot imagine this happening between people who promised to love, honor, and cherish each other, but it does. All the damned time."

"A woman is abused in this country every fifteen seconds, according to this morning's reading. I don't know how Trent stands it." And if the mother were abused, what chance did the children stand?

Mac sat back, as if seeking distance from the evidence James had been studying.

"Trent fights the good fight, and I imagine it helps for him to think of all those battered wives as somebody's little girl, somebody's Grace or Merle. It gives him an edge, a determination."

"Never thought of it like that." James stuffed the photos out of sight, back in the court file.

"You might have asked Trent about this. Did Vera press charges?"

"She didn't. She damned well should have, but she didn't. I haven't checked with District Court, but I'm guessing she would have invoked spousal privilege to avoid testifying against her husband. The divorce hadn't been filed when this happened, and the restraining order was by consent."

"Hard call to make," Mac said, his gaze straying to the court file. "Most guys don't get more reasonable when you put them behind bars, but this wasn't a wild punch after a long night at the bar. This was purposeful."

Like harassing Vera by phone had to be purposeful. "Her ex has kids. My guess is that carried weight with Vera." Two kids in the hellacious throes of adolescence.

Poor Vera, poor Twyla, and as for those teenagers… They needed horses, or dogs, and different parents.

Mac wrinkled his nose. "So Vera dumped the guy and left those kids to deal with him alone?"

James tipped back in his chair, feeling a headache start up at the base of his skull. "Vera had to choose between his kids and her kid, and she did what any sensible mom would do. She took her kid and got to high ground, but stays in touch with her stepchildren as best she can."

"Hard to do with a restraining order in place." Hard to do legally, was what Mac meant. "What prompted you to dig into this particular file?"

"I'm not used to being given the bum's rush," James said, closing the file. "This makes it easier to understand."

But not easier to accept.

"Vera Waltham turned down a chance to tango with Lance Romance himself?"

"You're just jealous." The ribbing was inevitable, and yet it grated. "When's the last time you enjoyed the intimate company of a willing woman, Mac?"

"That's a state secret. You truly never get turned down?"

"I don't do the asking. Less chance of rejection that way." Though right now, James did, indeed, feel rejected. He'd taken three days, a gallon of whole milk, and two batches of brownies to figure out even that much.

"You must have asked something," Mac said, "because she gave you the bum's rush. A lady doesn't turf a guy out for standing around looking adorable."

James felt about as adorable as a hungover porcupine. "Maybe she does, if she's so tired, disillusioned, and rattled she can't notice how adorable he is."

"Vera, a pleasure to see you again."

Trent Knightley got to his feet when a lady entered the room, but he didn't offer his hand. He was old-fashioned enough to wait until the woman made the overture first.

Which Vera did—she liked her lawyer, and had found his courtliness a much needed comfort when her second marriage had been in shambles. Then, too, to go with his fine manners, Trent Knightley had the litigating instincts of a buzz saw, and those had appealed to her just as strongly.

"Good to see you too," Vera said, "and these are a wedding present." She passed him a tin of turtle cookies, which he set aside to help her off with her coat.

"Partner cookies," he said, waggling dark eyebrows. "Not for distribution to the lowly associates, if I don't want my brothers giving me grief for the next three weeks. Have a seat."

He directed her to a conversational grouping and took the chair beside her. She appreciated that about him too—he didn't take the trappings of his profession to heart, didn't use the big, pretentious desk to put distance between him and his clients, didn't ask his paralegal to sit in and take notes for him.

"What's on your mind, lady? And don't try to pretty it up. James warned me you might make an appointment, but he didn't give me any details."

"May I congratulate you on your recent nuptials?" Because simply being here, in this office, made Vera's chest feel tight and her palms itch.

"You may," Trent said, his smile bashful. That

smile—not one Vera had seen on him before—
completely undermined his *GQ* legal-eagle look, and
made him more closely resemble James. "Not only did
I marry the woman of my dreams, but she's provided
Merle with the sister of her dreams."

"Blended families can be a challenge, but you sound
very happy." Why didn't they call them chopped,
pureed, or frapped families? Blended sounded calm and
smooth, though Vera's experience with Donal and his
children had been anything but.

"I didn't know it was possible to be this happy,"
Trent said, "but it seems in poor taste to toot my marital
bliss horn when your situation is so…different."

Weasel words—of course, he'd excel at weasel
words. "I was happy too, Trent, once upon a time, and
I'm not unhappy."

"How's Twyla?" He would remember. He was a dad
too, not only a lawyer.

"Thriving, complaining that school is boring, angling
for a dog."

"A dog might be a good idea."

No. It would not. Donal, of all people, liked dogs.
"Why do you say that?"

"You're not exactly in a crowded subdivision, Vera,
and dogs deter intruders."

The small talk was abruptly over—how had Trent
done that?—and it was time for Vera to once again
entrust her private business to a man she paid to care
about it. At least he did care—not all lawyers would.

"I suspect Donal of breaking the restraining order."

"In what regard?"

She laid it out for Trent, and he took notes, asked

questions, and when she plugged in her answering machine and played the last five messages for him, he listened.

"You're sure that's Donal's voice?"

"I'd bet my vintage Steinway on it, but not Twyla."

"Something about it sounds different from Donal, though. What kind of home security do you have?"

"Very stout locks on every door." *Now* Vera had stout locks on every door. "I thought I had a decent electronic system too, but I deactivate it during the day if I'm home. You're not rattling off motions and petitions and other lawyer-speak, Trent. Why not?"

"Because we need proof."

He set his yellow notepad aside, though Vera had heard the word "we." *We* meant she wasn't crazy—and it meant more legal fees.

"Donal doesn't fit the profile of a serial abuser," Trent said. "You had one incident of domestic violence, Vera, right at the time of separation, when it's most likely to occur to any couple."

God spare me from attorneys playing devil's advocate.

"But Donal wouldn't turn my money loose," she said. "He wouldn't let me take anything from the house except my piano, my computer, and our clothes. He damned near got me sued, because he booked performances knowing full well I was taking a hiatus."

Even reciting that litany had Vera's pulse rate accelerating. She didn't hate Donal, precisely, but she had a healthy loathing for the havoc he'd caused in her life.

Trent opened the tin of cookies and held them out to her.

Vera took one to be polite, though she felt like upending the entire tin.

"Donal's a first-class horse's behind," Trent said, munching on a cookie. "That doesn't make him a stalker. Anybody could have gotten into your garage, and we'll have a difficult time proving he's leaving these messages."

A difficult, expensive time was what Trent meant.

"So you want me to get an unlisted phone number? Stop all contact with his children? They're teenagers, Trent, and their own mother hardly gave them the time of day before her last round of rehab. They call me, and they come visit, and I don't want Twyla to think I've tossed them over the transom."

Though Vera had done that exactly. Left a pair of nearly motherless adolescents to deal with a man who was a stranger to charm on his good days. She got up, crossed the office, and pitched her uneaten cookie in the trash.

"All I want is for you to take a few precautions."

Trent sounded so damned reasonable, Vera wanted to bean him with the rhododendron thriving on the windowsill. The plant had grown at least half a foot wider and taller since the last time she'd been in this office, while Vera felt as if her life had only contracted.

"The ray of sunshine here," Trent said, "is that you know to within a three-hour window when your tire was slashed. I'll send a letter to Donal's attorney, asking him to prove Donal's whereabouts during that window, and threatening all manner of mischief if he can't."

"That might help." Vera hadn't thought about the timing. Hadn't been calm or logical enough to think it through. She resumed her seat, and perversely, now she wanted a damned cookie.

Also a glass of cold milk.

"You can afford the security cameras and motion sensors," Trent said. "I'm guessing you don't want to go that route."

He had a point. Trent Knightley was a good lawyer because the legalities never outran his common sense, but Vera resented his honesty mightily.

Of course, she resented everything these days, from the privacy of her home, to Twyla's chattering, to memories of James Knightley, whispering about hugs and kisses.

Life had been easier when Vera had limited herself to practice rooms and concert halls.

"I don't want to put that much energy into squashing a bug," she said. Or that much money—that much *more* money. "Even in that analogy, I'm thinking and talking like Donal does, in scarcity and survival terms. If I let that mindset take over, then I'll have nothing left for my music."

Trent sat back and considered her, and Vera knew the urge to squirm. God help his daughter's eventual boyfriends if they brought the young lady home ten minutes late.

"Are you playing again?"

"I practice." Vera busied her hands with packing up her answering machine. "I teach as many as a dozen lessons some weeks. I haven't booked any performances, and I don't know if I ever will again. Traveling and being a single parent don't mix."

Being a single parent and being broke didn't mix well either, though for now, Vera was doing well enough.

"You're a pianist, Vera. I can't imagine you being content without occasionally making music for an appreciative audience. DC, Baltimore, Richmond,

Philly, Pittsburgh, even New York—they're all within driving distance and full of concert halls."

"You didn't push this before." Vera's decision to take a hiatus from performing didn't come anywhere near qualifying as a legal issue, and yet, she'd had no one to discuss it with save Olga. "Why bring it up now?"

Trent put the lid back on the cookie tin. Vera had chosen the Winnie the Pooh tin for this batch because Trent often wore whimsical ties.

"A performance," he said, "even one booked two years in advance, will give you something to look forward to and take your mind off Donal's stupid maneuvers. Anticipating a professional future will make you stronger, in a sense, and less vulnerable, like a good security system."

"Very subtle, Trent, but you forget: Donal was my agent, and I wouldn't know the first thing about booking a gig. I was the talent. I came. I sat down. I played. All the contractual baloney, the fine print, the business details were beyond me, and I liked it that way."

She got to her feet, because the legal discussion was over, not because her lawyer was being too damned perceptive about matters outside the courtroom.

"So make a few phone calls," he said, rising. "Or I can make them. James is bound to know somebody in DC who does entertainment law, and they can hook you up with a new agent."

James could *hook her up*? "That's a very kind offer, but no thank you. I'm not ready."

He escorted her to the door—or followed her. "Your fans won't care if you play the 'Maple Leaf Rag.'"

"I like the 'Maple Leaf Rag'—it's tricky, in its way,

but I mean I'm not ready inside." She tapped her chest. "My technique is benefiting from time working on the basics, but the rest of me…"

The rest of Vera, as had been made clear over the weekend, was a nervous, cranky, ungracious, defensive wreck. She'd even gone so far as to draft a note of apology to James, then realized she'd have to send it to him at the office, where a secretary might open it.

"Yours was not a cordial divorce," Trent said when she trailed off. "Give it time, and then give it more time. I'll let you know what Donal's lawyer says, and thanks for the cookies."

He held her coat for her, held the door, and walked her out toward the reception area, but they took a left when she was used to taking a right, passing through a suite of offices she didn't recognize.

"Beulah, is James in?" Trent asked an older lady at a secretarial station.

"He's working on some indemnity language for those doctors, Trent. He worked through lunch, so approach with caution."

"Trenton Edwards Knightley—" Vera began.

"That will teach me to leave my diplomas hanging where anybody can see them. Come along." He took Vera gently by the wrist and towed her into James's office.

"Greetings, James, it's time you took a break from the dreaded indemnity clause."

"Damn it, Trent—" James slapped some fat volume closed and was on his feet before Vera could beat a retreat. "Vera Waltham. Hello."

This was his jungle, his briar patch, and he looked right at home in it.

The steel-blue suit had to have cost a pretty penny, the tie was silk, possibly Hermès—blue with an abstract pattern of intersecting red snaffle bits—and the loafers looked like Gucci's. Vera recognized the same scent she'd picked up on in her driveway. Sage with notes of smoke and spice, a masculine do-me fragrance if ever she'd inhaled one.

Expensive, maybe even a custom blend.

"We have a question," Trent said, his fingers around Vera's wrist still, preventing her from pelting out of the office at a dead run.

"Shoot," James said, settling back against the front of his desk. "I might have an answer."

"Vera needs to talk to somebody who handles entertainment contracts. Any ideas?"

From the gleam in Trent's eyes, Vera had an awful suspicion that James was an expert on entertainment law.

"Let me give it some thought. I'm in touch with half my law school class, and several of them had their sights on entertainment law. It's an interesting field."

"You have Vera's number?" Trent asked.

"I can get it from the file."

"Great. Vera, I'll be in touch, and you should consider that security system. It could get you the proof you need much more quickly than we'll find it otherwise."

Just like that, Vera's attorney, her zealous advocate, the man she entrusted with her dirty laundry and her personal fortune *shamelessly deserted her* in enemy territory.

"He means well," James said, closing the door after his brother. "I'd apologize for him, but I can't recall Trent pulling a stunt like this before."

So Trent had ambushed them both. Maybe that explained why they were both smiling.

"I have two brothers," Vera said. "They get odd notions, brothers do. Your office is different from Trent's."

"Different how?"

"Sleek where his is cozy, a little intimidating where his is comforting." Her gaze lit on a small colorful painting on the wall beside his desk, a luminous image of flowers adorning a country porch. "That's a signed original?"

"I inherited it, so don't ascribe any good taste to me. I do like it, or I wouldn't hang it."

When a student wasn't prepared for a lesson, they found endless ways to talk about the pieces they hadn't spent enough time working on. Vera had no patience with their prevarications, or with her own.

"About the entertainment law thing? You can forget it."

"All right," James said, without an instant's hesitation, which should not have been a disappointment.

"Just like that? Your brother came close to browbeating me over it."

"Trent's in love. He wants everybody to be as happy as he and Hannah are. Give it a few years, and he'll be as grumpy as the rest of us."

"Is that why you're not married?" Vera peered at James, past the French designer tie, the Italian shoes, and Savile Row tailoring, to the shrewd country boy— *hiding?*—beneath. "You don't believe in romance?"

"I believe in romance," he said, uncrossing his arms. "Sometimes I think I'm the last man standing who does, but marriage is hard, and I don't have to quote the divorce statistics at you. Trent's department turns away business."

"So you'll not even make the attempt? Do you ever intend to marry?" Why did his answer matter, when Vera wouldn't see him again after today?

"I don't know," James said, touching a corner of the painting's frame. "I haven't thought much about it. I assume you're soured on the whole marriage thing?"

"Your assumption is in error." Vera's answer surprised her and had one corner of James's mouth kicking up. "I had a good marriage the first time out. We weren't passionately in love, by any means, but we were a team, and we respected each other. Donal was a bad choice made out of grief and inexperience. I'm older and wiser now."

And buckets less confident.

James left off fussing his inheritance. "So it's me you don't approve of? You intend to get back on the horse. I'm simply not a suitable mount?"

Had he set her up for that question, as if she were a hostile witness on cross-examination? But, no, Vera had put her own foot in her own mouth.

"I don't disapprove of you. I…someday, I *might* remarry, but not… I'm not ready." Not ready for even a hamster, for God's sake.

James blatantly watched while a blush spread up Vera's neck and across her cheeks. When she was well and truly mortified, he offered her a shameless smile and winged an arm at her.

"While I'm enjoying this conversation immensely, I have three pages of insurance clauses to get through by midnight. I'll walk you to your car."

She took his arm, as if they were mincing up the aisle at some society wedding, and let him lead her through the building and out to her truck.

"I will not ask you if you've replaced your spare yet, and I will not ask you why Trent wants you to get a security system, and I will not point out that a dog would be a lot cheaper and more fun," he said as she stowed her gear.

"Good of you."

James leaned close again, exactly as he'd done in her driveway. Vera studied his gold tie tack—a rearing lion— rather than close her eyes and inhale through her nose.

"But, Vera, I *will* tell you I've been thinking about that hug I didn't cadge, and that kiss I didn't steal."

Vera had thought about them too. She continued to think about them all the way to the tire shop, all through the afternoon's lessons, and then all the way home.

Chapter 5

Donal MacKay considered himself a patient man. He'd waited years to snatch Veracity Winston from Alexander Waltham's overprotective managerial clutches, and the wait had been worthwhile, at least for a time.

Waiting for his attorney to finish reading some damned letter was not worthwhile.

"What does it say?"

Aaron Glover, Es-damned-squire, shoved the letter under Donal's nose.

"I swear, Donal, if you're tormenting that woman, I will drop you flat, and that will send a signal to any lawyer you attempt hire in this town. They will ask first if you've paid off my bill, and when you say yes, they will call me to catch you in the lie. They will ask next if you and I parted on tolerable terms, and when I hem and haw and say everything but yes, the lawyers willing to touch your domestic troubles will be rubes fresh out of law school or the nearly disbarred and suspended."

Donal tuned out the sermon—what was it that made lawyers feel like they alone, of all God's flawed creatures, were entitled to lecture and remonstrate?—and scanned the letter.

"It isn't me," Donal said, passing the letter back. "Tell her pet barracuda to back off. The last thing I want to do is antagonize that woman."

Aaron Glover stood and glared down at his client. "Don't hand me a line of bull, Donal. You want to intimidate the hell out of her, push her around, and generally act like you own her, but I'm tired of telling you slavery was outlawed in this country some time ago."

Slavery had been outlawed in Scotland long before the colonials took an entire war to settle the matter.

"I was her agent," Donal replied quietly, though he wanted to shout. "Everything I did was to further her career. You think classical music is big money, Glover? You think the concert halls fill up like they did fifty years ago?"

"Stow it," Glover said, pacing to the office window and turning his back on his client. For that alone, Donal would have fired him.

Would have, back when he was agenting the hottest classical musician to take the stage in twenty years.

But he'd not paid even half of Glover's fees from the divorce, and young Mr. Glover was too competent to be susceptible to a disciplinary complaint through the grievance committee.

More's the pity.

You land a single blow on a woman—a woman who had provoked you past all bearing—and you were labeled for the rest of your miserable, misbegotten life.

It wasn't as if Donal had meant to strike Vera, for pity's sake. He'd never laid a hand on a woman or a child before or since, and he would have apologized sincerely if she hadn't slapped that restraining order on him.

Then he'd dragged his miserable arse off to counseling—which he could not afford—because his attorney had strongly "suggested" it.

"If you didn't slash her tire, who did? If you didn't leave those messages, who did?"

"It is not my job to investigate every petty prank in Damson County," Donal said. "If you must know, when the restraining order expires, which it ought to in about six weeks, I want to approach Vera about honoring the concert dates she hasn't canceled yet."

Glover fiddled with some sort of high-tech blinds, softening the afternoon glare in an office that had likely cost more to furnish than Donal's entire downstairs.

"If you were at an AA meeting, just say so, Donal. I have it on good authority at least two of the judges sitting in this county are regular attendees."

Was that supposed to comfort a man drowning in legal bills?

"I do not attend AA meetings, Glover, though I'd put up with even those glorified pep rallies for the sadly afflicted if it would put me in a more flattering light in Vera's eyes."

Glover turned, his gaze roaming Donal's features with the flat curiosity of one who'd seen much despite his relative youth.

"Donal, you are either the ballsiest son of a bitch I've ever met, or you're stone stupid. What makes you think Vera would want you to represent her, even if she did take on those performances?"

One could be ballsy and stupid, if one were Scottish, broke, and weary to death of lawyers.

"Vera doesn't have a choice. If you knew the first thing about business law, you'd know I booked those dates in my capacity as her agent. She has a small window left when she can cancel them and pay a reasonable fee, but if she doesn't cancel soon, I get the commission on the advance due the agent. She's contractually bound, plain and simple. As agent, I have a lot of say in how those performances take place."

"Why would you want this?" Glover asked, folding his arms across his chest. He was a big man, fit, lean, and smart, a gladiator in his prime. He'd been chosen to be a suitable adversary to that snake Knightley, but he'd disappointed Donal. Who would have thought a gladiator played by a bunch of infernal rules?

"You think I'm obsessed with my former wife's charms?" Donal said. "I can assure you, ours was a practical union on both sides. The poor woman was too busy pining after her dead first husband or spoiling the children when she wasn't practicing. As far as I'm concerned, she can marry anybody who won't interfere with her talent."

With her revenue-generating ability. Donal wasn't proud of such a mercenary position, but his children needed to eat.

"As a commodity," he went on, "Vera's stock is going up now because she's on hiatus. She saves her passion for her music. Sales of her recordings are steady, when they should be nonexistent, and she's going completely to waste, teaching out in this benighted backwater. She could come back stronger than ever, line up performances five years out, and make me enough to retire comfortably. She agreed to do as much when I married her."

The prospect of a comfortable retirement—of any retirement—had made a fool of him. Donal wasn't proud of that either.

Glover scrubbed a hand over his face, glanced out the window, then back at Donal, and oh, mercy, Donal had failed once again to impress his counsel with selfless sentiments and bottomless remorse.

Donal would apologize to Vera all day long, sincerely and humbly, but that was none of this fellow's business.

"Whatever you do, Donal, do not approach her personally until that restraining order is expired. You will go to jail, no ifs, ands, or buts. The best attorney in the state could not ethically prevent that outcome. That your children have contact with her is over my objection, but the judge didn't place any restrictions on them. Now, where were you at the time Vera's car was vandalized?"

"None of your business."

"Donal, I cannot defend you if you don't give me the ammunition to do so."

"I am not charged with anything." Donal plucked an imaginary speck of lint from the sleeve of his best suit. "Really, Glover, must I do your lawyering for you? Send the appropriate letter fussing and fuming and claiming I want a cordial relationship with Vera when circumstances allow it. It's the damned truth." He rose, not waiting for Glover to be the one ending the meeting.

For a patient man, Donal was about at the end of his rope, regardless of the fees owed for services rendered. Had Glover done a better job, Vera would have been brought to heel, and this whole mess could have been avoided.

At the very least, Vera would be performing again, and happier for it.

Donal had reconciled himself to the divorce easily enough—they hadn't had much of marriage, after all—but if Glover had been more effective, then the financial mess might not have been so god-awfully complicated.

And Donal did so hate complications.

———∿∿∿———

When Trent Knightley needed a knock-down, drag-out, two-hand-tackle game of racquetball—when he was coming down off a bad loss or a tough win in court, for example—he called his brother James. Typically, Trent could hold his own against James, but had to battle for every point.

The difference in their ages was part of it, a small part, but James had a natural athleticism that defied fairness. Trent had long ago decided the better course was to be proud of his brother.

And he was.

Also worried about him.

"What in the hell has gotten into you?" Trent passed James a bottle of water and flopped down on the bench beside him. They were in a panting, stinking, righteous sweat, and Trent would be sore for days. "You were trying to kill me."

James chugged half the bottle. "Just playing for keeps."

"You weren't playing, James. What gives? Hannah won't like it if you cripple me for life."

"I'll be there to comfort her and serve as a father figure for the girls." James elbowed Trent ungently in the gut. "You go tend to your aches and pains, old man."

"Hannah already turned you down flat once. You gave it your best shot, and she chose the better man."

"My best shot? You call a few casual lines over lunch

a man's best shot? I wasn't half trying, and you'd best treat that lady like a queen unless you want her straying into my more appreciative arms."

"You're coming very close to crossing a line, James." Trent spoke quietly, because James was a flirt and maybe a slut, but he was also Trent's brother, and a gentleman.

A gentleman slut, if such a thing were possible. Maybe even a gentleman slut on slut-hiatus, if Mac's speculations were accurate.

"Put a sock in it, Trent. Hannah Knightley is your wife, for one thing, and ass over teakettle in love with you, for another. I have my standards. I'm just…"

"Just what?" Trent cracked open his own water bottle—even his hands were sore—and waited.

"I'm thinking of getting a dog."

"You love animals," Trent said, and yet James possessed none of his own. What did a dog have to do with playing racquetball like a rhinoceros on crack? "You have plenty of space, and a dog is good company."

"Dogs stink. They chew your favorite shoes, piss on the carpet, hurk on the porch, and either hump everything in sight or come in heat, and that's worse."

Too good an opening for a concerned older brother to pass up. "You don't want the competition?" Trent nudged James hard and let a little of his water spill on James's leg.

James nudged back harder. "For your information—"

"I know. Mac is fretting that civilization as we know it has come to an end because you're working a lot more than you're playing."

Playing. Something in Trent's mind connected, and his mild concern ratcheted up a notch. He would say

something to Hannah and see what her woman's intu-
ition suggested.

James chugged the rest of his water, crumpled up the
bottle, and lobbed it into the nearest trash can.

"My department is shorthanded," James said. "You
stole the perfect new hire away from me, and then you
married her. I'm taking up the slack."

"Take up bowling, come riding with us, or go
fishing with Mac. You need a hobby, James, or—I
can't believe I'm saying this—to get out and socialize more. You've got the biggest little black book in
the history of single men." Trent passed him another
water. "The single females of Damson County will
go into a collective mope if you continue to withhold
your favors."

This time, his nudge was playful, or intended to be.
James didn't nudge him back.

"No, Trent, they won't. They'll go shopping and buy
a new pair of shoes, and in the morning, their new shoes
will stay in their closet and still fit just fine."

James held up a fist to bump in parting, then rose and
walked away.

Slowly. At least James walked away slowly.

When Trent could, when he was done with his second
bottle of water and had properly inventoried his pulled
and aching muscles, he got up slowly too, and called
his wife.

—∿∿—

Rather than spend his morning staring at more
crossword puzzles or—James had resisted so far—
breaking out the sudoku, James sought the winter

woods because nothing soothed quite the way a quiet woods could, the dead leaves crunching underfoot, the occasional squirrel lecturing from the safety of a high, sturdy branch.

A dog would have enjoyed the chilly breeze, because to a dog, the wind always bore interesting information.

But, James reminded himself, a dog would have found something dead to roll in, and happily brought the stink into the house for the next three weeks.

Growing up, James's father had favored bull mastiffs as farm dogs. He'd said they were neither too dumb nor too bright. James had found them loyal and good-natured, if a little hard on the groundhog, rabbit, and squirrel populations.

But big. Too big to spend long days crated in the kitchen while James was off making his living at the office or the courthouse. And one dog wasn't enough, because they were pack animals, genetically predisposed to having others of their kind to socialize with.

So no bull mastiffs. No dogs, in fact.

A sound off to the left dragged James's attention away from the dogs he wasn't going to buy—a brindle pair would be nice, maybe breeding quality.

Whatever was moving around was big enough to be indifferent to how much noise it made in the woods.

A rabid animal might not care about making a racket, but a healthy animal ought to. The Maryland mountains provided a home to bears, and increasingly, to bobcats, mountain lions, and coyotes.

None of those big predators sang "Alice the Camel" as they hunted their next meal.

"Hullo, James!"

"Twyla, hello. You've wandered a long way from home."

"Not so far. Besides, I'm not lost. Home is right over that way."

She gestured vaguely over her shoulder. The girl wasn't wearing mittens or a scarf, and sneakers were not the wisest apparel for walking in the woods.

"Home is that way," James said, taking her by the shoulders and gently spinning her about 120 degrees. "You aren't dressed for hiking, my friend. Come on. I'll walk you to the tree line."

"Are you sure?"

"I'm sure. I've been walking these woods for years, and it isn't that hard to tell which way to head. What time of day is it?"

"Nine in the morning," Twyla said, giving him a patient look. "Mom will be doing her exercises for at least another hour."

So Vera was a woman who took her fitness seriously. "Where did the sun come up?"

"Over there," Twyla said, pointing generally east.

"Then that's east, and the woods are west of your property, right?"

"I guess so."

At least James wasn't the only one feeling a bit lost. "If you're exploring unfamiliar territory, Twy, you need to know how to find your way home. If that's east, you show me where west is."

He oriented her to the compass points, and led her through a series of questions that resulted in Twyla figuring out in which direction her home lay.

"If I had a dad, he'd show me things like that," Twyla said, kicking at the dead leaves as she walked along.

If James had a dad… But he hadn't had a dad since he'd turned thirteen.

"If you had a dad, he'd bless you out something fierce for leaving the house without telling your mom where you went."

"How did you know?"

"You're not the only person ever to be eight years old, Twyla Waltham." Or to heed a reckless impulse. "Allow me to point out, your mother was also eight once upon a time."

Twyla stumbled on a rock hidden beneath the carpet of leaves. James wasn't quick enough to catch her, but she righted herself and trudged on.

"Yeah, but Mom was perfect. I heard Donal telling her that once when I was supposed to be in bed. He said she used to be perfect, and he liked her better when she was a girl who listened to her elders."

"I take it Donal is older than your mom?" Did posing that question constitute prying? James was fairly sure it did.

"He was a geezer. My dad was a geezer too, but Mom liked him."

"I guess that makes me a dinosaur?"

She smiled up at him. "You're not a geezer yet, and you can do fractions."

Her smile reminded James of her mom, and that was both a joy and an irritation.

"Fractions are one of my greatest strengths," James said, smiling back. "You will tell your mom you took off this morning without letting her know, won't you?"

"I don't want to," Twyla replied, and the lawyer in James heard the hedging. "She'll say she's disappointed in me, and that's the worst thing ever. She gets this patient look on her face, and I want to cry."

Thank God, older brothers didn't cry. "But you broke a rule, didn't you, Twy?"

"Maybe."

At least two rules, then. Time to do a neighbor a kindness. "If your mom asks me, I won't lie to her. I'll tell her you were out prancing around in these woods, half lost, tempting any bear or mountain lion who came along."

"There are *bears* and *mountain lions* around here?"

"Black bears for sure. Don't worry about them, though, because they're shy. If you make a lot of noise—sing 'Alice the Camel' at the top of your lungs, for example—they'd probably only sniff you over without taking a very big bite."

Twyla slipped a small, cold hand into James's larger one. "If people are going to have bears in their woods, they should put up signs."

"These aren't my woods, and they aren't yours either. If people are going to trespass, they should be glad the woods aren't posted."

Twyla came to a halt but did not drop James's hand. "I thought this was our land."

"Your land stops just inside the tree line. You see this pile of rocks, here?" James pointed to a long, undulating line of rubble.

"I wondered what it was."

"This used to be a stone wall, and it marks the line between your land and Inskip's."

"What happened to it?"

How long had it been since James had enjoyed such a natural curiosity about his surroundings?

"Time happened to it," James said, turning them to walk along the ruin that was once a stout wall. Time happened to a lot of once-solid structures. "Back when they cleared the land and first put it to the plow, they built these walls with the rocks they turned up from the new fields. Over time, the wall would settle, the ground would freeze and thaw, and freeze and thaw, and the wall would shift, until it began to come undone. In spring, you be careful climbing over these rocks, because the blacksnakes like to come out and sun themselves."

"*Snakes?*"

Mission accomplished. "Big blacksnakes, and the occasional copperhead too. A bite from a copperhead might kill a little thing like you, and it would hurt something fierce. Then too, poison ivy loves to grow in these woods, and so does poison oak."

Also wildflowers, but James didn't tell Twyla that. She had his hand in a death grip now.

"Have you ever seen a snake for real?"

"As big around as my wrist," James said, holding out his free arm. "He was having a nice comfortable nap on a big, flat rock, but he heard me walking up, and came awake."

"How can he hear without ears?"

Leave it to a kid. "He can feel vibrations. He has organs right under his skin for that purpose, and then too, his whole body is lying on the ground, so he can feel things like you'd feel somebody walking on your bed when you're trying to nap."

Twyla was quiet, but because James was matching his stride to a child's, they weren't making very quick progress through the woods.

"You know a lot, James. Did you learn all this when you went to law school?"

"I'm not sure I learned anything important in law school. I do know you should not have wandered off alone, and you know it too." Spoken like a guy who'd wandered off alone into a lot of other people's beds.

"But staying home all the time is *boring*. Mom does her exercises every morning, no matter what, and it's the weekend. We should be having fun, and we never do."

Twyla's observation landed in the middle of James's mood with the jarring solidity of a rock lurking beneath the leaves. Yes, the weekend was supposed to be for fun. Crossword puzzles were not fun. Visiting Inskip's heifers was not fun.

"You could do the exercises with your mom."

"No. I can't. They're too hard, and they aren't fun."

"Then you have to negotiate," James said, feeling a little wicked. "You have to figure out what you each want, then find a way so you can both get it."

"I want a dog. If I had a dog, then those old bears wouldn't eat me. We could watch movies together and do homework together and everything. I'd name him Ralph."

"That's a fine name for a dog. Did you ever call my nieces?"

Twyla stopped in midstride and peered up at him. "I forgot. I still have the paper you gave me with their phone number on it, but I forgot to call them."

James boosted her over an enormous fallen oak, then climbed over himself. Inskip would turn the deadfall to firewood next year, and James would enjoy helping him. Not a hobby, not fun, but something to look forward to.

"If you want to call my nieces, I'm sure they're awake by now."

"I'll call them. You're going to tell Mom I went for a hike, aren't you?"

James wanted to, for the sake of Twyla's safety, but also because it was an excuse to call Vera and hear her voice. He'd probably succeeded in scaring the girl out of the woods for a couple of years though. His brothers had pulled the same routine on him when he'd been six.

"I won't bring it up, Twy, but if she asks me if I saw you out here half lost and bellowing 'Alice the Camel' to scare away the snakes and bears and mountain lions and coyotes and rabid raccoons, then I will tell her the truth."

"Coyotes aren't so bad," Twyla said, darting a glance in all directions.

Stubborn. She was Vera's daughter, after all.

"It's the dead of winter," James said, "and you aren't wearing gloves or mittens. What if you fell and twisted your ankle and were stuck out here for a week while we got out the bloodhounds to find you? You'd freeze, if a bear didn't eat you first."

"You aren't wearing gloves. You'd make a much bigger snack for a bear than I would."

He gave her credit for trying to lawyer the lawyer. "I know how to scare a bear off."

"You want to sing 'Alice the Camel' with me? My mom sings harmony to it, and it's a lot more fun than when I sing alone."

"We're at the tree line, Twy. I'll stand here and watch you walk right up to the house. Be sure you lock the door behind you when you go inside, and in my experience, the sooner you confess a sin, the easier it is to live with the penance."

"It isn't against the Commandments. I memorized them, and there's nothing in there about thou shalt not take a walk."

"Honor thy father and mother, or thy mother will be mighty disappointed in thee."

She scowled, dropped his hand, and trooped off toward the house.

Ambling around in subfreezing weather was no way to work out the stiffness James was developing from yesterday's racquetball session.

Getting old was hell.

He had the rest of Sunday to kill, and no idea how to kill it. He could go into the office—he could always go into the office. He'd gone into the office yesterday after he'd left the gym, and look what that had gotten him.

A sore ass and a draft subcontract that wasn't due until mid-week.

He could call somebody and get himself invited over for a relaxed afternoon of lovemaking, followed by dinner out, possibly finishing with a movie.

But which somebody? No particular somebody came to mind, and James didn't typically do the calling. In fact, he never did the calling anymore. Moreover, the whole idea of admitting he was that incapable of filling a day off with something worth doing was a blow he would not inflict on his pride.

Maybe he should lease a horse, a trail horse good for the occasional weekend waddle down the lane.

Except waddling down the lane had never appealed to James—hard to keep a horse fit when nobody broke a sweat—and the reasonable place to keep a horse was Adelia's therapeutic riding barn.

Adelia, whose number James had tossed. He had a hard copy of that phone-directory file somewhere, but he lacked the motivation to hunt it up. Instead, he got out the local paper and started on the crossword puzzle out of sheer boredom.

As he was trying to think of the British word for grain—four letters—he spotted an advertisement in the next column:

"Piano instruction. Serious students only. Reasonable rates." The phone number looked to be a cell from the exchange.

He needed a hobby that wouldn't kill him or freeze his parts off, and he'd always enjoyed music. He'd taken years of piano lessons—his mom had loved music almost as much as she'd enjoyed painting—and he still fiddled around from time to time.

He dialed the number, got one of those android messages, and left his cell number in response.

Piano lessons were a stupid idea, an impulse, and James almost hoped the lady didn't return his call—assuming it was a lady. He wandered over to his piano, opened the lid, and sat down. Two hours later, he was still fiddling and fussing with a Beethoven slow movement, one he'd never really been serious about but had always wanted to learn someday. It involved crossing the left hand over the right, weaving melodies in and around each other, and James had a recording of the piece that mesmerized him with its lyricism.

He was interrupted when his phone rang, and he very nearly didn't stop playing. Probably Trent, wanting to compare aches and pains. Well, Trent had Hannah to poor-baby him—

The phone would apparently ring all afternoon. "Knightley."

"I am calling to thank you, first, for seeing Twyla safely home. This is Vera Waltham."

An adolescent pang of pleasure hit James at the sound of her voice even if she was in mama-mode.

"You're welcome, Vera. What's second? You said you were calling first to thank me."

A pause, and James envisioned another dinner in that big spotless-but-cozy kitchen. Maybe play some Go Fish afterward and see if the Waltham ladies were inclined to cheat at cards. A little thank-you dinner to the man who single-handedly fended off hungry bears and rabid snakes—or he would if there were such things—to rescue fair damsels lost in the Great North Woods.

This lovely meal would be served with a small but artfully presented serving of crow for the hostess who'd told him they shouldn't socialize.

Hah. Hah. And Hah.

"Were you spying on us?" Vera asked.

"*What?*"

"I asked if you were spying on us, or…something."

The woman was batty—and then James's mind had to present him with images of the same woman with a dark purple shiner, a busted lip, and a swollen jaw.

"You mean was I standing guard to see if I spotted anybody lurking in your bushes?"

"I don't have bushes," Vera said. "I've been meaning

to landscape. I want to do it myself, but I haven't gotten around to it. I'm being an idiot, but, James, were you spying on us?"

She needed hugs, and endearments, and a good neighbor. Also the plain truth.

"No, Vera Waltham, I was not spying. I've been walking Hiram Inskip's woods since I moved in here years ago. I also walk his fence lines and stop and visit with his cows. They, however, do not call me up to accuse me of deviant behavior, though they are as pretty a batch of heifers as I've ever seen."

Though the most placid heifers would spook given enough provocation and barrel right through any obstacle in their race to find safety.

"I wasn't accusing." Vera's tone was tense, tinged with self-consciousness. "I was asking."

While James had been making a try for humor—an unsuccessful try. "Vera, do you expect a man to admit he's stalking you? That's criminal behavior, which is bad enough, but it's also damned pathetic."

"I know."

Two words, and yet they conveyed a world of misery. James hiked himself up to sit on the kitchen counter and wished he had some cookies to munch on.

"Vera, what's wrong?"

"Somebody has been here. My stepson is visiting for the afternoon, and when I opened the garage door so he could park inside, I noticed the service door had been damaged."

James did not allow himself to swear. Part of him was relieved that she'd called him—the other part was pissed that she'd needed to.

"What does that mean?" he asked. "Damaged how?"

It meant something bad, because James could hear the tremor in Vera's voice. A tremor of fear, of nerves held together by indignation and self-discipline.

"They must have tried to get in, then been frustrated when they found the dead bolt had been installed. And, James? This could have happened while Twyla was out wandering around alone in the woods this morning."

Nobody could awful-ize like a mom could awful-ize.

"It could have happened earlier this week, while you were closeted with my brother, and Twy was safely bored at school. Sit tight, and I'll be over in a few minutes."

"Not now," Vera said. "Darren will leave shortly. Wait an hour, then come. Darren has Twy upstairs, playing some video game, so I stole a minute to call."

Vera wanted James to come over. That was good. James wanted to go to her. That was…what a neighbor did.

"You sure you want me to wait, Vera?"

"I don't want to upset Darren, particularly if Donal is behind this. I tore a strip off Twyla this morning, and she's still not talking to me."

Thank God for moms who knew how to mom. "She needed to get the message, Vera. I wasn't going to rat her out, but neither would I cover for her."

"She probably wasn't going to rat herself out, but I spied her coming across the yard and was screeching before she was in the kitchen."

"Good. She probably doesn't see you screeching very often, and I'm sure it made a suitable impression. I'll see you in an hour or so, and I'll expect some fresh brownies when I get there."

And possibly even a hug.

James hung up, Beethoven forgotten, and debated whether he should call Mac. Breaking and entering was a crime, and Mac was the criminal expert. Except there'd been no entering—this time—but there was trouble. There was definitely trouble.

And there was good news too, because if nothing else, the morning's developments proved that this time, Vera Waltham hadn't thrown James's number away.

Chapter 6

VERA HUNG UP, FEELING MARGINALLY BETTER. NOW instead of stewing over who had tried to break into her garage, she could stew over that *and* why she'd asked James Knightley to inspect the damage.

Anger gradually calmed her down—anger and the routine of whipping up a fresh batch of brownies. Common sense tried to assure her James Knightley didn't need to stalk anybody. If anything, he needed to beat the women away with a stick.

Women prettier, younger, and more interesting than a washed-up musician coming off a failed farce of a marriage.

So what was the real reason she'd called James?

Rather than honestly answer that question, Vera cleaned up the kitchen and considered waving James off. What was he supposed to do, anyway? Stand around and confirm her garage door had been hacked at with something sharp?

She brought that unhappy thought to an abrupt cadence and bellowed up the stairs.

"Brownies are out of the oven!" A steady cacophony of explosions stopped, and the patter of not-so-little feet commenced.

"I could smell them all the way up in Twyla's room," Darren said. His feet—in loosely laced Timberlines—appeared first, clunking down the stairs. Black jeans came next, complete with rips and holes, followed by swinging chains, a studded belt, and an incongruously soft and comfy red-plaid flannel shirt.

His chin sported bristles, not quite a beard—seventeen could be an awkward age. Vera almost felt sorry for Donal, having created a son whose need to differentiate himself from his staid, stern father had resulted in such displays.

"Who wants ice cream?" Vera asked.

Though Twyla wasn't speaking to her mother, she communicated to the room at large that she'd like some vanilla ice cream on her brownie.

Darren looked up a few minutes later, spoon poised for the first bite. "You're not having any, Vera?"

"Not at the moment. What were you two playing?"

"Death and Destruction II," Twyla said, then shot a guilty glance at her former stepbrother. "It's not really that violent."

"Right," Vera said evenly. "Darren will take it home with him when he finishes his brownie."

Darren tousled Twyla's hair. "Good move, brat. For that, I might have to swipe a bite of your brownie."

That odd, awkward affection he showed a much younger child was part of what motivated Vera to stay in touch with both Darren and his sister Katie. They took after their mother in coloring—tall, slender, pale, and auburn-haired—but they were a stubborn pair too, and Vera suspected half the reason they maintained a relationship with her and Twyla was to thwart their father.

Or maybe brownies had something to do with it.

"Darren can have seconds, can't he, Mom? He doesn't have to steal from mine."

Twyla moved her bowl a few inches farther from Darren as he dodged his spoon in the air over her ice cream.

"He's a growing boy. They have hollow legs, and his dinner will probably be a couple of hot dogs wolfed down at midnight."

"It's a school night," Darren said, his mouth curving in a sullen line. "I'll be home by ten or get locked out again."

"In which case," Vera said, cutting herself a sliver of brownie, "you know you can come here if you run out of other options." Donal wouldn't think to look for his son here, would he?

"Thanks, but my friends put me up when Dad's a jerk."

Which, Vera knew, was much of the time, though Darren never missed an opportunity to try his father's patience, either.

"How's your mom doing?" Vera asked.

"She's great," Darren said, tossing his hair out of his eyes. "I'm taking Katie over there for dinner tonight."

"Please tell Tina I said hello."

Darren nodded, but the request likely made him feel awkward. Donal had proposed to Vera before his divorce from Tina MacKay had been final, though Tina apparently bore no grudge. If anything, Vera's few interactions with Tina suggested she'd earned Tina's pity.

Which in hindsight made perfect sense.

"Before you take off, Darren, I want to give you a house key. One for you and one for Katie."

His spoon clattered to his empty bowl. "You sure?"

"I'm sure. Your father and I are divorced, but you and Katie are still family to me and Twyla. I don't expect you to use it except in emergencies, and your dad might be upset to know I've done this. I can't tolerate the thought of you wandering the streets of Damson Valley at midnight in the dead of winter because your watch was five minutes slow."

Though nobody wore a watch anymore, and cell phones kept accurate time—if they didn't run out of juice.

"I can always sleep in the car," Darren said, scraping his spoon against the sides of the bowl. "I've done it before."

"I know, but it isn't safe." Vera brushed her hand over the top of his head, as much affection as his teenage pride would tolerate, and collected his empty bowl. She wanted him on his way before James showed up. If Darren casually mentioned her visitor to his father, all manner of grief might ensue for the boy.

Or for her.

"Someone's at the door!" Twyla shot off her stool and bolted up the hallway. Darren casually appropriated the last bite of her brownie.

"Finders, keepers," he said, grinning around a bite ice cream. "They're good brownies."

"I made a double batch. Take a couple for the road." Vera was putting them in a baggie when Twyla came steaming into the kitchen with James in tow.

"Mom, it's James! James, this is my brother, Darren. He's allowed to have seconds of the brownies too."

The kitchen grew smaller with James Knightley in it, but somehow calmer too. James was in jeans and a cream cable-knit sweater that did great things for a long torso and broad shoulders. His cheeks were rosy, suggesting he might have walked over.

"Darren, pleased to meet you. I'm James Knightley." James extended a hand, and for an instant, Darren merely stared at it. He recovered, wiping his palm on his jeans then shaking briefly.

Good Lord, was Donal unable to teach the kid even basic manners?

"Did you leave me any brownies?" James asked. "I was lured over here by the scent wafting on the breeze."

"James is our neighbor," Twyla said, still clinging to James's left hand. "He lives on the other side of the woods, and he can fix cars."

Something crossed Darren's features, respect maybe, for a guy who knew engines.

"Your brownies, Darren." Vera added a fourth and passed him the sealed baggie. "Please give Katie my love."

"Right," he said, taking the brownies. "See you, squirt." He stuck his tongue out at Twyla, who returned the gesture.

"Get him his video game, Twyla. And, Darren, you know she's not supposed to play anything I haven't vetted."

He colored obviously, as redheads will do. "There's no blood, Vera, honest."

"There are only death screams," Twyla said, her expression suggesting she was trying to be helpful. "And stuff explodes all over the place. It's cool."

"Thanks, Twy," Darren called as Twyla headed for the stairs.

Vera opened a drawer, wanting to move beyond the subject of the video game. "Your key and one for Katie."

Darren slipped them into his pocket. "I won't tell Dad we have them." He glanced around the kitchen, everywhere but at James, who was serving himself a rather large brownie. "The restraining order expires soon."

"Not for weeks," Vera replied, "and when it does expire, I still won't want anything to do with him." That needed to be said, and believed. Trent Knightley's best divorce advice had been practical rather than legal: No mixed messages.

"You could just, like, bury the hatchet, though, couldn't you?" Darren asked.

James had become diplomatically fascinated with his brownie, but simply having him in the room gave Vera a bit of vicarious fortitude.

"Darren, I understand you need the people in your family to get along, but I can't trust your father, and I doubt that will change for a long time. Your father and I can be civil, if he's willing to make that much of an effort, but he's not too happy with me either."

She spoke gently, well aware Darren would feel self-conscious about James's presence.

"I don't like or trust him either," Darren said, patting the keys in his breast pocket. "The feeling is mutual."

"Raising your parents is hard. Ask Twy."

"Ask me what?" Twyla came bumping down the stairs on her backside again, a disc case in her hand.

"How hard it is to be a kid," Darren said. "A little kid, with homework every night, no driver's license, and only a mom to call your family."

James paused in the act of slicing a second, smaller brownie from the pan, the first having apparently already met its fate.

Darren had meant to tease, but like a lot of older brothers, he could tease too damned hard.

"You're my family too," Twyla said, chin jutting. "Mom says, Katie too, and even old Donal and Tina, sorta."

Now James, to all appearances, was focused on the intricate art of spooning vanilla ice cream onto his second brownie.

"What Mom says, Twyla believes," Darren retorted. "I'll be on my way, and thanks for the brownies, Vera."

He gave an awkward bob, something that might turn into a hug or a pat on the arm in parting when he had more self-confidence. Vera moved in and gave him a one-armed hug.

"Drive carefully, Darren. I mean that. It would matter to me and to Twy if you ended up wrapped around a telephone pole."

"It would matter to Dad's insurance premiums." He gave James a two-fingered salute and departed through the garage door.

"I told him he should show you the game first," Twyla said, taking a stool beside James at the island. "He said he's my older brother, and I'm not supposed to tattle on him." She picked a crumb from the brownie pan. "Is that right?"

James—who had two older brothers of his own— tucked into his brownie with as much focus as if he were a professional brownie taste tester.

"Darren's not quite right," Vera said. "If he's asking you to break a rule, then you have to wonder if he's trying to keep himself out of trouble at your expense."

"Like when he had his friends buy that vodka for Tina?"

Vera took the third stool at the island, while James nibbled microscopic bites of his brownie.

"Tina is a recovering alcoholic." Explaining this situation to Twyla was an ongoing process. "She isn't supposed to have any alcohol, because it's a bad habit for her. She can't stop when she starts drinking. Buying alcohol for her, like when she asked Darren to, wasn't a good idea."

"Because she gets drunk," Twyla said, looking pleased to be able to finish the syllogism. "Then she does dangerous things, like drive, and she could kill people and run over dogs and kill herself and smash up the car."

"Right. Asking Darren to find her something to drink was like Darren asking you to break the video game rule. It got everybody in trouble."

"Contributing?" James asked quietly, and Vera knew exactly what the full question was: Was Tina charged with and convicted of contributing to the condition of a minor, and was Darren adjudicated a delinquent for procuring the alcohol?

Vera helped herself to one of the yellow napkins stacked in the middle of the island, and started folding it into an owl.

The owl was the symbol of wisdom, also a little spooky.

"Darren is as shrewd as his father," Vera said. "He had an older friend make the run, so he himself was never in possession of the booze." This was really a great deal more family business than she wanted to share with James.

With anybody. She and Twyla were due for a talk on the topic of family privacy—a private talk.

"What was your punishment for exploring the woods without permission, Twy?" James asked, relieving Vera of the need to change the subject.

"Mom is thinking about it," Twyla said, but she

didn't stop there. "Sometimes when she thinks about it, she forgets, and I don't get a punishment."

She grinned, but James didn't return her smile. Vera watched with a flare of parental satisfaction as Twyla realized she hadn't entertained their guest with her flippancy.

"Never hold an opinion *sub curia*," James said. "Trent recalls that as the best advice he heard when he was courted for a judgeship. You decide the case when it's fresh in your mind and get rid of it. Everybody gets closure that way and can either live with your decision or get busy appealing it."

"What's peeling it?" Twyla asked.

"Appealing the decision," James said. "Going over the judge's head to ask for a reconsideration."

"Who would I go to?"

"God," Vera interjected, giving up on her origami owl, which had come out looking like ET. "If you don't like something I decide, your only other recourse is to ask God to override me."

Twyla looked confused, but from the smile on James's face, Vera suspected she'd given the right answer.

"What do you think your punishment should be, Twy?" he asked.

Vera was half off her stool, but she sat back down to hear the answer.

"I don't know."

"What if your mom sneaked out on you? Didn't tell you where she was going, didn't let you know you were home alone, didn't tell you when she'd be back? What if she disappeared to some place you'd have a lot of trouble finding her? Some place not quite safe?"

Twyla's face became a mask of consternation. "Would you do that, Mom?"

"I haven't yet. I can't imagine I'd do it on purpose, either." Not when James described such behavior in terms of abandonment and danger.

"I was bad," Twyla said slowly, as if realizing the magnitude of her transgression for the first time.

"What you did was bad." James settled a large hand on the child's neck and shook her gently. "You made a mistake, Twy." He finished the gesture by running a hand over her crown.

His observation held expectation, though, and Twyla picked up on it.

"I'm sorry, Mom. I'm really, really sorry, but we've never explored the woods, and I didn't know about the bears and snakes, and you do your exercises forever."

"We've talked about my exercises. They're like brushing your teeth or taking a shower. I have to do them, Twy." The finger exercises comforted Vera too, the way meditation lowered stress levels and quieted the mind.

"But *forever*?" Twyla asked.

James shot Vera a glance, one asking permission to participate in the discussion. What a novel and lovely experience, to not be so alone in the wilds of the parental woods. She gave a small nod and started over with another napkin, aiming for a swan this time.

"We're talking about two different problems, Twy," James said. "The first is how you can apologize for breaking a no-wandering-off rule and worrying your mom. The second is what to do about you feeling bored and alone when your mom does her exercises."

James's words lit the proverbial lightbulb for Vera:

when she sat down at her piano, for Twyla, that was the same feeling as if her mother went off into the woods, leaving Twyla alone and uncertain.

Vera smoothed the center crease of her unfinished swan. "I get pretty focused when I do my exercises. They aren't boring to me."

"They are to me," Twyla said with a wealth of long-suffering. "I sit in school all day, and that's boring too."

"What about a list?" James asked Twyla. "Could you do your homework, or your chores, or take your shower, or otherwise get something you don't like to do out of the way while your mom is busy?"

"I'd rather make brownies."

"You have homework almost every weekend, Twy," Vera pointed out, folding the napkin into a tail and a neck. "We always end up arguing about it Sunday night." As the mom, Vera ought to have found a solution to that problem by now too.

"We don't always argue," Twyla retorted.

"Do you have homework this weekend?" James asked—when Vera would have taken the bickering bait.

"I do, and Mom is right. She usually has to remind me to do it, starting after lunch on Sunday."

James tossed his spoon into his empty bowl. "Maybe you want to make your mother a proposal?"

"What's that?" Twyla asked.

"You come up with how you want to solve the problem you've created. You apologized, and that's a start, but it's only words. What you did wrong was deeds."

Even a child could understand justice when it was put that simply. So could a mom.

"I can do extra chores," Twyla said. "Mom hates to do laundry, but I'm good at folding and putting away the clothes. I usually only do the socks, though."

The swan was turning out half decently, but then swans were easy—also the symbol of love, grace, and harmony.

"My nieces do the socks too," James said, "but they're only seven. They probably can't manage the big stuff like towels and bathrobes."

"I can," Twyla said. She went silent, leaning into James.

Vera set the swan down before Twyla and took James's bowl to the sink, a shameless though perhaps not quite obvious bid for space.

Maybe having a lawyer around sometimes wasn't entirely a bad idea. For a change, she and Twyla hadn't simply talked at each other—screeched at each other. They'd shared some real insights.

"I think I'll go do my homework," Twyla said, getting off her stool. She gave Vera a curious glance, then trotted up the stairs.

"Is that what you do for your clients?" Vera asked, running water into the bowl in the sink. "You sit them down and make them listen to each other?"

"Sometimes."

Vera hadn't heard James's stool scrape back, so she was surprised when his arms came around her.

"James Knightley, what are you doing?"

His chin parked on her crown, and he drew her against his chest. "The kid scared the living peedywaddles out of you."

Yes, she had. "I don't even know what peedywaddles are."

Vera knew this embrace took her in the opposite direction of independent self-sufficiency, made two giant steps backward from maintaining intended boundaries, and was a direct contradiction of at least two speeches about not getting involved.

She turned to face James, wrapped her arms around his middle, and rested her forehead against his throat.

James wore that delicious fragrance, masculinity in the high desert, and his hand stroked slowly down her back.

"Darren smelled funny to me," she said, making no move to draw away. How long had it been since a man had held her like this, without expectations and maneuvers up his sleeve?

"Funny how?"

Vera could feel James's voice resonate in his chest when he spoke. In the dark, that voice would—

She stepped back, and James let her go.

"He smelled like pipe smoke and burned lawn clippings when he first got here," she said, turning back to the sink to wash out the bowl. Or something.

James grabbed a towel and dried the bowl when she'd put it in the drain rack. "Like pot?"

"*What?*"

"Marijuana smells sweet and grassy. He probably lit up a joint on the way here."

"Pot?" Vera hissed, keeping her voice down with ingrained parental discipline. "You think he's doing drugs?"

"I got a faint whiff of it too, but I wouldn't condemn him on that evidence alone."

She returned to washing brownie dishes while James went on drying.

"What do I do?" she asked as the water swirled down the drain a few minutes later. "Darren is not of age and he's driving. He could mess up his whole life, and for what? To catch a buzz?"

James hung the towel on the handle of the oven. "Didn't you ever rebel, Vera? Didn't you ever take a risk to feel big and bad and all grown-up?"

"No," she said. She'd felt big and bad if she skipped practice—also really guilty. "Pot is serious. Very serious."

"It's serious only if he gets caught," James said, wringing out a rag and starting on the counters. "A little experimentation is not the end of the world, but you mentioned that his mom is an alcoholic. That might put a different complexion on the matter. In any case, it isn't your problem to solve."

"Blessed St. Mary." Vera subsided onto a stool. "He's genetically set up for addiction." Donal would not know how to deal with this either, and for all his faults, Donal loved that boy.

"We don't know about his genetics. You've never mentioned his father having any sort of problems with drugs or alcohol."

Watching James methodically wipe down the counters was soothing, or maybe Vera reacted to the calm in his voice. She set the yellow swan in the middle of the island, though it looked lonely there.

"Donal has all sorts of quirks," she said. "He has rigid routines and pet peeves, and I can almost understand why Tina took to drinking."

Vera had never admitted that to another soul, not even her lawyer.

"Nobody compels an alcoholic to drink, and this is

not a happy topic," James said, rinsing out the rag and draping it over the faucet. "While we're dwelling on the negative, and Twy is occupied upstairs, let's take a look at that garage door."

"Of course." This was why he'd come over. Not to mediate with her and Twy, not to diagnose Darren's inchoate addiction, not to hear a lot of miserable family history.

Not to hug her.

Vera grabbed a jacket from a peg near the door, only to find it taken from her grasp and obligingly held for her. When she'd slipped her arms into the sleeves, James gave her shoulders a pat and shrugged into his own jacket.

"Come on," he said, taking her by the hand. "It will be dark before we've solved the problems of the universe, and my new neighbor apparently hasn't invested in any motion sensors or outdoor lights."

His neighbor. Vera had never had a neighbor who'd taken her by the hand or held her.

"You think I should invest in all that?" She let James lead her into the garage, not really wanting to be in the space by herself.

"No. I do not. You'll have all manner of wild game setting off the motion sensors, unless you calibrate them for movement at shoulder height and above. The motion sensors will turn on the lights, but they'll also alert your intruder to the fact that he's been spotted— assuming you wake up, go to the window, and recognize him."

"But they'll scare him off." Or scare her off, or *them* off.

James opened the service door and stepped through to view it from the outside.

"Not good, Vera. Somebody used something sharp and mean to try to hack the hell out of your door. I'm surprised you didn't hear it inside."

"I'm glad I didn't hear anything." Had she practiced through this? "Maybe I wasn't here when this happened, which is a much more comforting prospect than that I slept through this."

James used a cell phone to take several pictures. "Have you touched it? We can have the doorknob dusted for prints."

"I haven't touched it lately." Only by coincidence, not because she'd thought that clearly. "I hate this."

James rose and wrapped his arms around her. The contrast between his warmth and the chilly winter air had Vera burrowing closer, though a small voice in her mind ranted about boundaries and self-sufficiency.

"Hugs don't fix anything," she said.

"They make me feel better. Call the sheriff's office, and I'll give a statement corroborating that the door was undamaged as of my last visit here. They'll recognize the Knightley name, if nothing else, because Mac is the bane of their prosecutorial existence and the best out-fielder on the bar association's softball team."

"I don't want to impose." Vera didn't want to cling either, but she stayed right where she was.

James was quiet, letting her impose to the tune of a long, solid embrace.

"James?"

"Honey?"

"This isn't why I asked you over."

"Of course it isn't."

Was he mocking her?

His lips, warm and soft, came down onto hers. Vera was so surprised she went still, letting out a sigh that sounded suspiciously of pleasure.

His kiss held worlds of patience and a slow, sweet, savoring quality that made everything else fall away—the brisk winter air, Vera's worry, the clamorings of rational thought. James parted his mouth, and Vera scented chocolate on a warm puff of his breath. A chocolate kiss, and for once not wrapped in foil.

His hands settled low on Vera's hips, steadying her as he came at the kiss from a different direction. James was tempting her, teasing her into parting her own lips even as he moved closer, pressing her back against the outside wall of the garage.

In the space of a heartbeat, Vera's pleasure was replaced by panic.

Her hands, fisted on his jacket lapels one moment, shoved him away from her the next. Tried to shove him—he barely moved, though he lifted his head.

"What in the *hell* do you think you're doing?" She scooted away from him along the wall, scuttling like a rat in a searchlight.

"Vera?"

"I didn't invite you over here so you could…could do *that*."

He took a few steps back, his expression puzzled. "Why did you invite me over here?"

"Because the lock was scratched to smithereens and the sheriff won't be out here until Wednesday and you're the only neighbor I know and because…*I don't know*!"

"Sweetie, calm down."

"Don't call me that."

"Vera, please calm down. I did not kiss you to upset you, and I'm sorry if I have."

"So am I." She crossed her arms and glowered across the wintry landscape to the bare trees edging the woods. They'd been pretty when she'd moved in, leafy guardians of her privacy. They looked sinister now. "Why did you kiss me?"

Why had *she* kissed him back?

James rubbed a hand across his nape. "To comfort you, to distract you, to give you something to think about besides the way your door has been vandalized. Because I wanted to."

Heaven help her, she'd wanted to too. "James, I like you—I like you a lot. Any woman would—but I'm not good at this. Whenever I think I'm putting my marriage behind me, I turn up all ridiculous, flustered, and confused again."

Good Lord, what if Twyla had come upon them kissing?

"A little affection between grown-ups isn't ridiculous, Vera."

That was *a little* affection to James Knightley? "If I can't manage a little affection without losing my cool," Vera retorted, "then I'm ridiculous. I'm sorry. I don't want to feel ridiculous, and—we're done kissing."

She couldn't quite bring herself to tell him they were done being neighbors.

"I do believe you're the first woman in the history of women to put me on the receiving end of an it's-not-you-it's-me speech." The smile James offered her was slight, dear, and even a little hurt.

Vera tucked her hands in her pockets rather than brush her fingers over that smile. Ridiculous was an understatement.

"I have to be very careful, James. I cannot trust my judgment where men are concerned, and there's Twyla to consider. I'm sorry."

Far more than she could admit where he was concerned, she was sorry.

He shifted so he stood beside her, both of their backs to the garage's outside wall. "You liked your first husband OK, and you can't berate yourself forever for choosing Donal. You said you were grieving, and Donal was someone you trusted."

She'd said that? Vera couldn't even recall thinking it, but James's version of events sounded plausible. It sounded true, in fact, and made her want to get away from James so she could think clearly about what he'd said.

Also so she could cry.

"The issue here is not Donal, it's me. I'm apparently still in no condition to be kissing you." Which was not James's fault, or his responsibility to ascertain.

Even B-flat minor wasn't sad enough for how Vera felt to be running James off again.

"You're a grown woman, Vera, and you're entitled to decide with whom you do and do not socialize. Don't apologize for speaking your mind."

Why couldn't he act even a teeny bit like a jerk and why, on this cold, stupid day, did the garage wall hold a hint of warmth?

"James, I *am* sorry. I never used to be like this. I was steady and confident. You deserve nothing but the best, and I won't bother you again."

A woman who wanted to kiss a guy good-bye after yelling at him for kissing her in the first place probably didn't qualify as sane, much less steady or confident.

"Yes, you will bother me, Vera Waltham. You might not call me again, but you surely to goodness will bother me."

B-flat minor minor minor.

Vera expected James would walk off, just disappear back through the woods, because his vehicle was nowhere in sight, but he paused long enough to gently squeeze her shoulder, and abruptly, Vera could no longer contain the urge to cry.

She dashed back through the damaged door rather than watch him leave her property.

Chapter 7

THE SORRY SCENE WITH JAMES MARKED A TURNING point for Vera. She was frustrated with Donal and his silly games, but more to the point, she was frustrated with *herself*. The next time a sweet, sexy, lovely guy kissed her, no matter how rattled she got, she would not send him packing over a bout of nerves.

She'd blown it with James Knightley, but she could learn from her mistakes.

In that spirit, when Tuesday morning came, Vera was tooling east to Baltimore on Interstate 70, the fields and farms of central Maryland rolling past in their drab winter plumage.

Will she ask me to play? Ask being a euphemism, of course. Vera had never suffered the sharp edge of Olga's tongue, but she'd seen her mentor put many a musician in his or her place with a look, a word, an excruciating silence.

A lesson with Olga Strausser was not for the faint of heart.

Serious students only.

And yet, the old woman vibrated with joy, courage, and vitality Vera craved like sunshine. The joy was there when Olga hugged her hello.

"My Vera, my lovely Vera. How glad I am that you do not live in California, or Texas with all those cowboys. Come, we will have chocolate and sweets, and you will tell me of my little Twyla."

For a small woman, Olga had a fierce embrace.

"Twyla's hardly little anymore," Vera said, draping her coat over a chair. "This weekend she went off into the woods by herself and was lost until a neighbor found her."

Given that opening, the interrogation commenced immediately. Gently, relentlessly, Olga prodded and questioned, and Vera spilled the story.

Leaving out an awkward epilogue involving yet another first—and last—kiss with James Knightly.

"An adventure, then," Olga said, "but safely concluded like all good adventures. Now to our sweets."

James's kiss had been sweet.

They had chocolate, because Olga eschewed tea and coffee—and because Vera deserved to be haunted by a sweet, final kiss.

"You are done with the divorce from that Scot?" Olga asked.

How had she known to ask? "I am, mostly. The restraining order expires in a few weeks, and I expect Donal will pressure me to honor the few dates I haven't canceled yet."

"You are stubborn, so you think, no, not for him shall I play."

"I am stubborn." Vera set her empty cup down, though she'd barely tasted her chocolate. James's kiss had tasted better. "I'm also enjoying the time off, Olga. I love raising my daughter, like having a real home, not simply a retreat between tours, and relish having students I can watch progress."

"These are important things to a woman," Olga said, pushing the tray of buttery madeleines closer to Vera's elbow. "You need to eat, Vera. Music takes energy."

Life took energy, but to Olga, music and life were of the same magic.

"Olga, did you ever want to quit all together? Just let it all go, the performing, the practicing, the touring, the teaching?"

"Oh, yes," Olga said, taking a slow sip of her chocolate.

The older woman was still beautiful. Not because she had lovely features, though good bones served her well, but because she still embraced life with verve and humor. She enjoyed her chocolate; she ogled cowboys; she flirted with her doorman; she played the hell out of anything she set her hands to, be it music or cards or life.

But was Olga ever lonely? "You *wanted* to quit?" Vera asked instead.

"I did quit, three times. The last time I retired I was eighty-eight. What did I know? You think you shall die tomorrow, and then it's six years later, and here you are still rattling around in your much vaunted retirement. This is a great joke on God's part, but the humor is subtle."

"I'm not eighty-eight."

While Vera studied a cookie, she knew Olga was studying her.

To admit the possibility of not being a musician, not being a pianist, much less a concert soloist, was a relief. Music was a lovely place to hide, an enchanted forest, but that forest had an admission price that was never paid in full and came with a full complement of trolls and warlocks.

"You think next time, maybe a neighbor will not find our Twyla?"

Vera had thought it, dreamed it, had probably played it a few times in B-flat minor too.

"Donal took something out of me," Vera said, putting the cookie back on the tray. "Something precious. I trusted him, I'd known him forever, I even found things to like about him, and he betrayed me."

Olga swatted Vera's knee. "Play for me."

Ah, the keyboard, the ultimate dissection table. But with Olga, there was no refusing, none at all. One could bargain, though.

"What would you like to hear?" Vera asked, rising and opening the cover of the vintage Bösendorfer that Olga had once toured with. "Some technique to warm up?"

"Nothing too technical today. Maybe a little late Brahms, some dear old Chopin."

Blessed St. Cecilia. *Those* two. The musician who thought to approach either composer without technique well in hand was doomed.

So, a test, and not simply of technique.

Vera chose Brahms's Opus 116, a suite of short works that was by turns tender, lyrical, and full of good old Teutonic bombast, leavened with the occasional contrapuntal passage just for fun. She'd liked these pieces since she'd met them as an adolescent. Liked them for their expressiveness and their challenge.

Olga listened to three pieces in succession, eyes closed, humming softly as Rudolph Serkin had done even in concert. When Vera had played the final cadence, she closed the keyboard cover and remained on the piano bench, hands in her lap as she'd been taught.

Judgment would come; no need to hurry it.

After a dramatically long silence, Olga opened her eyes. "We are so serious. Come sit with me."

She patted the place beside her, and Vera obeyed,

feeling more satisfaction than she ought. For the first time in three years, she'd played for Olga and played well. James would have been proud of her.

"Vera, my dear, do you think Johann Sebastian wanted to bury eight of his twenty children?" Johann Sebastian Bach, to differentiate him in Olga's parlance from the dabbling pack of offspring by the same last name.

"Eight?"

"His first wife, too, of course. Do you think Frédéric Chopin wanted to spend *ten years* rotting to death of consumption as he both composed and toured? Did Beethoven wake up one day and think what great fun it would be to lose his hearing? Did Brahms set out as a young fellow to go his whole life without the comfort of a wife to love him? And what of Mozart? A childhood spent being paraded around Europe like his papa's trained monkey followed by poverty and heartache. And yet we have such music from him!"

Vera's Old Testament was shaky, but her music history was fairly solid.

"They were great men, and great musicians," Vera said. "They triumphed over hardship."

"They were merely human." Olga smacked Vera's knee again, harder this time. "They *chose* music, or it chose them, and they learned to be *happy* with their fates."

Vera was not happy. That's the real reason she'd panicked at James's kiss. She knew herself well enough to say that much with conviction, but the rest of the problem was harder to articulate.

"This isn't like when I've blown a performance, Olga. This is my life that's in shambles."

"What shambles? You buried a husband, and a car

accident was a hard way to lose him, but you were ready
to be out from under his wing, just as you were ready to
throw over that Scot whom you married in a momentary
lapse of judgment. I have had two such lapses, but twice
I also chose more wisely. But you, now you are *free*, and
all you can do is doubt yourself. Humility is a virtue, but
this fear, Vera… Is this what you want your daughter to
know? That life can toss you off your piano bench like
a bucking horse?"

A direct, telling hit. Vera sat back and let her gaze
roam over the great black grand piano across the room.
How many people had it taken to move that one instrument here to Olga's living room?

"I want Twyla to be safe. I want to be safe."

"So you married Alexander, and he sheltered you and
protected you and exploited you. The Scot exploited you
more—though give the devil his due, he also worked
hard to build your career. You might have allowed his
exploitation endlessly, had he known how to care for
you. Better that he didn't."

Caring had never been part of the bargain with Donal,
but neither had abuse. "I might still be performing if
Donal had been less of a tyrant."

"So you'd perform, but would you be happy?"

Vera thought about it for three seconds. "I'd be
miserable."

"All right, then you stopped performing, but are you
happy now?"

No, and Vera didn't need even three seconds to reach
that conclusion. "I am content."

"Content is for men who are one hundred and three
with bad knees," Olga spat. "Listen to me. You are

trying to refresh your playing and your confidence by hiding in the technique. It's a good strategy. More of us should resort to it more often, though you will only partially succeed."

Partial success was better than no success at all. "I'm playing better. I am more confident with the notes than I ever knew I could be."

"The notes, bah!" Olga waved a hand that was still as strong and graceful as a young man's. "When good musicians are young, they have the passion of the music. They play and play until they are drunk and reeling with it, with their talent, with their ambition. This is good. To learn the repertoire and perform it well takes stamina.

"But then life sweeps you along, and you have a choice, Vera. You can try to sustain your career on a passion for the music alone, or you can allow yourself a passion for life. I say this because of who you are. Another must content himself with only correct notes, but you are capable of more."

Olga sat back, offering an endearingly self-deprecating smile. "I have become a preacher in my dotage. I do not recommend this retirement business. One soon bores not only oneself, but one's guests. Will you play at my benefit next year?"

The smile had been a decoy, and Vera was unprepared for the salvo that followed. Olga's yearly benefit raised money for all manner of deserving charities. She recruited shamelessly from all musical walks, and performing for her was an honor.

"I am old enough that I recall how it was years ago," Olga said, studying her hands. "Nobody took a baby's continued life for granted. Children died with alarming frequency where I grew up, and their first few birthdays and name days were celebrated with a certain caution. It's the same now, at the end of life."

Vera helped herself to two more buttery, sweet madeleines. "Stop it, Olga. The death and dying speech will not get me to play."

"Then play for your daughter," Olga said, dropping the lugubrious air as easily as she'd put it on. "Twyla takes a walk in the woods, and instead of being proud of her adventurous spirit, you fret yourself into a dark, dank little corner. I blame this on the Scot. Though you divorced him, he still controls you. Snap your fingers at him, Vera, and make him disappear from your life."

Olga gave a loud, crisp snap of her fingers right in Vera's face.

"I'm trying, Olga. He's not disappearing as obediently as he should." If anything, Donal's presence loomed larger as the restraining order expiration date approached.

Another part of the reason Vera had blundered so badly with James.

"Then keep trying. Be more stubborn than Donal is, and take some of these cookies. They grow stale if I'm left to eat them all. I wish Sting had come to one of my benefits. Such an attractive man, and that voice…"

If he had come, he might have found himself sharing the stage with some country music great, or the up-and-coming world music act to catch Olga's ear most recently. The benefit would be a no-pressure venue to perform in, where Vera could play anything she chose and be guaranteed a positive reception. Olga had never extended this invitation to her before.

And Vera hadn't accepted.

You're snakebit... Snakebit was the name for when the enchanted forest turned dark and scary, and Vera no longer viewed getting home in one piece as a merry adventure.

As the week wore on, James tried to focus on his work, but all the ladies whose numbers he'd tossed out were abruptly determined to look him up.

He let them, every single one of them, ring through to voice mail, and he did not return the calls. This behavior was quintessential Clueless Guy, and only a year earlier, it would have been unthinkable for James.

Now he could not *rise* to the challenge.

He did, however, exchange texts with his prospective piano teacher. She would come to his house—though he still hadn't even a name to go with his mental image of her: sensible shoes; hair in an iron-gray bun that no grown man had ever seen down, even before she'd gone gray; no figure to speak of, and a metronome where her heart should be. She would be a relief as females went, and her name would be Irmantrude—Fraulein Piano Teacher, to him. James wouldn't have to charm her.

He wouldn't be able to, if she held to his estimation of her.

Though compared to a fidgety eight-year-old boy, James could be plenty serious when he put his mind to it. Trent liked music and bought the CDs James picked out for him, but only James had inherited their mother's musical talent.

So he ground through contracts, drafted articles of incorporation, argued with his clients' tax attorneys—corporate returns being due March 15, not April 15—and he did not walk in Hiram Inskip's woods.

He did not lease a trail horse. He did not buy a dog either, though he did peruse the "free to good home" ads on the same page as the crossword puzzle of the local newspaper.

A cat, maybe. Cats dealt well with periodic abandonment, such as when James had a marathon contract negotiation for a client. Cats looked nice in an aloof and inscrutable way.

James drove home at midday Friday, wondering what Vera Waltham would think of him, taking up a musical instrument to replace his usual social agenda. He wasn't sure what he made of it himself, but he didn't cancel his lesson.

If Vera hadn't collapsed in a fit of rebound nerves, but had instead kissed him back with half the fire he sensed in her, would he have canceled this lesson? Kept his evenings and weekends free for a budding relationship with her rather than a never-ending struggle with eighty-eight keys and only ten fingers?

He'd thought about that kiss and thought about it.

Vera had been shy, true, but interested. He was almost certain she'd been interested.

Trapping her up against the house, however innocently he'd intended it, had tripped her defensive responses, and that had been game, set, and match point to the lady's insecurities. He'd crowded her, not comforted her, and that rankled.

James was plodding through his major scales—all except F major, which he saved for last because of the fingering—when his doorbell rang.

Vera Waltham stood on his porch, a satchel in her hand.

"Hello, Vera." He stepped back, mentally cursing the timing, because his piano teacher was due any minute. He did not, however, curse the identity of his caller. "This is an unexpected pleasure."

She stood on the front porch, looking stylish in low-heeled boots, jeans, and a leather bomber jacket.

Stylish and horrified.

"If you want to bless me out again," James said, holding his ground, "let's not do it where the neighbors will be entertained." The neighbors being Inskip's heifers, at present.

She stepped into the house and peered into his living room. "*This* is where you live?"

"Have for the past eight years. The place needed a lot of work, but Trent and Mac helped. I love an old farmhouse treated properly, and it's comfortable enough for a bachelor. Not to be obtuse, but to what do I owe the honor, and can I get you something to drink?"

Her gaze fell on the Baldwin baby grand in what should have been his dining room.

"This isn't a mistake, is it?" she said, crossing to the piano. "I got the address right, and you're my one o'clock. Did you do this on purpose?"

To James's expert eye, Vera was getting worked up about something, but she'd mentioned one o'clock and…a gleaming full-size grand piano occupied her front room.

She did *exercises* every day without fail. Finger exercises?

She'd needed an entertainment lawyer.

She been married to a man who'd been her agent. Not her literary agent, as James had assumed, but some other kind of talent agent.

And in the same room as her big, black piano, James had seen shelves and shelves of music.

"*You're* my piano teacher?"

"You're my new student," she said, eyeing him as if he were a reluctant eight-year-old boy. Or something worse. "Did you really not know from whom you'd be taking lessons?"

Her expression rankled, because she ought to have faith in his honesty by now, even if she wasn't smitten with his kisses.

"Your ad doesn't give a name," James reminded her. "We never spoke in person on the phone about these lessons. I left voice mails, and I got your texts. No way I could recognize your cell phone number—or you, mine— because we've only traded landline numbers. Will you turn tail and run, or will you at least give me a fair hearing?"

Smooth, that, calling a snakebit woman a coward, but James was damned if he'd be sent packing for offenses he hadn't committed.

One of Inskip's heifers bawled, and Vera startled. James wanted to smirk—even the cows agreed with him—but didn't dare. After a long silence from the bovine peanut gallery, and from James's prospective piano teacher, Vera set her bag down on a cedar chest.

"Is this piano tuned?"

"Of course," James said, keeping his expression deadpan while his insides were spiking the ball and doing a happy dance. Vera Waltham was not turning tail and running.

Vera was his piano teacher. Not what he'd planned on, but it pleased him inordinately and lifted the sense of ennui that had plagued him all week.

"The piano was tuned after the first frost, and it will be tuned again when the weather changes," James said. "I take care of my equipment, Vera. All of my equipment."

—⁓—

Vera pretended to study the piano while ignoring any double entendres hidden in James's words, and any cows barking in his front yard.

The piano was dusted, the keys and finish gleaming in the winter sunshine. The closed lid had no rings where somebody had carelessly left a drink to sweat and wreck the veneer, no dings and dents from a casual move. The piano bench was adjusted to accommodate a man with long legs, suggesting James truly played this instrument.

James was silent while Vera inspected his piano, but when she turned to face him, his arms were crossed over his chest, his feet planted in a solid stance.

Abruptly, the spark of joy she'd felt at the simple sight of him—the bonfire, to be honest—winked out.

He was angry. Vera had established beyond all doubt that she could not deal with angry men.

"This won't work, James." Vera picked up her bag, but he stopped her by turning his back to her and facing out the big picture window that looked over black-and-white cows, fallow fields, and pasture in the distance.

"What is with you, Vera? We shared one kiss, nothing more, and not even a particularly erotic kiss. You're lying to yourself if you're calling that an assault."

Not even particularly erotic?

"It wasn't the kiss"—*must* he have such an elegant back?—"or not only that. You kiss very—you know what you're doing, and then I fell apart. Nobody assaulted anybody, and I fell apart."

He shot her a glance over his shoulder but didn't turn. "Was that a compliment? A complaint? Because as compliments go, you leave me a little uncertain."

"It was a statement of fact," Vera said, deciding some discussion—a brief, matter-of-fact discussion—was in order, because she could learn from her mistakes, and she was not neurotic.

She was snakebit, though. She sat on the piano bench, the place in life where she'd always felt most confident.

James sat beside her. Right beside her. "I kissed you once, Vera, and after sampling my wares, you waved me off. I can get past that. Can you?"

His tone was indifferent, and his right index finger skimmed over the white keys without making a sound. His hands embodied male competence, and Vera was inordinately interested to know if he was any kind of musician.

Then too, he'd spun her meltdown into a casual instance of a lady changing her mind.

"I didn't sample your wares, James. You surprised me is all."

"I won't surprise you like that again." Now his left index finger skimmed down to low A, which meant Vera either suffered his arm to bump against her side, or she leaned back as if she had an allergy to his touch.

Which she did not, but they wouldn't be tackling the four-hands literature, that's for sure.

"Play me something." Vera hadn't planned to issue a command, but music would help her make up her mind about James as a student, and give her time to get an utterly groundless bout of nerves, glee, mortification, and other inconvenient emotions under control.

"Let's get your coat off," he said, rising. "You never told me if you'd like something to drink."

"I'm not a guest, James. I'm like a contractor who's come here to install your washing machine."

The left corner of his mouth quirked up, and Vera's upset subsided half an octave. If James could overlook her wrong notes, she'd be better able to forgive them in herself.

"My mama," James said, "of the famed mashed-potato recipe, claimed anybody welcomed under our roof was a guest, and to be treated as such."

"A glass of water then." If he set it on the piano, Vera would lecture him up one side and down the other, and enjoy every second of it.

James disappeared into the kitchen, and came back with one glass and a wooden coaster, both of which he handed to her. Vera had not watched his backside as he'd sauntered away, not for more than a single moment.

"What should I play for you?" he asked, resuming his seat on the bench.

"I'll need a chair so I don't crowd you on the bench."

He popped back up and fetched a chair from the kitchen.

"Are you warmed up?" she asked. "If I don't like what I hear, then we'll agree I'm not the teacher for you."

"We will?" He sat back down square in the middle of the bench, right where he was supposed to be, nose aligned with middle C. "How 'bout if I play something anyway, before we agree to that? I'll play you a piece I'm working on, so you can give me some pointers, before we go agreeing on anything."

"Fair enough." More than fair. Vera did like this man—liked him a lot.

She mentally squared her shoulders, prepared to hear him limp through some pop tune, or maybe—if God's humor was to be inflicted on her today—a butchery of the *Marche Militaire*. A thumping piece, because boys without the musical gene invariably viewed the piano as an excuse to thump. The ones with the gene were inclined to thump occasionally too.

James dug through some music and opened a book to a middle movement. A slow movement?

After rubbing his palms down the denim on his thighs once, he set his hands on the keyboard, and in that instant, Vera realized she did not want James to make a fool of himself. She wanted him to be musical, to be proficient, and she wanted even more to teach him what he sought to learn.

She closed her eyes and waited.

The introduction was stately, almost baroque in its reserve and self-possession. Beethoven, fairly early, when he could look back to the classical more easily than he could forward to the romantic.

Then the lyrical first theme, a lilting descant above a rippling middle register, and thank God and all the saints, James could *play* it. He was up to Beethoven's weight, technically, and that was a relief.

That he'd even choose a classical piece was a wonderful surprise. He stumbled, and Vera rejoiced to hear that too, because she could help him with the fingering. He came to the first cadence, and glanced over at her.

"Finish the movement," she said—another command. "It's not that long."

So James played through the short development, and the melody grew befuddled when he had to cross his hands more consistently. He soldiered on without losing his focus, bringing the piece to a sweet, decorous conclusion.

Then he put his hands in his lap and let the last few notes linger in memory, like any well-schooled performer would.

"Beethoven had a fondness for, and genius with, the violin," Vera said. "Think of this melody, here"—she pointed to the notes on the page—"as a violin, lilting along to the accompaniment of a submissive and admiring keyboard. Moonlight over water, a breeze ruffling the golden wheat. Touches so gentle you sense them emotionally more than tactilely."

His slow smile distracted her.

"What?" She searched over the piece to find the exact place where James had lost his ear for the melody.

"So I passed?"

"We'll see," she said, flipping pages, but, yes, indeed, he'd passed. "Play that."

"I don't know it."

"Sight-read it."

To demand that James sight-read in the first lesson was cruel, but highly diagnostic too. Vera had turned to the Trio in the same sonata—the C Major. A tricky, fun two pages full of pitfalls for the unwary disguised as rapid arpeggios.

James sailed into the opening measures gamely, reading the notes fairly well, but missing the punch lines to the phrasing the composer had set up.

"I like it. You want to choose something else?" he asked when he'd finished.

"No."

James looked good on the piano bench, relaxed, confident, competent. The easy choice would be to shuffle him off to one of Vera's advanced students, to tell him he wasn't ready for a teacher who'd demand as much as she would, except that would be dishonest.

Vera demanded progress only, not virtuosity. Anybody who put in a reasonable amount of time with the instrument each week would make some progress.

Olga's distinction, between humility and fear, came to mind, as did her admonition to be the kind of musician Twyla could respect. James had done nothing wrong. He'd kissed Vera once, and when she'd told him to desist, he had. The fault—*if there were one*—lay with her.

Vera had learned about James by listening to him play, seen aspects of him she hadn't sensed even when he'd kissed her.

James Knightley valued proficiency, and he valued privacy. For a man who hadn't been taking lessons for some time, he'd retained good basics, and somehow kept his hand in beyond the typical amateur.

And yet, emotionally his music lacked the joyful abandon of the devoted amateur.

Soul. James's music lacked the added extra that transcended wrong notes, muddy pedaling, and cavalier phrasing. He was conscientious with the music, respectful of the composer's intentions, but he held back too.

The music lacked a piece of his heart.

Vera knew what she was listening for, because for the past two years, her music had lacked the same quality.

Well, damn.

"You sight-read well enough," Vera said, "but you

don't listen as consistently as you could. Listening helps
you pick up the patterns in the music, and that helps you
read more smoothly. Read through the whole sonata at
least a couple of times this week, and do it at one sitting."

"It's thirty pages!"

A mere warm-up, thirty pages. "We're working on
your stamina too. When you get to the Trio—move
over—pay attention to the phrasing. Listen."

Vera took the middle of the bench, leaving James a
corner into which he didn't quite fit.

"You did let the phrase rise and fall," she said as she
played, "but the accents are on three and one. Beethoven
gave it a two beat, off-kilter feel. We're in the Scherzo—
the lightest moment of the piece—so musical humor
should be expected. The proper term is hemiola. Hear it?"

Vera played at easily twice the tempo James had—
though not up to performance tempo—the better to show
him the lift and lilt of the music. James didn't have the
control to play at such speed, but she wanted him to hear
how the music was meant to be played.

"Jesus God, Vera, you play the hell out of a piano."

She stopped at a cadence, though she was tempted to
finish the movement. "Thank you—it's a fun piece. Did
you get the phrasing?"

"I will eventually, but I still won't sound like that."

James's consternation pleased her inordinately, as if he'd
just learned she had both a CPA and a law degree in piano.

"You are not to rush the arpeggios," she said sternly.
"You understand about making haste slowly? You play
it seven times slowly before you even attempt once at
a slightly faster tempo, and you keep that seven to one
ratio until I say otherwise."

Was he trying not to smile?

"How much do you expect me to practice each day?"

Fair question. "You have a foundation. You should practice the same amount you did to reach this point, but I am a fiend for technique."

James closed the volume of Beethoven and set it aside. "Finger exercises, you mean?"

"Drills, finger exercises, technique, call it what you will. You have to confirm the motor skills before you can tackle any real repertoire." Vera fished in her bag and produced a worn volume of good old Pischna. "These are butt-ugly exercises, but they'll get your hands in shape faster than anything else I know."

She made him work through the first three drills, and told him to play them in a different major key each day. They went back over the Beethoven slow movement, measure by measure, with Vera doubling the melody an octave above, until James began to hear it as a melody, not simply as pretty notes tinkling around in the higher range.

"You can borrow my Pischna for this week," she said, though she typically did not lend her own books. "Order the same edition off the Internet, because I assure you, Pischna will become an old friend."

James took her dog-eared volume of finger exercises and leafed through it. "That's it? Finger exercises and Beethoven?"

Like folding socks and doing fractions? "You think your sentence is too light?"

"I'd like to work on more than one piece. Get a little variety in my playing."

A restless mind. Of course, for all his slow speech

and graceful manners, James Knightley's mind would
need variety.

"What about Chopin?"

He made a face. "Too damned prissy."

Too emotionally transparent. "You've done the Bach
two-part inventions?"

"A half dozen or so."

"Then pick up the *Well-Tempered Clavier*, and start
reading in the major keys." Vera explained how the
series was set up, with a prelude and fugue in each key.
Bach was emotionally safe, nearly mathematical in his
structure, and he wouldn't challenge the artist in James
unduly, though he would gratify the lawyer.

"Ever work on any Brahms?" she asked.

"Nope."

"You might like him. Let me think about it, and next
week I'll bring you some suggestions." Next week…
When had she decided that, and why?

"Suggestions?" James was back to tracing a fingertip
silently over the white keys.

"I'm a benevolent dictator. You'll need a notebook,
James, to keep track of your assignments, and from time
to time, I'll bring you CDs to listen to, and I might even
send you to the occasional concert."

"I've seen you perform, you know."

Vera was so mesmerized with the repetitive stroke
of his hand, up two octaves, down two octaves—in the
same rhythm as he'd once stroked her back—that his
words took a moment to register.

Then she needed another moment to recover from
the shock.

Chapter 8

VERA HADN'T BEEN BEFORE AN AUDIENCE FOR SEVERAL years, and yet James had just told her he'd heard her perform. She felt ambushed rather than pleased. Classical performers never became household names in America, and she'd treasured that increment of privacy.

"Where did you hear me?"

"The only place I could hear you live was when you played in DC, nine years ago, and six years ago. Your hair was a lot longer, not that I could see much from the back of the second balcony. You weren't much more than a kid the first time, but you had fire."

Vera hadn't expected this, hadn't foreseen that her divorce lawyer's brother would be a fan. "Did Trent tell you?"

Did she have any of that fire—wonderful term—left?

James opened the book of finger exercises, and pointed to her maiden name scrawled in the corner.

"Veracity Winston," he said, tapping the letters. "I suspected when I heard you ripping through the Beethoven, because I got the same rush as I did both times when I heard you live."

Vera looked not at James, but around the room, a space that combined country comfort with a certain elegance, and views of muddy black-and-white cows with bleak, uncultivated land.

"I'm on hiatus," she said, feeling miserable and

pleased at the same time. That James liked her music was a stroke to her ego; that she had to admit to him she wasn't performing was awkward.

Like a first kiss neither party had seen coming and couldn't get quite right.

James sat beside her on the piano bench, hip to hip, close enough she could catch the scent and warmth of him.

"Was it your choice to go on hiatus?" he asked.

He didn't politely dance around the topic, but he'd tread lightly, and Vera hadn't ever considered exactly *who* had put her on hiatus.

"I more or less backed into it. Donal booked a series of dates without my approval, and I didn't feel I could honor them all. I started canceling them, and didn't stop until very little remained on my calendar."

Vera had had a tantrum, in other words, maybe one long overdue.

James closed the book of finger exercises and propped it front and center on the music stand. "Very little remains on your calendar?"

"I still have a few option dates. Donal will want me to play them, so he gets the commission, and I'm not wild about that idea."

"The issue isn't simply him and the money, is it?"

Lawyers heard people's personal business all day long. They worked with the wreckage of human relationships, and James, as a lawyer, wouldn't be squeamish about Vera's personal business.

Though—lovely man—he wasn't raising the topic as a lawyer. He was asking, as a friend would ask. A good friend.

"Every time I try to wrap my mind around *the issue*, James, it gets more complicated. Grief, anger, fear, naiveté, inexperience, and even laziness have brought me to where I am. Until the divorce came along, I never dreamed that I might have a life away from the piano."

And until James had come along, the matter of Vera's *happiness* hadn't gained her notice either.

"Your talent is beyond doubt, Vera, but if you no longer enjoy performing, then you shouldn't perform."

You're a grown woman, and you're entitled to decide with whom you do and do not socialize.

To James, Vera's independence, her right to base her life on her own judgments, was beyond question. How could she not treasure that about him, even as the standard he set daunted her?

"From my family I get the you-owe-it-to-the-world speech, or the get-back-on-the-horse speech," Vera said, which accounted for the infrequency of her phone calls to her mom and brothers. "I get it from everybody else but Twyla." She'd more or less heard it from Olga, except Olga's version was subtle.

"I was in general practice when I first got out of law school," James said, patting her knee—a very different touch from Olga's use of the same gesture. Comforting, not the least admonitory.

"I was a crackerjack at divorces," he went on. "Tore through them like hell on wheels, and got one badass reputation as the son of a bitch to go to when you wanted to stick it to your ex."

Another pat to her knee, even gentler. "I hated it, Vera. I can't be that person, the terminator of marriages. I was more relieved than I can say when Trent stepped up to the domestic law plate. I owe him more than he knows. Same thing with the criminal cases. I could not—*could not*—live with myself when I knew my low-down, rotten, conniving client had gotten off on a technicality. That ate me up, despite the money rolling in from all directions."

"Did you choose business law?"

"About as much as you chose to go on hiatus."

Vera hadn't talked with anybody about the decision to stop performing, but with James, the topic was comfortable. The entire lesson had been comfortable, in fact.

"Your music helped," he said, sliding the cover over the keys.

"I beg your pardon?"

"You'd won some big award right as I finished law school, and you did a lot of recording in a very short time. I have every one of your CDs, and bought sets for Trent and Mac. Trent says nothing helps him change gears at the end of the day like popping in a classical CD on the way home."

"He's never said a word to me about this."

"He wouldn't want to crowd you," James said, nudging her with his shoulder. He had broad shoulders, heavy with muscle.

"Practice your little fanny off this week," Vera said. James had a lovely fanny too. "As my student, you're on permanent probation."

"Because of one barely-worth-mentioning kiss?"

Now it was barely worth mentioning? "No, not because of that."

"Then why?"

"Because I'm Veracity Winston, and I say so."

"Good enough." He smiled, just as he had when she'd said something to Twyla of which he approved. He had Vera follow him into the big, tidy kitchen so he could get his checkbook, then walked her to her truck. He thanked her twice for taking him on, though he didn't shake her hand, and he made no move to touch her.

Which was oddly disappointing.

***

Trent motioned to his wife to come into his office while he cradled the phone against his shoulder. "Trent Knightley here."

"Glover here," said a gravelly baritone. "I'd hoped I was done with your love letters, Trent."

"I'd hoped I was done sending them to you, at least as regards the Walthams."

"But it's family law, so the cases never die," Glover said on a sigh. "I wanted you to know I'm sending along the appropriate reply. You can start peeling Ms. Waltham off the ceiling in anticipation."

"That reply would be?"

"My boy is innocent. Innocent, I tell you!" Glover infused his voice with mocking irony. "Donal says the last thing he wants to do is antagonize the golden goose so close to when the restraining order expires and he can actually brow…talk to her again."

Hannah meandered into the office, closing the door behind her. She'd taken to wearing her dark auburn hair down, which was nearly as much of a distraction to Trent as when she'd worn in it in a tidy bun.

"Aaron, I know you have a client to represent," Trent said, "but Vera doesn't want to talk to him, doesn't want to see him, doesn't want to have jack to do with him. She's been very clear about that, and given the injuries—"

Trent had seen far more serious injuries in domestic altercations, but a single blow could leave unseen damage that never healed.

"I know," Glover interrupted. "Believe me, Trent, if I could back out of this case or hand it on to successor counsel, I would, but there's a problem with Rule One that my client and I are resolving over time."

Rule One in private practice: Get Paid.

"I sympathize," Trent said as Hannah took a seat opposite his desk and crossed the prettiest legs in the known universe. "But don't think if MacKay goes after his ex-wife to start performing again that it will have any impact on your Rule One problem. She's as done with Donal as an agent as she is with him as a husband."

A silence, and Trent realized he'd probably been a little too zealous. Aaron Glover had balls of steel, but he had the ethics to go with them.

"For the record, Knightley, I told Donal to his unsmiling face that if he violates the restraining order, he will go to jail. Not even your brilliant and charm-free older brother could save Donal from his own stupidity if he violates that order."

Hannah began messing with the Rubik's cube Trent had borrowed from James's office.

"So what's Donal's alibi?" Trent asked. "Where was he when somebody, who shall remain nameless and had no discernible motive, was slashing Vera's tire?"

A pause on the other end of the line, as if Glover were closing a document, or making an entry in a client file.

"Wish to hell I knew. Donal claims he's innocent until proven guilty, a quaint but popular notion in some quarters. I didn't lean on him very hard, though. I expect he was looking at naughty pictures or having a hair-loss treatment."

"So your letter will tell me, essentially, to buzz off?"

"I like that. Buzz off. Marriage must be agreeing with you, but yes, you can buzz off, and warn your client that my client intends to resume cordial relations when the order expires."

Across the office, Hannah let her pump come partway off, so it hung by her toes while she swung her foot in an impatient rhythm.

"Vera will be posting her property if I have anything to do with it. I'm serious, Aaron. Donal is not welcome back in her life on any terms."

"Yeah, yeah. She wouldn't pee in his face if it were on fire. I'm a divorce lawyer too, Knightley."

"When's the last time you had a vacation, Aaron?"

"About the last time you had one. The way I hear it, you and the new Mrs. Knightley haven't even had a honeymoon, but fear not: you know at least one good divorce lawyer if things with the lovely Hannah go south."

Hannah's pump, a raspberry confection with a hint of heel, slipped off her foot.

"Not funny, Aaron."

"Skipping your own honeymoon is?"

He ended the call, leaving Trent with the mixed feelings common to a profession where his adversaries were also his colleagues, and the only people who could truly sympathize with the burdens of being in practice.

"That was Aaron Glover?" Hannah asked.

"On the Waltham case. He's done a yeoman's job with what Donal has given him to work with, but I suspect Aaron does not have control of his client."

"Never a good thing."

"Not when your client has violent tendencies. May I ask you something?"

Hannah slipped her shoe back on, glanced behind her at the closed door, and nodded.

"Can we ditch the girls with James and Mac over spring break and go on a damned honeymoon?"

Hannah made a pretense of considering the question, but then she leaned forward and pitched her voice for his ears only.

"Hell, yeah."

———

"I've noticed something." Mac set his lunch tray down across from Trent, then took the chair opposite in the cafeteria in the basement of the Damson County courthouse.

Trent hadn't planned to share a meal with Mac, but the timing was fortuitous.

"You're always noticing things, MacKenzie. You're constitutionally incapable of turning off the ability to notice, unless it has to do with females. You don't notice them."

"I notice your new wife is happy," Mac said, accordion-folding the paper on a plastic drinking straw until it was compressed into a small wad. He used his straw to let a single drop of water touch the paper, causing it to expand.

"Hannah's female," Mac went on. "I notice your daughters aren't bothered with sibling rivalry, though by rights they ought to be a couple of screaming meemies."

"Give it a few years," Trent said, wondering if Mac would do the same thing to his straw papers when he was an old man. "Adolescence looms close at hand."

"True, though your girls are blessed with uncles who will bust the chops of any young swain who thinks to take inappropriate liberties, so rest easy."

Trent was more than capable of busting said chops. "Hadn't thought of that. Hannah will be relieved."

"Hannah will?"

"She worries," Trent said, being purposely obtuse, of course. "She's worried about leaving the girls with James and you when we leave town next week too."

"We'll manage," Mac said, unfolding a napkin over his lap. "Let her make a bunch of lists, but take her cell phone when the plane lands, and don't give it back to her unless she makes a real effort to enjoy herself."

Thus spoke a bachelor of the subspecies Hopelessly Clueless.

"I don't think taking her phone will go over very well with Hannah." Trent put some fries on Mac's plate, because some forces of nature were not worth fighting.

"Then she'll have to accidentally lose her phone, won't she?" Mac took the longest fry on his plate and began to munch it down from the end, the same way he'd eaten his fries since toddlerhood. "Today's Friday," he said.

"Praise Jesus for that. Jenelle came back from maternity leave just in time. If Hannah had to do one more child-support case, she would have turned in her license to practice."

"You've been at court the past few Fridays, but I've been back at the office, and I have noticed that James is taking leave on Friday afternoons."

Trent looked up from dabbling a fry in his ketchup. "You mean he's off seeing a client, or shagging some woman, or doing both?"

"Neither. I mean on his time sheet, he marks Friday afternoon as leave without pay, though he has plenty enough billable hours that it doesn't affect revenue."

Trent sketched a unicorn in his ketchup. "He isn't burning the midnight oil quite as steadily either. I've put in some late hours, and it used to be James was always right down the hall, beavering away on some pleading or correspondence, or having serial phone sex with his flavors of the evening. For the past few weeks, you're right: no James."

"I am mildly concerned," Mac said, starting that munching-from-one-end thing with a second fry—the second longest of the pile on his plate.

"You're beside yourself, wondering why James has abruptly taken holy orders. I wondered if he'd picked up an STD."

Mac's eyebrows rose, then came crashing down. "I taught you both better than that."

"Condoms aren't foolproof. I have two daughters, Mac, and I practice family law. I know more than I ever wanted to about certain subjects."

"Give me the criminals any day. You don't really think James is…afflicted?"

"Not with an STD, exactly. Do you recall when he took an order out to Vera Waltham for me?"

Fry number three met its fate. "That was a while ago."

"And James is not a man to waste time, but he has patience and determination to burn when it really matters. I have a theory, and Hannah agrees with me."

Mac chewed through the rest of Trent's fries, but he also listened. When Trent was done setting forth his theory, Mac was looking very thoughtful indeed.

"I told you, Chopin's too damned frilly for me." James wiggled his fingers in the air at eye level, his expression disgusted.

"You don't get to choose." Vera nearly rapped his knuckles with a rolled-up volume of Bach. "You will at least read through the nocturnes, one a week, or I'll make you do the waltzes, and they are frilly."

"I like the C-sharp minor waltz," James mumbled. Vera's assignment had him sitting before the keyboard like a big, sulky boy kept from his sandlot ball game.

He was beyond the waltzes, though the C-sharp minor was lovely.

"You can read through the longest nocturne in about twenty minutes," Vera said. "Twenty minutes out of your whole, entire week, James, so stop pouting."

Brooding rather. James was a grown man.

"Why'd he call them nocturnes?"

Ah, a glimmer of interest. "The form was first used by an Irish composer, Field, though there was an Italian form, the *notturno*, to which it might have borne some relation. To me, nocturne suggests music for the evening, a brooding, sunset mood. Have you heard them?"

"You haven't recorded them."

So…that would be a flattering sort of no?

"Budge over." Vera scooted onto the bench beside James, though he didn't budge far at all. "This one's in E minor, and it's underrated as party pieces go. Only two pages, and less saccharine than the E flat major."

She launched into the music, which to her evoked billowing seas and pewter skies with the odd ray of sunshine making a hopeful appearance in the contrasting theme.

The nocturne was a muscular little piece, substantial, and hard to ignore.

"That's not background music," James said when Vera brought her playing to an end. "Are they all like that?"

"Some are bigger, some are longer, but yes, they all have that balance of substance and grace. If I were to record something, these would be near the top of the list."

James flipped through the volume of Chopin until he found the one Vera had just played at the back of the book.

"Why don't you record them, Vera?"

Well, of course he'd ask. "People think recording is easy compared to a live performance, because if you muff it up, you can just try again, but it isn't like that."

He closed the music and set the book aside. "What's it like to record beautiful music, Vera?"

This was another question nobody had asked her. Vera dreaded recording sessions, always had, and couldn't bear to listen to the results for fear she'd hear mistakes.

"Donal and Alexander never understood this," she said, or maybe they hadn't wanted to understand it. "In the concert hall, you make mistakes, but they're forgiven, they're almost expected. The occasional wrong note, the appoggiatura that doesn't quite come off, the pedaling that ends up sounding sloppy in live acoustics, they happen. You learn to play on, and sometimes, it's the best you've done with that piece, despite the booboos. The audiences and the critics get that, mostly."

For one, startling instant, Vera missed that. Missed the thunder of applause, the passionate appreciation from a packed house, the satisfaction of having played the hell out of a tough program.

"Is there a but?" James asked.

One of the cows bawled out in the pasture, a homely, lonely sound.

"But in the studio," Vera said, "you must be perfect. I have a friend who was performing seventy-five years ago, and she says the old guys, the generation who first recorded classical music, they were more confident of their reception, closer to their audiences, and they'd leave in a little mistake every once in a while, like blowing a kiss to the audience, or winking. You don't get away with that anymore."

"It has to be perfect?"

"Donal thought so, and so did Alexander, though he was more subtle about it. He'd look disappointed if I'd done an imperfect job, and in some ways that was worse than Donal's ranting."

James closed the lid over the keys, a small act of consideration for the piano many people neglected to do.

"What you think should be what matters," he said. "For the record, I've never heard an obvious error in your recordings or your performances."

She stared at him sitting so innocently beside her. James would not lie to her, but he could not know—*she hadn't known*—how much she needed to hear those words.

"Say that again."

"I've never heard an obvious error in your performances."

"No, the other."

"What you think should be what matters. Isn't that why you're the teacher, Vera? Your judgment is the most trustworthy when it comes to music. You've devoted your life to it. You've had the best instruction. You've performed all over the world. You love music passionately and would play every day, even if you didn't get paid for it…what?"

Vera fumbled in her bag for a tissue, only to find James was holding out a monogrammed cotton hankie, his expression grave.

She took the hankie and sniffed and blinked, and tried to think up a saint to invoke appropriate to this loss of dignity, and still James sat beside her. He'd taken the wind out of her sails, shown her in a few words how low her emotional reserves had sunk.

And he'd offered her some fortification too.

"What I think should be what matters."

Slowly, slowly, Vera let her head fall to his shoulder. His expression didn't change, and his gaze remained fixed on the keyboard, but just as slowly, his arm stole around her waist.

James waited while she composed herself, and still she didn't want to sit back. He stayed right there beside her too.

"Which nocturne was it that you played?" James asked after a few minutes of silence.

"The E minor. You found it at the end of the book."

"Right. I'll start with that one."

※

"You should be looking at small horses," James said. "But you're stubborn, so feel free to drag me around to look at every foundered pony in western Maryland before you admit I'm right."

Trent kept driving, not sparing James even a glance, so James plowed on.

"Ponies are what happens to decent, law-abiding horses when for untold generations, they can't find adequate fodder. You try being hungry for thousands of years and see if it improves your disposition. Why are we looking exclusively at grays? They're prone to skin trouble."

"Grace's imaginary unicorn is white."

"With spots on his butt and wings," James said, humor warring with a sense of avuncular doom. "If you're looking to fulfill your stepdaughter's fantasies, then you can drop me back at my house, and I'll leave the unicorn shopping to you."

"You don't understand." Trent fell momentarily silent as they passed a tractor hauling a load of manure to the fields. "I want to find Grace the perfect horse. She's had a tough start in life, and I'm the new guy, and this is important."

Those same sentiments regarding Vera had kept James on the piano bench until midnight last night.

"You won't find another Pasha," James said. You used up your entire quotient of dad luck when that old duffer fell into your hands."

"He's a prince, but he can't be the only prince within shopping distance."

Yeah, he could. "Does your stepdaughter know you're looking?"

"No, and Hannah and I agreed we're not incorporating step-anything into our vocabulary. The girls can pick and choose labels as they see fit, but Hannah and I have two daughters, period."

Interesting, when James had decided he wasn't a *step*uncle, either. "What does Merle's mother make of this development?"

James posed the question because a brother could ask it, under the right circumstances, and who else was Trent going to talk it over with? Mac tended to get either silent or violent when the topic of Trent's ex came up.

"She was surprisingly gracious, or she was relieved. Now she can be even less attentive to her daughter, because Hannah will love Merle the way a mom ought to love her children. The way we were loved."

"Your turnoff's coming up."

This time, Trent did glance at James, but James didn't take the bait.

Nearly five years younger than Trent, James had long since concluded they'd been raised by different parents. Trent's parents had been hardworking, loving, devoted to their children, and tolerant of them within sensible limits. James's father had been too.

"The place needs a little work," Trent said as they bumped up a rutted lane between two lines of sagging board fence.

"Spring hasn't arrived yet," James said. "Nobody fixes their fences until the grass starts coming in."

They parked the truck near a bank barn whose standing-seam tin roof sported a thick coat of rust. Russet bantams huddled on a fence rail looked cold and scrawny, even for bantams, and a lone dog on a thirty-foot rope was tied on the other side of the barn.

"Why would you tie up a farm dog?" James asked.

"Because he bites."

"Right." How could the dog possibly be happy, tied in a barnyard with acres of liberty—and dead groundhogs—all around him?

"Does this charming and carefree mood of yours have anything to do with Vera Waltham?" Trent asked.

James was saved from making a reply by a woman coming out of the nearby farmhouse, the screen door banging closed behind her.

"Let me do the talking," James said. She was in that transition from middle-aged to older, a life on the farm taking its toll at the same time it imbued her with a certain purposeful energy. James suspected her name might rhyme with Irmantrude.

"You fellas come to look at the pony?"

"Hello, ma'am, James and Trent Knightley." James stuck out a hand, which she took, eyeing him up and down.

"You didn't bring a trailer. I was told if you were buying for slaughter, you'd have a stock trailer and offer cash on the spot. I'm only selling to a good home."

Charming, carefree moods were apparently thick on the cold, hard ground today. "We're looking for a first horse for my niece."

"I only advertised the pony," she said, glancing at Trent, who, understanding his role, nodded affably. "The pony has some years left in him. The horse is like me, seen better days."

"We need something with a lot of experience," James said. "My niece hasn't been riding very long, but she'll love any horse put into her care."

"Sure she will." The lady scuffed a worn tennis shoe

in the dirt. "Until she takes a notion to chase boys. We got the pony and the horse for our granddaughters, but they don't come around much anymore."

Or their parents didn't bring them. "Grace is seven," James said. "She'd better not discover boys any time soon, or her daddy will take exception."

This earned James a fleeting twist of the lips that might have passed for a smile.

"Come along, then. The paddock's out back." She walked off, her gait uneven, and James moved along beside her.

Why were there no tall old women? "May I ask why you're selling the pony?" James's tone was deferential, and he slowed his steps to keep pace with her.

"My husband had a stroke right before Christmas. He's up and around some now, but he tires easily, and horses are a lot of work if you take proper care of them. Planting is coming up, and it will be all we can do to keep up with the crop farming this year."

Horses were a damned lot of work, though Trent seemed to manage that work easily enough.

They rounded the corner of the barn, coming up to another sagging fence enclosing a few barren acres. A dozen muddy Angus steers milled around, along with one very muddy horse and an even muddier pony.

"Who's your farrier?" James asked, extending a hand over the top rail. The horse eyed him curiously, the pony turned its mud-caked butt toward the fence.

Thousands of years of short rations did take toll on a gal's mood—or a fellow's.

"Mr. Dean did the horseshoeing, but he moved away first of the year."

The first order of business was a visit from Mac, then, who'd picked up farriery in college as a way to earn extra money.

"Mind if I introduce myself?" James asked.

"Watch that mud. This time of year, it's nothing but mud everywhere." As James clambered over the fence, the lady glared at her farmyard as if the mud fairy would catch a stern lecture for all this mess.

James had dressed with the weather and outing in mind, and waded through the indifferent bovines to reach the horse first. The beast's mane hung to its shoulders in dreadlocks of mud, its forelock was a solid mass of burrs, and beneath a coarse gray winter coat, the animal wasn't carrying any extra weight.

The pony, a shaggy gray, was in only slightly better shape, and both were overdue for a foot trimming. James scratched the horse's withers, which inspired the pony to amble closer.

"You had their teeth floated lately, ma'am?"

"Maybe last year."

Two years ago, then, at least. "May I ask where you bought them?"

"An ad in the paper about five years ago. The pony is the one we're selling."

The pony, who was now nuzzling James's back pockets, from which James withdrew a lump of sugar. "You mind if I feed them a treat?"

"Go on ahead. They won't bite. My husband wouldn't put up with anything that bites."

"You have a bridle for either one of them?"

"Yes, we do, and you can have the bridle if you buy the pony. I'll fetch the bridles, if you're interested."

Nobody should be interested in this pair, based on their appearance. "A saddle for the horse would be nice, if you have one."

She nodded, her expression disgruntled.

"Are you being polite," Trent asked when the woman was out of earshot, "or are you really considering one of these warthogs for my daughter?"

"Hush. You'll hurt the lady's feelings."

"Not if I pay cash, but, James, you can't be serious. These two are out of condition, ugly, neglected, and filthy. They even smell like cows."

James had long enjoyed the smell of cows. "You can fix all that. Look beneath the mud to the disposition, which you can't fix very easily once it's been soured." When Mrs. Farmer-the-Charmer returned, James took the pony out of the paddock first, which left the horse pacing the fence.

"We're not going far," James said to the horse. "You can cheer us on, but your turn is next. What's the pony's name, ma'am?"

"Josephine. We call her Jo for short."

James bridled the pony, rigged long lines from bailing twine, and hand-drove the little beast all over the barnyard, using a broken-off cane of sumac for his driving whip.

Josephine was quiet, obedient, and happy to take any reasonable order. When James asked her to hop a log, she cast him one questioning glance, then cleared it willingly enough.

He fed her another lump of sugar and gave Trent a pointed look.

"She's a perfect lady," James said to the owner. "Do you mind if I work with the horse for a few minutes?"

"I don't see where it would hurt, but he's seventeen. That's getting old for a horse."

For some horses, but by no means for all horses. James peered into the gelding's mouth before slipping the bridle on, then swung up onto the animal's back without benefit of a saddle.

The horse stood docilely. "How long did you say it's been since he was ridden?"

"Years."

The gelding recalled his manners, and packed James around the barnyard at the walk, trot, and canter, both directions. He stopped on cue, he backed, he side passed, he even half passed.

A gentleman fallen on hard times, then, one who'd never make an impression on the ladies in his present state. James liked the horse for trying and for maintaining his equine dignity in the midst of humble circumstances.

Also for being protective of the little mare.

Chapter 9

"What's his name?" James asked, petting the gelding on its shaggy, muddy neck.

"Wellington," the lady replied. "When he loses his winter coat, you can see he probably started out as a strawberry roan, but he's mostly white now. He used to be a fine animal."

James could sympathize with that sentiment, but not for any amount of money or attack of softheartedness would he saddle his brother with a lame horse. The next step was an inspection tour of the gelding, picking up each foot, peering into its ears, running hands over flanks, legs and belly, lifting the tail, and listening to the animal breathe.

"Mind if I have a word with my brother?" James asked their hostess.

"Not at all. I got chickens to feed." She half limped off in the direction of the barn.

"You're going to tell me to buy them?" Trent asked as James slipped the bridle off the horse. "This guy is breathing hard, and you barely worked him ten minutes."

"I worked him nonstop for ten minutes. I'm six foot three, and he's been out of work for years. Give the guy a break. Seventeen is a perfect age, and he's a gentleman."

"He's not for sale."

Damned lawyers, always getting focused on the minutiae. "I never met a horse that wasn't for sale at some price. The pony will be a nice little driving horse when nobody wants to ride her."

"A guest horse," Trent said, jamming his hands into the back pockets of his jeans. "Now that we have two girls, the house is overrun with children on weekends and days off."

"A guest horse, then. These two are solid citizens, and you can get them for a song. Have the vet out to take a bunch of X-rays and charge you a lot of money, but for what you're going to pay, they're worth it."

The pony remained by the fence, aiming hopeful, hungry-pony looks at James, while the horse took to scratching a shoulder against a fence post.

"What were you looking for under the horse's tail?" Trent asked.

"A pot of gold."

Trent smacked his arm.

"Melanomas. Pink skin is prone to them, but he's in good shape."

"What did you think of the horse's gaits?"

A prospective buyer's question. "Grace can sit them with a little practice," James said. "The canter is particularly nice, considering the boy's feet are overdue for some attention."

Trent scrubbed a hand across his chin as the pony lifted its burr-laden tail and let go a sulfurous, sibilant fart.

Ponies were not known for their diplomacy.

"You think I should get both? I can't take them home looking like this, and the present owner hasn't so much as taken a brush to them in years."

While James's hands fairly itched to start combing the burrs out of their manes.

"They're a couple, Trent. You saw how the horse fretted when he thought the mare was being taken away."

"So they'll be buddy sour."

Was that what being a couple meant to James's newly married brother? "Not in a herd, and not once they get the routine down. Do you want your daughter to have a horse or not?"

"I do."

"Then I'll take them to my place for a while first," James said. "I'll get 'em cleaned up, have Mac get after their feet, bring their shots up-to-date, and have the horsey dentist look at their teeth. These are good horses. They just need some time and TLC."

Same as most people did after a rough patch.

"You said you never wanted pets," Trent retorted, confirming that litigating attorneys had good memories for what was better forgotten. "You haven't had an animal of your own since you were kid."

The horse and pony wouldn't be James's either.

"Who needs a pet, when both of my brothers escaped from the primate house? If you don't like these horses, then you can leave them with me. I'm offering to guarantee the sale, because I feel that confident you won't regret buying these two."

Trent turned a baleful eye on the cows, which had that half-indolent, half-wild quality typical of the livestock on small, tired farms.

"How much cash you have on you?" he asked.

"Enough."

James convinced the woman the horse and pony would be happier together, and she was threatening

James with coffee cake and pictures of the grandkids by the time he and Trent climbed back into the truck.

"What is it with you and women, James? They love you on sight."

"Gertrude's lonely and tired. Most of them are just lonely and tired." James hadn't meant to put it quite like that, but Trent—older brother at large—seized the opening.

"Which brings us back to Vera Waltham. You haven't asked me the first thing about her."

"Because you're her lawyer, and unless Vera's case comes up in one of our partner meetings, I don't want to know about her legal problems." Also because James was mentally rehearsing a negotiation with Mr. Inskip about use of a pasture and shed for a couple of months.

Or maybe longer.

"But I'm your brother," Trent said, slowing down to ease the truck over the rutted lane. "I won't discuss Vera's case, but I might answer some general questions."

James's questions regarding Vera were not general. "Why would I ask about your client?"

"Why would you buy a battery for a Ford Falcon a few weeks back, if not for Vera?"

"The girls told you?" James sure hadn't let that slip—or had he?

"You told me," Trent retorted. "Though little people have perfect recall for all the things you shouldn't say in front of them. Ask any parent. They forget their chores, their homework, their socks, and their own names, but don't drop the f-bomb around a kid, or you'll soon be famous for it."

"Must be awful, having your every inconvenient word played back for you. I wouldn't drop the f-bomb around the girls." Though did Trent have to sound so happy to have his own junior censorship board underfoot?

"You wouldn't ask me about Vera, either," Trent said.

"I don't have to. I googled her, Alexander Waltham, and Donal MacKay."

"And?"

And James *did* want to discuss Vera's circumstances, now that Trent had brought her up.

"She was the third woman Waltham married," James said. "The odd thing is, all of his wives were the same age when he married them."

Trent hit a button on the dashboard when they reached the road, and soft strains of Rachmaninoff filled the truck.

"Why is the age of a man's wives significant?" Trent asked.

"Vera was barely of age when she married him. He was forty-two. What kind of man has his first kid when he's forty-four?"

"Kids happen," Trent said with the pragmatic tolerance of a family law practitioner. "What did your research tell you about Donal?"

James turned the music down so it was barely audible. "Donal's another guy who prefers lamb to mutton. He's fifty, and Vera's twenty-eight. I gather as Vera's manager, Alex was some kind of check on Donal, who would have had her doing four hundred performances a year, left to his own devices."

"They both passed up other promising clients to focus on her. Some might say that was a sacrifice on their parts."

"Then some would be idiots," James retorted.

"Vera's the real thing, Trent. She has music in her soul, and talent coming out her ears. Alex and Donal knew a once-in-a-lifetime opportunity when they found it. They differed only over how quickly they were going to burn her out."

Did Vera admit that, even to herself?

Trent turned the music up just a bit. "I don't think she's burned out, exactly. Heartbroken is more like it."

Not the observation of a lawyer, but the observation of a guy who'd taken his turn on the heartbroken bench.

"Don't tell me you think she was in love with Donal?" Every instinct James had—and his instincts regarding women were formidable—told him the marriage had been as pragmatic as the divorce had been messy.

Trent brought the truck to a stop at a four-way, and waited for another tractor-cum-manure spreader to lumber through the intersection.

"I think Vera wanted to at least hold Donal in high regard," Trent said, pulling forward. "She was simply too stubborn to admit she'd made a mistake until he lost his temper with her."

"We need to change the subject." James studied the fallow fields on the passenger side of the truck, which looked like a thousand other fallow fields all over Maryland. "When I think of him raising a hand to her, putting his hands on her in anger—Why didn't he go to jail, Trent? Why the hell didn't he go to jail?"

Why didn't they all go to jail? A man who had to ask that question was much better off down the hall from both family law and criminal law, buried in the desiccated catacombs of subrogation and assignment clauses.

Or out of the practice of law altogether.

Trent was silent for a mile or so before he answered.

"We cut a deal. Vera allowed the criminal charges to go to the inactive docket, and Donal agreed to the maximum length of time for the restraining order. Donal's kids would have had to go back to their mother full time if he'd been locked up, and Tina MacKay hadn't been out of rehab very long at the time."

Did Donal make every woman who married him miserable?

"That restraining order expires shortly." James could not help sounding pissed about it. "How quickly time flies when you're having a divorce. How do you stand working with this crap every day?"

They hit a construction zone and more ruts, though the truck's suspension was equal to the challenge.

"Family law is hard sometimes." Even that much was an admission from Trent, an admission he probably would not have made before marrying Hannah.

"What gets to you the most?"

"The kids," Trent said, no hesitation. "They invariably want Mom and Dad back together, and they go to awful lengths to see it happen. They get sick. They get straight A's carrying a heavy course load. They get into trouble. They become promiscuous. They flunk out of school. They develop mental illnesses and eating disorders. They cut themselves. They run. They try to be perfect. If you ask them, most of them will say they want their parents to be happy, but their actions tell a different story."

The family law department referred a lot of cases over to Mac's criminal defense team for delinquency issues. Did everybody regard that as a mere coincidence? James certainly didn't.

"You do this work," he said, "when you yourself are divorced. Can you wonder why Mac and I worry about you?"

"Don't worry about me," Trent said, flashing a cat-in-the-cream smile. "Hannah and I are away on our honeymoon next week, and it's you and Mac who'll be deserving of worry."

"Because we're taking on two perfectly wonderful little girls for a straight week?" When had James ever looked forward to female company more? "It'll be a walk in the park."

"I don't do underdoggies," Mac muttered, but of course, Merle and Grace, both in the backseat, heard him.

"That's OK, Uncle Mac," Grace said. "Uncle James can be in charge of underdoggies, and you can be in charge of pushing the merry-go-round."

"And no fair hopping on and riding it," James chimed in from behind the wheel. "You make it slow down sooner when you do that."

"Yeah. No fair, Uncle Mac," Merle echoed.

They arrived at the park, and when the girls were tearing across the grass to the swings, Mac took a bench, and James came down beside him.

"How do they do it?" Mac asked softly. "Trent and Hannah keep up with these two and work full-time jobs. It boggles the mind."

"Puts a few things in perspective," James said. "I am more concerned for how they do the jobs they do, having children. Hannah's wading hip-deep into mediation, which will mean a steady diet of families trying to reorganize themselves in the midst of litigation. Trent deals with the cases that can't be resolved in mediation, and they both come home each night and interact with not only each other, but the girls."

"Takes stamina."

"Takes love and courage."

Mac would doubtless have leveraged that comment into some sort of older-brother lecture about James's personal life, but—thank the unicorns—Merle bellowed from her swing.

"Uncle Jaaaaaammmmeees. Time for underdoggies!"

"Whoever invented underdoggies should be shot," James muttered. Then, "Be right there, pumpkin!"

Mac's smile was more of a smirk. "Go get 'em, Uncle James."

When both uncles were exhausted from the park, and the girls were chattering away happily in the backseat with ice cream cones, James drove back to Trent's farm. The top scoop of Merle's double-dip ended up all over James's leather seat, and when he cleaned that up, he found the sprinkles from Grace's sundae necessitated vacuuming the backseat as well.

Thank God he wasn't trying to deal with both girls entirely alone, and thank God that Gertrude had let him keep Wellington and Josephine with her for another couple of weeks. Mac took on the barn chores, while James took on the cooking and the housework, and both uncles were cheerfully "assisted" by their nieces.

When the girls were tucked in and both uncles were sitting on the couch, too tired to even reach for the remote, James leaned his head back and closed his eyes.

"The silence. Listen to the sweet, sweet silence."

"We have about sixty-eight hours until Trent and Hannah are back," Mac said, stifling a yawn. "I figure the kids will sleep for at least twenty-four of those hours, which means forty-four big ones to go."

"Forty-four is a lot."

"Look how far we've come."

A short, awestruck silence ensued, while James contemplated getting up and making himself a cup of decaf tea. He'd cut back on his caffeine at the suggestion of, of all people, his piano teacher.

"Did Grace seem fidgety to you?" Mac asked.

"Neither one of them stopped moving all day. Fidgety when?"

"After dinner, when Merle and I were annihilating you and Grace at Concentration."

James hadn't felt this wamped since beating Trent at racquetball, but he could not let that pass. "You weren't annihilating us. We were letting you develop a false sense of security."

"You lost three in a row."

"The championships are coming up. Perfect setup for you and Merle to get overconfident." Grace *had* been fidgety. She'd sat next to James and been twitching and rocking the whole time.

"Damn." James shot to his feet.

"You said a bad word, Uncle James."

"I'll be saying more, because I didn't remind the girls to use the bathroom before they turned in."

Mac stayed right where he was. "Uh-oh."

"Yeah, uh-oh. They're probably still awake. Why don't you go remind them?"

Mac rearranged himself so he was sprawled on the

couch, flat on his back. "You're the nighty-night expert. You remind them."

"I'm not the nighty-night—You are such a sissy, MacKenzie."

James headed up the stairs, more so Mac wouldn't see him smiling than anything else. The past four days had shown James a shyness in his brother he hadn't known was there, and the knowledge was precious. They hadn't shared a roof for years, hadn't been on a joint vacation, hadn't spent this much time together in a long, long while, and James was reassured that he still truly liked and enjoyed Mac's company.

The girls had chosen to share a room—yet another decision to be made when two families joined forces—so James knocked softly, then cracked open the door.

"We're awake," Merle said, though the room was lit only by the night-lights beside each bed.

Had they had to negotiate that too?

"You're supposed to be asleep, cast into the arms of Sweet Morpheus by the ordeal of managing two uncles all by your lonesomes."

"Was she one of your girlfriends?" Merle asked, sitting up.

"A friend, anyway. The Greeks put Morpheus in charge of sleep, and those who slept." James sat on the edge of Grace's bed and peered down at her in the gloom. "Sweetheart, have you been crying?"

"She has," Merle said.

"You miss your mom?" James asked, brushing a thumb over Grace's damp little cheek.

Grace burrowed closer to her pillow.

"That's not why she's crying."

"You're not supposed to tell, Merle." Grace sniffed. "It's a secret."

"You're going to wet the bed, and then it won't be a secret," Merle said.

"I'm not going to wet the bed, because I'm not going to pee."

"Why aren't you going to pee?" James asked, but his insides were not half so calm as his voice.

"She won't pee because it hurts."

"Merle." James and Grace both spoke her name at once, James gently, Grace with considerable animosity.

"She's worried for you, Grace, and so am I. Does it hurt to pee?"

Grace pulled the covers over her head.

"She's embarrassed," Merle said. "She says she just got you as uncles, and she's not going to tell you about it. She wanted to tell Mom, but not over the phone with everybody listening."

Her mom, who was hundreds of miles away. "Of course she didn't," James said. "It's personal."

"Yeah." Grace peeked out from the covers and stuck her tongue out at Merle. "It's personal."

Then James had a truly terrifying, sickening thought.

"Grace, has your mom talked to you about good touches and bad touches?"

"Sure."

His heart thumping against his ribs, James put the next question as neutrally as he could. "Have there been any bad touches you need to tell someone about?"

"No, and if there ever are, I can tell Mom, or Dad, or my teacher. But Bronco looks after me, and bad touches are yucky."

Bronco being the winged, spotted unicorn no uncle dared denigrate.

Grace pulled the covers back up, then lowered them. "Am I going to have to go to the hospital?"

"I doubt it."

Merle sat up crossed-legged amid her covers. "Grace hates the hospital. I do too."

"It isn't anybody's favorite place, but they can help when you're not feeling well," James said, and thank God, both Trent and Hannah had left notarized statements providing James and Mac the authority to consent to medical treatment.

The immediate practicalities needed to be dealt with too. "Do you need to pee now, Grace?"

"No. I haven't had anything to drink since lunch."

Lunch had been eons ago. "That's not so good. You must be thirsty."

Grace's chin jutted in a mulish fashion that put James in mind of her mother with a tough case. "I'm not going to drink anything, and you can't make me."

"I wouldn't even think to try," James said, running a hand over her tousled braid. "Let me talk to Uncle Mac, and we'll see what our next move is. Would you take a drink to get down some painkiller?"

"Yeah. Mom showed me how to take grown-up medicine."

"Dad showed me," Merle chimed in.

"Then I'll be right back with some pills." James tweaked each nose and took his leave, the girls whispering furiously in his wake.

"Houston, we have a problem," he said to Mac, who was still horizontal on the couch.

"Somebody have an accident already?"

"No. Somebody has a little-girl problem. Grace says it hurts to pee, and she means business. She hasn't had anything to drink since lunch."

Mac got to his feet in one lithe motion.

"Where are you going?" James asked.

Mac stopped halfway to the stairs. "I don't know. I was going to cross-examine the witness. I guess you already did that?"

"Abetted by Merle. What makes it hurt to pee, Mac? Grace said there hadn't been any bad touches."

Mac dropped back onto the couch like he'd been clobbered with sack of feed. "Bad—Christ on a pogo stick."

"Do we call Trent and Hannah?" James asked.

"Trent and Hannah can't help. I guess we go to the emergency room because the urgent care has closed by now. The insurance cards are on the fridge."

They couldn't *both* go to the emergency room, because somebody had to stay with Merle.

"How will Grace deal with that?" James asked. "She says she just got us as uncles, and they'll want a urine sample, and I'm a grown man, and I can't even…"

"Shy bladder," Mac said, nodding once and not meeting James's gaze. "It's genetic. They have nurses, though, at the hospital. Haven't you dated any nurses you could call?"

James stifled the urge to deck dear old Uncle Mac. "I avoid the medical types. Too controlling, while they call it a helping profession."

Mac was on his feet again. "What are we in, if not a helping profession?"

"Deep doo-doo."

They fell silent, though Mac was pacing. Mac didn't pace when his client was charged with first-degree murder.

"We need a mom," Mac said. "You've dated moms, surely?"

"I tried to pick up Hannah, once, just to test her intentions toward Trent, but she laughed in my face, which was a much bigger relief than it should have been."

"Does Trent know this?" Mac asked. "I've kind of enjoyed having you for a brother. Gotten used to it, in fact."

Kind of good to know. "Trent laughed too. I don't date moms. They have no use for me."

Mac looked puzzled, then his expression brightened entirely too much. "Vera Waltham is a mom, and she lives not five miles away. We could call her."

A drop of calm landed on James's roiling insides. "What is this *we* shit, Uncle Mac?"

"Bad word, Uncle James."

"F-Phooey… Sh-Sugar, I just nearly dropped the f-bomb. It's almost nine o'clock, and Vera has her own kid to tuck in." Though Vera would come. If James asked her to, she'd come.

"So bring the kid here." Mac said. "We'll have a slumber party, and you and Vera can nip off to the ER and take care of Grace's whatever."

Managing partner, indeed. "A fine plan, MacKenzie. I'm dealing with a whimpery little girl and a pack of nosy doctors, while you're up past your bedtime, eating popcorn and watching princess movies."

Mac's bright expression dimmed. "Princess movies?"

"Merle will be too worried to sleep until Grace gets home, and Bronco's coming with us," James said. "How do I explain an imaginary winged unicorn who's in truth a guardian angel, and not have the hospital think the kid is nuts?"

"It's the spots on his butt that people just don't understand. You'd better call Vera."

You, not we.

Grace was upstairs, needing her mother, afraid to pee, mortified, in pain, and too worried to sleep. James didn't want to call Vera Waltham, not really, but he'd better.

Yeah, he'd better.

—◆◆◆—

Vera accompanied James into Trent's house, with James carrying a sleeping Grace. He'd been so worried over a simple bladder infection, Vera had been hard put to credit it.

Cool, calm, sexy James Knightley had been nearly unglued at the prospect of asking a little girl to pee in a cup at the local urgent-care facility. Or maybe— possibly?—Grace was feeling miserable, and James was too tenderhearted to deal with it.

Fortunately, Vera had met Trent's daughter Merle months ago in Trent's office, and Grace had been too relieved to see a friendly adult female on the scene to stand much on her dignity.

MacKenzie Knightley looked the worse for wear as he rose from the couch. "Is Grace OK?"

"She has a bladder infection," James said quietly, because Grace was dozing against his shoulder. "It's a little-girl thing, and antibiotics will fix her right up."

"Thank God," Mac said, "and thank you, Vera Waltham. Your daughter is fast asleep upstairs, and what a delightful child she is."

"She spared you having to watch princess movies," James said, kissing Grace's crown. "You're in Twyla Waltham's debt, old man."

How protectively he held the child, and how comfortable Grace was in his embrace. At the hospital, the physician had assumed they were father and daughter.

"I am happy to be in Twyla's debt," Mac said, "but I'm also happy to head off to bed. Want me to tuck the patient in?"

Grace yawned without opening her eyes.

"Now you're the Chief Tucker Inner?" James asked. "I don't think so, Mac the Wimp. Make Vera a cup of decaf tea, and I'll be back down shortly." He sauntered off with his burden, while Grace roused enough to wave a sleepy good night to Vera and Mac.

"James has never been the possessive sort before," Mac said. "The kitchen is this way, though I've left James a few dishes in the sink for form's sake."

"You are brothers, after all, aren't you?"

Mac's smile was astoundingly sweet, transforming his otherwise forbidding features. "Now more than ever, we're brothers, though I'm thinking a princess-movie marathon might be the ultimate bonding experience. Decaf or high octane? Or would you prefer coffee?"

Vera would prefer hot chocolate with whipped cream and a dash of nutmeg.

"Anything without caffeine," she said, struggling a bit with the novelty of having a man wait on her.

Kitchens told the tale of the family, and until recently, this had been exclusively Trent's kitchen. It was spacious, tidy, and inviting, with a liberal sprinkling of African violets on the counters and shelves. The refrigerator door held photos and drawings, his and hers already on the way to being ours.

"James and I were in a panic," Mac said as he put on the kettle. "James cannot stand to see a female in distress, much less a little girl whom he loves."

"He's known Grace, what, only a few months?"

"How can anybody not love Grace?" Mac asked.

Mac was genuinely perplexed, God and the unicorns—James had explained about that part—bless him.

"Grace is very dear," Vera said, "but maybe you were equally upset to see James rattled."

Mac stopped in the middle of setting mugs and the sugar bowl on a tray and shot Vera a look over his shoulder.

"Trent likes you," he said. "I should have realize that means you're a bright lady. I think James likes you too, though the theory did not originate with me."

"Oh?" This was interesting.

"Trent takes credit for it, but Hannah was doubtless the one who put the pieces together, so it's marital property."

Hadn't James said anything to his family about his piano lessons? And if not, why not?

"James is six years my junior," Mac went on. "Dad died when James was thirteen, and Trent and I were focused on college. When classes started in the fall, that left James home with our mother, whose grief took her in some unhealthy directions."

"James was only thirteen?" And he'd lost father and both brothers. No wonder Chopin's flooding emotion spooked him.

"Unlucky thirteen," Mac said, "and he became the little man. Trent and I were too stupid and too young to understand the position we'd left him in."

"What position was that?" What position was Mac putting Vera in with this family history chat?

Mac took the kettle off before the whistle sounded loudly, and poured two mugs of boiling water. He knew his way around a kitchen, and wasn't too proud to leave a dish towel draped over his shoulder.

"Mom held it together OK for the first year after Dad died," he said, "but then it was like she expected her grief to up and go away, and it didn't. My sense is she'd go for months without a slip, then fall off the wagon in a spectacular way. I didn't know how bad it was until I came home for the weekend unexpectedly one Easter break, and she was a wreck."

Mac paused, teakettle in hand, steam curling up from both cups. Inside a criminal defense mastermind lurked the heart of a worried older brother—and a touch of Martha Stewart.

"There was my little brother," he went on, "doing all the housework, managing the help we hired to do the farm work, pulling straight A's in advanced placement courses, and not saying one damned word to me or Trent, because Mom wouldn't want us to know. Excuse my language. I'm an uncle. I should know better."

He fished a quarter out of his pocket and put it in a mason jar on the counter labeled, "Bad Word Restitution Fund," with the *d* in "fund" crossed out.

"Why are you telling me this?" Even as she asked the question, Vera tried to square what she knew of James with this sad and yet somehow predictable tale.

Mac brought the tea tray to the table and gestured for Vera to have a seat. "I suppose this is in the nature of a confession," he said. "I let my brother down, and feel responsible for some of his shortcomings."

"James has shortcomings?" Vera meant it as a joke, but Mac only looked thoughtful.

"He's a caretaker," Mac said, as if a family were allotted only one of those oddities. "We were all raised to be responsible. It's hard to grow up on a farm and not be responsible, but James cares almost too much, which is why we don't let him have the family law cases, though he dealt with them brilliantly. He's never had a pet, you know?"

Vera hadn't known, but Mac wasn't finished.

"He rode like a demon, or he did as a younger man, but the competition horse he leased in college colicked and had to be put down, and James stopped riding altogether. Just walked away from the whole business, and he was very good at it. Sugar?"

At first Vera didn't understand what Mac was asking, because a picture was forming of the boy James had been, openhearted, probably sheltered by his older brothers, and then—bam!—his entire family dead or off to college, except for a mother who didn't cope well.

"Just a dash of sugar," Vera said. "And a drop of milk would be appreciated too." The conversation needed brownies though, or homemade cookies.

Mac got to his feet and went to the fridge, bringing back a full gallon jug of milk and thunking it on the table. Vera hadn't seen her own brothers for two years, but she knew they would have done the same.

"Thanks." Very carefully, she added a dollop of milk to her tea. "Will James want some tea?"

"He can fix his own."

Vera put the milk away, contemplating the strange blend of gruff concern and casual indifference that was fraternal love.

"What happened to the farm?" she asked when she returned to the table.

"We sold it when Mom died, and divided the proceeds to pay for our various educations," Mac said. "It's ironic, because our great-great-grandfather was a lawyer, and in his later years a judge, and his profession was sufficiently lucrative to allow him to buy that ground. In hindsight, selling was a mistake, though a well-intended one."

Hindsight and mistakes went hand in hand, and everybody hit wrong notes. "Why do you say that?"

Mac stirred his tea slowly, staring at the mug as if it held answers.

"Our dad said we could be anything we chose, anything at all, but we had to get an education first, so off to college I went, and Trent followed, but James…" Mac made a face at his tea. "Trent and I started off on loans, scholarships, and part-time jobs, and our shares of Dad's life insurance. When Mom died, we assumed James should get himself to college, but if we'd asked him, he might have stayed on the farm, at least for a few years."

Vera's tea was delightful, an Earl Grey that managed to savor wonderfully of black tea and bergamot, even though it was decaf.

"You didn't ask him if he was ready to give up his home?" she asked. Had anybody asked Vera if she wanted to perform?

"Do you have older brothers?"

"Two."

"I don't need to explain the caring that masquerades as bravado, then, do I? Trent and I were eighteen and nineteen when Dad died, legally adult, but emotionally very much orphaned. Trent says I'm wrong, says James had some very unhappy memories of the farm and would not have wanted to stay, but we denied him a choice."

More than a decade later, Perry Mason was still passing judgment on himself. "MacKenzie, I think James would have spoken up if he'd wanted to stay."

Though maybe not. Maybe James would look after the brothers who'd failed to look after him.

Mac met her gaze, his expression curious. Did any of his female clients notice that Mac Knightley had lovely eyes?

"Why do you say that?" he asked.

"James isn't farming now, is he? He isn't raising horses, or cows, or whatever farmers do around here. He could if he wanted to, and he doesn't."

"Now he's the business partner at the firm, and sees himself as responsible for both of his older brothers, if not every single person on the payroll."

As well as his nieces and his new neighbor. "In what regard is James responsible?"

Though why was Vera probing into this aspect of James's life? He was a piano student.

Who had kissed her.

Who guarded his heart.

Who sweat bullets over a little girl's welfare.

Who'd come without hesitation when Vera had asked him to.

Who'd called upon Vera when he'd been backed into a corner.

"A law firm is an interesting entity," Mac said, taking his empty mug to the sink. "Its day-to-day operations are concerned with handling cases, going to court, meeting with clients, and making money doing that, but if the venture is to be profitable, somebody had better also have a firm grasp of management principles and business law. Somebody had better have some *vision*. For us, that somebody is James."

"He told me he's a CPA," Vera said. Which in itself was astounding. Now Mac said James was a CPA with *vision*, surely a rarity among bean counters. "How does having a partner who knows tax law make you more competitive?"

Mac glanced at the clock, a sunflower ceramic which pointed to nearly midnight.

"I'll give you an example," he said, leaning back against the sink. "Every other firm in the county rents office space. This is sensible when office space is abundant and you have responsible landlords who keep up the property. James pointed out that the attorneys are all concentrated within a couple of blocks of the courthouse, which is in a historic district. Office space there consists of rickety old houses with narrow corridors and uneven floors, and little in the way of handicapped accessibility."

Vera knew the exact area Mac described. Early Dilapidated masquerading as Civil War Historic.

"So you serve the handicapped clients more easily in your present offices?" she asked.

"We can, but those historic downtown properties are prohibitively expensive to buy, and very dear to rent and maintain. James did the research, talked to the banks, and figured out we could create a landlord company of our own to build the facility we have, state of the art, plenty of parking, all the amenities, and pay rent to ourselves while we're building up equity in the property and claiming all sorts of tax benefits."

"So you're financially healthier," Vera said, though the whole arrangement sounded more complicated than a four-voice fugue. "You wonder why the other firms aren't doing the same."

She took another sip of very good tea, and wondered what James was doing while she interrogated Mac.

"The other firms don't have James figuring the angles, pitching the banks like only a CPA can pitch them. James has us leasing our cars from ourselves. He chose our payroll and accounting software and keeps it up to date. He developed the five-year plan for the business and fine-tunes it as we go. Because we have James, we work smarter than the competitors. Ergo, we have more money to plow back into benefits, salary, and training. Ergo, we attract the best people and can charge accordingly."

Did people who'd never been to law school use *ergo*?

"James is your secret weapon?" Did he see himself in that regard, or was he still the youngest brother, trying to pull his share of a load he'd never chosen?

"I would have said family loyalty is our secret weapon," Mac said. "Upon reflection, I worry that James has been more loyal to me and to Trent than we have to him."

While Vera had figured out too late where her agent's and manger's loyalties had lain.

"You should ask James, then," Vera said. "He'll be

honest with you." But kind, too, because in addition to his other fine qualities, James was a gentleman.

The gentleman himself walked into the kitchen, looking tired and worn around the edges, but no less handsome—no less sexy—for the fatigue.

"Ask me what?"

Chapter 10

"IF YOU'RE ENJOYING THE PRACTICE OF LAW," VERA said, "or doing it only to support your brothers." She aimed a glance at Mac, but he had turned his back to rinse out his mug—again.

Oopsie.

"What kind of sorry question is that?" James shot back.

"An honest one," Mac said, abandoning the pretense of domesticity. "Trent and I have niches we enjoy and do well, but you more or less took up the business law because we neglected it, and it has occurred to me you might not particularly enjoy it."

"Did I sit for the CPA exam because you neglected that?" James replied. "Did I advertise us as having business law expertise because you neglected that too? Did I court the damned banks and accounting firms because you and Trent forgot to do it?"

James was answering a question with a question, which could be perceived as a dodge, and his tone was challenging, though he kept his voice down.

"We're tired," Vera said, "and it has been a long, long evening. Maybe there's a better time for this discussion."

James sent Mac the kind of disgusted glance a bull might have cast at a matador backing out of the bullring, but Mac took the olive branch.

"We've imposed on Vera long enough," Mac said. "I can take her home."

"I'm the one who imposed on her," James retorted. "I'll take her home. I wouldn't have stayed upstairs so long, but Grace woke up and asked me to sit with her until she fell back to sleep."

Mac looked like he wanted to say more but thought better of it. "I'll thank Vera one last time then, and bid you both good night."

Tension that had been filling the kitchen left with him, the fraternal sort that could flare or dissipate with a word or a look.

James put a quarter in the mason jar—probably for the "damned" banks—then crossed to the stove and put on the teakettle.

"I'm not sure what Mac told you," he said, "but I'm sorry you had to witness that last exchange. Would you like some tea? We have decaf."

"I'm still working on my last mug," Vera said. "The essence of what Mac said is that he worries about you." Mac loved James too. Ferociously.

"He worries." James stared at the teakettle, a plain metal teakettle like a million others. "He's prone to fretting, is our MacKenzie. That's part of what makes him hell in a three-piece suit in the courtroom. You don't catch him unprepared, not with the latest changes in the law, not with fresh appellate opinions. He's damned good."

No quarter this time. James was apparently damned irritated with his brother.

"Mac thinks you're damned good too," Vera said.

This late, and after the evening they'd had, some of James's smoothness had eroded, leaving Vera a slightly different companion than she'd known previously.

James set an oversized Winnie the Pooh mug on the counter and fired two stringless tea bags into it.

"Mac thinks I'm sixteen years old and barely holding it together. Trent's not quite as bad, but sometimes I want to grab one brother in this hand, another brother in that, and ..." He pantomimed banging two fraternal heads together. Hard.

"I felt the same way about my brothers," Vera said, "until Alex took over as my manager and Donal became my agent, and then I realized brothers have their uses."

"Your brothers are older than you?"

"A few years, and we used to be close, but then I started competing and touring, and they couldn't come to every performance anymore, and life has moved us in different directions."

That hurt. Every time Vera came to that realization, it hurt. Twy had cousins she barely knew, and the time had come to fix that.

"You're reminding me to be grateful I have the brothers I do," James said, scrubbing a hand down his face. "Believe me, I am, but tonight, I was more than grateful to have you along. I've heard of bladder infections, but when Grace first said how she hurt..." He hiked himself up to sit on the counter, then leaned back against the cupboards with an air of utter weariness. "I don't know how you people raise children. The whole idea scares the hell out of me."

You people? "When Grace told you it hurt to pee, what did you think, James?"

The teakettle started to hiss. James flipped the burner off and let his head fall back against the cupboards.

"I thought someone might have hurt her intimately, and,

Vera, the idea, merely the idea—I can honestly say that was one of the worst moments of my life. Simply having to consider the possibility made my stomach heave."

He poured the boiling water into the oversized mug. The scent of peppermint wafted across the kitchen as he squeezed a few drops from a bottle on the counter into the fragrant tea.

"Grace will be fine," Vera said, using the tone that usually worked on a student threatening to choke at a recital. "You got spooked, and you should be glad you knew enough to be spooked. Bad things happen to good little girls every day, James. Not everyone can even face that possibility."

While the worst thing that had happened to Vera as a girl had been the occasional poor showing in a concert hall. Some consolation lay in that thought, some perspective.

"I'm a lawyer," James said, holding the squeeze bottle as if he might hurl it against the wall. "I know about all the bad, awful things people do to each other, but bad things shouldn't happen to Grace." He set the squeeze bottle down a little too hard and scooted off the counter. "Not to Merle, not to Grace, not to Twyla, and not to *you*."

He picked up his tea, brought it to his mouth, but didn't drink. "I'm sorry." He set Pooh away from him. "I'm more tired than I know and wound up and rattled."

Rattled. Vera knew exactly how that felt, and could not stand for James to wrestle with the same over-whelming, unfocused demons while she watched and did nothing.

She was across the kitchen without having made a deci-sion to go to him, her arms wrapped around his middle.

"She's all right," Vera said, bundling in close. "Grace is all right. You and Mac got her the help she needed. I'm all right. I got spooked too—you had a word for it—and I'm not one hundred percent yet, but I will be."

Tension vibrated through James, and dark, unhappy emotion as well, but he closed his arms around Vera slowly as she laid her cheek against his chest.

His heart was pounding, at midnight, in his brother's kitchen; when to appearances, James would look merely tired, his heart was pounding.

Vera smoothed her cheek over the flannel of his shirt twice. His breath fanned past her neck in a long, slow sigh, and still she held him while he stood immobile in her embrace. Vera was about to drop her arms and start stammering her apologies, when James's hand landed on her nape.

She remained quiet and waited as he sank his fingers into her hair. A few heartbeats went by before he pulled her close.

She stroked his back and his hair while he held her—held on to her—and she tried not to breathe too deeply lest he realize how tightly they embraced. It felt good—it felt *wonderful*—to be held so fervently, to be pressed this close against another human being in a moment of sheer, honest emotion.

This close to a man Vera…cared for.

"I'm not at my best," James said, his voice low and very near Vera's ear. "I'm sorry. My stomach won't settle, and I keep thinking what if it were serious? What if that dear little girl was hurt on my watch? What if she'd been admitted to the hospital with a bad appendix and I had to tell Hannah?"

"Hush, you. Stop awfulizing. You coped. You kept your head. You're tormenting yourself for nothing."

Very likely reliving old torments too, of being that kid stuck on the farm with a grieving mother and oblivious older brothers off at college.

"I'm an idiot."

James's voice held such a wealth of fatigue and resignation, Vera had to smile.

"You're an uncle who loves his niece and got stuck with a tough night. If it's any consolation, I went through the same thing almost to the minute with Twyla last year."

He was quiet for a moment; his breathing slowed, and his heartbeat calmed.

"Who gave you tea and sympathy at midnight?" he asked, offering Vera a sip of his tea. "You would have been in the middle of a nasty divorce, living by yourselves in the back corner of those woods, late at night…"

Vera took a taste of peppermint, both soothing and reviving, rather like a stout hug. She stepped back but not far.

"Tough nights go with being a parent, James." She passed him the mug. "Do you have an extra bedroom here?"

"We're not full up. The master bedroom is unoccupied, because I'm taking the sofa bed in Trent's study. I assumed you'd want to sleep in your own bed tonight."

The mug went another round. If they kissed right now, it would be a peppermint kiss, but a kiss would be…superfluous?

"It's near midnight," Vera said. "We're both bushed, and now that the moment to leave Twyla here is upon me, if it's all the same to you—"

James set the tea aside and fired off another round from his arsenal of smiles, this one tired, understanding, and hopelessly dear.

"When was the last time you two were separated?" he asked.

"When I last toured, which was several years ago. Then Twyla had Katie and Darren at home with her, as well as the au pair, but Twy had reached school-age, so I made myself go off and leave her."

Or had Vera allowed Donal and even Alexander's ghost make her go?

"You don't have to leave Twyla now. The sheets on the bed are clean, and we'll find you the extra toothbrush."

James was a good host, and Vera hoped she wasn't imagining his relief at not having to stay up yet later to get her home.

To a cold bed, alone, no one to wake up to but dog-eared, old Pischna.

James gave her one of his flannel shirts to sleep in, and loaned her a bathrobe of his that hung nearly to the floor on her. The garment was flannel and smelled of cedary aftershave and fabric softener. Vera was reminded of the times she'd borrowed Alexander's clothing, and the thought made her more glad she hadn't gone home to sleep all by herself in her own bed.

"This bed has more controls than a lunar module," James said, sitting on the wide bed and picking up a gadget from the night table. "It heats, and it changes firmness on each side, and probably makes you breakfast."

"You will not figure it out for me at this hour," Vera said, settling beside him. "What is it with men and equipment?"

"Not men. It's me. I can't resist a machine, a tool, or anything that lights up, beeps, or makes noise."

Vera did none of those things, though around her heart, liking for James glowed softly. "I'm too tired to play with the bed, James."

"Are you too tired to play on the bed?"

The glow warmed to fondness. "*Idiot.* You felt compelled to flirt, didn't you?"

James wrapped a purely friendly arm around Vera's waist, and the moment was perfect, like that shared cup of tea. Like a Bach two-part invention.

"Habit, probably," James said. "That reflects poorly on me, not present company."

"Not habit," she said, patting his knee. "Coping mechanism. Go to bed. You can run me home in the morning before the girls wake up, and I'll get my exercises done first thing. As a gesture of good will on my part—and not to encourage your silliness further—I'll take the girls starting about mid-morning. You and Mac can sit around in your sweats and belch and scratch like real men all day."

While Vera would make cookies, read through the Chopin nocturnes, and call her family.

"I ought to tell you that won't be necessary," James said, setting the bed's remote control on the nightstand. "I ought to turn you down flat, stand up for the pride of uncles everywhere, but Mac will kiss your feet, and that I have got to see. Then too, I might take one of Trent's horses out for a trail ride, and even get Mac to go with me."

Lucky MacKenzie.

"Now shoo," Vera said, getting off the bed. She'd meant it when she'd said she was too tired to play.

Though how lovely, to know she could ask for space and have her request respected.

"I'm shooing," James said, standing in the space between Vera and the bed. He brushed a hand over Vera's brow, a grace note of a caress.

"I owe you, Vera Waltham. Not only for coming along with us tonight."

"You don't owe me. You've been my friend too, James."

"I *am* your friend, and you are my friend." He kissed her cheek and left, closing the door quietly.

In the kitchen earlier, he'd been wrung out, nearing the end of his emotional rope, and he hadn't pushed Vera away. How long had it been since she'd felt a purely affectionate impulse toward a grown man?

Not quite purely affectionate—*protective*. Vera had felt protective of big-but-not-so-bad James Knightley, and surely when a victim of domestic violence feels protective of a man like James, she's making progress toward her own recovery.

Better yet, Vera expected to spend half her night dreaming of James, his smiles, his kisses, and the feel of his callused fingers brushing softly over her brow.

Progress, indeed.

⸺ᴠᴠᴠ⸺

James had fallen asleep like a farm boy who'd stacked the hay wagons in ninety-five-degree heat when rain threatened. One moment he'd been sorting through what Vera Waltham's version of friendship meant; the next he'd been dreaming of a man in a top hat playing Chopin.

He woke the same way, immediately aware of his

surroundings, fully cognizant of the developments of the night before.

As he tended to his morning routine, James silently thanked a benevolent deity for antibiotics and late-night ER staff and *friends* who came to help when they were asked.

Could have used some of those friends when he was seventeen.

And sixteen.

Vera was puttering in the kitchen when James came downstairs. She wore a bathrobe "Merle" had given James for Christmas a couple of years back—Disney characters, including Tinker Bell. Surely the work of a twisted fraternal mind.

"Good morning." Vera smiled at him as she filled the kettle at the sink. "I'm surprised you're up so early."

"Old farm boy habits die hard. You putting enough in there for two?"

"I am." She set the kettle on the stove and turned on the burner. Her dark hair hung down her back in a soft mess of curls and waves, and James wanted to touch it so badly he…got out the milk.

"You slept all right?" he asked.

"Like a log. You?"

"Like a tired log. I spy with my hungry eye a batch of pancake batter in here, and some blueberries to throw in it. The maple syrup and the butter are local, organic, and fresh."

James wanted to cook for Vera, to share a meal with her.

"A real breakfast would be a nice change." Vera unbelted her robe and retightened the sash, giving James a glimpse of his new favorite flannel shirt, shapely calves, feminine knees, and a bit of thigh.

James set the bowl of batter on the counter and cast about for witty repartee. "Behold, breakfast."

He simply wasn't used to being around a lady in the morning.

"Should I water the violets?" Vera asked.

"The violets?" *What violets?* James's gaze landed on pots of purple flowers gracing the windowsill above the sink. "That would be a good idea."

She filled a glass at the sink. "Because you haven't done it all week?"

"Me, personally? No, I haven't. Hannah left lists, but the violets are Trent's domain, and his instructions were to listen to Hannah."

James tried to keep his cooking racket to a minimum, lest someone, for example some nosy older brother who was worthless in a crisis for once—that made James smile at his pancake batter—come thumping down the stairs and ruin this breakfast tête-à-tête.

"What kind of tea for you?" Vera asked when she'd finished giving the flowers a drink.

"With blueberry pancakes? Lemon decaf. I put a squeeze of cactus juice in mine. You're barefoot."

She looked down at her feet as if this oversight had been committed by somebody else. "I'm fine."

He and Vera were beyond "I'm fine." James had seen to that last night, and Vera had come through for him with flying colors.

"Watch the pancakes, please." James fetched a pair of his organic wool socks. They were thick enough to keep feet warm in the worst weather and in the least insulated boots. Also big enough to fit a draft horse.

"Sit," he said, patting the back of a chair.

Vera sat, and let him—*let him*—put the socks on her feet. She had graceful feet, with high arches and the second toe longer than the first. Feminine feet, and James enjoyed handling them just a little too much.

He enjoyed even more that she *let him* handle her feet.

"I think your pancakes are done, James."

"And, thank the unicorns, no hordes of little girls to eat them faster than I can cook them," James said. "You pour us some OJ. I'll find the silverware."

Had he ever made breakfast with a woman before? As a younger man, he'd occasionally hung around in the morning long enough to grab a cup of coffee, but in recent years, he'd taken to stealing away in the night, or if he lingered until dawn, hitting a drive-through rather than creating awkwardness in the morning.

Awkwardness for whom?

Everybody, he decided, dividing the first batch of pancakes between two plates, turning the heat down, and starting a second.

With Vera, for all she'd taken exception weeks ago to his first attempt to kiss her, he felt the opposite of awkwardness, whatever that was.

"It's Friday," he said, taking the plates to the table. "If the girls are underfoot at your place, do you want to postpone my lesson?"

Vera put the orange juice back in the fridge, and when she turned to face him, she managed to look very much like his demanding piano teacher, even in thick socks and a Tinker Bell bathrobe.

"I do not favor skipping lessons, James. If you fail to prepare, you need to suffer the consequences, but in this case, I'll leave it to you.

"I'm prepared," he said, setting out cutlery as quietly as he could. "Mac and I took turns with the girls when they weren't in school, and I got in my practicing."

He'd also cleared out the loafing shed in Hiram Inskip's pasture, a smelly, gratifyingly physical job that neither Wellington nor Josephine would appreciate, though the heifers had seemed entertained.

"You haven't told your family you're taking lessons, have you?" Vera asked.

"It hasn't come up. Shall we sit?"

She said nothing, which was cause for concern. James adored the female body. Adored it in all its variety and details. The female mind was mysterious to him, though, as he supposed it was to every other male over the age of seven. He held Vera's chair for her out of habit, and she waited until he sat to put her napkin on her lap.

Like a date, but not like any date James had been on.

"Are Trent and Hannah enjoying their time away?" she asked.

"They're enjoying each other. Their marital bliss would be nauseating, but they both deserve somebody to appreciate them, and their road hasn't been easy."

Vera drizzled maple syrup in a figure-eight pattern over her pancakes.

"Alexander suggested we squeeze in a honeymoon, but I suspect he was looking for another excuse to see and be seen so soon after the wedding."

Alas, not such a saint after all. "What about Donal?" James tucked into his pancakes, rather than revisit the topic of his piano lessons.

"No honeymoon," Vera said. "It wasn't that kind of marriage. We had children to keep an eye on, and we were due for a tour that would include Honolulu. Donal gave us an extra two days on the island to remark our marriage."

"That's not a honeymoon."

"It was a nice break, even so. Have you ever been to Hawaii?"

They navigated a conversation around various personal sensitivities and land mines, while James enjoyed watching Vera devour something he'd prepared for her. She wasn't a picky eater and wasn't shy about the butter and syrup, either.

How many women had he bought dinner for, only to have them excuse themselves immediately after, leaving James to wonder if there were any single women left who didn't have eating disorders?

"You're a very good cook," Vera said, taking the last swallow of her orange juice. "Kitchen skills seem to go with musical ability."

James poured half his remaining orange juice into her glass. "Cooking and music go together?"

"And a talent for algebra. That makes no sense to me, but ask around, and you'll find a pattern."

"I do believe you've admitted I have some musical talent," James said, taking their dishes to the sink. *Could the morning be any cheerier?*

"I'll do those."

"No, you won't. You're a guest." Who begrudged James even a sidewise compliment, silly woman.

"I'm an uninvited guest and enough of a mom to need to pick up after myself, and I haven't made up my mind about your musical ability."

"You'll dump me if I'm without talent?" Vera's answer mattered to James more than his casual tone implied, though if she dumped him as a student, she wouldn't dump him as a friend.

James knew that now. Maybe Vera knew it too.

"Everybody has some talent," Vera said, putting the milk away, "even if it's only the ability to tap their toe in time with the rhythm. You have plenty of intellectual sense for the music, you understand what's going on with the notes, and you render them accurately on the keyboard."

She took a towel as James passed her a washed plate and half his masculine ego.

"Now comes the bad news," he murmured.

"Many, many people would kill for as much ability as you've shown so far, James. Don't be greedy."

"You're greedy," he said, resisting the urge to touch her hand when he passed over the second clean plate. "With your music, you're a shameless, plundering pirate. You want everything it has to give. You give it all you've got."

"I do, don't I?" Vera preened at her reflection in the clean plate. "I'm a pirate. Maybe even a pirate princess." She put the dry plate up on the shelf. "You're a lawyer."

And a CPA. Also a mucker of cow sheds. "A lawyer is a bad thing?"

"You hide in the notes, James Knightley, you don't surrender to the music."

"Maybe I don't like being taken prisoner." This conversation wasn't going to James's liking either. He passed Vera another plate, this time letting their hands brush.

He liked that just fine.

"Surrendering to the music isn't being taken prisoner," Vera said. "It's being set free. When did you become so domestic? Doing dishes doesn't fit with my image of you."

What was her image of him? Lawyer and CPA? Was that his image of himself?

"I was the last son at home on the farm for about five years," James said, "and that meant a lot of domestic chores. Then too, I like good food, so I had to learn to cook."

"Mac mentioned something about your years at home last night."

James mentally made a date to take his nieces bathrobe shopping for Uncle Mac. "Mac talks too much."

Except Mac never talked too much, not to anybody, and most especially not to women. A suspicion formed in James's mind about why Mac had developed a sudden penchant for loquacity, one James would explore with his brother when they had a grassy surface to wrestle on, and a referee who could be trusted to call the fight a draw before James disgraced Mac too badly.

"Mac loves you," Vera said, taking a glass from James's hand because he was not fool enough to put it directly in the drain rack.

"I love Mac too, but that doesn't excuse him from gossiping. I could tell you stories about him that would put his entire personal fortune at your disposal, but because he's already going to kiss your feet before witnesses, I will exercise my vast stores of fraternal discretion."

For now.

"We never did decide what to do about your piano lesson."

"I'll come to your house," James said. "The girls won't mind, will they?"

"Twyla hasn't had company over of her own since we moved to that house," Vera said. "She'll be in transports."

Doing dishes with Vera before the sun was even truly over the horizon, James was in a few transports of his own.

—◇◇◇—

"You can go back to bed," Katie MacKay told her brother. "Dad was out later last night than you were, and he won't be down for hours."

Darren dug the heels of his hands into his eyes and cracked his neck. Though he wore sweats and an under-shirt, Katie could see he was beginning to fill out, start-ing to lose his adolescent gauntness, or maybe it was the divorces that had honed him down. Katie's friends thought Darren was hot.

Katie thought he was lucky to be leaving for college in the fall.

"How do you know when I got in?" he asked.

"You forgot to turn off your headlights when you pulled up the driveway." She put water on to boil, because Darren did not wake up without liberal doses of joe. "I'm told pot affects memory and sperm count first."

"Shut up." Darren bopped Katie on the shoulder, though his tone was affectionate. "Do I have any clean clothes?"

"In the dryer. You want some coffee?"

"Yeah." He disappeared into the laundry room, leav-ing Katie to fix his coffee. Being lady of the house at age fifteen was sort of cool—she did the housework, she and Darren did the shopping, she did what cooking her father and brother expected, and she was proud of her efforts.

Most of the time. Then there were times like last night, an increasingly frequent occasion of being left home alone. Donal had wanted a McMansion this time around, and so the house sat in lonely splendor in the middle of a five-acre parcel. Katie would not have felt safe walking to a friend's house after dark.

She didn't quite feel safe in her own home that late at night, but what could she do about that? Call her mother and hope Mom wasn't at a support group meeting?

Or passed out?

Katie could call Vera, but that seemed disloyal, and the last thing Katie wanted to do was piss anybody off—again.

"You eat all the muffins?" Darren asked, emerging from the laundry room. He'd bothered to put on socks and carried off a rumpled sort of cool.

"I made more. Butter's on the table."

"What do you suppose Donal's doing out past his curfew?" Darren asked.

"He says he's doing the concerts and recitals in DC and Baltimore, looking for fresh talent."

"You don't believe him?"

"Check the odometer," Katie said, measuring out fresh grounds. "Last time I looked, you had to go more than thirty miles round-trip to get to either city from here."

"My, my, my." Darren saluted with his muffin. "Quite the little sneak you are."

Katie resealed the bag of muffins, though Darren would probably eat half the batch before he went back up to bed.

"You're the one who taught me to do that when we were still living with Mom," she said.

"Maybe we have two parents with drinking problems," Darren mused around a mouthful of blueberry muffin. "Could be worse. Vera might turn lush on us."

"That isn't funny," Katie said, pouring the boiling water over the coffee grounds. "Why you insist on being so friendly with her is beyond me. She was our stepmother for less than two years."

"We've known her since we were little, Katie, and she's not a bad person. You feel guilty because Dad lost his temper with her over your sneaking out."

Katie felt horrible about that and had never apologized to Vera for it.

So Katie smacked Darren on the back of the head. "Who told me everybody sneaks out when they turn thirteen, and I must be some sort of dweeb, actually sleeping all night in my own bed?"

Darren opened the bag of muffins and took out the last three.

"They don't sneak out with nineteen-year-olds, Katie-did."

Katie took one of his muffins. "Who introduced me to him?"

"He's not my friend now, is he? Where are the rest of the muffins?"

She got the basket out of the breadbox—where else would it be?—and passed it to him. "What do you think Dad is doing when he's gone five nights a week?"

"Only five? Old age must be slowing him down. Maybe he's visiting Vera."

No, he wasn't. Of that, Katie was certain. "He'll get put in jail if he's caught."

Darren dabbed liberal amounts of butter on a muffin.

"Not for long. The restraining order runs out soon. They can be as cozy as they want after that."

His words were spoken with the casual disregard of a hungry young man intent on his breakfast, but Katie sensed unease beneath them.

"Mom said Vera didn't deserve what she got from Donal," Katie said as Darren demolished yet another muffin and about a quarter of a stick of butter.

"Mom's too nice for her own good, drunk or sober. These are not bad," he said, gesturing with his muffin and leaving crumbs on the floor. "What are you doing for fun today, Katie-did?"

Cleaning up after my brother. "Thought I'd vacuum the whole house, maybe make some soda bread, get all my homework out of the way, and look for your stash when you nod off around lunchtime."

"You won't find it. I'm not that stupid."

Katie had already found it. "Yeah, but if you weren't doped up so much of the time, we might have something left to eat when I get an honest case of the munchies."

"Keep your voice down, or Donal will hear you, and he'll be as pissed at you for not telling him as he will be at me for spending my own money the way I please."

Some of his own money. Katie knew Donal took a portion of Darren's wages too, saying he was saving it toward Darren's college tuition, but Katie had her doubts. Without Vera to represent, Donal's income was in the toilet.

"What will you do with the day?" she asked.

"Same thing I do every day," Darren said, getting down a coffee mug. "Avoid Dad, cruise, coast, loaf, *score*." He winked.

Katie stuck her tongue out at him. "While you get straight A's. It isn't fair." Though the only thing he was scoring was pot. Katie knew that much.

"Yeah, but I got saddled with you for a sister, so things balance out."

The hell of it was, Katie would miss Darren when he went off to college. "What did I ever do to deserve you for a brother?"

"I don't know, but at least you have one family member who gets up in the morning, most days."

Darren sauntered out with his coffee, probably going upstairs to roll himself another joint. He kept his stash in his own room, between the mattresses with his dirty magazines, which was hardly original. Katie had friends whose brothers hid drugs in their sisters' rooms.

And Darren did get up most mornings.

Vera got up every morning though. Katie had liked that about her. Vera got up, made sure the kids were decently fed, clothed, and off to school, and then she started practicing. With Vera as a stepmom, it had been a very different less-than-two years, and Katie's grades had never been better.

She finished her coffee, put away the butter and the muffins, wiped off the table, made sure the pot was on simmer, and got out the vacuum.

Chapter 11

JAMES'S SUV WAS WARM WHEN VERA CLIMBED IN, HER side's seat heater already toasty.

"Spring is just around the corner," James said as she buckled up. "You can feel winter losing its grip almost by the day. Days are getting longer. Birds are coming back. Ground's getting soft where the sun can get to it. This is one of my favorite times of year."

"You miss the farm, don't you?" Vera asked

"I go by the farm every day, most days twice."

Maybe James was glad to be free of it?

"I didn't realize the property was this close," Vera said.

James was relaxed behind the wheel, making even driving an exercise in effortless competence.

"I wish the farm weren't quite so near," he said. "The property has been sold twice since we put it on the market, and my guess is whoever has their hands on it now is trying to hold on until development picks up again out this way. You warm enough?"

"Warm and full of delicious pancakes." Vera let James turn the subject to what the girls might find to do, and what he and Mac would do with their Uncles' Day Off.

"Mac will go into the office, and I will get ready for my piano lesson."

"You can't cram, James. It doesn't work like that."

"I'm not cramming. I'll read Chopin's nocturnes

so I won't have to suffer through them for the next few weeks, or maybe those Bach fugues. They're nice and complicated."

The fugues were also highly technical, all the passion in them going into their structure. Now that Vera had seen what emotion James was capable of—what caring—she was more bothered that he was so reserved with his music.

"Want to listen to something?" James asked.

"Something of mine?"

"You choose." He gestured to a CD case between the passenger's and driver's seats. She flipped through them, pausing at a recording by Ashkenazy of the Chopin nocturnes and ballades.

She passed over that one without comment—a recent purchase, no doubt—and chose The Academy of St. Martin in the Fields orchestra performing Vivaldi. Cheerful, energetic, and beautifully nuanced, it made for a good start to the day.

They rode along without conversation for a few minutes until James spoke again.

"That used to be our property," he said, nodding toward the right. "You can see the neglect. Nobody has graded the lane lately, the fences are getting tentative, the winter wheat went in late, and I haven't seen any lime on the pastures in forever."

Set back from the road about a quarter of a mile, the farmstead itself looked picturesque and serene. The house was a big gray fieldstone structure that might have been called a mansion in the proper setting. A few hundred feet from the house sat a stone bank barn with a tin roof, and a few scattered outbuildings, some also made of stone. The occasional stately oak punctuated a post-card pretty scene, even at the end of winter.

"What kind of cows are those?" Vera asked. They were stocky with a unique red-and-black brindle coat pattern.

"Limousine. A bit of a boutique breed for this region, but they're handsome."

The farm passed from sight, though Vera would study it every time she drove by.

"The property is still salvageable," James said, "but the day that barn comes down so somebody can put up a damned subdivision, I don't know what I'll do."

"Maybe you'll play Chopin then." Why would James mourn the barn more than the house where he grew up? Vera was still pondering that question when he turned up her lane.

"Putting up a gate here would be easy, Vera. Your property would be a lot less accessible then, and a tres-passer would have to park in plain sight on the road a mile from the house."

"The restraining order runs out soon, James. Whom would I be trying to keep out?"

"Donal," James said as the SUV bumped along her lane. "You can put him behind bars or get an extension on the restraining order if he threatens you in any way, and trespassing on posted, gated land is threatening. You prove that, and you can reactivate the assault charges."

More lawyering, which hadn't resolved anything where Donal was concerned. Where *anything* of impor-tance was concerned.

"I have to deal with Donal sooner or later, and we can't prove he violated the order."

James parked right in front of the garage, set the brake *hard*, and came around to open Vera's door. She liked that he'd let the argument drop, and liked more that he had such an automatic grasp of old-fashioned manners. Alex had been capable of gallant manners, but within six months of the wedding, he'd put them on and taken them off, depending on mood and situation.

Or the presence of the press.

"I could do with another cup of tea," James said. "Or maybe even a brownie chaser, not that I'm shamelessly begging for a few more minutes of adult companionship free of the thunder of little feet, mind you."

He gave her one of his charming, crooked smiles, and Vera was about to admit that she was susceptible to the same temptation, when her gaze fell on light glinting off the walkway at the side of the house.

"What's that?" She was already moving when James's fingers wrapped around her wrist.

"Slow down." He fell in step beside her, but Vera was still pulling him along when her mind figured out what her eyes had been trying to tell her: both windows on the side wall of the garage had been shattered.

"Vera, don't touch anything."

"But somebody… Somebody's been…" Rage welled like an orchestral crescendo. "My house has been… My house. James, somebody tried to break into my house."

"They succeeded," he said, peering in one jagged, broken pane. "Look at the shatter pattern, Vera. There's more glass out here than on the garage floor. The windows were broken from the inside."

The window on the service door was shattered as well, and all the glass from that blow was on the sidewalk.

If Donal had been standing before her, Vera might well have raised her hand to him.

"James, let me go. I have to see."

"You can't touch anything," he said, his grip not easing in the least. "Vera, you can't go in there."

She dreaded going inside, but she *needed* to. "It's my damned house, and I'll go in there if I want to."

"It's your house," James said gently, "but, Vera, it's a crime scene now. You could disturb evidence that will help the cops catch whoever did this to you."

She wrenched free of his grasp but made no move to approach the house. "As if there's any question who's at fault?"

"There's always question," James said. "Donal is innocent until proven guilty, and we don't know if whoever did this has left the scene."

For the first time, Vera felt a sense of resentment when she looked at her lovely old stone house. She took a step away from the house, closer to James.

"I can't bring Twyla home to this." Twyla *played* in that garage sometimes, while Vera was absorbed with her damned Pischna.

"Let's get back in the car," James suggested. "We can call the sheriff and let Mac know what's afoot. Hannah's mom can probably stay with the girls, and we can sort the rest out later."

Vera wanted to smack him, just whale on him, beat her fists on his muscular chest, backhand his handsome, grave face with a violence that frightened her more than Donal's idiocy ever would. She also wanted James to hold her, and make her house the safe, welcoming place it was supposed to be.

She settled for being led back to the car and driven to the foot of the lane, while James called the sheriff's office and calmly reported evidence of a break-in. His next call was to Hannah's mother, Judge Louise Merriman, who was all too happy to spend some time with her granddaughters and their friend. The last call was to Mac, who promised to come over as soon as Louise posted at Trent and Hannah's house.

"Don't say anything to Twyla," James admonished his brother. "We haven't sorted out what to say to her yet, or where Vera and she will go from here."

He put his phone away and draped a wrist over the steering wheel. "We don't know it was Donal. Why would he antagonize you now, when he ought to be currying your favor?"

James was determined to be rational, to manage, to deal with the situation calmly. Vera both treasured and resented that about him, and would save for another day the question of where he'd learned to cope like this.

"Donal is furious with me," she said, worrying a nail. "Nobody can hold a grudge like a Scot when his livelihood is threatened."

"He's pissed, maybe," James replied, "and ashamed, but to do this, he'd have to have lost his mind, Vera. Was the man who agented you for years and the man you married crazy?"

Another wave of resentment welled up, but Vera understood this one better: perhaps she *had* married a crazy man, and what did that make her? Stupid, at the very least.

She'd gone through Band-Aid counseling when Donal had assaulted her. Three sessions of what to look for and what to expect after being the victim of a violent crime. Shame went with the territory: I should have known better. I should have fought back. I should have avoided the whole situation. I should have seen it coming. I should. I ought. Why didn't I?

Then more second guessing when she'd let Donal off without criminal prosecution. Was that the best outcome for all concerned? For the children? For her? For Donal? His ex had called to thank her on behalf of the children, though Tina had also said Donal had never once in their seventeen years of marriage raised a hand to her or the children, and the assault was surely an aberration.

That call had been awkward but oddly comforting too.

"Cavalry's arrived," James said. A cruiser turned into the lane, lights flashing, but no siren, for which Vera was grateful. At first she thought it simple kindness, but then she recalled James saying the intruder might still be inside.

Protocol, then. Nothing to do with consideration for her or her privacy.

James consulted with the officers, then drove the SUV back to the house, the cruiser in the lead.

"Mrs. Waltham." The deputy sheriff looked familiar to her. "Corporal Winters. I believe we've met."

Oh, they'd met. Corporal Winters had been the first to respond to Katie's 911 call when Donal had lost his temper with Vera. The corporal had seen Vera bruised, crying, and more distraught than she'd ever been in her life.

Another tough night. The toughest.

"We have met," she said, shaking his proffered hand.

The two deputies first made sure the house was empty, then while his partner called for an evidence tech, Winters took a preliminary statement from Vera. Mac showed up at some point and attached himself to Winters's partner, whom he seemed to know, and James…

James stood beside Vera the entire time, and when Winters had finished with his questions, James sat beside her on the front steps.

Such a pretty spring morning, brilliant sunshine showing every promise of chasing the chill from the air in weeks if not days. Birds sang, and even the loamy country air smelled happy.

"Would you rather wait in the car?" James asked. "Those heated seats have to be more comfortable than cold concrete."

"You wait in the car if you want. I'll wait here."

"What are you waiting for, Vera?"

She sensed from James's careful, quiet tone that he wasn't being smart; he was trying to ask her something more subtle than she comprehended.

For his consideration, she'd walloped him with a load of attitude.

Or nerves. "I want these strangers out of my house." Vera took a deep breath and let it out, the same as she would when facing a daunting program before a packed house. "This might be a crime scene, but it's my crime scene, and where I live. Where Twyla lives. I perfected that brownie recipe here."

Her voice caught, but she plowed on. "I want my house back, James. I want my property back. I want my privacy and my peace of mind. I need to see that my piano has not been vandalized, that my music is still where I shelved it, and my CDs are in order. I want to b-bake brownies… Oh, God, James. I am so angry. When will I stop being angry?"

She pitched into him and let the tears come, and all the while he held her and stroked her hair.

Vera had nearly composed herself when Mac came out the front door and down the steps, taking a seat on the side of Vera that James wasn't occupying.

"How're we doing?" Mac asked.

"We're pissed and miserable," Vera said. If she could have located genuine fear, she would have added that to the list, but maybe that was the morning's lesson. Fear never solved a problem, never helped a marriage, never improved a performance.

So why give it a front-row reserved seat? Make the bastard cower in the obstructed-view seats, at least.

Mac looped an arm across Vera's shoulders, while James's stayed at her waist.

"Is James making you cry? If he is, I'll beat him up for you." Mac's voice held a thread of hope.

"James hasn't made me cry, MacKenzie. I'm weeping over having my house broken into, and my peace of mind stolen again, just when I thought life was settling down."

"As if Mac could beat me up," James scoffed.

"With one hand tied behind my back and giving you first swing," Mac said. "The windows are the worst of it, but we found a message on your computer."

"My computer?" Vera lifted her head from James's shoulder. "I turned it off before I left last night. I'm sure of it. I always wipe down the screen and the keyboard at the end of the day, because Twyla can leave it sticky."

"Somebody knew your password, then, because they opened the word-processing program and typed four words in forty-eight-point type: It's all your fault. The 'your' was misspelled, made into the contraction."

James shot a puzzled glance at his brother. "Fingerprints on the keyboard?"

"A few partials, and that might be enough. I assume Donal's are on file?"

"They are," Vera said. "He was arrested the night he assaulted me, and they took his prints. Maybe that was my fault too." Though a detail bothered her: Donal had an excellent command of spelling and grammar.

"Taking prints is standard procedure," Mac replied. "The damage inside is mostly shattered glass."

"Mostly?" Vera had to ask, and also had to huddle closer to James.

"The deputies think there was some attempt to make this look like a robbery—a few drawers opened, the desk in your study rifled, but if it were a robbery, a pro would have covered his tracks. The longer a thief goes undetected, the harder it is to catch him. As break-ins go, you don't have the wanton destruction of crackheads desperate for cash, either. The deputies are honestly puzzled as to motive."

"The motive was to rattle me," Vera said. "I refuse to accommodate whoever did this."

A silence fell, and Vera realized that despite what had happened to her house, as she sat on the steps bookended by James and Mac, she felt safe. At that moment, she felt safe, if furious, but what about when darkness fell, and she was home alone with Twyla?

"You should come back to Trent's with us," Mac said. "We can get a gate up across your lane by tonight, and you can start making arrangements to have a security firm out here alarming the place to the teeth."

James shifted in reaction to Mac's words, but he said nothing.

"I don't want to impose." Vera had nearly said, *I'll be fine*. She was not damned *fine*.

"So you'll stay with us only when we're the ones imposing?" James asked. "You'd sleep in the same bed, at the same house, with the same people in it as last night, Vera."

Dratted lawyers. "It isn't that," she said, trying to sit up, but neither brother had removed his arm. "I need a piano. I haven't practiced today, and the weekend's coming, and I try not to do anything but my technique on weekends, because I want to spend the time with Twyla. That leaves only weekdays for repertoire, and with recital season coming up, the teaching schedule—you both think I'm silly."

"We think you're dedicated," James said. "I have a piano and plenty of space. Stay with me."

Three little words, but when she heard them, Vera's insides rearranged themselves. The upheaval of once again being the victim of a crime settled down, but a different set of butterflies took flight.

"Thank you, but I don't want to be parted from Twyla."

"You and Twyla, stay with me. I have the room, I'm close to your house if you need anything, and I will physically tear the limbs off anybody who tries to harm you or your daughter."

Ergo, the idea had significant appeal.

"That's a sensible suggestion," Mac said, his tone a little too casual. "You probably don't want to be alone in this house until it's thoroughly secured."

Vera glanced over her shoulder at the house. She hadn't lived there long enough to really turn it into a home, to domesticate and detail and build up the memories that made where she and her daughter slept into a *home*.

A strong, independent, self-sufficient woman knew when to accept help. "You're right. You're both right."

"If you'd rather, I can stay with you here," James said, "but you shouldn't have to deal with this alone."

"If you don't want his ugly face staring at you over breakfast, I can make the same offer to stay here with you," Mac said.

Vera thought back to breakfast with James, though it felt like another year, not mere hours ago. Cozy, pleasant, intimate.

And comfortable. Marvelously comfortable. "We can stay with James, but only until the house is fitted out with more security."

"One of my clients owns a security firm," James said. "I can call them for you now, or give you the number."

"You two take care of that," Mac said, rising in one lithe move. "I'll find a broom and a dust pan and make a first pass at cleaning up the glass. Where's the vacuum cleaner?"

"In the broom closet in the laundry room. But you don't have to—"

He was already up the stairs and through the front door.

"Let him do it," James said. "I am very much aware this is not the first time Mac has walked through a crime scene, but it's probably the first time he's known the victim on a first-name basis. Might be a good perspective for him to gain. You can do a walk through and determine if anything's missing once Mac has finished."

"He's a criminal defense attorney, isn't he?" Vera asked.

"One of the best in the state," James said. "Let me

find you the number for the security firm." He passed Vera his phone a moment later.

When she said James Knightley had recommended the company to her, she was put through immediately to customer service. The rep knew the questions to ask, and promised to have someone at Vera's door within the hour.

"And if you don't mind," James said, "I would like to be in evidence when that discussion takes place. Howard will cut you a better deal if I eavesdrop."

An independent, self-sufficient woman who knew when to accept help also didn't mind saving a buck here and there.

Thus Vera spent much of the day with James. He shooed his brother off to the farm-and-feed store, and finished cleaning up with Vera. By the time they were done, the estimator had arrived from the security firm. The cost wasn't as bad as Vera had anticipated, but she attributed the reasonableness of the price to the occasional question from James.

They'd no sooner finished with the security firm rep than Mac arrived with lunch from a sub shop, the SUV loaded down with a haul from the local farm supply.

"They'll drop the gate off at the foot of the lane before sunset," Mac said. "We can hang it before dark, assuming I got the rest of James's list right."

"You can help," James said to Vera. "We'll use less bad language if you're lending a hand."

Vera liked their bad language, tame as it was. She mostly watched while Mac and James sank posts in concrete, wired a solar cell, and otherwise installed and assembled a reasonably attractive gate across her lane.

"Do they teach you how to do this in law school?" she asked when the job was done and most of the day gone.

"They do not," Mac said. "This is Farm Boy 101, and you'll have to ask James where he picked up the wiring."

"Farm Boy 102," James said, "which is for when you absolutely, positively must at least glance at the assembly instructions. We also learned, when it's supper time, to put the tools away, or we might miss dessert."

"Be dark soon," Mac said. "I'd get what you need from the house now, Vera, and you and Twyla can head to James's place after dinner."

"And don't say it." James latched his two-ton tool case closed. "You can so impose for dinner. You barely ate any of your lunch, and Mac snitched half your fries. He spends too much time around criminals and claims some old property law case says if it's a potato fried in oil, it belongs to him. Louise will have wamped up a huge pot of spaghetti, and she does her garlic bread from scratch, so no sass from you, please."

"Going Neanderthal on you," Mac muttered. "Sure sign of low blood sugar."

"And, you"—James rounded on his oldest brother— "am-scray, otherbray."

"A bilingual Neanderthal," Mac said, grinning. "I'll see both of you back at the ranch, as they say."

Mac kissed Vera's cheek then sauntered off, leaving a whiff of clove and cinnamon on the air.

"He smells good." Vera put a hand to her cheek, wondering how many other people shortchanged MacKenzie Knightley on first acquaintance. "He's a very dear man, and he smells good."

James caught her off guard when he leaned in right next to her ear. "I smell better."

But he didn't kiss her on the cheek, or anywhere else, either.

Twyla was quiet on the ride to James's house, and James realized he had no idea what had been said to the child to explain their destination. As soon as they arrived, Vera went upstairs with Twyla while James fired up the wood stove and checked his email—his personal account, which few people had access to—and then his business account.

"You never made it to the office today," Vera said, leaning on the doorjamb to his study twenty minutes later. "Are the messages piled up twenty deep?"

"Nothing that won't wait until Tuesday." James sternly admonished himself to ignore the sight of Vera Waltham wearing only an Eeyore nightie and a filmy excuse for a pink bathrobe. "That's one of the perks of doing business law. Your clients work mostly business hours, and they seldom get arrested or have late-night domestic disputes. How's Twyla?"

"Exhausted," Vera said, coming into the room. "A few broken windows didn't seem to bother her. She's probably asleep already, and dreaming of barn chores and making spaghetti with Aunt Louise."

"Aunt Judge," James said, avoiding the study of Vera's bare feet. Did she *want* him to lend her another pair of socks? "Louise's vanity prefers that to Grandma Judge, which would be the more accurate title."

"She's a recent addition to Hannah and Grace's lives, though, isn't she?" Vera dropped onto what James thought of as his Pondering Couch. One end of that couch was the sweet spot in his house, the place where he could idle with a newspaper, a book, or the details of a tough case.

"Louise is recently recognized as Hannah's mom," James explained, "and Judge Monihan as her dad. They're nice additions."

Vera drew her feet up under her—a mercy, that.

"What about your folks, Vera? I know you've mentioned brothers."

"Two, and they live on the West Coast. When I was touring, we'd get together if I played San Francisco or LA, but it has been a few years."

And no airplane had ever flown from LAX to Dulles? "What about your parents?"

"My mom was a single mom. Dad succumbed to cancer when I was three, and I barely remember him."

Well, crap. Fatherless, widowed, and divorced. Three for three in the guys-not-to-lean-on department.

"You've seen the single-parent drill from both sides," James said, wondering if he could join her on that couch. "As the kid and the mom. That probably helps."

"It helps, and it doesn't," Vera said, expression thoughtful. "You don't want to make the mistakes your mom made, so you make the same mistake in a different direction."

"Give me an example." Because at long last, they'd reached the hour of the day reserved for grown-ups to talk to each other.

"I was performing by the time I was eight. I was determined Twyla would have a normal childhood, not be forced onto a stage before a lot of strangers, not tied to a piano bench when she ought to be playing with dolls. She doesn't sit on a piano bench hours a day, but I'm not sure what she should do with her time instead."

"You do the best you can," James said, taking the place beside her. Vera didn't move away, but neither did she jump into his lap. "My mom must have said that to me a million times after Dad died, always with regret."

"You miss her?"

He nodded, but he hadn't seen that question coming. He'd started missing his mother the day they'd buried his father.

"We never did get to my piano lesson," James said.

That lure was adequate to distract Vera from interrogating him about his family. "We didn't. May I ask you a favor?"

"Of course."

"Play for me?"

Nowhere near *play with me*, but this was Vera. "You want to do a lesson now? Won't the racket keep Twyla up?"

"Twyla has fallen asleep to the sound of a distant piano more often than not. If I can squeeze in a couple of hours after she goes to bed, and couple of hours after I've done my technique, then I almost feel like I'm approaching my quota."

"What's your quota?" James asked, getting to his feet and extending a hand to Vera.

"My quota? Always a little bit more than I've done."

James kept their hands joined as he led Vera to his music room. He knew in his bones what never reaching a goal, never being quite adequate felt like, and he wished he could assume the burden for her.

God in heaven—performing at *eight years old*? Twyla was eight, and Grace and Merle were about to turn eight.

"What shall we start with?" he asked.

Vera didn't take her customary seat in the chair beside the piano bench.

"This isn't a lesson. I'm asking you to *play* for me. Get out your old favorites, the friends you turn to when you're heartsore and soul weary, the consolation pieces that aren't for everybody else. You play them for yourself."

She curled up across the room in a papa-san chair and pulled an old quilt around her.

Could he do this?

If Vera had asked James to go to bed with her, he would have known he was competent to bring her pleasure, to satisfy her most intimate wishes and secret, sexual desires. But this? To play? *For her?*

She wanted the music that had called to James, spoken to his soul and become a part of him. Pieces of his heart.

James set his hands on the keyboard, took a slow, deep breath, and began to play. He played from memory, his fingers finding the notes easily in the dim light. He could play this waltz with his eyes closed, and he had, many times. He hadn't heard it since the night his mother had died, but she'd loved it too, and his hands would never forget how to craft the phrases and melodies.

"Oh, James, the Chopin." Vera sighed her pleasure at his choice, and James's heart sighed with her. He could do this for her, soothe her with music the way she'd made music to soothe and delight so many others. The waltz shifted from a work he'd set aside years ago—a grieving piece—to a gift from him to Vera.

Only to Vera.

When the last rippling rise of notes died away, Vera remained curled up, eyes closed, mouth slightly parted.

James had played her to sleep. He took a moment to memorize the sight of her, safe and at peace under the quilt his mother had made for her hope chest.

Then he thought back over other pieces he'd set aside, the ones that were too sweet or too sorrowful or both, and he began to play again.

—∿—

"Kathleen Fiona MacKay, are you up past your bedtime?"

At Donal's question, the girl looked up from whatever novel she'd been reading, her expression wary.

"Child, I'm teasing you," Donal said, the weight of a thousand regrets pressing on his heart. What did it say about a father, that his own daughter *expected* him to be in a foul humor?

"I'm waiting for the bread to come out of the oven," she said, putting her book cover-side down on the counter. "Are you hungry? I made macaroni and cheese."

The smell of baking bread was delightful, though Donal was not hungry. His daughter had apparently taken to whiling away her evenings with vampires and dukes. The vampires Donal could tolerate—he was a businessman, after all—the damned dukes, though, were likely *English*.

"You made your mother's macaroni recipe?" Donal asked.

"Darren likes it."

How did a female learn at such a young age to build such stout walls? "I like it too. Your mother's a good cook. I wouldn't mind a small portion, if your brother left any."

Katie retreated to the refrigerator rather than offer an explanation for Darren's second violation of curfew in a week.

"Will you join me, Katie?"

The blue ceramic bowl in her hands nearly dropped to the counter. "You shouldn't eat carbohydrates this late at night."

"Very likely, I shouldn't eat carbohydrates ever again. Don't eat with me then, but tell me how you're going on."

Donal had to try. Darren would be off to college in less than six short months, while Katie might well end up rattling around this mausoleum with her old dad for the next five years. Mediocre grades limited her options to the community college, not that she seemed to mind.

She scooped out a generous serving of pasta and cheese. "I'm passing all my classes."

"You always pass your classes, you've your mother's flair in the kitchen, and this house is spotless. If I haven't said thank you before, I'm saying it now."

The serving of macaroni went for its microwave carousel ride, which seemed to fascinate Katie.

"If you're saying thank you, why does it sound like you're yelling at me?" she asked.

Brave girl. She got her courage from her mother.

"Because I'm not very good at it." And months of trying apparently hadn't resulted in any improvement. "Your mother loved to read, you know."

Still did.

The microwave chimed. "When she was my age?"

"From little up. I met her at a library, or came upon her asleep in a library." He'd kissed Tina awake, another imbecile college boy earning his highest marks in strutting and preening.

"You should smile more often," Katie said, passing Donal the warm bowl. "Do you miss Mom?"

Tricky ground, indeed, but his little girl was all but grown up, and Donal was no better at spinning lies than he was at saying thank you.

"Aye, I miss her. I don't miss her drinking." Donal took a bite of very good macaroni and cheese, then stirred the bowl's contents, the better to distribute the heat.

"Neither do I."

Time to change the subject, before Katie ventured on to questions about her father's activities of late.

"Do you know if your brother has a summer job lined up yet?" Donal asked.

Katie put the rest of the macaroni away, and clicked on the oven light to peer at her bread.

"Ask him. He only talks to me if he can't find a clean pair of socks."

"You'll have his car when he goes to college," Donal said, provided the damned vehicle hadn't been repossessed. "Humor the lad for now."

"*I'll* have his car?"

She was so pretty when she smiled, the very image of her mother.

"Darren can walk about campus the same as any other freshman," Donal said. "Out here in the country, a car makes finding a job or passing the time with friends easier, though you'll have to buy your own gas, and I'll only show you how to change the oil once. The bread smells good."

"Ten more minutes," Katie said. "Then I have to wait for the bread to cool before I can turn it out of the pan."

"I'll be up for a while yet. I'll tend to it."

Her incredulous expression might have been humorous, were it not so sad. "You'll turn out the bread?"

When Tina had been at her worst, Donal had made the macaroni and cheese, done the wash, checked the homework, kept the money coming in—everything. Katie had forgotten that, which was probably a mercy. Donal hadn't forgotten.

"I'll look after your bread, and I won't kill your brother when he comes creeping in from his latest spree of pointless rebellion. I was young once too, Katie Fiona, but I worry that the boy will fall in with bad company and follow in his mother's footsteps."

That would break Tina's heart, all over again, and when Tina's heart broke, awful and often expensive things happened.

"I worry too, Dad," Katie said. "And not only about Darren."

With that telling farewell, Katie left Donal to his carbohydrates.

Chapter 12

VERA WAS A NICE TIDY BUNDLE IN JAMES'S ARMS AS he carried her up to his larger guest bedroom. She'd sleep across the hall from Twyla, and right beside his own bedroom.

"James?"

"Hush, sweetheart." He turned to slip through the doorway with his burden. The door had been left open for warmth, and Twyla's door was ajar as well. In the bedroom, the night-light cast shadows against the headboard.

"Cold," Vera muttered.

"You'll be warm soon," James said, drawing the covers over her shoulders.

"Don't go."

Those words, Vera had spoken clearly, but she was still more asleep than awake. James had played for more than an hour—Chopin, Beethoven, Bach. Her friends, his challenges—maybe his friends someday too.

"I don't want—" She levered up on her elbows and stuffed her bathrobe into James's hands. "You played for me." She lay back, smiling a sweet, dreamy smile, not one she'd graced him with before.

Thank you, Frédéric, Ludwig, and Johann.

Then Vera held up the covers. "Come cuddle, James."

James sat on the bed, not because he'd anticipated that invitation, but because those were the last words he expected to hear from her.

"That might not be a good idea." Making love with Vera would be a fantastic idea. His cock leaped at it, in fact.

"I'm not out to have my way with you." Behind Vera's quaint word choice, her tone was puzzled and hurt. "You're probably right. Go on, James. Go shiver yourself to sleep in your own bed. Shoo."

She flopped over to her side, giving James her back and leaving him with a decision.

She wasn't after sex. This should not have been a relief, but it was.

Interesting. Confusing, but interesting.

James ditched his shirt, and then his socks and jeans, leaving him in a pair of silk boxers. Normally, he liked stripping down, and the prospect of climbing into bed with a willing female had been his favorite way to end a day.

A female *willing to use him.* Another confusing, interesting insight for pondering later.

"Budge over," he said.

Vera obliged, but she did not turn to face him.

Here he was—by some lights the greatest lover in Damson County—in bed with the first woman to truly catch his eye, and what was he supposed to do with himself?

With her?

Vera reached behind her and took James's hand, then brought his arm around her waist under the covers.

"Cuddle," she said as if she'd read his mind. "It isn't complicated."

The hell it isn't.

But James did know the tune, he simply wasn't familiar with it outside of a post- or precoital maneuver. He spooned himself around Vera, and if she detected the beginnings of an erection snuggled against her backside, then maybe this night would get complicated—nicely, wonderfully complicated—after all.

"James?" Vera settled her hand over his arm at her waist.

"I'm here." *Brilliant response, Knightley.*

"You were kind to me today. Very kind. You're being kind now. I understand that, and I thank you."

He bundled her closer, comprehension dawning. This overture was not about teasing him, or about cold sheets, or about being too coy to acknowledge desire.

"You're scared," he said. "You have reason to be."

"I'm tired of being scared, tired of coping, dodging punches, and paying your dear brother to do my legal shadow boxing. I'm tired of being angry, even, and tired of trying to prove something to myself."

Tired. James understood Vera in a way he would not have predicted. Heartsore and soul weary, she'd called it.

"Rest now. Your troubles won't find you here." He threaded his free arm under her neck, and slipped his other hand away from hers to bring it to her shoulder blades. He pushed her hair aside and started a slow, wandering caress to the soft skin of her nape.

"I should be wiser," Vera said, some of her tension easing beneath his touch. "More resourceful, tougher. More resilient. I hate that word—resilient, like a foam pillow. That feels wonderful."

James no longer did this with his casual hookups, didn't linger, pet, and cuddle. Never for more than the obligatory few minutes—and neither did they invite him to.

"Can you sleep, Vera?"

"I dozed downstairs, which was not smart. Now I'll lie awake fretting."

"Don't fret. Tell me about Donal." She might not be comfortable with the topic, but she probably didn't bring it up with anybody else. Then too, talk of old Donal would keep James's nascent lust in check.

"Donal MacKay." Another sigh, this one not happy at all. "He looks like a cross between a history professor and a bouncer, and he's about twenty years your senior. I was a little intimidated by him when I was young, but as I matured, I saw that he was simply gruff, graceless in the way of an old-fashioned man. He has odd touches of humor and self-deprecation, though if I had to choose one word to characterize him, it would be shrewd."

Shrewd was not the worst way to describe a man—or the best. "He managed your money then?"

"Much of it, and he did fairly well. Money became complicated when we married, though. He thought my money should be marital property, but his commission on my money should not, because he'd had the position as my agent before we married."

Donal's position under Maryland law was ridiculous. "Is that what you and Donal fought about?" For Donal was apparently still in a very un-shrewd snit about something.

"We didn't fight. We argued, and he decked me. Nobody asks about it. A grown woman is backhanded by the man who promised to cherish her, and my publicist told me to deny it happened."

"I'm asking about it." James shifted her, so her

head was pillowed on his shoulder, and he could get his arms around her and his hands in her hair. "What happened, Vera?"

She rubbed her cheek against his bare chest, probably not intending it as an erotic gesture, but James felt it, felt the informality and the dearness of it.

"We were not intimate," she said. "Donal offered to marry me when Alexander died, as he said, to shelter me from those who would prey on my grief. I was barely functioning, and his idea made sense at the time. We shared a house, and while I took a hand in raising his children, he continued to organize my calendar, and to structure my day so I could find the time to practice, go to rehearsals, and record."

They were not intimate. To her, that was a casual recitation of old business, while to James, the words bore an entire fascinating sunrise of new and intriguing information.

"You were intimate in the sense of sharing a household," James said, "sharing the business of your music, and sharing responsibility for his children?"

"Yes. And when two people who are by no means in love with each other seek to parent the same children, clashes are inevitable. I had no legal authority over his children, nor he over Twyla, but while he was out scouting new venues, or listening to what he called my competition, I was home with those kids, going over homework, making dinner, washing their dishes, and otherwise being the parent."

Vera was good at those activities, and they were important. James knew they were important.

"You quarreled over child-rearing issues?" James

brushed his lips against Vera's hair. The fragrance of honeysuckle teased at his nose, and lust, his party piece between the sheets, was overtaken by protectiveness.

"Donal's approach to parenting is to look at the report card," Vera said, "and if the grades are good, then he doesn't look further. His job is to pay bills. The children's jobs are to get decent grades. Darren is a good student without trying, but Katie has to work hard at school. Donal has no appreciation for this."

"He doesn't *see* her." James knew what it was to be invisible to his own parent. To his own brothers.

"Donal doesn't see anybody but Donal, though I'm convinced somewhere beneath all his bluster and crankiness remains a man capable of kindness and decency."

"Why do you think that?" Keeping the question neutral took effort, because Donal had put his hands on Vera in anger, and sent her to the emergency room.

"Except for that one incident, James, Donal was civil to me. I honestly don't think he regarded marrying me as exploiting me, but rather, consolidating complementary interests."

Sometimes, James was not at all proud to be a guy. "A win-win for the history books."

"I didn't say his judgment was faultless. Mine certainly hasn't been." Vera did that thing again with her cheek, then she drew her knee up, so her leg half rested on James's thigh.

The woman took her cuddling seriously, and that was a fine quality to end up in bed with. A fine quality, though it challenged a guy's focus.

"Donal's judgment sucked if he thought hitting you was acceptable," James said.

"He was furious with Katie. She'd sneaked out with one of Darren's older friends, and was only thirteen at the time. I came home to find Donal ranting, Darren hovering, the whole argument escalating the longer it went on. Then Donal slapped his daughter—Trent has assured me that's entirely legal if there's no injury—but when I stepped between them, he backhanded me. For some reason, it is legally acceptable to hit your kid, but not your wife, or even the husband who is twice your weight."

What was legal and what was right did not always converge, the first disappointment most law students grappled with in law school.

"You can't use excessive force with your child," James said, but that was the lawyer in him talking— which was why the observation was worse than lame.

"Donal slapped Katie nearly off her feet. And that *upset* me, so I raised my voice, stood between them, and told him in no uncertain terms he could not treat his daughter that way or I'd report him to every authority known to man, and he just let me have it."

James did not want to hear this, but as Vera had said, *nobody* wanted to hear a woman's experiences of abuse.

"What did he do, Vera?"

"One stout backhand," she said. "Wham, backhanded into next week, as the saying goes. He struck me so hard, I went down and banged my face on something as I landed. He kept yelling at me as I lay there, blood pouring from my nose, my lip laid open. He bellowed about how he'd raise the children as he saw fit, and I was not their mother, and half the time he felt as if he'd raised me, and on and on. Donal absolutely lost it, and a lot of ugliness resulted."

"I'm sorry, Vera." Sorry for her, for the children with a lush of a mother, even for Donal, for James knew what an alcoholic could do to the other members of her family.

Though what if that hopeless bastard had kicked Vera in the face? What if Donal had damaged her hearing? Stepped on her hands? How would Vera have coped without the ability to play the piano?

Gently tracing her features, James tactilely assured himself Vera was well and whole, recovered at least physically from an assault that could have been permanently disabling.

"The part I can't forget"—Vera's voice dropped to a whisper—"the part that's worse even than being struck, is Katie screaming, 'Daddy, please stop!' over and over. Darren grabbed her around the waist and dragged her back, but the child would have put herself in harm's way again, trying to defend me from her own father. Katie was the one who dialed 911, and she was still crying when the cops arrived. It was awful."

Vera turned her face to James's shoulder and stayed liked that while the first shiver went through her.

"James, I've been so worried about those children. I abandoned them, and Katie won't visit me. Twyla never asks me about her."

James let her cry, murmuring meaningless comforts against her hair, wiping the tears from her cheeks. He'd been with women who cried after sex, sweet, quiet, passing tears that he'd found a little silly.

What an utter ass. Women cried because they hurt—because they'd been hurt.

"What would help, Vera? What would make it not hurt so much?"

"Time has helped."

"What else?"

"I want to know the children are all right. I've thought of calling their mother, but Tina and I—she was always cordial, and I always felt guilty."

Guilt, the fifth apocalyptic horseman. "So you need to know the children are safe. What else?"

"I want an apology," she said. "Restraining orders are fine for a cooling-off period, but I've known Donal for most of my life, and one incident has overshadowed everything else in our lives. As long as that restraining order is in place, he can feel like a victim, and I can be a victim."

Vera wasn't blaming herself, exactly, but she was tormenting herself.

"You're human, Vera. Donal can't control his temper, and you're not responsible for making him learn how to."

"He *could* control his temper—for years he'd fuss and rant and carry on at some house manager angling for a better deal, or at Alexander for neglecting details. Donal never lost control before, not with me, not with the children, not with Tina."

She'd spoken quietly, but James was holding her closely and heard every word.

"*It's not your fault, Vera.* You said it yourself: the man was capable of self-restraint. You are not to blame for his bad behavior."

James eased his fingertips over her face again, replaying a melody in his heart: big, expressive eyes; full lips that parted in a lovely smile; graceful, swooping eyebrows; a strong jaw and determined chin.

"I'd asked Donal for a divorce earlier that day, James. I had no idea he'd blow up. No idea what a financial house of cards he was living in. He came into the marriage broke from paying for Tina's rehab and from the damage she'd done to their credit. I had no clue what a Pandora's box I was opening. He'd kept his hands off my money, but other than that, he—and Tina—had made poor choices."

James knew the litany well, for alcoholism was mother to many poor choices.

"Why did you want a divorce, Vera?" Why wouldn't she? Surely the entire marriage was an artifact of grief?

"My reasons weren't profound," she said, and in the casualness of her tone, James heard how precious this confidence was. "I was lonely, James. I'd had my mother, then Alexander as my constant companion. In a few short years, Twyla would be growing up, and I saw the rest of my life, decades, filled with nothing but practicing, folding laundry, accepting every date Donal booked, smiling on command for my publicist, and sitting at home by myself night after night when nobody else had a use for me."

She seemed to be waiting for James to react, though what she'd said made perfect sense.

"I understand." *Sitting at home by myself night after night when nobody else had a use for me...* "I really do understand, Vera. Loneliness can make fools of us all."

Vera let out a breath, a long, slow exhalation as she relaxed along his side. Had she expected *James* to criticize her for the bad decisions loneliness could inspire?

She yawned and drew her leg higher on his thigh.

"You're not the most comfortable pillow in the world, James Knightley, but you do give off a wonderful amount of heat."

"Roll over." If she moved her leg two inches higher, he'd not be accountable for the heat he gave off.

Vera rearranged herself obligingly, and James shifted to his side, so they were once more loosely spooned. He settled a hand on the middle of her back and caressed the bones and muscles along her spine.

"You'll have me asleep in no time, James."

An accomplishment James would take pride in come morning. "That's the idea. Close your eyes, Vera, and dream."

—⁂—

They made such a sweet picture, the tall man and the young child. Twyla would dart around exploring, then come back and seize James's hand and no doubt pepper him with questions. Even from a distance and watching through the kitchen window, Vera could see Twyla's cheeks were rosy. Twy gestured animatedly toward a pair of black-and-white cows meandering, nose down, across the bottom of James's yard.

Across his yard?

Two more cows followed, then a few more, until the entire herd of about two dozen was lined up, waiting for a chance to pass through an opening in the fence between the two properties.

Blessed St. Isadore, those enormous beasts were getting loose, and Vera's only child would be trampled. Vera was on her feet, ready to do she knew not what just as James and Twyla began trotting toward the cows from different directions. The cows looked up, then went back to ingesting James's lawn.

Twyla raised her arm and shooed the cows toward James, who deflected them back toward the gap in the fence. A ponderous variety of pandemonium ensued, with the cows trying to avoid being sent back into their pasture, other cows trying to get out of that same enclosure, and the two humans herding, coaxing, and hazing the bovines into accepting defeat and strolling placidly back into the pasture while snatching a few last bites of James's grass.

When the final cow hopped over the boards to join her sisters, Twyla punched a fist into the air. James grabbed her and swung her in a fast circle by her wrists, then bent to pounding on the fence with a hefty rock while Twyla stood by.

Vera dropped back into her chair.

Twyla hadn't been trampled. She'd had fun, and she'd helped James keep the cows where the cows were supposed to be.

Vera tried to take a sip of her tea, but her hands were shaking.

She would not rant. She would not berate. She would not screech. She would be reasonable, and ask James very calmly what in the infernal key of C-flat minor he thought he was doing, putting Twyla in the middle of a herd of enormous, stampeding, little-girl-eating cows.

Vera said a quick prayer to Saint Francis, then took her tea upstairs and finished dressing. When she came back downstairs, the wanderers had returned.

She hugged her daughter hard then rose. Mustn't cling. Mustn't screech; mustn't rant in any key.

"Good morning," Vera said.

"Do I get one of those hugs?" James was smiling at her, abruptly reminding her of their conversation the night before.

She wrapped James in a ferocious embrace. "You two scared me. I saw the whole roundup from the kitchen, and I about ran through the window."

"They were just Mr. Inskip's yearling heifers," Twyla said. "They're like kids who want to wander off the playground at recess, and they prefer James's grass because nobody poops in it."

Vera raised her head from James's chest to peer at her daughter.

"We had a nice old morning constitutional," James said, as if he'd been chasing cows since childhood, which, maybe, he had. "Twy said something about drawing the cows to show Grace and Merle."

"I did. Do we have my crayons, Mom?"

Why was Twy smiling like that?

"I have crayons," James said, easing from Vera's clutches. "I keep them around for Merle, and I suppose Grace will use them now too." He gave Twyla directions to the proper drawer in his study.

"Twyla's never chased cows before," Vera said, cradling her tea, because the mug was still warm and her hands were cold.

"Well, it's about damned time she did," James replied. "The girl's a natural. If she were a quarter horse, we'd say she has *cow*."

The last of the tea was tepid, but sweet. "What does that mean?"

"Twy has an instinctive sense of what the bovine will

do before the animal does it, and knows how to move in response. You hungry?"

So James had *cuddle*. "I am hungry."

"Let's take care of that while there's peace and quiet to be had. You never know when the grass pirates will plunder my yard again." James moved off toward the kitchen, leaving Vera to follow. His eyes held a smile even when he wasn't grinning, and his cheeks bore a rosy flush from his exertions.

"You enjoyed that," Vera said. He would have enjoyed it even if Twyla hadn't helped.

"I can match wits with just about any attorney in town and come out on top," James said, taking a pitcher of orange juice out of the fridge. "But two-dozen hungry young heifers, now there's a real challenge. Twyla and I had omelets. You want one, I can make you one, or we can do fruit and cereal, get out the waffle iron...what?"

"You made her breakfast. You took her for a walk so I could sleep. You both left me a note." Vera turned to look out the window, noting the cows were staying on their side of the fence. For now. "I'm not used to this."

"You pissed off?" James went about refilling the teapot and setting himself up a mug with a teabag and agave nectar.

Vera was *not* angry, not even a little. "Disconcerted. It doesn't make sense, but I feel sad, maybe. Also happy."

"Bereft." James stopped making his kitchen racket and came to stand beside her. "Trent mentioned something similar. He's had Merle all to himself for years, and now he has to share her with Hannah and with Grace—odd man out, sometimes. He was off stride until Hannah got him sorted out."

"How'd she do that?"

"Hannah's an interesting lady," James said, going back to the stove. "She was raised in foster care, and that meant one transition after another. For the first twenty years of her life, she was never in any one place for more than a couple of years, so she knows all about transitions. She pointed out to her new husband that every change—every change you can imagine, even if it's hitting the lottery—involves loss, and is a cause for some minor grieving. I have my own theories about what's going on with my brother, though. You want some more tea?"

"Please, the jasmine green tea is lovely."

"Hannah's favorite," James said, plucking the empty mug from Vera's grasp. "I suspect Trent was coping and bearing up and soldiering on, but being a single parent is hard. When Hannah and Grace came along, he had to admit how hard it had been, and how much of a relief it was to have some backup." James slapped a second tea bag into his mug and two into Vera's. "That's a heartache, look-ing back and wishing things could have been different."

Verily. "Your brother gave me a similar explanation for Donal's loss of temper."

James filled both mugs with hot water, and the sooth-ing fragrance of jasmine wafted through the emotions filling the kitchen.

"I hope to God my brother did not make excuses for your husband, or Trent and I will have a very pointed discussion."

James was doing it again, championing Vera's causes unbidden, before she'd even perceived her interests might be jeopardized.

"Vera, did you ever describe to Trent exactly what happened?" James watched her now, rather than the steam curling up from the tea.

"No, I did not."

"He's your lawyer. Why wouldn't you have told him?"

"He said he read the police report and didn't need to make me rehash it. I was relieved not to have to explain to him why I let Donal get the better of me. You're scowling at me."

If Vera had been a heifer, that scowl would have sent her right back where she belonged.

"You're blaming yourself, Vera." James crossed the kitchen, and she wasn't sure of his intent until he settled both arms around her shoulders. "It was not your fault. Say it for me." He spoke very close to her ear, quietly but clearly.

"It was not my fault." The words were hard to get out, and that was…that was something to think about.

"Now believe it for me." James stepped back and fixed their tea, stirring the milk in before he handed Vera hers. "What do you want for breakfast?"

"Cereal with fruit. Winter makes me hungry for fresh fruit and vegetables." The change of topic was appreciated as well.

"I'll join you. Rounding up strays is hard work, though keeping up with Twyla will be harder."

He was looking forward to that hard work, clearly. "Do you two have plans?" Vera asked.

"Now, don't get your dander up. I thought I'd ask Twyla's mother if I might take the child with me to the office. I want to pick up some files before I go in on Tuesday, and we can maybe sneak an ice cream cone or a trip to the park. I'm the Damson County champ at under-doggies, though besting Mac wasn't much of a challenge."

Was *anything* a challenge for this guy? "Why are you doing this?"

"Making breakfast? Because you're hungry. Entertaining Twyla? Because you want to practice, and you didn't get a chance to yesterday, and you'll feel better once you get your butt on that piano bench for a couple of hours."

Vera didn't merely want to practice, she needed to, and would feel immensely more in control if she did. James poured two enormous bowls of granola cereal before she could stop him.

"Half that much for me, James."

"You'll waste away to nothing," he said, pouring half of her bowl back into the box. "We have strawberries, blueberries, and bananas. I put chocolate chips on mine, but you mustn't tell Twy where my stash is."

How did he know not to leave temptation where Twy would find it? "Maybe just a few."

"That's my lady." He gave her a quick, wicked smile, a little knowing and a lot smug, and Vera's middle filled with happy, colorful F-major-major butterflies.

James had played for her.

He'd listened to her.

He'd held her when she'd cried.

And he'd smiled at her.

James had *cuddle* and *smile*. When breakfast was finished and the dishes washed, Vera sent Twyla off with James, which sparked novel feelings of both anxiety and gratitude.

Vera didn't puzzle over her emotions, she instead plowed into limbering-up exercises passed down from her teachers and not found in any books. She practiced, she played, she read over old friends, and practiced some more. She got out the Schumann A minor concerto and brushed up, spotting passages that would challenge her students.

Vera was at the keyboard when she heard the kitchen door bang closed, and though she didn't want to stop, she brought the music to a cadence.

A pretty auburn-haired lady stood in the kitchen doorway, her hand wrapped around little Grace's.

"Good God, you are something else, Vera," the woman said. "No wonder James wanted you all to himself. Don't stop for us. I'm Hannah, and yes, we're back early. The honeymoon was terrific, but Trent and I both got an irresistible urge to come home."

"Hannah, a pleasure to meet you." Vera rose from the piano bench, resisting the urge to scrub her hands over her stiff backside. Her gaze drifted past Hannah's shoulder to the clock as they shook hands.

She'd been playing for five hours.

Five hours?

"James has kidnapped Twyla and taken her on a round of errands," Vera said. "I suppose Mac explained the situation to you?"

"He did. My thanks for being Grace's angel of mercy the other night."

"Mom says we ladies have to stick together when there's trouble," Grace piped up. "That's why I brought Twy my drawing pencils." She held them up for Vera's inspection, presenting a wooden box with, of course, a unicorn carved on the lid.

"I can offer you a cup of tea," Vera said. "I'm fairly certain James and Twy will be back soon."

"Mom has pictures of her honeymoon," Grace said. "She and Dad got all dressed up, and Dad took a picture of her for me."

"And I took a picture of your dad for you too," Hannah said, tousling Grace's hair. "Vera, are you sure you don't want to get back to your music? You sounded wonderful, and we can leave you in peace if you'd rather."

Part of Vera did want to get back to her music, and not because she *had* to, but because she *longed* to—an F major realization.

"I'm hungry, truth be told," she said. "Let's raid the kitchen and see what James's larder reveals about him as a person."

"He hides his chocolate chips," Grace volunteered. "Can I put my pencils in the study with the crayons? Merle told me where they go."

"Don't touch Uncle James's computer," Hannah said. "If you want to draw him a picture, you can use the printer paper."

Grace scampered off, pencil box rattling, rather like Vera's wits. Abruptly, she faced the prospect of kitchen small talk with another woman.

Another mom.

"I'll put the kettle on," Hannah said. "Trent took Merle off on some secret mission, which I suspect has to do with finding tack for the horses he's buying to add to our herd."

"You're dividing and conquering," Vera said. "I've always wondered how parents manage when that third child shows up. You have to go to a zone defense as opposed to man-to-man."

"We're still trying to blend the families," Hannah

said. "We figured each child would want some exclusive time with their more familiar parent, hence Grace and I are visiting Uncle James before we head off on our own errands."

"Checking me out?" Vera asked.

Hannah got down the jasmine green tea, clearly at home in James's kitchen.

"Making sure Uncle James is coloring inside the lines. Don't believe everything you hear about him or Mac. I suspect they're both capable of mischief if left unsupervised too long, but they're gentlemen too."

Hannah was wrong, at least about James. He was capable of such gallantry he ought to be knighted for it.

"That brings up the interesting question of what would constitute mischief in the eyes of MacKenzie Knightley," Vera said. "You take milk and sugar?"

They chatted about Hannah's travels, and the differences between second and third grade, and the pleasures and challenges for Hannah of working at the law firm her husband and his brothers owned.

"Not long ago, virtually every small business was a family business," Hannah said. "Now I see the advantages of a family business rather than the disadvantages."

"One of them being you get to see me regularly." James stood in the door, beaming at his sister-in-law. He held out his arms, and Hannah was hugging him hard before Vera was even on her feet.

"James!" Hannah held on tight, and James patted her back, his expression that of a man holding a woman precious to him. "I missed you, James, and I've heard all about your big adventure at the ER. Grace is now officially among the hordes of unfortunates smitten by you."

"As long as you're smitten too. Twy lit out for the study when she heard she had company. Vera, your daughter was a perfect angel, and utterly exhausting. I remain in awe of both you ladies for your parenting abilities."

He also remained standing beside Hannah, his arm around her shoulders, as if he were afraid she'd bolt, leaving him to once again impersonate a parent himself.

"Vera, is there enough in the kettle for three?" he asked.

"Of course, and I was scrounging up a late lunch."

"I confess Twy had a double-dip Meanie Beanie Vanilla about an hour ago," James said, "but I refrained out of respect for my once pristine leather seats. Let's grill some ham-and-cheese sandwiches, and a batch of your brownies wouldn't go amiss either."

Vera's stomach broke into a metabolic version of the Hallelujah Chorus. "I don't want you to spoil your dinner."

"He can't spoil his dinner," Hannah said. "The Knightley menfolk are bottomless pits. Start making double batches routinely. You'll see what I mean."

James made the sandwiches while Vera put together the brownies, though she was surprised that James had the fixings, including some high-quality baking chocolate. They ate off paper plates, everybody snitching potato chips from the communal bag, James getting up to make a chaser of hard-boiled eggs.

"Bad for your cholesterol," Hannah said.

"I was run ragged all day by a merciless slave driver," James countered. "My bottomless pit can't be content with a mere couple of Dagwoods, half a batch of brownies, and one-third of a bag of potato chips."

"What did you and your slave driver get up to?" Vera asked.

"It's a secret. We can show you eventually, but I am sworn on my honor not to tell."

"He's good at keeping secrets," Hannah said.

They exchanged a peculiar pair of smiles, James's self-conscious, Hannah's sad. Hannah collected her daughter and left shortly thereafter, though James walked her and Grace to their car.

Vera sat peeling a hard-boiled egg and watching out the window as James hugged Grace, then held her giggling above his head before letting her climb into the backseat of her mother's Prius. James and Hannah stood outside the car a few feet off, their postures and expressions suggesting earnest conversation.

He was trying to convince Hannah of something, was Vera's guess, and that seemed an unlikely discussion for a new brother-in-law to have with his brother's wife. The exchange became even more unlikely when James pulled Hannah in for a hug, and Hannah's forehead dropped to his shoulder.

The embrace was intimate, protective maybe. More than cordial or even affectionate family members might share.

But James didn't kiss Hannah, and when Hannah climbed into her car, she was smiling.

None of my business. James was affectionate by nature, and he hadn't seen Hannah for a week. He'd had Hannah's daughter in his care for most of that time, and of course, Hannah would be grateful.

But was that gratitude Vera had seen, or something else?

Chapter 13

"FOR GOD'S SAKE, DONAL, MACKENZIE KNIGHTLEY called me at home over the weekend as a courtesy, the same courtesy I'm extending to you before the cops show up on your doorstep."

Aaron Glover's voice betrayed a hint of exasperation, which suited Donal just fine. Smug bastards like Glover deserved to have their ears pinned back periodically in the interests of the common good.

Donal put his feet up on the corner of his antique oak desk, which he'd had shipped over from his grandfather's estate in Perthshire. If a man couldn't be comfortable in his own study, matters were at a sorry pass.

"According to you, Glover, the damage was done between 9 p.m. and 9 a.m.," Donal said. "For most of that time, I was home sleeping in my bed." Tossing and turning at any rate. "I suggest if you want to be useful, you find out who is menacing poor Vera, and quit harassing me at an ungodly hourly rate."

"I am not charging you for this call. It's a courtesy, Donal, because you are suspect number one, and if you can only account for *most* of your time, you might soon be facing charges. Where were you?"

"That is none of your affair, Glover, and exactly how much criminal defense experience do you have, anyway?"

A low shot, but nothing less than Glover deserved, for Donal had never once been caught in a lie to the man.

"Enough to know you're whistling in the dark, and the best criminal defense attorney in the county won't represent you, because he's Trent Knightley's brother. Start getting an alibi together, Donal, an airtight alibi that *poor Vera* will believe."

"I am not accountable to her any longer, if I ever was. I bid you good day."

Donal hung up only to see his firstborn and only son regarding him with an unreadable expression from the doorway of the study.

"Why aren't you dressed, young man?"

"Because it's Sunday," Darren said, his slouching stance becoming more defiant. "Because the more I get dressed, the more laundry Katie has to do. Because I know it bothers you when I hang out in comfortable clothes. Was that your lawyer?"

The little rooster was a chip off the old block, though far better-looking than Donal had ever been.

"Somebody is making a nuisance of themselves to Vera," Donal said. "Mischief that under the circumstances is being attributed to me."

"Why you?"

Because for one instant, under a deluge of stress, worry, disappointment, shame, and rage, Donal had lost control. He was still ashamed—also frustrated and worried—but no longer enraged.

"I'm a suspect, laddie, because nothing is deader than a dead business arrangement, as you will soon learn."

"Vera was never in love with you," Darren said, cocking his head. "Not like Mom was."

Donal wanted badly to correct him, but a prudent parent chose his battles.

"Perhaps not, but Vera was fond of me, and of you children, and now I am the logical choice as her present detractor. I am the pathetic, spurned, and appreciably older former husband. I hope you learn from this example."

Donal had learned from it.

"What am I supposed to learn?" Darren asked.

"That if you look guilty, it will make little difference whether or not you are guilty."

Darren rolled his eyes and sauntered off to the kitchen, where the boy would no doubt consume enough to keep a small army on forced march. Darren would leave in the autumn, assuming the money to pay for tuition fell from some benevolent cloud, and Donal would miss him. Not only did Darren keep a close eye on Katie, his presence in the home also allowed Donal freedom to be out and about of an evening.

Though Donal dearly wished the boy would stop hooking school and smoking marijuana.

Some things were predictable. For Donal, cigarettes and good whiskey had tempted him at an early age, both vices he'd learned to eschew. Darren would learn too, and do it before he was caught misbehaving by the authorities.

Like father, like son, after all.

———

Having spent nearly a week in close proximity with his nieces, James was beginning to appreciate that parents either developed the ability to mentally multitask, or they suffered a complete annihilation of their productivity.

While he'd been out with Twyla, he'd conversed with reasonable coherence on such topics as his favorite flower, what boys liked about sports—besides swearing and slapping each other's butts—what a lawyer really did other than strut around in court, and why Grace and Merle's uncle Mac only ever laughed with his eyes.

All the while, James's adult mind had also been circling around the time he'd spent in bed with Twyla's mother.

He and Vera had talked, they'd touched, and the emotion that passed between them was different from any James had associated with sharing a bed. As Vera had put it, they'd cuddled—emotionally as well as physically.

Holding her, listening to her, having the time to pet and caress and feel her body relaxed and warm in his arms...that had been lovely. The time spent with Vera had left James with a profound sense of peace, which he would not have anticipated in the absence of sexual intimacy.

They'd shared something that surpassed a mere union of bodies, though it left James hungrier than ever for that intimacy as well.

To be Vera's friend and her lover, not simply her convenience...the idea fascinated him.

"You're preoccupied," Vera said as dinnertime approached. "Was it ratios or proportions that put that look on your face?" She stirred a pot on the stove, one redolent of chocolate and calories.

James slipped his arms around her from behind. "I'm thinking of you. How are you?"

She leaned back against him. "You were right. I needed to play the piano today. Maybe having a different instrument to work on, maybe knowing Twy was adequately supervised helped, but I was still playing when Hannah and Grace arrived."

He let her go, because the stuff on the stove was beginning to boil. "What is that? It smells good."

"You cook it into candy, then pour it over the oatmeal and peanut butter in that bowl, and it makes cookies."

"Raccoon droppings. My house is honored to host their creation, and I will happily see to their demolition. Shall I set the table?" James asked.

"Twy usually takes that job if I don't get to it."

"You'd hail her in here, when we're having a perfectly civilized adult discussion and she's happily organizing my desk drawers?"

The mixture on the stove was bubbling madly, though Vera merely watched the kitchen clock as she stirred with a wooden spoon.

"Excellent point," she said, "and Twy has an eye for organization. James, if I asked you to play for me again tonight, would you?"

"Yes." He got out place mats and matching napkins— orange and brown, because he'd had his brothers over for Thanksgiving and to watch the game a couple of years ago. "Would you play for me?"

"Yes." She poured the chocolate into the bowl and stirred quickly. "But not too late. I want some time to cuddle with you tonight."

"Vera…" Place mats and napkins were a nice touch for company, but James drew the line at two forks when they were having tacos, for God's sake. "My motives for sharing a bed with you aren't entirely pure. You need to know that."

They weren't entirely clear, either, even to James himself.

Vera spooned chocolate goo onto a cookie sheet in rapid, deft strokes, and the scent was positively divine.

"My motives aren't entirely pure either, James." Her lips quirked up in smile that drove James's insides into a happy, bucking-pony dance.

Very carefully, he arranged the cutlery on the place mat. "Just so we're on the same page."

"I'm not sure what page I'm on, James, but I'm willing to see what develops."

Ah. Development was what happened in a sonata once the themes had been introduced.

A *maybe*. Vera was giving him a definite, very encouraging maybe, and that was so far from ordering him off her property that James wanted to ball up the napkin and spike it into the wastebasket sitting outside the laundry room.

"I'm willing to see where it goes too," he said. "How soon can I have one of those cookies?"

Vera served him another Mona Lisa smile.

James resisted the urge to wrap his arms around her again, because this time he'd nudge at her backside with his hips, and let her feel the happy anticipation her *maybe* had sparked behind the buttons of his 501s.

"I'm done!" Twyla came swinging into the kitchen, wreathed in smiles, and James shifted his gaze from Vera's fanny to the wrinkled ball of napkin in his hand. "Your desk was a mess, James. Mom would never let me keep my desk like that."

"Sure she would," Vera said, not breaking rhythm as she spooned cookies onto the tray. "Provided you could find everything you needed when you needed it. Did you thank James for helping you with your math?"

"Thanks, James. Those are raccoon droppings."

"I called dibs," James said, "but I think they're for dessert. Here." He fired the napkin at Twyla. "I'm not sure what to do with these things, except for tucking them under the fork."

"You can make a fan with them," Twyla said, taking a place at the table, "or you can make a flower, or just…" Her tongue went to the corner of her mouth, and James passed her two more napkins as she went to work.

Vera's smile was no longer seductive; it was parental and adult and still intimate, bearing thanks for having distracted Twyla, and for heading off the battle of Your Dinner Will Be Ruined If You Eat Cookies.

James took a snitch of a gooey cookie, then brushed his lips across Vera's, all behind Twyla's back.

And that was…fun. Teasing and cooperating and anticipating a meal together and keeping one eye on Twy and having a completely silent grown-up conversation in the same room with the child was fun.

The cookie was sweet, warm, and richly chocolate. James could hardly wait to have another, except he was a grown man. He could wait to get his cookies.

He hoped.

———⁓———

"Play me the Chopin."

As she made the request, Vera curled up in what had taken only twenty-four hours to become "her" chair and pulled the old quilt around her.

"I played that for you last night." James's tone was more teasing than cranky.

"I enjoyed it then too. That waltz is special to you."

"I'll get around to playing it again if you behave."

"What constitutes behaving?" Vera asked.

"Being quiet would be a nice start. Unlike some people, I can't deliver entire musicology lectures while I'm trying to get the notes right."

Vera fell silent, because playing for her couldn't be easy. They'd skipped James's lesson this week, but she hardly cared. Listening to James like this was more important than repertoire or technique. What he played for Vera now would be music, not mere notes.

James started with his Beethoven slow movement, something the past weeks had seen bloom in his hands. The melody glided up over the right hand in the left and hung suspended in sheer grace above its accompaniment, only to nestle back down in the right hand, then rise again. He was playing the work entirely from memory too.

Vera closed her eyes and considered which sonata she'd turn him loose on next. He'd soon be ready for the big ones, the *Pathétique*, the *Appassionata*, the…

The beauty of the music distracted her, stealing thoughts and worries and tension from her mind, and from her body. The next thing she knew, she was lifted into James's arms, and again carried up the stairs.

"You'll hurt your back."

"If loading a wagon of Hiram Inskip's baled alfalfa doesn't hurt my back, a little bitty thing like you won't do it any damage." James brought her to her bed and closed the door behind them with his hip, then set Vera on the mattress.

"It's warmer in here tonight," she said. "Somebody turned down the bed."

"I put a little heat on." James sat on the bed at her hip. "I turned the covers down so the sheets would warm up too."

"You won't warm them up with me?" Vera took her time getting out of her bathrobe, mostly so she wouldn't have to meet his gaze. She'd all but thrown herself at him in the kitchen, and now it was well after dark, Twyla was fast asleep, and they were alone, *in a bedroom*.

Maybe James had simply been flirting with her—he was an accomplished flirt.

Maybe he'd been being kind—he was endlessly kind.

Maybe he'd wanted to reassure—

His mouth settled over Vera's, warm, soft, and easy. A slow kiss, an introduction to getting started kiss.

Vera slid her fingers into his hair as he eased her to her back.

"I've been wanting to do that," she said when he pulled away and hung his head so his cheek lay against her chest.

"Wanting to kiss me? You didn't have to wait until bedtime to do that, Vera. I'm open twenty-four seven for your kissing convenience."

"That too. I meant get my hands in your hair. You have the sexiest natural tousle I have ever seen."

"I have a tousle." James sighed against her skin, his breath a warm tickle. "I'm a lucky guy."

"Are you about to get luckier still?" Oh, how she hated the insecurity in her voice. Hated it.

"Tell me about Alex."

Vera wanted to pull James's head up by his ears and study his expression, for his invitation left her uncertain and much in need of reassurance. A man didn't kiss like that and then turn down sex, or did he?

Maybe James did.

Maybe he should have.

"For this discussion, I at least want the light out," Vera said. She also wanted James's arms around her.

James killed the light. Vera heard the sound of clothes tossed onto the foot of the bed and wished James had reversed the sequence of his actions. Next time, she'd undress him herself before anybody turned off lights.

If there was a next time.

She had never undressed Alexander, and the very notion applied to Donal made her shudder. That James was in a different, better category than those two was cheering.

James climbed in beside her and scooped her against him, gently pushing her head to his shoulder.

"Tomorrow night, you play for me, Vera. I want that on the record."

Yes, Your Honor. "Tomorrow night, I play for you." She took a whiff of his shoulder. How James always managed to smell good was a pleasurable mystery, though she'd never enjoyed mysteries before. "Tonight, I suppose you want another variation on the Life and Times of Vera Winston?"

Her maiden name, and it had just slipped out.

"A brief variation, if that's all you're comfortable with."

"What about the Life and Times of James Knightley? Will we rehearse those etudes?"

"There isn't much to tell," he said, taking her hand and bringing her knuckles to his lips. "I have no former spouses, no children. I've gone on no world tours, never recorded a classical album that went platinum. I've never been physically beaten, except once by Mac when I mouthed off to my mother at the age of sixteen, and even then he pulled his punches and eventually apologized."

"Mac apologized?" James had put Vera's hand over his heart, the beat slow and steady against her palm.

"Mac apologized, for him. He said he'd overreacted, and he was remiss for not keeping a closer eye on things. My loss of temper with Mom was understandable, though I was still wrong to give her the lip I did."

James giving a woman lip? "Were you truly wrong?"

"I don't know. I was sixteen and dealing with a lot. God knows, asking Mom nicely wasn't getting me anywhere." His tone held uncertainty and a hint of desolation.

Maybe having the light off had been a good choice after all.

"That's one of the worst things about the death of a loved one," Vera said. "You don't realize as you're going along, sometimes carping and sniping at each other, that someday when you apologize and get it right may never arrive. You bank on that someday, and then you lose your loved one, and you lose all the somedays too. Lose them forever."

"Was it like that with Alexander?"

"Very much." Vera fell silent, choosing her words and snuggling closer to the man sharing the darkness with her. James's hand settled in her hair, and his fingers began slow circles on the side of her neck. She felt the patience in him, even as she knew he was listening to her silences as well as her words.

"I had a terrible crush on Alexander when I was a girl. He was so very debonair, and his wives were kind to me. They thought it endearing that I was so taken with my manager. He was courtly and acted as a buffer between

me and Donal when I wasn't happy with Donal's decisions, or my mother's. Alexander was old-fashioned in
the protective sense, and that can be good."

Also smothering and hypocritical.

"But still, you were banking on the somedays?"
James asked.

James's heartbeat was a like a metronome set at sixty
beats, a relaxed, comfortable tempo.

"At first," Vera said, "I thought the best someday
would be someday when I wasn't touring so much, then
I realized Alexander loved the touring, loved the seeing
and being seen, the drama and tension of a looming performance before a full house."

"You were the one bearing the tension." James's
hands shifted to her scalp, and Vera was momentarily
struck dumb by the sheer pleasure of his hands in her
hair. Nobody had touched her like this, and she hadn't
the sophistication or the self-discipline to ignore it.

"You learn to work the performance adrenaline
to your advantage," she said after a moment, "or you
quickly crash. Alexander knew he could count on me. I
was paid handsomely for what I did well, what I believed
I was born to do."

"Believed? Past tense?"

Damned lawyers. He would pick up on that.

"I'm not sure anymore, James. The two years I've
had away from it have been the most peaceful in my life,
despite the divorce and moving and all the upheaval.
Hotel rooms, even nice hotel rooms, carry a certain loneliness. Alexander distracted me from that loneliness, at
least for a while."

Though he hadn't always distracted her in a good way.

"How long were you married to him?"

"A few years, mostly good years, because I was on the road a lot. My star was rising, Donal was happy, and Alexander was showing off his newest trophy wife. Then we had Twyla to look forward to."

"So the bloom hadn't worn off the rose when Alex died," James guessed. "That must have been hard."

An entire chord of wrong notes sounded in Vera's head. "It wasn't quite like that."

"Come here." James shifted her, so she was straddling him, her nightgown bunched between them. He wrapped his arms around her and gently pulled her down to his chest. "Tell me, Vera, and don't pretty it up."

His embrace was warm and sweet, and yet Vera knew she wouldn't escape the bed without parting with a few painful truths. Maybe a lot of painful truths.

"A few weeks after we were married, I had a series of concerts scheduled around southern France and northern Italy. Spring is a beautiful time to be in a beautiful part of the world, and I was newly married. The critics were kind, the audiences wildly appreciative. We came back to the hotel after I'd played a lovely matinee, and life was perfect. My handsome, attentive husband was at my side. I had my music, my fans. A beautiful life."

James drew her a shade closer.

"Alex suggested I lay down for a nap while he went for a walk along the water, and we'd have dinner later on the balcony as the sun went down. A fine plan, full of romance, but I was too wound up to sleep, though I was plenty tired. I went out on the balcony to wait for Alex, to enjoy the wonderful breeze and the wonderful life I'd landed in."

James said nothing; but then, he was a very perceptive man.

"The hotel was built in a U shape, facing the beach, which meant I could see down onto the balconies of many of the other rooms, because we were in the penthouse. At first I could not believe what my eyes were telling me, but the hotel provided field glasses for watching the beach. My husband was on somebody else's balcony, shamelessly making love—if you can call it that—with a woman I'd never seen before."

"And you were twenty years old and in love with him."

A lump rose, hard and painful, in Vera's throat.

"Not for long. When he came sauntering back into the hotel room, I confronted him, and he was very *understanding*. That was the worst part, his unflappable conclusion that his peccadillo had been no slight to me, but merely his considerate way of indulging my need for rest. Casual encounters were something a sensible wife tolerated. I had my music, after all, and he loved me. He would never infringe on my practice schedule, never publicly embarrass me. According to him, his devotion to me was beyond doubt, and my silly notions of fidelity were quaint and immature."

"That bastard. I hope you kneed him in the balls and threatened to take your music and get the hell out of Dodge."

Vera spoke the next words against his throat. "I ordered room service. Oh, James, *I ordered room service*."

The tears leaked from her eyes as she cried silently yet again. James held her, and soothed and caressed and, God bless him, he did not try to talk her out of her sorrow or her anger.

"I've cried for him," she said a few minutes later when James had tucked a tissue in her hand. "I have cried and cried for Alex, but I was twenty-two when he died, my daughter not even toddling, and I was so scared and lonely. I never thought to cry for *me*."

"No wonder Donal seemed like a safe bet," James murmured. "The marriage you set up with him was at least immune from the kind of betrayal Alexander handed you."

"Betrayal." She turned the word over in her mind, finding it a perfect fit with her feelings. "I've never put that label on it, but yes, Alex betrayed me not only with his infidelity, but also with his condescending assumption that I should get used to it."

James tucked the covers up over Vera's shoulders, cocooning her in warmth, softness, and a hint of lavender. "I have never understood why, when a man cheats, the lady he cheats on is ashamed of herself."

Vera found that word startlingly apt too. "Ashamed? Yes. I was ashamed. I had assumed I'd be enough to hold Alex's intimate interest, but I soon found out that growing up on a piano bench does not make for a sophisticated outlook on life. I had little experience when I married, and the sense that Alex was being tolerant of my virginal overtures became unbearable, when I knew he was taking his needs elsewhere as well."

"And yet, you've told me it was a good marriage."

And James had paid attention. "I did, didn't I?"

Vera recalled her words, and at the time, she'd meant them. "Maybe compared to what I ended up with in Donal's house, it was, and maybe compared to being alone, it had some benefits. My revenge was that I would never initiate sex with Alexander. He had to come to me, and the occasions became infrequent. My playing blossomed."

"How did that work?"

James's hands moved on her back in the same lyrical, tender mode as those hands played the Beethoven slow movement.

Vera had to mentally replay his question before she could answer.

"I was mightily, mightily hurt," she said, "and became ruthless in my practicing. If Alexander wanted to cheat with some Hungarian countess, I would cheat with Franz Liszt, a notorious womanizer in his day. I'd cheat with Rachmaninoff and the entire London Philharmonic. I'd cheat and cheat and cheat until Alex was so lonely for me, he'd leave off his wandering. He was getting the message before he died."

"While you were growing bitter. At the age of twenty-two, the concert world at your feet, you were growing bitter."

Bitter, lonely, and hollow. A violin was hollow too, and could make beautiful melodies, though it shattered upon the slightest impact.

"Alex apologized for that," Vera said, the memory a sad comfort. "The day before he died, we were having breakfast, again in the South of France, again in the middle of a successful tour, and he told me he regretted not appreciating the beauty he had in his wife, and would I forgive him and start over?"

James's caresses on Vera's back paused. "Did you lay down terms?"

"I told him I didn't know if I could start over, which was honest, but then he died, and my honesty only created that much more guilt. If I'd been less honest, would he have been driving more carefully? Would his reflexes have been quicker? Would he have watched his speed more closely? Would he have been home with his wife?"

Would Twyla be growing up, knowing her father rather than half-orphaned as Vera had been?

James's arms closed around her. "God Almighty, Vera, you can't do that. You can't torture yourself that way."

His embrace was swift, certain, and a better balm to her heart than even Chopin.

"That's what Donal told me. He said he'd watched Alexander moving in, watched him dimming the light in my eyes, watched the change in my playing, and hadn't known how to stop it. Donal offered marriage by way of apology."

James brushed Vera's hair back over her shoulder. "You believed him?"

Yes, she'd believed him, because Donal had been telling the truth. Donal was many things, but a liar was not among them.

"I still think Donal's motives were at least partly above reproach," she said. "Donal is not given to displays of sentiment, but he has some decency."

"If you say so."

James had decency to spare, decency enough not to argue.

They fell silent, but Vera was intensely aware of the man over whose body she was draped. Physically, she was relaxed, and mentally, for all the misery and tears in their discussion, she felt lighter, more at peace.

"You think I'm damaged goods," she said. "This

wasn't what I had in mind when I asked you to cuddle with me."

"Not what I had in mind either," James said, his tone bemused. "You're not damaged goods, Vera Waltham."

She sat up and organized her nightgown, which had bunched up between them. "I've kept Alexander's name because of Twyla, but I'm thinking of going back to Winston."

"I wouldn't if I were you. Twyla won't understand, and forever after, you'll have to prove to the school and the soccer team and the summer camp that you have custody of her."

"I hadn't thought of that."

James urged Vera back down, and she went willingly into his embrace.

"Family law teaches you that children see things differently from adults. And, Vera, I want you to listen to me."

James rolled her, so fast she hadn't felt it coming, and then he was looming above her, braced on his elbows.

"You were married to a spoiled boy and then to a cranky old bully. They weren't, either one of them, the right man for you. You were too young or too upset to see their agendas clearly enough to protect yourself, but the fault for the harm you suffered lies with them and with life, not with you."

James's mouth descended on Vera's, a very different kiss from anything they'd shared previously. This was a claiming kiss, openmouthed, ravenous, plundering; Jesus, God, and all the angel choruses, this kiss was full-orchestra *competent*. Vera twined her arms around him, wanting more of the kiss and more of *him*.

"James…"

"Enough talk," he growled, sealing his mouth to hers again.

She wanted to tell him she lacked confidence, she wasn't sure of herself, and she'd probably disappoint them both, but then her hands slipped down his sides, intent on fastening themselves to his luscious, muscular behind.

And froze.

"James, you're completely…you don't have any… You're *naked*."

—⁓—

James heard surprise and dismay in Vera's voice, and that cut through the fog of lust clouding his brain.

"This bothers you?" he asked. "Because I'm telling you right now, if I had my druthers, you'd be naked too."

Silence, but beneath him, Vera wasn't tense or squirming. A tentative hand landed on his backside, and then a second hand.

"Answer me a question, Vera." He nuzzled around until he found her nose with his nose, then kissed her nose for good measure.

"What question?"

Her voice was breathy, a good sign. "Did the selfish idiot at least take care of you?"

"I don't… James, you're aroused, aren't you? I don't know what the question means."

"Then he didn't," James said, sorry for her to draw that conclusion, not sorry for himself at all. "I will."

"You will what?"

He rolled them again, but this time Vera moved with

him, straddling his lap much more gingerly than she had earlier.

"I will take care of you, but I'd like to ditch the nightgown."

"It's pitch-dark in here, James. What do you think you'll see if I take it off?"

"Sweetheart, I don't want old Eeyore to get torn. Donkeys and I go way back."

She thought about this for about two seconds, and then James heard the slip and swish of fabric moving while she pulled the nightgown over her head.

"Stuff it under the pillow to keep track of it," he suggested. This of course had the delightful effect of making her lean forward, and James's mouth found a succulent nipple without even trying.

"James Knightley."

"Under the pillow," he muttered, not turning loose of his prize. He used one hand on her bare flank, warning himself this would be the most excruciatingly deliberate joining he'd ever inflicted on a woman, or on himself.

An adagio, rather than an allegro con brio.

Instead of exploring the full curves under his hand, he settled his palm on her hip and let her get used to the feel of his touch.

With his free hand, he gently captured her breast, holding her still for his oral delectation.

She held him too, with a hand wrapped around the back of his head, the other braced on his shoulder.

"James, James…"

She was sighing his name, purring it, and James gave her a hint of his teeth scraped along the underside of her breast.

The sighing shifted closer to a groan, and James's arousal crested higher. He switched breasts, and she obliged, arching her back and threading her fingers through his hair. When he drew on her nipple, she whimpered.

The music of a woman letting herself experience pleasure.

"Saints and angels!"

That was neither a sigh nor a whimper, but more of a squeak, occasioned by the brush of James's arousal against Vera's sex.

"I'm interested, Vera, and you're getting interested too. I like it when your body touches mine."

She settled over him gingerly. "Like this?"

Exactly like that. "I want to feel your weight on me," James said, running his hands up her arms. "I want to feel you getting wet and needy and hot for me."

"Hush."

"Come here." He guided her to him by her nape. "I'll whisper what I want to do to you, what I want you to do to me." Was he moving too fast for her? He surely wasn't moving as fast as his cock begged him to move.

"Tell me," she murmured against his neck.

James pretended he hadn't heard her, and palmed both her breasts in the darkness. By damn, the next time he made love with Vera would be in blazing daylight, because he had to know if her nipples were as delicately pink as they tasted.

"James, tell me."

"I'll show you." He stroked every inch of her breasts, varying the pressure and the focus of his caresses, then closing his fingers gently around her nipples.

"James…that feels… God."

"You like it?"

"Umm." She encircled his fingers with her own and increased the pressure. "Fortissimo. E-flat major."

"You do like it."

James pleasured Vera a while longer, probably more aware than she that her body was resting fully on his. His erection was nestled right up against the hot glory of her sex, and everything in James wanted to plunge into her heat and start pounding away.

Next time. You can screw your brains out next time; this time, you give her the music.

Experimentally, and without abandoning her breasts, James lifted his hips to press closer to her. He held himself there, then relaxed.

"Do that again, James."

"Do what?"

She pushed herself down on him more firmly, then lifted up. "That thing you just did with your…"

"With the part of me that's screaming to bury itself inside you, Vera? The part of me that wants to make you scream with pleasure too?"

Two coherent sentences, more or less, which should have been impressive under the circumstances. Vera was still capable of speech too, though, so James set up a rhythm against her, sliding the entire length of his erection slowly over her damp folds, pausing, then sliding back.

"I want you to come, Vera."

He let go of one breast, and slid his hand slowly down her ribs to brush his thumb through her curls.

"This is too much," Vera panted. "I'm not sure…"

"Not enough," James countered, finding her with

his thumb. Vera went still above him, and he felt every particle of her listening for what his thumb was about to do. "Not nearly enough, Vera."

She remained unmoving, like a grand pause before the final cadenza, and James let her gather what wits she could before he moved his thumb again. Just a whisper, just a brush.

"*James!*" Soft and low, mostly a moan, so James moved his thumb again. Vera's head fell forward enough that he could close the distance between them and find her mouth with his. He used his tongue in the same rhythm as his thumb, a slow, soft slide of parts on parts.

She began to move her hips in a languid thrust along his cock, wetting him thoroughly, and requiring of him yet another increment of discipline. Months of celibacy did not entitle him to be selfish and greedy with the first woman to truly need his consideration.

"James…I can't…"

"You can. Let go for me, Vera." He added a hint more pressure and a touch more speed, and her control slipped its moorings on a soft glissando.

"Sweet… Sweet saints… James…"

Vera keened against his neck while he drove two fingers inside her, and felt her body fisting around them. By the time she slumped in a boneless heap on his chest, James's entire body was aching with a combination of tenderness and frustrated lust.

No, not lust. Desire. He was only now learning the difference; one he would consider later, when he was capable of pondering something besides intimacy with Vera Waltham.

"Sweetheart, you all right?"

"It's never been like that, James." Vera sounded bewildered, and not particularly pleased.

"Did I hurt you? I'm sorry. I wasn't trying to be rough, but there at the end I thought…" Heaven help him, if he'd screwed this up, it would be divine retribution for all his casual romps and flings and hookups and…

Vera put two fingers to his lips.

"Sex with my husband was a speed bump, a little thrill, maybe. This was the big roller coaster at the amusement park, the one people drive all day to ride and then talk about for years."

"That's a good thing? That you rode the roller coaster?"

James wasn't sure, because Vera's voice was dreamy and introspective. She kissed him, and some of his confidence returned, because her kissing had grown more bold, more passionate.

"The roller coaster is wonderful and precious, but now I want to ride the space shuttle, James. Buckle up."

Chapter 14

BENEATH VERA, JAMES'S CHEST RUMBLED WITH HUMOR.

"Reach into the drawer on the nightstand, sweetheart, and get us some protection."

She blushed against his chest, but thank goodness for the darkness, because she'd never—

"I can feel that," James said, affection in his voice. "Protection is part of being intimate, Vera, and, no, I don't keep condoms in my guest rooms routinely. I was hopeful after your comments before dinner."

"You can be casual about this," she said, levering up to grope for the drawer pull. "It's new territory for me, James." Though she was glad he could be so matter of fact about something this important, and something she hadn't quite known how to bring up.

"Vera Waltham." He gently imprisoned her wrists in his grasp, and brought her knuckles to his lips. "Being with you like this is not casual. In. Any. Regard."

He let her wrists go, but his voice in the dark—low, sexy, and utterly serious—sent a frisson of pleasure down her spine.

Vera found a condom in the drawer—one of *several*? "What do I do with this?"

"Scoot back a bit. You tear off a corner of the foil and toss that into the drawer, then roll the condom down on me from the tip."

"Why can't you see to it?"

"We'll do this together." James's hands found hers, and his fingers tore the little packet.

"This end up," he said, taking her fingers and showing her which way he'd oriented the condom. "Now unroll it on me."

To do that, Vera would have to put her hands on his erection, something he seemed perfectly happy for her to do.

"Is this necessary, James?"

"Yes. Like those finger exercises you're so devoted to. Not glamorous, but it pays off."

Even in one syllable, she could tell her reticence amused him. They'd reached the scherzo, the humorous part.

Vera slid a hand down his flat belly until something velvety smooth brushed the back of her knuckles. She used her index finger to trace down the length of him and back up.

"Is this one of the concert grands with an extra octave?" she asked.

James's belly bounced, which had his cock leaping.

"If you're asking about my John Henry, then I'm not in a position to comment, because you've probably seen more of these instruments ready to perform than I have. Vera Waltham, you are stalling. You having performance anxiety?"

"Yes." If Vera were more sophisticated, she'd have humor and savoir faire to match James's aplomb, but all she had was the certain knowledge she wanted to be his lover. For that she needed to get past this latex moment.

"Vera?"

The teasing was gone, and her hand was enveloped in James's.

"Like this, sweetheart." He positioned the condom and unrolled it down his shaft.

"We can turn the lights on if you'd rather," James went on. "I'm dressed for the party now, so tell me what your pleasure is. In about two minutes, if you stay where you are, I will no longer be able to respond intelligibly."

"I want you," Vera said, unable to banter any longer. "I just… I want you, James, and I trust you to see to the details."

"Pleasing you isn't a detail, Vera. Let's start with the traditional approach, and if that isn't working for you, you tell me."

Vera treasured this about James, that he was so calm and assured about matters Vera seldom let herself think about, much less dwell on. A corner of her mind—an insecure, out-of-tune corner of her mind—worried about how he'd acquired such self-assurance.

James rolled her under him and settled himself over her, and abruptly, Vera's awareness was filled with James, James, and only James.

"I want this to last," he said, grazing her eyebrows with his nose, "but you are more inspiration than a mortal man can withstand for long, Vera. Be patient with me, and I'll make it up to you."

She was spared a reply by James's mouth fastening itself to hers. She was glad for the darkness, because shadows allowed her to focus on the sensation of his lips brushing softly over hers, then his mouth, landing on hers at a slight angle. James might have wanted it to last, but Vera's own simmering desire needed only the touch of his mouth to gallop back to life. She traced the seam of his lips with her tongue, and both felt and heard him growl in satisfaction.

"More of that," he said against her mouth. "Devour me, Vera."

He opened his mouth over hers, and plundered with his tongue, even as Vera became aware of the weight and length of him along her stomach. She arched up and clamped a hand on his backside to urge him closer.

"I like your hands on my ass. Love it." James levered up so he was surrounding her with man, muscle, and warmth. "I want to be inside you too, Vera."

Vera understood he was leaving the timing up to her, that she'd been invited to take a small but important initiative, the way a good conductor defers to the soloist. She twined a leg over his flank and started moving her hips in a slow undulation under him, but that wasn't enough. She shifted, until his cock nudged at her sex, the sensation exquisitely arousing.

"Now, James, please."

He slid an arm under her neck. "Guide me, sweetheart. Show me where."

She reached between them and positioned him exactly where she wanted him. "Right there, James, and right now."

He pushed forward slowly, then retreated, making slow, steady progress as he penetrated her heat. The sensations were indescribable, bliss and longing radiating from where they joined, up through Vera's middle, and down to the soles of her feet.

The emotions were more complicated, because along with joy and desire came compassion for the younger, less confident woman Vera had been, and for the choices that woman had made. The trust and closeness James offered had been denied Vera by her first husband, though at the time she'd sensed their absence only through a tug of insecure instinct.

Regret was nudged aside by pleasure, by a growing loss of ability to do anything but *feel*.

"James, I think I'm about to…"

"Then let it happen," he said, not breaking rhythm. "As much and as often as you want, Vera. I'm yours."

She tucked her face into his shoulder and shuddered through a slow, sweet orgasm, made longer and more intense by the way James kept moving inside her. As the pleasure ebbed, he surged forward and began to thrust with force.

"Oh, holy… James, I can't… Damn you…not so soon, I can't…"

She did. The space shuttle, the roller coaster, the Damson County Philharmonic, and entire meteor showers of blinding, tearing pleasure. When James let her finish, Vera lay limp and dazed beneath him.

"No more." She brushed his hair back from his brow, and the damned man hadn't even broken a sweat. "I'm not used to this, James, and this much satisfaction can't be good."

"It's wonderful." He dipped his head to kiss her temple. "I will let you catch your breath before we make it even better."

"James, you're scaring me."

He lowered his cheek against hers. "Why scared, sweetheart? I would never hurt you."

Joined like this, she heard the promise in those words, the vow in them, and felt tears threaten.

I'm yours, he'd said. Did he know what those words might mean to her?

"This isn't me. I'm not…I'm not a passionate woman. I accept that."

James's reply was to flex his spine, a slow, deep thrust that had Vera sighing against his neck. She *did* want him, again and again and again. Maybe this was a fluke caused by years of celibacy; maybe it was a testament to his skill; maybe it was—

"Move with me, Vera. Let me have it, as hard and as long as you want."

Dirty words, arousing words, growled right in her ear as James ground himself into her. She caught his rhythm, abruptly realizing she could torment him as much as he was tormenting—and pleasuring—her.

"God, yes," he muttered, his rhythm intensifying. She matched him, and locked her ankles at his back, even as she clutched at his backside until she knew he could feel her nails digging into his flesh. They made the bed shake in the dark, and just as Vera was beginning to hope she might outlast him, he tucked a big hand beneath her, shifted his angle, and sent her off like a Roman candle.

But by God, she wouldn't be the only one to launch. She bucked hard against him, demanding that the finale be a duet, wringing pleasure from him, and bearing down purposefully on him inside.

"For the love of… *Damn*, Vera…"

His hilted himself inside her and pushed hard against her a half-dozen times while Vera went dizzy and helpless with her pleasure. James's breath came hoarsely against her ear as he shuddered out his own satisfaction, and she clung to him through it all.

So *that* was pleasure beyond bearing.

Except she had borne it. Vera licked James's neck and rubbed her cheek over his shoulder. James nuzzled her temple and ruffled her hair with his breathing.

The world made more sense to Vera. The *Emperor Concerto*, the Schubert A minor, the grand, tender Chopin ballades. They all, every note of them, made more sense.

"How in the ever-loving hell could you think you're not passionate, Vera Waltham? If you were any more passionate, I'd be the happiest dead man in Damson County."

Not tender words, but in the genuine bewilderment with which James offered them, Vera heard tenderness anyway. Happy bewilderment, a mirror of Vera's own sentiments, or some of them.

She kissed James's cheek lingeringly when no reply came to mind, though intimacy with him was unlike any lovemaking she'd experienced. More compelling, more daring. To share passion like this took courage, and if James was doing anything, he was helping her find her courage again.

"You're quiet," James said, levering up on his elbows. "I have to be squashing you."

Was that a hint of uncertainty in his voice?

"Don't go." Vera managed that much, and backed it up by tightening her arms and legs around him.

"I'll be right back. What Vera puts on me, I have to take off."

He was referring to the condom, of course, something else Vera hadn't known how to talk about. She let her arms go slack, glad in her bones James was the one who had to navigate climbing out of the bed. She heard him snatch a tissue from the box on the night table, and then he was back, the mattress dipping with his weight.

"Women are supposed to want to talk after sex," he said, sliding an arm under Vera's neck. "Or maybe I'm behind the times. You going to roll over and go to sleep on me?"

He was teasing, but Vera wrestled him atop her again when he would have spooned himself around her.

"I feel sentimental, James. Like I'm about to say something stupid or cry or both." Like she'd better not sit down at a keyboard until she had these feeling under control.

He let her get situated beneath him. She scooted down so James was above and around her.

"If what you want to say is the truth, Vera, then it can't be foolish, and your tears would never be foolish to me." He palmed the back of her head and cradled her face to his shoulder.

That was what Vera wanted, exactly, precisely what she wanted, to be held and cherished and *cosseted*, by God. At long last, finally and thoroughly, she'd found a man who knew how to cosset her.

"James?"

"Sweetheart?"

"The space shuttle's got nothing on you."

He kissed her cheek, and Vera fell asleep beneath him to the feel of his hand caressing her hair. Her last thought was that it was *bliss* to be held in the arms of the only man to ever figure out how to…cosset her.

—◇◇◇—

James poured Twyla a bowl of granola, sliced a few bites of banana and strawberry onto it, tossed on some chocolate chips, and set it in front of the girl.

"Wow. My cereal at home isn't this fancy. Thanks, James." Twyla picked up her spoon and dug in. "Mom sure likes to sleep in at your house."

James rinsed out his own bowl. He'd indulged in an entire handful of chocolate chips on his cereal, because a guy needed to keep up his strength.

"Any change of routine can be tiring," James said. Then too, multiple shuttle launches in the course of a night could also wear a gal out. "You want to get eggs with me?"

"You buy them at the store?"

The child's education had been neglected. "I most assuredly do not. Not a quarter mile that-a-way is a genuine working henhouse, and Monday is my day to fetch the eggs. Hiram lets me take what I need and keeps me in butter and milk too, in exchange for the occasional hand with his farm work."

"Like when you fixed the fence yesterday?"

"That was simply defending my castle," James said, putting the milk away. "But, yes, mending fence, stacking hay, running the manure spreader over the fields when it's too cold for an old man's bones."

Twyla paused in an effort to spoon-mine the chocolate chips from her granola. "You spread manure? *On purpose?*"

"Finish your cereal, and we'll go for a ramble. I'll write your mom a note."

James would not sign the note with *love*, though it was tempting. Last night had been...unprecedented. James usually concluded a sexual interlude feeling he'd scratched his itch, provided the same relief to the lady, and could go happily on his way.

He'd wanted to linger, wanted to hear Vera call his name one more time, wanted to feel her hands on him, wanted to be the man who proved to her she was extraordinarily passionate for all her innocence.

Maybe because of her innocence.

"James, are you going to write the note?" Twyla asked.

"Sometimes it's hard to get started. Why don't you write this for me, and I'll tidy up the kitchen."

"I washed out my bowl." Twyla said, taking the chair James abandoned, and sliding over the pen and legal pad James had appropriated from the phone stand. "You begin with Dear Mom, except she's not your mom."

"She's my Vera," James said, that truth inordinately satisfying. "My dear Vera."

He wished he'd not delegated the note writing to Twyla, so he could put those words on paper: My dear Vera. *My own Vera.*

The sentiment echoed as he introduced Twy to Inskip's hens and the proper method of parting a biddy from her egg. Twyla looked at but didn't touch the manure spreader, and peered into the pungent gloom of the heifers' loafing shed for the source of the manure. James stopped by the milking parlor for a gallon of raw milk, explaining to Twy as they returned to the house about homogenization, pasteurization, and cream rising to the top.

"You know a lot," Twyla said. "Grace says both her uncles are smart, but not as smart as her dad."

"That's because her dad was smart enough to marry her mom," James said as they walked into the kitchen. "That makes Trent the brightest guy in the family. Look who's awake."

He smiled at his Vera, who sat at the table in her nightie and bathrobe, a pair of James's wool socks on her feet, and a cup of tea in her hand.

What a perfectly gorgeous sight. James resisted the urge to kiss her only because Twyla was there and Vera's gaze held shyness.

"Good morning, beautiful lady," he said. "We come bearing gifts from the neighbor ladies."

"I got the eggs myself," Twyla added. "James says small hands are better for raiding the boxes. I had chocolate chips on my cereal, and can Grace come over and play today?"

Vera peered into the pail James held. "Did you thank the hens?"

"We did," Twyla said, beaming. "Eggs have to be washed. I never knew that."

"You're headed for the office today, aren't you, James?" Vera asked.

"I am not," he said, putting the eggs in a colander in the sink. "I have to run over to West Virginia for a client, and that will pretty much ruin the day. I can stick around for a couple hours, though, while you get started on your practicing."

"That would be helpful."

Twyla looked from one adult to the other. "Would it be helpful if Grace came and played with me? I promise we'd stay out of your hair, Mom."

James shot Twyla a sardonic glance over his shoulder. "You'll pester her for brownies and cookies, and probably sneak out and chase the heifers. I'm leaving this house in the hands of a pair of hooligans."

Twyla grinned at her mother. "I've never been a hooligan before. I'll text Grace she can come."

"How about," Vera said, a touch of authority in her voice, "you will let me call Grace's mom, and see if Grace is free to come play? Hannah probably has to go to work this morning herself, Twy. Not everyone is still on spring break today."

"I'll go make my bed, so when Grace comes, that will already be done," Twyla said, bouncing out of the kitchen in great good spirits.

"Somebody slept well," James said, abandoning his post at the sink. "How is somebody's mother?"

Vera rose from the table and faced away from him. "How do we do this part, James?"

"This part?"

"This is the proverbial morning after, and I am…all at sea. I found the note. Thanks for taking Twy on a walk, and thanks for…"

He was across the kitchen in two strides, his arms around her. "The pleasure was entirely mine." If he had to listen to her thank him for hauling her ashes, it would cast a pall on an otherwise lovely day. "I can't postpone this business in West Virginia, or else Twyla would be off to play at Grace's, I assure you."

"I have to practice." Vera's arms stole around James's waist. "I cannot think straight, but somehow, I have to practice."

James rested his chin on her crown, pleased beyond words to have muddled her so. Thinking straight was vastly overrated.

"First you have to tell me you enjoyed last night, Vera, and you have to tell me you're better than just fine."

She smiled up at him. He snitched a kiss while Twyla

was occupied elsewhere, though it left him wanting to snitch more than a first kiss of the day, to hoist Vera onto the counter, undo his jeans, and—

He needed to get back into the habit of keeping a condom in his wallet.

"Now, I'm better than fine." She closed her eyes and rested against him.

This affection and closeness, this warmth, this was how Trent started every day of his married life. Lucky, lucky bastard. Smart, lucky bastard.

"I can wave Grace off," James said. "Hannah wouldn't mind if we wanted to send Twyla to her for the morning."

"I'm going to practice," Vera said, slipping free of his embrace. "Practicing will be a complete waste of time, because I won't be able to focus at all, but I have my standards, James."

"Anticipation isn't entirely a bad thing." He went back to washing the eggs, mostly because dirty eggs might quell the uproar starting behind his zipper. "I'll also stop by your place on my way west and make sure the security firm has gotten started."

"Any idea how long that will take?"

Years, if I have any say. Though prevaricating like that with Vera held no appeal, not even if foot-dragging by the security firm assured James more nights in her bed.

Entire nights, which was a switch. He'd awakened with a silky strand of Vera's hair across his mouth, her leg cast over his thigh, and her soft snoring inches from his ear. Leaving her undisturbed had been an act of sheer discipline, one made possible only by the knowledge that little kids went to bed earlier than grown-ups.

And woke up earlier too.

"I'll get a schedule from Howard's crew chief today," James said. "You in a hurry to get home?"

Vera grimaced at her tea. "I want to get it over with. Those eggs must be spotless by now, James. Where's Hannah's number, and is it too early to call?"

"Nah. They have livestock. They'll be up." James passed Vera his cell. "She's on my contact list, but, Vera?"

She glanced up, her gaze wary, and James hated that.

"This is the proverbial morning after," he said, purposely not touching her. "There was nothing proverbial about last night though. Last night was special, and you are special, and seeing you here in my kitchen this morning is special, and taking your daughter with me to raid the henhouse is special…and I'm saying stupid things, aren't I?"

She looked puzzled, then the corners of her lips turned up, and a smile broke over her whole face, illuminating every feature and shining out of her dark eyes.

"Yes, James. Yes, you are saying stupid things. Very stupid things for such a brilliant, *sexy* man." She went up on her toes and kissed him on the mouth, a fat, sassy, Hello-Buster of a kiss that had James smiling right back at her.

⁓⁓⁓

Vera admitted she'd been wrong.

While James puttered in his study with Twyla on the computer, Vera had sat down to do her finger exercises. She'd expected the familiar comfort of a manual routine, not that they'd come off all flourish-y and polished. Olga could make technique sound that way, as if it had its own drive and will to shine, exactly like concert repertoire.

Vera hadn't known how to pull off such a feat.

She attributed this aberration in her playing to a wonderful night's sleep in James's arms. He'd stayed with her, a pleasure in itself, and kept her warm and occasionally rubbed her back or her scalp.

He was a natural at team sleeping, tucking an arm around her, running his foot up her calf, kneading her backside gently as she dozed beside him. The sex had been dazzling and disorienting, but the sharing a bed… with James; that was the bodily equivalent of the way he talked to her, involving courage and trust and something magic she hadn't shared with anybody in her twenty-eight years on earth.

A four-hand rendition of happily ever after.

Vera was falling in love with James plain and simple. He'd said she hadn't had the experience to defend herself against Alex and Donal, and he'd been right. But all the experience in the world wouldn't be enough to protect her against James's combination of charm, sex appeal, and sheer male presence.

She got out some Bach fugues, and even they sounded more…polished, competent…brilliant?

"Mom, Grace is here!" Twyla knew to time her bellows to the pauses between pieces, but Vera merely bellowed back. "I'll be along in a minute."

She had no desire to leave the piano bench and was still playing twenty minutes later when James sat beside her.

"You're a maniac today," he said, when Vera reached a cadence. "What's gotten into you?"

A who, not a what. "Spring fever, maybe."

He pushed a lock of Vera's hair over her shoulder. "The girls are up in Twy's room. I moved the DVD player in there, and I think they're having a princess marathon. I should be back by dinner, and Hannah will pick Grace up on her way home from work."

While Vera impersonated a maniac pirate pianist. Vera liked that image just fine. "Hannah's working today?"

"She and Trent are both the kind you can't keep out of the office for too long. You ladies will be OK while I'm gone?"

"We'll manage." Then a thought intruded, the trombone making its dolorous entrance on the day's concerto. "James, what do we know of Grace's father?"

A funny expression flickered across James's face. "Why do you ask?"

Why hadn't this come up earlier? "Because Grace is in my care for the day. What if he shows up? Are there restraining orders? Does he have any kind of custody? Do I have to watch what I say about him in front of Grace?"

"Tangled webs," James said. "As far as I know, Grace's father does not know she's alive, and Hannah wants it that way. Grace's conception was not a happy occasion for Hannah, but the details are hers to share."

A gentle reprimand, not quite a scold, but an understandable one. Family business was family business.

"Then I don't need to worry about him, do I?" Vera asked.

"You do not, particularly when you are sounding so ferociously good at the keyboard."

"I am, then? It isn't just my imagination?" Vera could ask James, because he'd be honest. Kind, but honest, because he had no stake in manipulating her, showing her off, or exploiting her talents.

"You're in rare form, Vera. Recall that you promised to play for me tonight. Save a little of your fire for when the sun goes down."

He gave her a look that would incinerate her concert grand on the spot, and Vera had to stare hard at middle C.

"Drive safely, James."

He kissed her cheek and sauntered off, while Vera watched his backside and knew that James knew she was ogling him.

She turned resolutely back to her playing, but what was she thinking, anyway, trotting out musty old Bach? She mentally dug through her stacks of music, came up with the finale to the *Emperor Concerto*, and started romping away with Beethoven at his exuberant best.

"Your mom is terrific," Grace said, remote in her hand. "She can play like that, and she makes great brownies."

"She hasn't played that piece since I was little," Twyla replied. "It's long, and there're a lot of other instruments that go with it. I like it."

"We can watch the movie later. You wanna just listen?"

"You wouldn't mind?"

"I'm going to tell Merle she missed bee-yoo-ti-ful music," Grace said, tossing the remote up and catching it. "It makes Bronco want to dance in the Cloud Pasture."

"It makes me want to learn to play the piano."

Vera spent the day playing old friends, trying to pinpoint what, exactly, was different about her music.

What was better.

She hadn't solved the mystery by the time she made the girls lunch, and she still hadn't solved it when she spotted Hannah's blue Prius pulling into the driveway, but she'd had great fun—something Vera couldn't recall doing on a piano bench for years.

"Hullo," Hannah said. "I gather the girls are still friends?"

"No sulks or pouts yet today," Vera replied. "Can you stay for a cup of tea?"

Said like a perfectly normal mom too.

"Yes, please. Reentry is hard after a vacation, and probably harder still after a honeymoon."

They shared a cup of tea as darkness fell, and as Hannah took her mug to the sink, she tossed a question over her shoulder.

"I don't suppose James is underfoot somewhere? He wasn't in the office today."

"He had an errand in West Virginia, and said it would take most of the day. Business for some client. He ought to be back any minute."

"West Virginia?" Hannah's hand went to her middle, as if the tea disagreed with her.

West Virginia was less than fifteen miles away. "I didn't ask for details. Are you all right?"

"I'm fine, probably jet-lagged, and ready for a quiet evening with family. It's odd, to have family. Real family."

Yes, odd. "Odd good, or odd peculiar?"

"Odd wonderful," Hannah said. "Probably like the difference between playing one of those big pieces where the piano sits in front of the orchestra with the other instruments, and trying the same piece solo. The work was meant to be played with an ensemble, but you can't tell that until you hear the difference."

"A concerto. Interesting analogy."

"Mom!" Grace came racing across the kitchen, sliding up to her mother on stocking feet. "Twy and me wrote a story on Uncle James's computer, and I drew the pictures, and we're going to send it to Dad and Uncle Mac."

Hannah knelt and hugged her daughter. "Does this story have unicorns in it?"

"'Course it does. And ducks and turtles and cows."

"Maybe you'll give me a preview in the car?"

After a few parting flurries of promises between the girls, and a thank-you to Vera, mother and daughter moved off, leaving a ringing silence behind.

"You had a fun day," Vera said to Twyla. They'd *all* had a fun day.

"Grace has a little kid's imagination," Twyla said. "But she's fun, and I liked the carpet picnic you made for us for lunch."

PBJs, carrot sticks—in the event any unicorns crashed the party—and cookies with milk.

"Pretty soon, the weather will be warm enough to take the Falcon out and do a real picnic." Vera slid an arm around her daughter's shoulders, and Twyla leaned against her mother's hip.

"May I bring Grace and Merle?" Twyla asked.

"Sometimes. I'd still like to have my little girl all to myself sometimes too."

Or maybe all to herself and James?

Twyla's smile was bashful, leaving Vera to realize that in recent days, she'd almost lost track of her daughter.

"How 'bout you set the table, Twy, and I'll put the bread in the oven, and we can look at the calendar to see when our first outing will be?"

"'Kay." Twyla skipped away, going to the silverware drawer. She'd taken no time at all to orient herself to James's home, and for that Vera was grateful.

Vera punched down the loaf rising on the counter's built-in cutting board, the feel of the dough a pleasure in her hands. Everything had been a pleasure today, despite all the upheaval in her life.

She shaped the loaf and tucked it into a buttered pan, a question wafting through her rosy mood as she opened the oven door: Was it a good thing that she was already listening for the sound of James's SUV coming up the drive, or a very good thing?

———※———

James parked and shut off the engine, then sat for a moment with the window cracked, listening for the sound of piano music drifting from his house, and hearing none.

Well, damn. Vera had said she'd play for him later, and he could look forward to that. To that *too*. Having somebody—two somebodies—to come home to was different. Different, wonderful, and disorienting.

He paused in the kitchen doorway, watching while Twyla set out place mats and napkins, and Vera mashed the hell out of a batch of potatoes. She was using James's antique potato masher, not the mixer, and making quite a racket.

"Is that fresh bread I smell?" he asked.

"James!" Twyla dropped her place mat and pelted

over to hug him around the waist. He lifted her to his hip and extended an arm to Vera, who crossed the kitchen more slowly.

"Hello, ladies." He limited himself to giving Vera's shoulders a one-armed squeeze. "I'm relieved to see the house is still standing, but I suspect it had a few narrow escapes. What's for dinner?"

He set Twyla down and bussed Vera's cheek, though Twy was already chattering about picnics and unicorns.

"I saw that," Twyla said, smirking at her napkins. So James kissed her cheek too, then blew a raspberry on her neck.

Dinner was delicious, a tad noisy, and thoroughly enjoyable, even though Vera was subdued. Still, James was relieved to see Vera shepherd Twy up to bed a couple of hours later. He fussed around with his email, deleted yet another version of his social phone list, and checked the time every five minutes.

When he looked up, Vera was leaning in the doorway of his study, watching him with an expression that looked almost sad.

"How was your day, Mrs. Waltham?" James asked. "Twyla hardly let you get a word in edgewise at dinner."

Vera sidled into the room like she didn't know quite what to do with herself, so James shifted to the sofa and patted the place beside him.

"I spent most of the day playing the piano," she said, settling in and tucking up one foot. "I haven't done that for a while."

Her mood was difficult to decipher, but James wasn't about to keep his hands to himself.

"I missed you today, Vera." He underscored the

sentiment by putting his arm around her and nudging her head to his shoulder.

"You took care of your errand in West Virginia?"

"I did, and it was as successful as I'd hoped it would be." He hardly wanted to dwell on business, though, so he asked again about her day, and kept up a subtle cross-examination until Vera drew her knees up and curled in to his side.

"Trent asked me to come in to see him tomorrow," she said, pressing her face into his shoulder. "He has the police report."

Well, shit. "Did he give you any details?"

"He was on his way to court, so no. I'm to meet him at eleven."

"I'll take Twy to school so you can get your practicing done first."

She raised her head to peer at him, and then leaned up and gave him a soft kiss on the mouth.

"Thank you, James. Thank you for making us welcome. Thank you for being who you are."

"Sweetheart, is something wrong?"

She got to her feet and stretched, then extended a hand down to him, drew him to his feet, and kept his hand in hers.

"Being here in your house…"

"Yes?"

"I realize how lonely I've been, James. I think Twy was lonely too, but I'm also anxious to get home. It doesn't make sense."

Mixed feelings never did. "Howard said he can probably have the place done by Wednesday. You know I'll bunk in with you if you ask it, Vera."

She nodded, but when she didn't say anything more, James scooped her up against his chest and carried her toward the stairs. She let him help her undress, let him brush out her hair, let him spoon himself around her.

And before she drifted off to sleep, she let him love her gently and thoroughly, until she was clinging to him and whispering his name over and over in the darkness.

Chapter 15

"THEY'RE NOT DONAL'S PRINTS," TRENT SAID. "I WISH I could tell you something different, Vera, but the evidence techs know what they're doing, and they didn't find these prints on file anywhere."

"I was sure they were his," Vera said. "I'd reached the point that I was almost sorry they were his, and now *this*? You're telling me a stranger was in my house, leaving threats on my computer? Impersonating Donal's voice on my phone?"

Trent had seen a lot of upset women, and he was looking at a very upset woman now. Oh, Vera was keeping a lid on her nerves—a veteran concert soloist wouldn't give way to hysterics, after all—but her knuckles were white as they gripped her purse, and her expression was tense.

"Not necessarily a stranger, but not somebody with an arrest record either. And, Vera?"

She pulled a wilting leaf off Trent's rhododendron and tucked it into the soil. "More bad news?"

"You know the restraining order has expired?"

She paused, another yellowing leaf in her grasp. "Blessed St. Jude."

"Who's he?"

"Patron saint of lost causes."

She'd been wandering around Trent's office, picking up law books, leafing through them, setting them down, her purse still hanging from her shoulder. Mac had the same habit of touching everything in sight, as did James. She ripped off the second leaf, tossed it into the pot, and dropped onto Trent's sofa.

"What do I do now, Trent? I'm the victim of some stalker, but if I turned every disgruntled student or unkind critic in to the cops, the list would be endless."

Trent took the place beside her, though she was giving off a stay-out-of-my-space vibe. "You have more security in place now?" he asked.

"They'll finish up by tomorrow, and James assures me it's a state-of-the-art system."

Good move, James. "And you document all the emails and nasty messages and break-ins. I'm not sure there's more you can do, besides go about your life and send the signal that whoever is doing this hasn't intimidated you one bit."

How Trent hated having nothing else to offer her.

Vera gazed at her hands, which might look like any other mom's hands, though Trent knew how talented they were.

"I have a daughter, Trent. Whoever is doing this has intimidated the hell out of me and made me angrier than I've ever been."

"I know." If anybody had threatened Merle, Grace, or Hannah… Trent put that thought far to the side. "James is keeping a close eye on you. That has to be some reassurance."

Reassurance to Vera's lawyer, not necessarily to James's brother.

"I am not James's responsibility," Vera said, rising. "You are telling me there's essentially nothing you can do."

She was bright woman—a bright, upset woman—and she was right.

"Mac has put out some feelers, and if it's any comfort, the established criminal element, such as it is in Damson County, isn't admitting to any familiarity with Donal or his schemes."

Mac had damned near gone cruising the open-air drug markets, trolling for information.

"Do we have an established criminal community here?" Vera went back to pacing the room, tactilely inventorying the portables.

Trent opted for honesty over diplomacy. "Wherever you have easy access to major cities by interstate, you have drug trafficking, and that pretty much guarantees ongoing criminal activity. And, Vera, I hate to be the one to tell you this, but I spoke with Aaron Glover again yesterday. He thinks Donal is up to something legal, something that will force you to honor the dates you haven't canceled."

Vera picked up a small glass figure of Justice, complete with blindfold, scales, and sword. "What can Donal possibly do?"

"I don't know. I suffered through a year of contract law back in law school, but it's really and truly not my area, beyond separation agreements. Until Donal files something, we can assume he's blowing smoke for the sake of aggravating you."

Vera set Justice down on the windowsill, where it could catch the morning sun and cast a prism at Trent's feet.

"I hate to interrogate the children," she said, turning Justice so it faced out the window. "Darren will probably come see Twy this weekend."

"He's almost an adult, Vera. You don't have to tie him to the rack. Simply ask him if there's anything he wants you to know. Children usually pick up a lot more than we give them credit for."

"Spoken like a dad."

A dad who noticed that the tip of Justice's sword had become chipped. "How's the playing going?"

Trent asked the question to change the topic, but also because Hannah had raved about Vera's ability. Trent had some of Vera's CDs, though he'd never heard Vera perform live. James had.

Lucky bastard.

"I don't know how to answer that, Trent," Vera said. "During the times in my life when everything went to hell, my playing only got better. My life is in transition, and all the practicing I'm doing is bearing fruit, though not the fruit I'd anticipated."

Vera had never struck Trent as a flighty musician, but he suspected she could wax as loquacious as the next artist about her craft, and he had lunch with a certain lovely wife in ten minutes. He got to his feet and took Vera's coat off the rack near his door.

"A surprise gift then. Do you have any more questions about the police report?" He'd given her a copy and Mac a copy, but the document itself was useless.

"No, thank you. I'll keep the alarms turned on when I'm sleeping or not at home, and maybe even put the house on the market."

Did James know that? Should Trent tell James that? "Shall I walk you to your car, Vera?"

"James and I are having lunch, our first meal without an eight-year-old chaperone, as it turns out."

Good move, James. "You know where his office is?"

"I do. Thanks, Trent, and I'll keep you posted regarding any crime sprees."

He parted from her, frustrated that he couldn't do much about her problems. He half hoped Donal did try some contractual maneuvering, because the business lawsuit hadn't been brought that James Knightley couldn't try the hell out of.

—⁂—

Vera hadn't expected Trent to have good news, but neither had she expected him to be absolutely useless when it came to stopping the harassment and mischief. Trent wasn't a criminal lawyer, but Mac was, and the retainer agreement she'd signed months ago specified that members of the firm consulted among themselves when a case called for it.

She made her way to the suite of offices reserved for business law. James had told her he was interviewing prospective new associates this morning, so she wasn't surprised his door was closed.

"We sent the last interviewee packing half an hour ago," the secretary said, coming around her desk. "He's probably in there working on his short game. The golf courses will soon be open for business, and James takes his recreation seriously. Yo, boss!" She rapped on the door twice with her knuckles then pushed it right open, but stopped abruptly.

The tableau Vera saw over the secretary's shoulder was becoming familiar: James, his expression unreadable, had his arms around Hannah, whose face was pressed to his shoulder. When Hannah turned and stepped back, Vera would have sworn the woman had been crying.

At least they'd had their clothes on.

Vera wasn't convinced the embrace was innocent, but neither could she conclude anything incriminating. Hannah's expression was luminously happy, for all her cheeks were streaked with tears.

While James looked more pleased than guilty, if a little sheepish.

"My lunch date arrives," James said, holding out a hand to Vera even as Hannah peeled herself off her brother-in-law. "Hannah, we'll talk more later, but I wish you'd reconsider."

"I can't," Hannah said. "Not yet. Maybe when the thirty days are up, not now. But, James—thank you. Thank you, thank you, *thank you*."

She looked like she'd hug him again, but James draped his arm over Vera's shoulders.

"I think your spouse is pacing the carpet in anticipation of lunch with you," Vera said, and she honestly, truly did not mean it to sound catty, and must have succeeded, because Hannah's smile became even brighter as she sighed, squared her shoulders, and left without another word.

"We're working on a tough case," James said. "She is one stubborn woman."

"You say that like you admire her for it."

"I do." James pulled Vera closer with an arm around her shoulders. "You should know by now I enjoy stubborn, determined, unstoppable women. Now get me out of here before I close that door and my couch loses its virginity."

Vera debated for about two seconds before letting
the matter with Hannah drop. James might fall in love
with his brother's wife, but he would not trespass, of that
Vera was almost certain.

———✺———

James left the office promptly at five and did not stop
at either Trent's or Mac's offices on the way out.
Tomorrow, Vera and Twy would move back to Vera's
house, and tonight was the last night James had to enjoy
their company. When he turned up his driveway though,
by the last of the light, he saw several of Hiram's heifers
loose in the front yard.

He let them graze, hoping they'd find their way back
to their herd before too much longer.

Or maybe they wouldn't, and James frankly did not
care. He wasn't about to spend the next hour playing
border collie to a dozen wayward Holsteins, when his
womenfolk—

He paused just shy of slamming the door to the
SUV closed.

His. Womenfolk.

Two quaint concepts—that the females under his roof
were womenfolk, and that they were his to look after and
be looked after by. Up at the house, the kitchen lights
were on for a change. Most weeknights, he'd head down
to the basement, work out, then check email before he
went into the kitchen to make himself a sandwich. He'd
eat standing up, alone, or take "dinner" to the study to
munch on while he went back to the computer.

He'd come to prefer those nights to evenings when
he spent several hours flattering and teasing and flirting

before falling into bed with whichever woman had dialed him up.

What in the *hell* had all that been about?

Rather than ponder his past, he walked up to the house, letting himself in through the kitchen door.

A burned smell was the first clue his kingdom was not at peace, and the way Vera was banging pots and pans around on the stove was the second. The mutinous glare Twyla shot him was the third.

"Hello, ladies. Are we not speaking to each other?" James was used to dealing with tense situations, but this was not simply a logistical puzzle or case study.

"Unless Twyla has an apology to share, I don't need to hear what she has to say." Vera spared James a brief, disgruntled glance and went back to stirring her cauldron.

"What about you, Twyla?" James inquired pleasantly. "Have your cannon at the ready?"

"Mom said I wasn't allowed to call Grace, because it's almost dinnertime. I didn't call Grace."

"You called Merle?"

Twyla's frown became confused. "How did you guess?"

Clever kid. "I guessed because I'm a lawyer. Maybe you'll be one too."

"Heaven forefend." That from Baba Yaga at the stove.

"Oh, come on now," James said. "Not all lawyers are weasels. Why did you call Merle, Twy, when you knew she was likely sitting down to dinner too?"

Twy fiddled with a folded napkin. "Because I…forgot…book."

"Twyla Scholastica Waltham." Vera propped both hands on her hips. "If you forgot your book at school, then what is the rule?"

"I have to learn the consequences of my behavior," Twyla muttered, but then she put *her* fists on *her* hips in an exact imitation of her mother's posture. "But I didn't forget my stupid book at school, and *you never listen!*"

She bolted for the door, but James caught her by one wrist.

"When people bellow at me like that," he said, "I am less inclined to listen, and if raising your voice to your mother isn't against a rule, in this house it will be from now on. What were you saying about your book?"

James dropped her wrist, and to give the kid credit, she stood her ground.

"I didn't leave it at stupid school, I put it in my stupid backpack to take home, but started doing my homework while we waited for the bus. Grace wanted to see, and I started talking to Merle while Grace looked at my book, and Grace stuffed my book in her backpack by mistake just as the bus came, and it's not her fault, but I don't want to get in trouble either, because I didn't leave my *stupid, idiotic, moronic* book at school."

Vera's fists dropped from her hips and her expression became bewildered, which James considered an improvement over that god-awful thunderous frown.

"Why didn't you say so, Twy?" Vera asked.

"Because"—Twyla screwed up her face in a sneer and pitched her voice higher—"I don't want to hear any excuses, Twyla Scholastica Waltham. You're too smart a girl to be so forgetful, Twyla. This is little-girl behavior, Twyla. That's why."

Twyla's lip quivered, and she turned into James's side, a miserable little ball of overwhelmed righteous indignation. Vera's expression shaded toward despairing, and James held out an arm to her.

She'd been distant at lunch, probably still processing her discussion with Trent, which James knew from Vera's recounting had been frustrating. As Vera leaned in against his other side, he put an arm around each female.

"You're both tired and hungry, and on edge about going home tomorrow. Am I right?"

"You're right," Vera said, her hand straying over Twyla's hair.

Twyla nodded.

"Then this is a misunderstanding, and can be easily fixed with a few apologies."

"Right again," Vera said, crouching down. "I will try to listen more patiently, Twy. You haven't forgotten a book in a long time, and I overreacted when you called Merle. I'm sorry."

Twyla shifted from a grip on James to twine her arms around her mother's neck. "You never yell at me anymore. Why did you yell at me? It's just a stupid book, and I only talked to Merle for three seconds."

"Holy shit!" James crossed the kitchen in two strides, not quickly enough to prevent a pot from boiling over. He lifted the sizzling, bubbling mess off the stove until the boiling slowed, and then turned down the burner.

"You're not supposed to cuss," Twyla said, a ghost of a grin tracing her mouth.

"Then I have something to apologize for too," James said. "But let's sit down to dinner before something else goes amiss."

Or James said more bad words.

"You won't get into your jeans first?" Twyla asked.

"Not tonight. Tonight I'm hungry as a bear." And James was *damned* if he'd leave these two alone unsupervised when he didn't have to. Still, dinner was a subdued business, with Twyla yawning over her dessert and leaving the table for her bath without a word of protest.

"You stay right there," James said to Vera. "I'll get the dishes, and you can tell me what a bad mother you think you are."

This earned him a wan smile.

"You heard her. I never yell *anymore*. That means I used to yell, and now I don't—as much."

James collected plates and cutlery into a stack and took it to the sink, then put a mug of water into the microwave. An Eeyore mug, in honor of the prevailing mood.

"So we'll analyze one tired, bad—and might I add, at the risk of provoking you to glowering—rattled moment to death?" he asked.

"Rattled." Vera's very lack of fight concerned James more than burned dinner, raised voices, or missing schoolbooks. "I'm nervous about being in that house alone. I admit that."

The microwave dinged.

"I can stay with you for a few nights," James offered. "I'll sleep on the damned couch if you're worried what Twy will think."

Vera watched as James slapped a couple chamomile tea bags into the steaming mug and set it before her.

"Are you being sweet, or getting cold feet, James?"

He set the stack of dirty dishes in the dish tub and parked his frustrations somewhere out among the neighbor's heifers. Vera was tired, rattled, and facing multiple challenges, but she did not have to face them all alone.

Her bun was coming loose too. James braced his hands on either side of her, pushed her bun aside with his chin, and fastened his lips to her nape.

"I have been wanting to get my mouth on some part of you since I walked in that door. I am not getting cold feet, Vera Waltham. You are upset and out of sorts. If you want the bed to yourself tonight, I understand, but you don't have to pick a fight to get a little privacy. Thank Jesus, I am not eighteen years old and a walking erection."

She chuckled at this description, and then she laid her cheek against his biceps.

"Can I make up my mind about this offer to sleep on the couch when I'm actually in the house?"

"You may, and if you decide to fly solo, I'm only a phone call away. Drink your tea, and when Twy is done with her bath, why don't you run one for yourself? I can read her a story or play I Spy, or whatever the secret ritual is."

From the look on Vera's face, James had offered her the crown jewels or the keys to Grace's cloud pasture.

"Twy sometimes reads to herself, but mostly it's just nighty-night and lights out," Vera said

"I can manage that." James finished up the dishes, aware of Vera behind him at the table, sipping her tea and staring out the window at nothing. She hadn't settled in her mind whatever had transpired with Trent, that much James could figure out, but something else was bothering her.

"You OK?" he asked as he put the last dish in the drain rack. "I don't know when I've ever seen you so quiet, Vera."

"Just thinking. I'll go check on Twy."

She passed him her mug and left him alone in the kitchen.

Thinking about what? About the spat with Twy, about returning to a house where she didn't feel safe, about the restraining order expiring—she'd laid that one on him at lunch—or about something musical?

For all James was falling in love with her, he didn't know her as well as he—

Falling in love?

Was it falling in love when he was happy to smell even a burning dinner because *she* made it? Was it falling in love when he spent the entire workday watching the clock just so he could be home doing dishes in the same room as his lady? Was it falling in love when he offered to sleep on the damned couch?

When he didn't want to let her go, not even to her own house one and a half farms away?

The door to the fridge now sported three drawings, two by Twy, one by Grace, of unicorns and cows. The autumn cookie tin had somehow migrated from the top of Vera's fridge to his own, and a magnet in the shape of a gold eighth note held one corner of the drawings. James had shared a hot meal with Vera and Twy for the last three nights, and Twyla's zoo collage lunch pail sat open on the counter.

Yes, it was falling in love. If, after eight years, it turned James's house into a home, then what he felt for Vera Waltham couldn't be anything other than falling in love.

~~~

Vera came downstairs after a truly wonderful bath to find James at the piano, his fingers coaxing a soft, sonorous version of Brahms's lullaby from the keys.

"Did Twy ask you for that?"

He nodded as he brought the piece to a sighing, twinkling close.

"We missed your last lesson, James," she said, taking the place beside him.

"We'll make it up." He slid an arm around her waist. "Twy was out like a light, but we called Hannah and made sure the errant book will be at school tomorrow too."

"Good thought." A thought Vera should have had, a practical thought aimed at solving the child's problem, not just yelling at the girl.

"Stop that," James said, jostling Vera gently. "The best mothers have bad days."

"You're not a mom." Though the protest was weak, and she laid her head on his broad and sturdy shoulder.

"I had a mom. I am coming to realize she was a good mom, for the most part, but she didn't plan on the loss of my father, and couldn't find her bearings after he died."

The comment caught Vera's notice, because James seldom brought up his past. For all he wandered Inskip's farm almost daily, he'd never discussed his own boyhood on a farm, never explained why he chose law over agriculture.

"Your mother never considered remarrying?" Vera asked.

"She never looked at another man, and loving that way—" James closed the cover over the keys. "I haven't been serious about a lady because I could not see past what happened to Mom when Dad died."

That had the ring of insight—of recent insight. "What happened?"

He touched the place where the cover could be locked

over the keys, except most piano owners lost the key to the mechanism. Vera's was in her wallet and had been for years.

"Mom held it together for a while," James said, "but she was white-knuckle widowing, pretending to function when anybody was looking. Widows are warned to watch the drinking, but alcohol got the better of her, and she never did shake it."

"Where were your brothers?" Where was anybody—neighbors, church, friends, extended family—who ought to have stepped in?

"Gone, off to college, then to law school. I'm younger. I was the one left at home."

"Mac said something about this." Vera laced her fingers with James's when she wanted instead to play him something comforting, soothing, and healing. "How bad was it?"

He stared at their joined hands.

"Worse than Mac or Trent know. They assume she'd genteelly fall off the wagon every few months, at the holidays, on their anniversary, around the time of Dad's death, but she drank every day too. There were all manner of anniversaries Trent and Mac couldn't see."

And James probably remarked each one, still. "Such as?"

"When the peepers start singing in the spring. The first frost, planting, when the corn comes down in the fall, when the corn tassels midsummer, the first haying, the first calf, the first crocus, the last cutting of hay, the first robin in spring. The entire agricultural year was a reminder of her loss, and I wasn't—"

He used his free hand to trace the gleaming curves of

the piano's empty music stand. "You sure you want to hear this?"

"I want to hear this. It's part of your music, James, and I want to hear it." Part of why he was so naturally attentive, competent, *and sad*.

Why hadn't Vera seen that, when she herself had worn sadness like her favorite concert black outfit?

"I loved my piano lessons," James said. A lament in a handful of words. He'd loved his mother too, no doubt. "Somebody had to drive me to them, because farms are by nature isolated. By the time I was fifteen, Mom wasn't sober enough to drive more days than not when I got home from school, and the deputies caught me driving myself one too many times. They understood—no charges were brought—but I was ashamed. If the authorities had gotten involved, then Mom's situation would become common knowledge."

He turned off the lamp illuminating the music rack, and his grip on Vera's hand became painfully tight.

"I can see now I was only a kid," James said. "At the time, I recall wondering: What would ever be enough for her? I wasn't enough to keep her out of that bottle, the prettiest farm on earth wasn't enough, pride wasn't enough, good health, so many blessings, and still, she hurt and hurt and hurt."

And she'd hurt her youngest son.

"I'm so sorry."

Vera wrapped her arms around him, not knowing what else to say. Was this James's way of explaining that he could never commit to one woman, or was it a confidence he'd share only if he were thinking of committing?

He kissed her knuckles. "This is not a romantic tale."

A change of subject, then. Vera allowed James that dignity before she began weeping on behalf of his younger self.

"It's an honest tale, James, one worth acknowledging. We should be getting to bed, though."

"You want me to stick to my own bed? I can behave, Vera, if that's your concern, but I'd just as soon… You'll be back at your own house tomorrow, and the chance to spend…hell and damnation, this isn't coming out right."

Yes, it was. It was coming out exactly right, though they needed one of those bad-words mason jars for each of their kitchens.

"What are you trying to say, James?"

"I'd like to share a bed with you, and I'm not out to pester you tonight. You're tired, and tomorrow will be a challenge. I've moved some things at work around so I can take Twy to school and you can get your practicing done here, if you like, and I can stop by—"

She put a finger to his lips. "Come up to bed, James. Please?"

Vera had her doubts about James, about his feelings for her, his feelings for his own sister-in-law, his ability to sustain a long-term interest in a woman, given what he'd disclosed about his past.

Those doubts seemed petty when James was spooned around her, drawing patterns of such tenderness on her back and shoulders that Vera almost put off moving back to her own house.

An independent, self-sufficient woman could grow to love sleeping with James Knightley all too easily.

She rose in the morning, feeling more confident of James for having spent the night together, and having thought some about his confessions. He'd shared a story with her Mac and Trent didn't know, and that had to mean something.

When she came downstairs, James was again seated at the piano, but Twyla was beside him, and they were both dressed for the day.

"Your nose goes right here, at middle C," James said. "If you look at where the manufacturer's name is, that will be the C you're looking for."

"This one?" Twyla depressed middle C.

"Right, and we have a system for marking which finger to use on which note, because you only have a few fingers to work with, and there are many keys."

"How many?"

"Eighty-eight on a standard modern piano." He went on to explain how piano fingering symbols worked, and while Vera silently watched, he also matched notes to their places on the bass and the treble clefs.

"I know this one," Twyla chirped. "Every good boy does fine. E-G-B-D-F."

"Yes, but this is my favorite: All cows eat grass because. A-C-E-G-B."

"You're a farmer," Twyla said, giggling. "I'm going to make up a different sentence for the left-hand spaces."

"You're going to eat breakfast while you do," James said, "or you'll be too late to snag your book from Grace."

Twyla's mouth formed into an O, and then her gaze fell on her mother. "Hi, Mom. James is teaching me how to play."

"Good morning." Vera held out her arms to her daughter, and when Twy crossed the music room, Vera hugged her tightly. "Sounded like you're making great progress, Twy."

"James said he didn't start taking lessons until he was nine, and boys are slower than girls. I'm only eight."

"You're also very smart," Vera said around the lump in her throat. "You'll be smarter if you eat breakfast before you take the world by storm."

"Great minds thinking alike," James said. "Or great stomachs. Come on, Twy, and I'll let you have a few of my chocolate chips."

The looming remove back to her house meant Vera didn't taste her granola and strawberries. She was doing the dishes when she felt James's arms come around her from behind.

"I'm taking the prodigy to school," he said. "You'll be here when I get back?"

Of course, she would. "Cavorting with Pischna."

"You know you don't have to leave, Vera? Not today, not until you feel comfortable going back there?"

And if she never wanted to leave? "I'll do it today. Get it over with. Remind Twy where to get off the bus this afternoon."

"Right." James kissed Vera's cheek and stepped away. "You can leave those dishes and start practicing, if you'd rather."

How could she doubt James's interest in her when he was so considerate? But then, he was always a gentleman, always responsible, always kind.

Vera tried to focus on her technique when she had the house to herself, but the idea of playing the same exercises tomorrow under her own roof distracted her. Would the enhanced alarm system make her feel safer than James's presence did?

No, it would not.

She gave up on her music, went upstairs, and packed what few belongings she and Twy had brought over to James's house. They'd been happy here, Twy especially, and James had seemed happy to have the company too.

Vera wanted to make a gesture of thanks, and racked her brain for what would be personal, but not too presumptuous. James had all her CDs; his house was tidy; she'd put some meals in his freezer.

The cookie recipe!

Twy had passed along a brownie recipe, but never completed the one for the raccoon droppings.

Vera beelined for the study, thinking to find pencil and paper. Sure enough, James had a neat stack of scrap paper on one side of his computer. Each page had printing on one side—legalese, it looked like—and the back side was blank.

Vera took a few sheets and brought them to the kitchen table as James came in the back door.

"Mission accomplished," he said, smiling. "We even managed to retrieve that blasted social studies book well in advance of the first bell."

"I'm writing you a recipe," Vera said, sitting down. "Not that I'll leave your cookie tin empty, but I want you to have it." *Her* cookie tin, but she wanted to give James something of her own—besides her heart."

"Anything ready for me to haul out to the car?"

"In the hallway, but take your time." Vera chewed the pencil's eraser, trying to recall a recipe she'd made by heart for years. She turned the paper over and perused the printout on the back side while she thought.

A list of…phone numbers? Every name on the list was female.

Every single one, and there were dozens, and beside each name, a few words: reverse cowgirl, G.O.T., silk necktie…

"James?"

"Sweetheart?" He stood in the doorway, Vera's overnight case in his hand.

"What is this?"

Chapter 16

VERA WORE A PECULIAR EXPRESSION. THAT EXPRESSION made James's insides slide around, though he could not have said why.

"What's what?" he asked, setting down her overnight case.

"What's this list? I found it in the scrap-paper pile beside your computer."

Without even looking, James guessed what was on the page and felt his life—his entire, stupid life—grinding to a halt.

"It's a list." The Chopin Funeral March started in his head.

"I can see that. What sort of list?"

"A scrap-paper sort of list. You ready to go yet?"

Vera wasn't buying it, and any prevaricating would just dig him a deeper, colder hole.

"What sort of scrap-paper list?"

"It's old business, Vera, over and done. I don't use that list anymore, and I never really did. Can we drop it?"

She stood and backed away from the table, as if that single sheet of paper carried a deadly toxin.

"You kept a list, a long, detailed list, but you never used it. What's reverse cowgirl?"

Oh, God. "A position, an intimate position."

"G.O.T.?"

James wanted to lie, to prevaricate, to disappear. "Girl on top."

Vera crossed her arms. "Silk necktie, I suppose that speaks for itself. What would you put beside my name, James?"

Wife. What he wanted to put beside her name was his own, but he was increasingly doubtful he could make that happen, and all over a stupid, stupid, stupid piece of paper.

"I threw the list out because I won't use it ever again, Vera. I have no former spouses, I'm not raising a child, I'm not dragging around the dregs of a nasty divorce or a failed restraining order, but I also wasn't born yesterday. That list is part of my past, but I'm standing here still hoping you're my future."

He'd beg if that would help—but it wouldn't. Vera was three for three in the guys-who'd-let-her-down department. She clearly intended to maintain her streak.

"You kept a list of their favorite positions and their favorite games." She bent over the table and began counting names, until James snatched the paper away from her, balled it up, and fired it at the wastebasket.

"You're hurt because you think this reduces what I feel for you to a name on a list or some bedroom toy, but, Vera, it isn't like that."

"It's never like that, is it?" She stared out the window at Inskip's heifers, who were for once behind their assigned fences. "Take me home, James."

"Vera, I was the toy. Me. James. I was the one they called when they needed a pity night or a flirt or a wingman to flaunt before their exes. I don't take their calls anymore. They've stopped calling, in fact."

He was desperate to make her understand, but this was Vera. Her own confidence was none too sturdy, and all his protestations were having the wrong effect.

"Take me home *now*, James, or so help me, I will call your brothers to come fetch me, and they will ask questions, which I will be happy to answer."

Old hurt, from dealing with a grieving, unreasonable woman and having no idea how to get through to her, made James desperate.

"Vera, will you at least *listen*?"

"I am listening, James, and what I'm hearing is that you pick up wounded birds and get off on fixing their broken wings. I'm not a bird, and I'm not wounded in any way your magic wand can fix. Take. Me. Home."

"For God's sake, Vera, *I'm the damned wounded bird*." He picked up her satchel and Twyla's smaller bag and made for his car. They drove the short distance in silence, and when they got out at her house, James felt ten times a fool.

"I suppose you and Twy planted these?" Vera's tone gave nothing away as she stood gazing at the flowers bordering her front walk, her porch, and the beds around the front of the house.

"Pansies are hardy as hell," James said. "They can take frost and even snow. My—my mother always had them out in buckets well before April Fool's Day."

Which had apparently come early this year, in colors of blue, yellow, white, orange, purple, brown, and even peach.

"You had to have bought out the store, James." Was there a question in Vera's eyes?

"This is your home. I wanted you to feel happy to be here. I'll put your bags inside."

Vera spent a few minutes wandering among the flowers, and James used the time to check each room of the house. The alarm system was installed, and the stickers were up on the windows to let all potential intruders know it.

Assuming the intruders were literate and could read in the dark.

"I've been through the house," James said when he joined Vera in the kitchen. "The place is secure, and you're the only one here besides me."

"My thanks."

Vera Waltham's chilly side was close to absolute zero, but James was damned if he'd let her freeze him out entirely.

"Are we back where we started, Vera? With me trespassing and you kicking me out?" He didn't want to see her impassive expression, so he stood at the kitchen window and started counting the idiot pansies in the bed outside. He knew how many he'd planted, because he had indeed bought out the store's entire inventory.

Pansies. How appropriate was that?

Vera took the place beside him.

"I like you, James, and yet I hate that list. I hate knowing that about you."

"I'm not too proud of it myself." He was ashamed, in fact. The admission cost him. Men were supposed to thrive on notching their bedposts, swinging their mighty swords with reckless abandon, but in reality—

He'd let himself be a notch on far too many bedposts.

Vera said nothing for a long moment, until James was mentally squirming and fighting back useless declarations. If he opened his mouth now, he'd plead, and that was too pathetic to be borne.

"I need to think about this, James. We're adults, we each have pasts, but those pasts have made us who we are. I might not be so upset if you'd told me about this yourself."

Well, of course. Let her think she would have responded more reasonably when he casually dropped the list on her over their one real lunch date. When, between the salads and the entrées, he'd confessed to being a well-dressed, well-educated tramp.

"Shall I stop by after work tonight?" He managed that question in a level tone.

"I think not. Let me and Twy get back to the routine here, and then maybe…we'll see."

"My lesson on Friday?" That was begging, of course. Shameless begging.

"I don't know."

He told himself an I-don't-know was worlds better than a damn-you-get-off-my-property, but it didn't feel much better.

"I will answer any question you ask, Vera. I didn't bring up the details of my past because they didn't seem relevant to what's growing between us."

"You'd say that, no matter how or when I found your list."

In other words, she had listened as much as she could for one day, and though a prudent man would understand all hope was lost, James was not given to prudence where Vera was concerned.

"Call me if you need anything, Vera. Anything at all, at any hour."

"Call you?" She shook her head. But when James bent his head to kiss her cheek, she turned her face so their mouths met.

That kiss gave him hope. As kisses went, it was a detail, one more kiss in a long string of kisses. Maybe the kiss should have meant farewell, or it should have meant nothing.

To James, it meant the world.

—⁓—

Vera made herself walk through every room of the house, unpack her clothes, and sit down at the piano to work through her finger exercises before Twyla came home. While one part of her mind attended to her practicing, another part circled around questions without any answers.

Why had James kept that list? Or had he truly tossed it out, left it in his pile of scrap paper because it honestly held no more meaning for him?

Did all men keep such a list, or were they more like Alexander, freelance philanderers?

Why had James left that list in a place Vera might find it? Or had the list simply slipped his mind, because James could not have foreseen that she and Twyla would be his house guests?

Why was he so inordinately prone to embracing his new sister-in-law? Family histories revolved endlessly around tales of a woman who married the wrong brother.

Who was Grace's father?

Vera tortured herself for an entire two-hour practice session, then turned to her repertoire and tortured herself some more.

How could a man make love the way James had made love with her, when he was emotionally entangled with other women, possibly with his own brother's wife?

Or was that the reason James was in such demand—
because he was *that good* in bed? A virtuoso, capable
of creating in every woman he was with the fiction that
he loved her.

What on earth did it mean that James himself was the
wounded bird?

Vera stewed and fretted and fussed, thrashing through
questions and music and more questions until Twyla
came banging in the door.

"You weren't at the bottom of the lane," Twyla said,
looking puzzled. "I like the gate, though."

"I'm sorry." Guilt punched through Vera's preoccu-
pations and questions. "I lost track of the time, and I
should have been there."

"You don't have to be. I don't like the walk so much
when it's pouring, but I'm not little anymore. I can
ramble up the lane by myself."

Ramble. James's word.

"I put your things on your bed," Vera said. "I forgot
the cookie tin at James's though, so we'll have to make
do without until I can replace it."

"I'll call James, and he can bring it over." A grin split
Twyla's face as she turned toward the kitchen.

Vera rose from the piano bench and trotted after her.
"That might not be such a good idea, Twy."

The child paused in the middle of dialing James's
number. "Why not?"

"He might think we left the cookies for him, as a
thank-you." James might not be gracious when he
returned the tin, and Vera did not trust herself to handle
that well.

Not yet.

Twyla put the phone down. "Should I send him a thank-you note?"

"That would be polite. And thank you very much for all the pansies. They really make the property look brighter."

"James said they'd cheer the house up, but he was being silly. Did you make brownies yet?"

"Not yet." More guilt, or preoccupation. "Why don't you start a batch? I'll put my music away and then join you."

"Deal." Twyla whisked up the steps two at a time.

How long would Vera be haunted by James Knightley? Being stalked by Donal was bad, but in some ways, the lingering questions between her and James were worse.

—∿∿—

"First you're not dating," Mac said, "now the secretaries are complaining that you're not even flirting. What's wrong?"

James looked up from the real estate ads marching down his computer screen when he ought to be…doing some damned piece of legal bullshit.

"I don't recall inviting you into my confessional, MacKenzie. How about you go make us some money off a crime wave somewhere?"

Though the only crime wave James cared about was happening on Vera's property.

"For shame, maligning defendant's rights." Mac perched a hip on James's desk, making the wood creak and James's sense of irritation spike. "Hannah mentioned that she hasn't caught you practicing your putts. The golf courses will be open in less than a month, James."

"Hannah's concerned about my game?"

James really, truly wanted his brother to leave him the hell alone, but Mac was more perceptive than he let on, and he meant well—usually.

Mac picked up a commercial law periodical and flipped through the pages. "The home place is for sale again."

Casual as a stampeding herd of heifers, that observation. "I know, MacKenzie."

"You want to buy it?"

"Why would I buy it? I spent five years trying to farm that place when I was little more than a child, and my memories of it leave something to be desired."

Mac eyed the door, which was…closed.

Crap.

"I always have the sense you haven't put all your cards on the table, James. Mom took to tippling, but Southern ladies will do that, discreetly of course. Why can't you just be relieved she didn't start hanging out on hookup websites, or going on clothing-optional cruises?"

An image of James's mother assailed him. "For God's sake, Mac, leave it alone."

"The anniversary of her death is next week," Mac said, putting the magazine down. "It's been more than a decade, James. When will you let her rest in peace?"

"Shut your mouth, MacKenzie. If you want to go best out of three falls, I'm game. I can afford to replace whatever furniture we damage."

"But I cannot afford to replace you," Mac said softly, "and every year, I feel a little more like I'm losing my brother. Oh, I have a crack-shot law partner to show for it, but law partners are thick on the ground compared to the number of people I love. Now what in the goddamn hopeless hell is it going to take to get through to you?"

James rose, had to move, had to move away from his brother before he decked the guy. "Vera found my phone list."

Mac waved a hand in circles. "The list with all the…"

"Yeah, that list. I've deleted it from every place I recall storing it, but I kept hard-copy backups. I thought I'd shredded all of those, but one lurked in the scrap-paper pile at home. She was writing down a damned cookie recipe for me… Crap and half. Why am I telling you this?"

Mac stayed planted on the corner of James's desk when any other man would have sauntered out the door.

"You're telling me this because you're going nuts, stewing in your own juices. Can you fix this?"

James didn't need to turn to see the rare light of sympathy in Mac's eyes. He could hear it in his brother's voice.

"I don't know, Mac. Mom taught me something."

"She taught us all a lot of things."

"She taught me you can't make a woman care, not about you, not about living, not about her own land, not about anything."

"Harsh, James." Now Mac got his ass off the desk and came to stand beside James at the window. "Mom didn't want to contract ovarian cancer."

"And she didn't accept a single experimental protocol they offered her, either, did she? Didn't even consider them for twenty-four hours."

"Ovarian cancer is bad, James."

James's mother had not died of ovarian cancer, she'd died of a broken heart. To be the only Knightley brother who understood that had abruptly become too great a burden.

"MacKenzie, do you know what it's like to be fifteen years old, having to give your mother a bath because she's passed out in her own vomit again? Gotten it in her hair, her clothes, left broken glass all over the kitchen floor?"

"So she had a bad moment." Mac dropped like a boulder onto James's couch, and he was repeatedly scrubbing his hand over his face. "Losing someone you love is hard."

"After a few years, that happened more nights than not, Mac, and as for losing someone you love, we all lost Dad, then I lost you, Trent, and the mother I grew up with." James said it quietly, gently almost, but he could not keep the words behind his teeth. "Mom would have no recollection the next day—I hope she had no recollection—and yet she'd get into the car and go buy herself more liquor, no matter how often I destroyed her stash. I had to go to school—just to get away from her. I had to go to school—but I hated leaving her alone."

Mac was staring straight ahead, as if by visually ignoring James, he could make the words less true.

"You never said anything."

"She begged me not to, told me time and again she was going to stop, she was going to get help, she was going to pray for the strength to deal with it. She'd even straighten up for a time if you or Trent were coming home between terms."

"I'm—" Mac swallowed and sat forward, his forearms braced on his thighs. "I thought it was the occasional lapse, an embarrassment, or an indulgence she was due. I never—Christ on a John Deere tractor."

"I disabled the stove when I wasn't home," James said.

"She nearly burned the house down twice, trying to cook while she was drunk. Toward the end, I took her keys, but she called a locksmith and claimed she'd misplaced her set. I took her money, took her credit cards, and she cried and asked me what she was supposed to do in an emergency. Then she was off again, always able to buy her booze but somehow completely uninterested in buying groceries. I hated her, Mac. *I hated my own mother.* You think it's grief I feel at the thought of her death, but I assure you, there's as much guilt as anything else."

James found himself sitting beside his brother. The spoken words, for all they were words of sorrow rather than anger, shocked him in their honesty.

They must have shocked Mac too, because he was silent for long moments.

"You must hate me and Trent too," Mac said eventually, "but, James, you did not kill that woman. Now that I hear what you've been carrying around, I'm not even sure it was the cancer that got her."

A glimmer of truth, and all James felt was a crushing sadness. "You saw her, that one Easter."

"I told myself it was the holiday, the sense of life renewing itself in the spring for everybody but not for Dad. I didn't want to see what was in front of my eyes, and so I cleaned your clock when you tore into her."

"She and I went at it much worse than that," James said tiredly. "Then she'd forget, until the next blowup."

"Every night, James?"

For years, nearly every night, unless Mac or Trent was due home for a visit. "Sometimes, she'd get so mad she'd smack me when I hid her bottles or took a bottle away. Then she'd cry and start in with the promises.

Getting smacked was so much easier than listening to her promises, Mac, and, God almighty, I wanted to belt some sense into her."

"But you didn't."

James was not so far gone into introspection and memory that his brother's words were lost to him, but for some reason, they didn't land easily in his mind.

"Say that again, Mac."

"You did not strike her, did not give in to the urge to slap her. You kept her confidences, though she was abusing you and betraying you as a mother at every turn. Of course you hated her, James. But you also loved her."

James had to clear his throat. Allergies were starting early this year. "Did not. Could not."

"Bullshit. You don't care for a woman that way, watch her fall to pieces time after time, keep her secrets, and protect her dignity as best you can without loving her. You were a *child*, James. You were her child, regardless of how strong, tall, smart, and clever you were. *You loved her.*"

James rose to put some space between him and a brother who saw too much too late. "I did not. I could not."

Because if he'd loved his mother, she'd turned her back on his love too. The love of the only child remaining under her roof, the only member of her family to still share her home.

"You loved her," Mac said again. "You did, and, James, I am so damned sorry."

⌒⌒⌒

Mac spent almost two hours in James's office, mostly listening, occasionally asking a question. James would have said there was nothing to talk about, but he admitted to himself he would have been wrong. The staff had the good sense to see they were undisturbed, and when James got to his feet, he could not recall what he'd been doing when Mac had walked in.

"What about Vera?" Mac asked as James made a slow circuit of the room.

"She's had a couple of rough marriages, Mac. Trust isn't her strong suit." Nor apparently was it James's, so they were zero for two in the long-term commitment category. Not good odds.

Mac was back to roosting on the corner of the desk. "So that's it? You'll ride off into the sunset, older and wiser?"

"And sadder. But grateful too." Also minus one long, sorry list of wrong turns.

"That is pure, unadulterated tripe, James Knightley. Vera is not Mom. She won't let you go just because she hit a rough patch with you."

This from the guy who'd not been on date in years? "Vera did let me go, Mac."

"So get up on your hind legs and fight for her."

"Easy for you to say." James collected a stray belly putter and nine iron from his umbrella stand and stashed them into the coat closet. This was a law office, after all.

"No, it is not easy for me to say," Mac retorted. "Neither is this: I would rather you up and quit the firm than watch you go through another year like last year. You hit on Hannah."

"That was"—stupid wrapped in pathetic tied up in asinine—"that was a trial balloon to see if she was serious about Trent." A mashie that had belonged to James's grandfather lurked behind the door. James hefted the club, rather than consign it to the closet.

"Right, a trial balloon." Mac did sarcasm well, well enough that James was back to wanting to deck him. "*You hit on Hannah.* You hit on every secretary in this building and half the female associates who weren't nailed down in a marriage. You dated your clients, your competition, and I had my doubts about your neighbor's heifers."

"*MacKenzie.*"

"What I'm trying to say is this: you were going to pieces, James, and all Trent and I could do was watch while you worked harder and played harder. Vera Waltham waltzes into your life, and suddenly, you're taking time off. You're playing the piano. You're finally interviewing the associates who can take some of the load off your shoulders. You're taking in those equine Chia Pets Trent bought. You did most of the parenting when we watched Grace and Merle, you've taken the time to make a big impression on Vera's daughter, and for the first time in more than ten goddamned benighted years, *you've talked to me.*"

Mac was on his feet, staring out the window as a muscle jumped in his jaw. Had they really not *talked* since their mother had died?

"I like Vera Waltham," Mac went on. "I don't like anybody, except my family. I think Vera could be family, James. Your family, and thus mine too. You've never been a quitter. Never. You didn't give up on Mom, and I hope to God you haven't given up on Trent and me. If you need to bow out of the practice of law, go. We'll manage without a corporate law partner. We will not manage without our brother."

Those words were precious, also unnecessary. "You finished, MacKenzie?"

Mac scowled at him over his shoulder. "I am, and it will take me another decade to recover from this little tête-à-tête, James."

While James would recall it for the rest of his life. "You going to buy the home place, Mac?"

Another scowl, more thoughtful.

"Nah. Farms take family, and that means recruiting a brood mare, and I'm getting too old for that."

James took a half swing with the vintage golf club. "You're ancient. Remember me in your will."

"Shut up, and make Vera give you another chance."

"Maybe I will, and, Mac?" Mac turned this time. The Knightley men could be first-class fools and even sluts, but they weren't cowards.

"What now?" Mac asked.

"Thanks."

James's words lodged in Vera's memory like a vamp, a few bars of music repeated over and over until the actor on stage was ready to burst into song. What did it mean when a man called himself a wounded bird?

She made herself wait a few more days, teaching lessons that were hard to focus on, watering the pansies when they went five days without rain, and listening to Twyla mention James in every other sentence.

When Friday rolled around, Vera got her technique out of the way, made a batch of brownies, and squared her mental shoulders. If James was home, she'd ask him for an explanation, and for some assurances.

For the first time in her life, she was in love, not with a piece of music, not with an instrument of wood and metal, but with a flesh-and-blood man who was only human. If she loved James, she owed him an open mind, and some trust. Not a lot, but more than she'd shown him so far.

And if he loved her—

She cut that thought off as she turned her truck up his lane. As Vera drove by, Inskip's cows placidly chewed their cud while they eyed the greener pasture of James's front lawn. Vera's foot hit the brake, her car rocking on its tires.

Hannah's blue Prius sat in James's driveway in the middle of a Friday. The children were in school, and Vera knew the law office was open, because Trent had left her a message earlier in the day.

What could possibly explain why Hannah's car was parked in James's driveway, when by rights, both Hannah and James ought to be at work?

James paused in his playing, bringing Beethoven to a resonate cadence. He could have sworn he'd heard something, tires maybe on his gravel driveway, but when he looked, he saw nothing but Hannah's little Prius sitting where he'd left it last night.

He went back to his playing. He'd tuned up the car, changed the oil, and would trade cars with Hannah again tonight, but for now…

He played Chopin. He played the waltzes, and the nocturnes, going through the little E minor at the end of the book repeatedly. The passion of it reminded him of Vera, and of the few nights he'd spent with her.

Since he and Mac had passed most of an afternoon rehashing family business, his brothers had found reasons to keep an eye on him, aided and abetted by Hannah. His brothers, James could have easily dodged—he'd spent more than a decade dodging them, hadn't he?— but Hannah looked at him with those big brown eyes, and he could not find it in himself to bark at her.

Hannah brought him cookies. Trent stopped by to pick up Grace's unicorn box of pencils. Mac had to borrow a tool, when Mac's own shop was a shade-tree mechanic's paradise.

Then Mac had to return the tool; Hannah had to fetch her cookie tin; and Trent had to come by and inspect Wellie and Jo as James groomed, long-lined, lunged, and coaxed them into a semblance of their former glory.

Trent said the horse and pony were ready to be added to the family herd, while James was reluctant to part with them. Josephine in particular was a treat-hussy, and needed patience if she was to mend her ways.

Grace told James that Twyla had passed along greetings to him, and James damned near adopted himself a dog so they'd all back off.

When he wasn't at work, breaking in his new underlings, he was home playing the piano, fussing Wellie and Jo, or out walking the greening fields.

The winter wheat was reaching for the sky again; the daffodils were up all along the lanes and hedgerows. Canada geese honked on their way homeward, and James spotted robins in his yard. When he heard the first peepers chirping in the woods one night, he realized Vera wasn't going to come to him.

He would have to go to her, and soon.

"I cannot believe he'd do this to me." Vera heard the tremor in her voice and unclenched her fingers from the strap of her purse.

"Slow, deep breaths," Trent said in the exact, well-meant tone of voice guaranteed to piss Vera off. "Anybody can bring suit against anybody, Vera. It's supposedly how our society handles conflict without violence."

"But, Trent, this is worse than when Donal raised his hand to me. That was a blow, plain and simple. It hurt, I knew it was wrong, and I suspect Donal would admit as much if I confronted him."

"Which you will not do." Now, he used his Stern Daddy voice, which was no improvement. "Suing you over the performance contracts is a way to stay connected to you, Vera, a legal way. Donal probably anticipates that you'll attempt to confront him, and he'll have what he wants."

"Which is?" And why did what Donal wanted matter?

"Maybe he wants a sense that he controls you? Or a renewed connection? The satisfaction of getting your goat once and for all?"

Vera tried to follow Trent's reasoning when she'd rather have thrown his little glass statue of Justice against the wall.

"Getting my goat by making me perform?" She loved to perform, mostly. Or she had once upon a time.

"You haven't canceled these dates," Trent reminded her, "and Donal does have third-party beneficiary status with respect to your performance contracts."

The pear trees in the parking lot were starting to

bloom, the grass was turning green, and the tops of the oak trees were showing a pale, reddish cast. Why did trees that would eventually leaf out green look red—and what did it matter if Donal was a third-party whatever?

"You OK?" Trent spoke from close enough beside her that Vera could catch a whiff of his aftershave. Something of James echoed in him, in his tone of voice, in his build, in his blue eyes, but the scent was wrong.

The feel was wrong.

"I'm rattled," she said, missing James very much, particularly when she knew he was likely right down the hall, possibly on the phone with one of the ladies on his infernal list.

"You look a little tired, Vera. Things going OK with the music?"

"That's not a legal question."

"There's more to me than my law degree."

Was Trent *scolding* her? Reminding her he was James's brother?

Vera paced back to the couch and took a seat. Where was a piano when she needed one?

"My music is doing better than ever, at least in my own opinion. Something has come together, between my heart and my hands, something I don't know how to teach my students, something I can't even properly describe with words."

Olga approved though. Vera had played for her twice in recent days, and Olga's praise had been nerve-rackingly effusive, while her sly references to Vera's "young man" had been simply nerve-racking.

Whatever was afoot with Vera's music, a grieving

Bach, a deaf Beethoven, and a lonely Brahms had all understood it well.

James might have understood what Vera was saying; Trent could not. But then, Trent was happy practicing law, and with respect to James's sense of a legal vocation, the jury was still out.

"I'm tempted to keep the damned dates," she said. "It's what Donal wants, and while you say he's trying to control me, his agenda could well be purely financial. He's broke, and without me to represent, all he has is that damned house." And two teenagers in a world of hurt.

"That house is worth a pretty penny," Trent commented.

"*If* he can sell it, but then where do his children finish growing up? Does he make Katie change schools halfway through high school?"

Katie, who hadn't exchanged a word with Vera for months.

Trent took a seat not beside her, but in the armchair at an angle to the couch.

"That is not your problem, Vera. They are not your children. They have a mother and a father, and they're not infants." Trent spoke gently, but his words were no comfort. Had he told himself James was not his problem when his younger brother struggled to keep an alcoholic mother from harm, while he also ran a farm and carried a full load of advanced placement classes?

That thought was petty, unkind, *and none of Vera's business*.

"I'll think about this, Trent. How long do I have to file something in response?"

"Thirty days, but, Vera, I want you to consider something else." His expression was cautious, something of a novelty in Vera's experience with her lawyer.

"Spit it out, Trent. I'm a big girl. Donal can't go after custody of Twy, and not much else matters."

Except James. He mattered, and Vera didn't know what to do about that.

"I am not an expert on contract law," Trent said. "I know enough to navigate the ins and outs of separation agreements, but Donal is referencing the contract you signed that made him your agent—years ago—and there will be clauses in that document I've never seen. I've never tried a case involving third-party beneficiary rights. I don't know the case law. I'm not an expert on the laws of agency, which is a fairly complicated concept from a legal standpoint."

"You're dumping me?" Every man in her life had been dumping her or disappointing her since her own father had—

Insight rippled over her, half chill, half tingle. If the first man in a girl's life leaves her, does she then choose men who can fulfill an expectation of disappointment?

Does she shoehorn every guy she cares about into that same posture?

Chapter 17

"I'M NOT DUMPING YOU," TRENT SAID, THE VERY IRRI-
tability of his tone assuring Vera he was sincere. "I
accepted service of process on your behalf, and that
means we're joined at the legal wrist, if you want it that
way, for the duration of the litigation. You have a wiser
choice though."

Vera's heart sped up as that skittery tingle suffused
her limbs. "You want me to retain James?"

"I want you to have the most competent representation this firm can offer, and that would be James. No
question, your best hope of getting what you want out
of this suit is to entrust yourself to James."

Tried that… Or had she? "Trent, you're talking like a
lawyer, and I appreciate that, but James and I aren't… I
don't think we're…"

He crossed his arms. Vera had seen him do the same
thing when he was making a witness squirm on cross-
examination, so she tried again.

"Whatever was between your brother and me, I don't
think it's going anywhere."

Putting that into words hurt. Badly. B-flat-minor
badly.

"Then you shouldn't mind having him represent you.
James is a gentleman, and adept at keeping work and
play separate when he has to. Come on." Trent was at the
door, holding it open for her. "We'll brace him together,

and if he's uncomfortable at the thought of representing you, he'll be honest enough to say so."

Vera let Trent escort her to James's office, the door to which was open. James was on the phone, but he motioned Trent into the room, then came to his feet when Vera followed Trent.

"Then you tell them to call me," James said into the receiver. "I can explain it to them, their lawyers, their mamas, or their dancing pet ferrets, and when I do, they'll either sign the contract or walk."

His voice held a thread of steel, one Vera hadn't heard before. She used the moment while James concluded the call to examine him more closely.

Around his mouth and eyes, fatigue had left faint lines. His tie was loosened, his cuffs turned back, and his suit coat hung over the back of his chair. His desk, usually tidy in the extreme, sported a half-dozen files piled on top of each other, and two fat brown books that were opened to reveal tiny dark print in two columns on each page.

James really was a lawyer. Somehow, Vera hadn't realized it the way she was realizing it now.

"Vera, a pleasure, as always." He extended his hand to her but didn't move from behind the desk.

Ouch. When what Vera wanted was to feel James's arms around her, to breathe in his woodsy scent, to feel the warmth and strength of his body against hers. Ouch.

"Vera has a problem," Trent said, gesturing to one of James's guest chairs. Vera took the chair, and Trent took the second guest chair. "Donal is suing her for specific performance of her contracts with a half-dozen venues, using his status as third-party beneficiary to do so. She might be within her rights to cancel the dates, but I haven't seen the language, and this isn't my area of legal expertise."

James was quiet for a moment, then he swung his gaze to Vera. "Are you asking me to represent you?"

"Trent said you're the best."

Vera felt about two inches tall, like somebody ought to hold her accountable for the consequences of her actions, *Veracity Penelope Waltham*. She couldn't be bothered to talk to James about their personal problems, but here she was, willing to use his legal talent for her own benefit.

And oh, she'd pay him, of course. What did that make her?

"There you are." Hannah Knightley appeared in James's doorway, her gaze on her husband. "Vera, I didn't know you were here. I'm sorry for interrupting. Trent, I'll be in my office when you're ready to go."

She withdrew with a little wave, and Trent glanced at the clock on the wall. James looked, if anything, irritated at the interruption.

"Has Donal filed his complaint yet?" James asked.

"I have it," Trent said. "I'll pass it along to your assistant and leave you two to discuss strategy."

"Vera hasn't accepted my representation."

"Yes, I have," Vera said, "and you have my thanks as well for taking the case."

Trent followed his wife from the office, and a silence stretched. Awkward, jagged silence, full of wrong notes and regrets.

"You truly don't want to go back to performing?" James asked.

Insightful, of course. James was wickedly insightful. "You think I should?"

A question for a question. Vera was spending too much time around lawyers.

Or not enough.

"You enjoy the performing, Vera, but if you do go back to it, it should be on your terms. Where is this tour?"

Why was James the only person to ever insist on that—that the music be on her terms?

"This tour is in Europe, a four-week hitch, six performances, some master classes, lectures in England, a recital with an Irish tenor. It would be lucrative."

"Would you enjoy it?"

Blessed Saint Anthony, Vera had missed James badly. Missed the steady regard in his eyes, the way he cut to the quick of any issue and put it in perspective for her without getting his own agenda involved.

"I don't know, James. There's the whole business of what to do with Twy, but the dates aren't until next summer. I have time to figure that out."

James tidied up the case files and closed the law books, so his desk assumed a more orderly appearance.

"You also have time to think about this lawsuit," he said. "We don't have to file an answer for a few weeks, and I can usually make room for negotiation."

He hadn't tried to negotiate with Vera, not since she'd cut him loose weeks ago.

"What sort of room?"

James explained his thinking to her: A shorter tour, a smaller cut for Donal, an exchange of these venues for those much closer to home, all manner of variables and combinations that would avoid litigation, get Vera some concert exposure, and back Donal down, if not defeat him entirely.

"You truly are brilliant at this," she said when they'd spent some time parsing the possibilities. "But do *you* enjoy it?"

James pursed his lips—lips Vera had kissed on not enough occasions.

"I'm thinking about that lately. I don't know the answer." He settled back in his chair and regarded her from across his desk. "You doing OK, Vera?"

No. I miss you. I miss you. I miss you. Have you started a new list?

"I'm managing. You?"

He paced to the window, turning his back to her. "What do you want me to say, Vera? I can pretend I'm doing fine—I see now that I've become expert at that—but there's an ache—" He scrubbed his hand over his nape. His hair needed a trim. "I'm managing too. Tell Twyla I said hi, and that Inskip's cows are leaving babies all over the pasture."

"Which she will want to come see. She misses you." An admission, but James looked merely puzzled to hear it.

"James, what's going on between you and Hannah?" The question came out, no forethought, no planning. No warning to even Vera herself.

"Hannah? She's married to Trent. I love her, and I love her daughter. They're family." He looked more than puzzled now; he looked bewildered.

"You have her favorite tea, I've seen her in your embrace more frequently than her own husband's, you're the first person she came to visit after cutting her honeymoon short, and you look at her daughter as if—"

"You think I'd poach on my brother's preserves? You think I'd—But then, you've seen my list, and you probably think I'm the Damson Valley booty call of the decade."

No, Vera did not. At her most doubtful and upset, she hadn't quite been able to believe that about him.

"I don't know what to think," Vera said, "but I've seen you with that woman in your arms on more occasions than a mere brother-in-law could easily claim, and at least once, James, she was in tears."

Vera didn't tell him she'd seen Hannah's car in his driveway. Let him volunteer an explanation for that. Please, God, let him volunteer an innocent explanation for that.

"There's nothing clandestine between me and Hannah, and that's all I can tell you. I love her, she's family, and I love Grace. But it's not—it's nothing I would ever be ashamed of."

It's not what you think by any other name.

Also not the reassurance Vera had been longing to hear—far from it—but not protesting too much, either.

"There's something, James, isn't there?"

Unrequited passion on his part, maybe. A crush at least?

"Not something I can discuss. Not now."

"Someday?"

How pathetic was the catch in her voice? How painful was the thought of having no somedays with James, ever?

James shifted the painting of porch flowers a quarter inch, so it hung absolutely plumb.

"I can't promise that either, Vera. All I can tell you is I'm not in love with my sister-in-law." He gave the words particular emphasis, but still, he was holding back.

Withholding.

"Then I guess we're at a standstill. A grand pause."

"Which is usually followed by a virtuosic cadenza."

He would get the musical analogy. "If the piece features a soloist," Vera said. And apparently it did. Two soloists, who weren't to perform together. "I'll see myself out, James, and thanks again for taking this case."

He did not walk her to her truck. That was fortunate, because Vera was in tears before she crossed the parking lot.

James toyed with the idea of buying the home place, and even made an appointment to walk through it with a real estate agent. The previous owner had died, a sister had inherited, and the price suggested she was testing the waters more than looking to flip the place.

The house was in good shape, but James didn't make an offer. Mac had been right: a farm, a real working farm, was an enterprise for family, at least in western Maryland, and James could not envision starting a family with anybody but the lady who'd already lost faith him.

So he walked his own land, and after the moon rose, he walked Inskip's woods. The peepers were singing, the occasional owl hooted, and the deer came mincing down their trails to graze the pastures.

His steps took him nowhere in particular until he realized he was at the tree line facing Vera's property.

Again.

James found a fallen log and sat himself down on it, watching for the flickering shadows that would tell him Vera was still awake.

She'd had doubts about James's regard for Hannah, and if he'd known—if he'd had the *least* inkling of her suspicions, he might have done a better job of fielding her questions.

No, not might have. He *would have* spelled the situation out for her somehow without crossing the lines he could not ethically cross. He would have done better than a dumbstruck silence Vera could construe in only the worst possible light.

He would do better, in fact. He'd rehearsed his speech, polished it, learned it by heart, and even practiced it.

James was considering knocking on Vera's door when a shadow moved around the side of the house. The figure knelt, and James had to wait for the moon to come out from behind a cloud to make out what was happening.

Somebody was pulling up the pansies, plant by plant.

James was already on his feet when his cell phone buzzed.

He turned his body to make sure no telltale glow gave away his position, and hit answer.

"James?" Vera, and she was whispering.

"I'm right here."

"Thank God. I'm home, Twyla's upstairs asleep, and I swear there's somebody outside. I didn't want to bother you, but you're much closer than the sheriffs, and what if it's only a raccoon… Are you there?"

"Vera, are the doors locked?"

"Always, but I haven't enabled the alarm system yet for the night."

"You're safe as long as the house is locked up tight.

Stay away from the windows and get upstairs. I'm on my way, and the bastard won't know what hit him."

"Be careful, James."

"Always. Upstairs now, Vera, and away from the windows."

He closed the phone, slid it into a pocket, and with years of wandering in the woods and fields to his credit, made a soundless approach to the house. James was so silent, in fact, that he was able to creep right up on the intruder, knee the idiot flat to the sidewalk, and knock the breath right out of him.

"MacKay, if it weren't for the tenderheartedness of the woman in that house, I'd take pleasure in reading your beads until you were blind in both eyes and singing soprano. Now on your feet, and move."

James hauled his captive up by the scruff of the neck, kept him in a half nelson, and frog-marched him to Vera's front door.

"Ring the damned bell, MacKay, and start praying."

———※———

How could James have gotten to her property so fast?

Vera was halfway down the stairs before it occurred to her James might not be at her door. It could be a trap, a decoy…

She kept the lights off and went to the bay window in the music room, where she could peer out and see James Knightley on her front porch, a shorter man standing right in front of him.

She turned on lights and went to the foyer, keeping the chain over the top lock as she cracked the door.

"*Darren?* What on earth…?"

"Your vandal," James said. "Or one of them. At the very least he was pulling up your flowers, and God knows what else he's been up to."

Vera opened the door, feeling sucker-punched. Darren? The kid she'd struggled through quadratic equations with? The one she'd taught how to make coffee? The one who played video games with Twy and scarfed down brownies in her kitchen?

"I do not believe this," she muttered, leading the way to the kitchen. "I don't want to believe it. Did your father put you up to this?"

"It's not like that," Darren said. "Call off your pit bull, and I can explain."

James met Vera's gaze, and only then did she realize James had Darren's arm hiked halfway up his back.

"He deserves a chance to explain, James."

"He was vandalizing your property, which is thoroughly posted against trespassers, Vera. Can we at least call his parents, so you get the same explanation they do?"

The suggestion was reasonable, but James still had Darren in an uncomfortable grip. "Darren can call them, both of them."

James let the boy go.

"Use the phone in the study, Darren," Vera said. "Get your mom over here too."

The kid shuffled off, throwing a relieved look over his shoulder.

While Vera felt abruptly weak-kneed. What if James hadn't come, and how had he arrived so quickly, and what was she supposed to say to him now?

"You want me to leave?" James asked.

"*No.*" Vera had nearly shouted the word. "No," she said more quietly. "I do not want you to leave."

"Maybe you should have Trent here," James said. "He's your domestic relations attorney, and this promises to be domestic as hell, if not criminal."

James was angry on Vera's behalf, despite weeks of silence between them. She wanted to hug him, but didn't dare for fear she'd start bawling like one of Inskip's heifers.

"Why get Trent here?" she asked.

"I'm guessing if we compare Darren's prints with the ones left on your computer, we'll find he's been here at least once before—and you gave him a key to the house, Vera. That would explain how he got in, but not why he's been threatening you."

"Mom and Dad are on their way," Darren said, hanging in the kitchen doorway. "I can explain."

"Call Trent," James said, holding out his cell phone to Vera and not even looking at Darren. "Ask him to bring Hannah along."

Her again? Vera stared at his cell phone warily. "Why Hannah?"

"She's a professional mediator, and you're about to meet up with the man who nearly put you in the hospital, while you accuse his son of delinquent acts." James slapped the phone into her hand. "Unless you order me off the property again, all this will take place while the guy who's madder than a wet hen on your behalf is glowering at the lot of them. Call Trent."

Madder than a wet hen, and a lot dearer. Vera called Trent, who agreed to collect his wife and join them directly.

"Does that mean you're not ordering me off your property?" James put the question with chilling neutrality, and Vera was aware of Darren silently taking in the whole exchange.

"I'm not ordering you off the property, though Darren's fate is another matter."

"Darren can look forward to being tried as an adult," James said, swinging around to smile evilly at the youth. "He can look forward to taking a drug test upon his arrest later tonight, and explaining the presence of any controlled dangerous substances in his underaged possession, and any alcohol."

"I only had one beer."

"That's one too many, little man," James assured him, "and an admission before a hostile witness. I can only hope you were also stupid enough to drive here."

"Don't badger him." When Darren's shoulders dropped in relief, Vera regretted chiding James. "Don't think I'm not furious, Darren MacKay, just because I don't rant and stomp around like your father. There will be consequences to this night's folly, and you will not like them."

Darren swallowed and shot a glance at James, who was lounging back against the sink like a big, twitchy-tailed feline predator.

He stared at Darren without mercy, and Vera felt an unaccountable urge to laugh. James was so good at this posturing and strutting, such a skilled negotiator.

Just as quickly, she had to swallow past a lump in her throat, because what next? If she got Darren sorted out... *When* she got Darren sorted out, she was still being sued by Darren's father, still putting this pretty, lonely fortress up for sale, and still losing James.

Had still lost him.

"I'm going upstairs to check on Twyla," she said.

"You two behave, and don't do anything that would wake my daughter up."

Neither one had anything to say to that, so Vera left them to glare and snort at each other while she took a little privacy for herself. Darren hadn't apologized, and that rankled, but James had come when she'd called, no questions, no hesitation, and that comforted.

That James had come comforted Vera immeasurably.

"Think of it as the condemned's last meal." James held out the cookie tin to Donal MacKay's oldest child. The tin was new, because James was shamelessly hoarding the one Vera had left behind at his house, saving it for a last-ditch excuse to come over some fine day when his pride collapsed entirely and he'd rehearsed his groveling speech another hundred times.

Darren took three cookies; James took two and went to the fridge to get the milk.

"Will they really drug test me?" Darren asked.

"You betcha, and maybe even do a hair follicle test if you manage to dodge the urine screen." He set the milk on the island while Darren got down two glasses.

"I'm so screwed."

"Screwed about says it, though not in front of the ladies. What's your plan?" James poured two glasses of milk and put the jug away while the condemned stared at the cookies in his hands.

"I didn't have a plan. I just couldn't let Dad get back together with her."

James took a stool and popped a cookie in his mouth while he considered that confession. "Why not?"

Darren sat on the second stool, hooking his legs around the rungs. "It's complicated."

"It usually is, while ripping up pansies is just plain mean. Scaring Vera is mean, and scaring Twyla is worse than mean. What will you do about it?"

Darren's plan had, though, ensured that Vera regarded Donal with renewed animosity, which had apparently been the kid's aim.

Darren sniffed and swiped at his cheek. "Don't know."

"Eat up, kid. Never know when you'll get home cooking again."

The example of two older brothers intent on disciplining a younger sibling came in curiously handy.

James let Darren stew a while longer, until headlights came bouncing along the lane. He'd hoped Trent would beat Donal to the scene, but MacKay came steaming up the porch steps before James could fetch Vera from upstairs. He was a big guy, broad shouldered, with wavy iron-gray hair and a square jaw. James did not permit himself to envision Donal raising his hand to Vera in anger, lest James coldcock the bastard on the porch.

"Where's my son?" MacKay's belligerent stance was belied by the worry in his eyes.

"He's in the kitchen, having milk and cookies. I'm James Knightley, Vera's neighbor. You'd be Donal MacKay, and I assume this is Tina?" He held out his hand to the lady, a pretty, aging redhead with kind eyes and a weary smile.

"Are you the lawyer?" she asked.

"He's the other lawyer," Donal said. "The barracuda's brother. I want to see my son."

"I'm right here, Dad." Darren stood in the foyer, his hands tucked into his armpits. "Hi, Mom."

"You—" Donal pushed past James to stand right in front of his son. "Get in the car, and we'll deal with you at home."

"Not going to happen," James said. "Vera wants to hear an explanation, and I want to make sure she gets the same explanation Darren gives you two."

"Just who the hell do you think you are to—" Donal started, but Tina put a hand on his arm.

"Donal, it's a sensible suggestion."

The man calmed at her touch, which was interesting. "Where's Vera?" Donal asked, his tone approaching civil from the back side. "We'll be having this explanation, and then taking our son home with us."

"Unless the cops are called," James said, not looking at Darren's mother. "He was caught in the act of vandalizing Vera's property, and I'm fairly certain fingerprints we took off her computer will match his. If we get the cyber detectives busy on Darren's computer, we'll probably find interesting things in the server archives from his sent email queue too."

"They can do that?" Darren's voice was barely a whisper.

"Hello, everybody." Vera came down the front stairs. "I'll ask you to keep your voices down. Twyla is sleeping upstairs."

Vera ushered the small crowd into her living room just as Trent and Hannah arrived, leaving James nowhere to sit.

"What's the barracuda doing here?" Donal asked.

"My name is Trent, and you will recall I am the attorney who got the restraining order against you, among other things. This is a domestic relations situation, and Vera asked me to be present."

"And the lady?" Donal's eyes flitted over Hannah, who was in jeans and a black turtleneck.

"I'm Hannah Stark, Trent's wife, and the firm's professional mediator. My job is to help keep tempers in check and make the discussion as productive as possible."

Tina MacKay took Donal's hand in hers as they sat side by side on a love seat. Darren took a wing chair, Trent and Hannah had the sofa, while Vera took a place on the floor. James lowered himself beside her without asking her permission.

"I count three attorneys here, while my son has no representation at all," Donal said. "Nobody has read him his rights, and I won't let him say anything incriminating. We're wasting our time."

Darren shifted back in his chair. "I want to talk."

"Do you want to go to jail?" Donal shot back. "Do you want to contract AIDS while you're behind bars with men twice your age and twice your size?"

Donal's question was not, alas, far-fetched. Darren's pallor suggested he grasped that.

"I have a suggestion." Hannah's voice was quiet, as relaxed as her posture. "Why not see where this goes, Mr. MacKay? If Vera is satisfied with what she hears, she might not press charges. We can start with asking James to describe what he saw, and that won't incriminate anybody. It will just be James's recollection."

Donal shot a look at the woman holding his hand, then nodded.

"James, from your perspective, what happened?" Hannah asked.

"I was out walking in the woods—the tree frogs are singing, and the moon is almost full tonight—when Vera called and said she thought someone was outside her house. The alarm system hadn't been armed for the night, but she'd locked the doors, so I knew she and Twyla were safe upstairs. I approached the house and found Darren systematically pulling up the pansies. Twyla helped me plant those pansies for her mother after the last time the house was vandalized."

Vera's leg tensed against James's. Had he shifted closer to her, or had she been the one to move?

"What did you do then?" Hannah asked.

"I apprehended Darren and brought him into the house. He's made no admission of guilt about the flowers, but said he can explain. Vera went upstairs to check on Twy, and Darren and I got into the milk and cookies in the kitchen."

"What last time?" Donal asked.

Donal might have made a passable lawyer, which James did not consider to be a compliment, in his case.

"The last time the house was vandalized," James said. "A few weeks ago, windows were broken, and a threatening message was left on Vera's computer in forty-eight-point type. She'd wiped the keyboard down when she logged off for the night, so clean prints were taken by the evidence tech."

"Glover mentioned something about this. The police were involved?" Donal's voice was a tad less pugnacious, and his beefy hand rested snugly in Tina's.

"They were," Vera said. "Not for the first time. I've received threatening phone messages and threatening emails, all of which have been turned over to the state's attorney. The voice leaving the messages sounds like yours, Donal, but in hindsight, I realize you and Darren have similar speaking voices."

Donal sounded like the Scottish Inquisition when he addressed his son. "What have you to say for yourself, boy?"

"Just a minute," Trent said. "Donal, are you saying none of this is your fault?"

"Listen, barracuda, I've told Glover I had nothing to do with this, and I'm telling you. The last thing I want to do is give Vera more reason to shut me out."

"Mr. MacKay, my husband was introduced to you as Trent. It would be helpful if you'd refrain from the name-calling," Hannah said, but she was almost smiling, and James realized she *liked* the idea that to Vera's ex, Trent was a barracuda.

"Fine, then. *Trent*," Donal said, "I had nothing to do with the mischief here, except insofar as I probably sired the whelp responsible."

"Can you prove that?" Trent pressed.

"Of course, he's my son—"

Donal fell silent. James gave him credit for protectiveness toward his family, and for grasping the seriousness of the situation.

"You mean prove my innocence?" Donal asked. "Now see here, bar—*Trent*. You've tried to find me guilty of breaking the damned order, and failed miserably, and you'll not accuse a man of—"

"Donal?" Tina's voice broke in softly. "You can tell them."

"I'll not air family linen before this pack of jackals, Tina."

"Then I'll tell them."

Something passed between Darren's parents while James watched and waited and Vera remained quiet beside him.

But when had she tucked herself so close?

"Donal has been spending a great deal of time with me," Tina said. "We're considering a reconciliation, but it's a slow process. We're in counseling every week, Donal has completed nearly a year of anger-management classes, and that was two nights a week, and two of the remaining nights we often go to support groups, or share a meal."

"You're getting back together?" Darren's voice cracked.

"We're considering it," Donal said. "If your mother will have me."

Darren was on his feet. "*But you dumped her!* You tossed her over when she hit bottom, and took her children away, and went to live in a big, fancy house, and you married *her*"—he jabbed a finger toward Vera— "and you forgot all about Mom, and wanted me and Katie to forget her too."

"Now that's enough!" Donal was on his feet too, glaring at his son. "Your mother and I agreed mutually to separate, but it's the stupidest decision I ever made. She needed inpatient treatment, I couldn't afford that again, and she'd qualify for more services on her own. I needed to think…to just…to get some perspective."

"Donal." Tina's voice was soft. "This is our son."

"Ah, shite." Donal sank back into his chair. He took Tina's hand again, then swung his gaze to his son. "I gave up, Son. You're right, but your mama was losing the fight with the liquor, and I couldn't stand to watch it. Vera was alone and mopey, and I saw a chance to further everybody's interests. Or so I thought."

"Divorcing was also a way to reduce the cost of my treatment," Tina said. "The outpatient treatment was a Band-Aid. What I needed was more intense, and the sliding scale put it within my grasp when I no longer shared a household with Donal. Then Donal took out a line of credit against the house to pay the portion I couldn't manage."

"While you were married to *her*?" Darren flung a hand toward Vera. "I don't get this at all."

"I'm not sure I do either," Vera said from James's side. "Why stay married to me if what you really wanted was to reconcile with Tina?"

"I'd dug myself too big a hole," Donal said, sounding weary, old, and defeated. "Treatment is expensive, and Katie needed braces, and the lad must have his car, and pretty soon… You were my golden goose, Vera, and I damned near killed your music, for which I am so sorry. You deserved better."

"*This* is why you're suing me, because I deserve better?" Vera demanded. "Did I deserve for you to back-hand me in front of your children?"

She didn't raise her voice, but James could feel the tension vibrating through her. Behind her back, where the others could not see, he rested his hand below her shoulder blades.

I've got your back. If you'll let me, I will always have your back.

Chapter 18

JAMES KEPT UP HIS SLOW CARESSES, THOUGH HE WAS ready to jump into the verbal affray on Vera's behalf too.

"I was wrong," Donal said, looking Vera right in the eye. "I behaved shamefully toward you when you were under my roof, Vera. I lost my temper, lost my wits, lost my reason. The idea that my Katie, *my little girl*, was out with a boy of nineteen, and I hadn't even known—and you defended her behavior. I couldn't tolerate that, and you were leaving, and I walloped you, and I've hated myself ever since. You did not deserve to be treated that way—nobody does."

He shifted his gaze to Tina, who said nothing, but kept her hand in his.

"What about tonight?" Hannah asked, looking at Vera. "What was it like tonight, Vera, to be afraid in your own home, again, your daughter sleeping upstairs while you waited for James to get here?"

"It was bad," Vera said. "When you've been assaulted, it takes a long, long time to deal sensibly with fear again. You doubt yourself, then you over-react, then you chastise yourself for overreacting. It's rough. Every time I got one of those emails, every time I came home to a nasty message on my machine, I started down the same damned road. I considered medication, and I considered moving. I am considering moving, in fact. So I really want to know, Darren, what the hell you thought you were doing. Do you really hate me that much?"

James stroked Vera's back, though he wouldn't blame her for going after the kid with every legal, emotional, and moral weapon at her disposal.

"I don't hate you," Darren said, shoving a mop of red hair out of his eyes. "I wanted to hate you, but you were a good stepmom. I know Katie misses you, but she doesn't want to be disloyal."

"What about you, Darren?" Vera used a tone any prosecutor would have envied. "What was all that visiting with Twyla and me about?"

"Dad said how much easier things were when he was agenting you, and I thought that meant he'd try to get back together with you. He talked about it and you said you were willing to be civil."

"I talked about agenting her, ye dimwit. I never said—"

"Mr. MacKay," Hannah cut in coolly.

"You're not a dimwit," Donal said. "Except this scheme you concocted, it was dim-witted, lad. Why didn't you ever talk to me?"

Darren straightened, stole a glance at his mother, then glared at his father.

"When was I going to do that, Dad? Was I supposed to tell you when you were yelling at me for how I dress? For who I hang out with? For cutting classes I've already passed? When was I supposed to talk to either you or *my own mother* about how stupid it would be for you to get back together with Vera? You don't love her, and she doesn't love you. It was stupid of you to marry her, and if I'm a dimwit, maybe I inherited the tendency."

"Maybe you did," Donal said. "But you also inherited my backbone. Make your apologies to Vera."

"Sorry." The word was muttered, and Darren was back to staring at the floor. Nobody said anything, and James nearly felt sorry for the kid.

An alcoholic mother whom he loved, no dad on duty, nobody to help him sort out anything. Well, hell.

"What are you sorry for?" Hannah prodded gently.

"I'm sorry I scared you, Vera, and sorry I didn't just ask you whether you'd ever take Dad back. You would have been honest with me."

As Darren's own parents hadn't been.

"Yes, I would have," Vera said. "I accept your apology, but because of what you did, Darren, I spent thousands on a home security system I don't need. I wasted time making reports to the state's attorney's office, and talking to cops who probably think I'm the crime victim's version of a hypochondriac. I started neglecting my email because I was afraid of what I might find in it, and now I have to question my judgment all over again, because I gave a key to my house to a young man not worthy of my trust."

He nodded and kept his head down. The kid wasn't entirely stupid after all.

"So, Darren," Vera went on, her tone softer, "I want to know what you'll do to earn back my trust."

Another silence, while the rest of the room waited, and Darren shifted in his chair, the chains clipped to his jeans jingling.

"I'll pay you back," Darren said. "I can get another job. They won't give me the hours where I work now, but I can find something."

"It's several thousand dollars, Darren," Vera said. "That's just the security system."

"I can work all summer. I was going to put the money away for college, but college will be there or I can go to the community college for a couple years first."

Be a whole lot easier to make the family therapy sessions if the kid went to the local community college. James kept that observation to himself.

"I know something that pays pretty well," he said instead. "It's brutally hard work and dangerous sometimes, but it does pay. My neighbor will be taking on help for the summer, and he has four hundred acres under cultivation or pasture. If you can drive a tractor, he'll work your ass off."

"I can drive anything."

"You can landscape this property," Vera said. "That won't take much more than manual labor, and once the grass starts growing, you can keep it cut."

"You must have three acres of grass," Darren said.

"Fortunately for you," Vera shot back, "I have a riding mower in excellent repair."

"I can keep after your property," Darren said, "but are you going to the police?"

James would have recommended lenience, but the decision wasn't his. Trent—the only other dad in the room—spoke up.

"I'll advise my client not to go to the police as long as you hold up your end of the deal, Darren. Hannah can draw up a contract between you and Vera, and part of the contract will be that Vera won't pursue formal charges as long as you're making progress on the resti- tution and doing the work around this property you've agreed to do. Is that acceptable?"

Darren wiped his eyes on his sleeve. "That's fine."

"Then we'll be taking him home." Donal rose and drew Tina to her feet. "Miss Hannah, our thanks, and, Vera"—he fell momentarily silent, frowning at her—"I did sue you, didn't I? Now you'll be turning the bar—the *barrister* loose on me, and it will be the divorce all over again. I brought suit for two reasons, the first of which is simply money. At my age, I won't have an easy time of it, finding new talent, and that's the truth, though it shames me to admit it. You would never have discussed those dates with me civilly, but perhaps our lawyers can discuss them for us, aye?

"I also brought suit because, knowing you cowered out here in the countryside offended me, Veracity Winston, particularly when I'm to blame for this scandalous state of affairs. You need to be performing, sharing your music with the people who love you for it. You cannot allow one blow to knock you aside from what you love—or several blows, God forbid. Just an old man's opinion, but an old man who has seen and heard what you can do with a full house and a piano. Think about it."

He gave her an odd little bow from across the room, and shepherded Tina and their son out the door.

James wished them well, but he was not sorry to see them leave.

"I have the sense," Vera said, "I never knew that man at all."

"He probably didn't know himself, but true love and a good therapist can work wonders," Hannah said. "I could use some of those cookies, and maybe a cup of tea. Trent, can you jot down some notes?"

"Make mine decaf," Trent said, "and, Vera, scoot over here. You have to approve of the agreement before anybody else gets to see it." He patted the place beside him on the sofa, so James drew Vera to her feet, and knowing exactly how bad it would look, shamelessly followed his sister-in-law into the kitchen.

—〰—

Vera sat beside Trent and wanted to smack him for the simple fact that he wasn't James, and he hadn't batted an eyelash at the sight of his own brother trailing after Hannah into the kitchen—and Vera wasn't blind. She could plainly see James had something on his mind, something he wanted to share with Hannah in private.

"When do the seniors get out of school?" Trent asked. "Do you want Darren working at Inskip's five days a week and here one, or four and two—I guess that depends on how much rain we get, and how fast your lawn grows. We'll need the receipts for the security system to justify the sum of the restitution, but you should also be compensated something for—Vera, are you listening to me?"

"No."

He sat back, his expression puzzled.

"I've just been handed an explanation for months of harassment and vandalism, Trent. That's a little more significant to me than receipts and schedules."

James would have known that, but James had disappeared into the kitchen.

Trent's frown eased into a look of concern. "You want to cry? That's understandable, because I want to hit something on your behalf. I'll muster Hannah from defending the cookies, and make James show me your Falcon while you ladies talk, if you'd like."

James did not run from a woman's honest tears.

"Trent, doesn't it bother you that Hannah and James are off in corners, whispering and exchanging glances?"

He sat back and eyed her warily. "Noticed that, did you?"

So it wasn't her imagination. "You don't seem concerned."

"Oh, I'm concerned, all right. They are trying so hard to be discreet, and I appreciate that, but if Hannah doesn't admit what she's up to soon, I will have to throttle my brother—probably both of my brothers, come to think of it, and possibly a unicorn or two."

"I thought you wanted to tell Trent," Hannah said, eyeing James curiously.

"It's your place to tell him," James replied. He was on the stool at the island while Hannah leaned back against the sink, a towel over her shoulder and a turtle cookie in her hand. "All I need is permission to tell Vera I represent Grace, and Mac represents you, and that it's a legal proceeding within the family. She'll get the confidentiality part."

Hannah took a nibble of cookie. "I'm no litigator, James, but isn't your representation public record?"

"Not until we file the pleadings, and because Grace is under ten, she doesn't really need a lawyer."

"But she approached you before I even thought of this," Hannah said, taking a sip of her tea. "Have I ever thanked you?"

James picked up an orange origami owl that sat atop

the salt shaker. The folding was intricate, subtle, not obvious on even close inspection, and Vera had probably created this little owl in an idle moment.

"You can thank me by waiving confidentiality," James said, "insofar as I would really like to explain the situation to Vera, and sooner rather than later."

"There's some urgency?"

A light of mischief in Hannah's eyes confirmed to James that he was being gently needled.

"You heard her, Han. She's thinking of selling this house, and God knows where she'll get off to. She's traveled all over the world, and this is the only state where I'm admitted to practice. May I ask you something?"

The teasing in Hannah's eyes died. "Of course. Anything."

"Did I offend you when I tried to pick you up over lunch last fall?"

"You puzzled me," Hannah said slowly, "but you did not then nor have you ever offended me."

James set the owl back on the salt shaker, relief—or maybe absolution—washing through him.

"I apologize anyway. I knew you were interested in my brother, and I should have kept my pandering to myself."

"James, forgive yourself. Nobody uses words like pandering except Supreme Court judges. You have my permission to tell Vera whatever you need to. *Whatever*, James."

"Is somebody going to China to get my tea?" Trent asked, sauntering into the kitchen. "Should I even ask if there are any cookies left? Wife, you were magnificent."

"I asked about three questions," Hannah said. "When people are ready to talk, all they need is a safe place to do it, and this house, ironically, was that place."

Trent took a sip of her tea. She held up a cookie, and he took a bite of that too.

"Has anybody told you two to get a room?" James asked, shoving off his stool.

"We have a whole house, with lots of rooms. Has anybody told you to get a wife?" Trent replied, munching his cookie while he nuzzled his wife.

"Leave him alone, Husband. James has an excellent sense of timing, and so do we. Grab a cookie, and take me home. Mac will have hit his limit of princess movies, and we had better rescue him."

Five minutes later, Hannah and Trent were gone, and James was standing in Vera's foyer, waiting for her to ask him to leave her property, possibly for the last time.

"You OK?" James looked Vera up and down, taking inventory. Her eyes were tired, but she'd lost the haunted, wary look she'd had when he'd first met her. She wasn't smiling; neither was she precisely grim.

"Wrung out, but I cannot thank you enough for being here when I needed you."

To James, that sounded like the prelude to a good-bye, so he spoke quickly.

"If you have another minute, I have some things I need to explain to you. It's a little late—"

"I have as many minutes as you need, James."

He wasn't at all sure what that meant, but he followed her back to the kitchen.

"Is this your tea?" She picked up the cold mug on the island, the one James hadn't even touched.

"It is, or was."

She put it in the microwave and peered into the cookie tin. "My cookie arsenal has taken a serious hit."

"Vera, to hell with the tea and cookies. I need you to listen."

The microwave dinged, and James wanted to toss it through the window. Vera left the tea in the damned microwave and took a stool at the island.

"Sit with me, James, and take your time. I have no lessons tomorrow, and I have some things I want to say to you too."

He took the stool beside her, which was a smart move, because it meant he didn't have to look her in the eye while he made what amounted to his most important closing argument.

"When Hannah and Trent went on their honeymoon," he said, "Grace approached me about having Trent adopt her, so he'd be what she called her real dad. I took this to Hannah in confidence, and she agreed we could get Mac involved, though it scared her to death to even consider it. We'll have to find somebody to represent Trent, but Hannah won't turn us loose on that until we know we've got a valid consent from Grace's birth father."

"An *adoption*?" Vera said the word as if it were recently borrowed from Swahili.

"An adoption isn't as simple as you'd think. Grace's natural father is serving a fifty-year sentence in a West Virginia prison for attempted armed robbery of a bank."

"*That* was your errand in West Virginia? You had to meet with him?"

James wanted to put his arms around Vera, but if he did that, he'd never get out what needed to be said.

"I couldn't very well ask Hannah to approach him, and I didn't trust Mac to behave."

"You can behave?"

"I can, when it's important. Then too, armed guards stood within shouting distance at all times during my conversation with Grace's father."

Vera touched the little owl, tipping up the end of one of its short wings. "I cannot fathom the worlds in which you walk, James. What did he say?"

"He was surprisingly humble and contrite, but then, he's had years to experience the daily threat of victimhood himself. I appealed to his vanity, told him he had a chance to do right by a little girl who would one day have the ability to contact him if he got on the adoption registries. He went for it, and now we have a valid consent."

Not a negotiation James had enjoyed.

Vera drew out another napkin from the holder at the center of the island and started folding.

"Was there any question of the outcome?" she asked.

"There's always question. For something as serious as adoption, the law allows for buyer's remorse. He had a period of time in which he could revoke his consent, but that period has elapsed."

In a few deft moves, Vera folded napkin in on itself, into a diamond shape. "So you and Hannah—"

James couldn't bear for her to finish the question. "I love Hannah, I'd cheerfully die to protect her or Grace, but she's my brother's wife. I am not in love with her and never have been."

A few more folds, and an owl's head and a beak took shape. "Thank you for explaining it to me."

That was all he got? A polite, distracted thank-you? "You saw her car in my driveway, didn't you?"

Vera nodded, guilty as charged. She gave the owl wings, and from some hidden fold in the napkin, created a pair of little owl feet.

"My family has been trying to keep me busy, Vera, and that meant tuning up every God's blessed vehicle we own, which is a damned lot of cars. You convinced yourself I could make love to you as if my life depended on it, and then turn around and two-time my own brother, but I can hardly blame you, given what you read on that infernal phone list."

Reverse cowgirl, G.O.T. *Pathetic.*

Vera set the new owl on the pepper grinder, so a matched pair of birds perched side by side. She looked James over, though he was damned if he could read anything in her steady gaze.

"I'm not that bothered by the phone list, James. I married two men who didn't love me, though I will grant they each had some regard for me, or for my talent. I came to this conclusion while trying to explain to Olga that *my young man* was popular with the ladies, and I didn't trust myself to hold his attention."

Vera fished a cookie out of the tin, took a bite, and passed a second cookie to James. He didn't dare interrupt her, but she had the most distracting dab of chocolate on her lower lip.

"You haven't thrown my insecurities in my face," she said. "Haven't accused me of cowering or dodging, but blaming my cold feet on your past instead of my stage fright is wrong. I hate that list, but I don't like that I've married the wrong man twice either."

Was that the kind of pardon a woman handed out before running a guy off, or was it a glimmer of hope?

"My phone list was one long, misguided mistake," James said. "I haven't figured out entirely what it was about, but I know I don't need to do that anymore, ever."

"Loneliness was part of it," Vera said, sweeping cookie crumbs into her palm, then upending them back into the tin. "We do sorry things because we get lonely and scared, and we can't see any other way out."

She slid her fingers over James's knuckles, a grace note of a touch.

"I at least know what and who I'm lonely for, James. I consider that an improvement, and I also know Donal was right about one thing: I'm supposed to perform."

James tried to concentrate on Vera's words, tried to fumble for a reply, but he was too mesmerized by the slow glide of her fingers over his knuckles. Vera's hands were magic—on the keyboard, on his body, making cookies.

She'd said something about…

He grazed a thumb over the chocolate on her lip. "Performing means travel, Vera. You have a child to raise, and now isn't a good time to sell rural property. You don't owe Donal a thing. I've done the research, read the contracts. You were a minor when you signed with him, and you haven't validated the agency contract in writing since. He's shown bad faith, and the doctrine of clean hands means he can't…"

God help me, I'm babbling.

Vera laced her fingers through James's and brought the back of his hand to her cheek.

"Can you forgive me, James?" She spoke so softly, he had to bend closer to make out her words.

The fragrance of honeysuckle addled James's brain. "Forgive *you*, Vera?"

"I judged you and jumped to the worst conclusions, didn't give you a chance to explain, and tossed you aside when what I want most in this life is to have a future with you. You put the heart back in my music, James. You make me a better mother. You planted flowers for me. You played all the Chopin I could ever want. You shared your family with me. You explained about fractions and cows and chickens to Twy. You made love to me as if *my* life depended on it."

She turned their joined hands and kissed the back of his. "I need you, James Knightley."

James could not think. He could not do anything except lean closer to Vera, slip his free arm around her shoulders, and rest his cheek on her hair.

"Be sure about this, Vera." His voice shook, and tremors rocked his heart. "You have to be very sure, because I don't think I could take… I *can't* take another few weeks like the last ones. I've walked every inch of those woods, and told my troubles to the damned cows and to a shameless hog of a pony, barked at my new hires, and all the while, I ache. I ache…"

She turned her head so their lips met, and James had the purest, most intense sense of homecoming he'd ever felt. Vera was his, she was *his*, and she was promising all her tomorrows to him.

He drew back enough to rest his forehead against hers.

"I want this for keeps," he said. "I don't want to be your agent or your manager or even your lawyer, Vera. I want the solid gold ring. I want to be your husband, and Twyla's dad, and everybody else can go through me to get to you. We can tour in the summer, and take Twy with us, or she can stay with family, and there are all kinds of venues right here on the East Coast, and don't cry…" He kissed her damp cheek. "Please, sweetheart, don't cry. Just say yes. Say you'll marry me."

"Yes," Vera said, threading a hand into his hair and holding him to her. "I will be yours, and you will be mine, and we'll make music, and raise children, and yes, James. For the rest of my life and yours, yes."

Epilogue

"I LOVED THE PART WHERE YOU MADE A RAINBOW UP the keyboard," Twyla said from the backseat of James's vehicle. "I could almost see colors coming from the piano."

"It's called a glissando," Vera replied, wrapping her fingers around James's hand. "They are a lot of fun, when you get them right."

"*I* liked the part where Olga announced that you'd be managing next year's benefit," James said, though he'd already informed his womenfolk that he'd be assisting at every step along the way.

"Olga has delicious cookies in her purse," Twyla observed. "All buttery and sweet. I'd like to learn to make them. Can we go for a trail ride when we get home?"

Vera would be exhausted from the day's events, though happily exhausted. She'd concluded a stellar program, playing to a standing-room-only crowd at the benefit, and had to placate them with two encores before they'd left off stomping and cheering.

The donations had set a new record, and offers had already come in from some extraordinary talents to play for the next three years.

"I'm up for a trail ride," James said as he turned onto the lane to the house. His recently acquired steed, a retired race horse by the name of George, was always willing to go for an outing. "Your mom might be too tired to join us."

"I'm not tired," Twyla assured her parents. "Josephine is never tired."

Because Josephine seldom bestirred herself to move faster than a trot, though she and Twyla were already fast friends. Trent had been forced to find other mounts for his wife and daughter, because where Jo dwelled, Wellie lived too.

"Vera, will you come with us?" James asked. "After the way you played, you're entitled to toddle straight to bed until next Monday." Though next Monday, they were all heading up to Deep Creek for a family vacation.

Sweet pair of words: family vacation. Not something James could recall his family ever doing when he was boy.

"If Jo and George are game," Vera replied, "then Wellie and I will join you. I might need a nap first, though, and I'm declaring this a pizza-and-princess-movie night."

Vera had been napping a fair amount lately, a lovely quality in a new wife. James had developed a fondness for napping too.

"I've thought of a name," James said as they bumped up the lane. He spoke softly, because parents skilled in the art of adult conversation could get away with the occasional private chat when Twyla was busily texting her cousins.

"We have plenty of time to think of names," Vera said. She wore the dreamy, happy expression James had formerly associated with their many and varied bouts of lovemaking.

Or Brahms. Late Brahms could make her that happy.

"I like this name," he said, switching off the vehicle.

Twyla scrambled out, leaving her parents a moment of privacy. "You said I'd get to pick the name if we have a girl."

"I did say that. I think Hannah and Trent have the same arrangement."

Now all the Knightley family needed was to recruit a stout-hearted lady to make *arrangements* with Mac, and James already had a candidate in mind.

"If we have a girl, Mrs. Knightley, I'd like to name her Madeline Olga."

"I like that name," Vera said. "I like it a lot, but you have a few colorful glissandos of your own, James. You might need to think up some more names before Madeline Olga is very old."

James considered that for a moment. "We might need a second piano and more ponies and an addition on the barn. I could build you a studio, in fact, and that's—"

Vera kissed him. Since she'd first graced his cheek with a kiss on a chilly morning months ago, she'd developed an entire vocabulary of kisses.

"Make haste slowly," she said. "Madeline Olga is a lovely name, and you are a lovely man. You're playing a four-hands duet with me at next year's benefit, James."

A challenge. James and challenges went way back, so he came around to open Vera's door and kissed her back.

"Four hands it is," he said, "and a duet every night and day until then, and a happily ever after for one and all."

**Read on for excerpts from the
other books in the Sweetest Kisses
series from Grace Burrowes and
Sourcebooks Casablanca:**

a
single
Kiss

Kiss
me
hello

From *A Single Kiss*

"SHE HAD THAT TWITCHY, NOTHING-GETS-BY-HER quality." MacKenzie Knightley flipped a fountain pen through his fingers in a slow, thoughtful rhythm. "I liked her."

Trenton Knightley left off doodling Celtic knots on his legal pad to peer at his older brother. "You liked her? You *liked* this woman? You don't like anybody, particularly females."

"I respected her," Mac said, "which, because you were once upon a time a husband, you ought to know is more important to the ladies than whether I like them."

"Has judge written all over him," James, their younger brother, muttered. "The criminals in this town would howl to lose their best defense counsel, though. I liked the lady's résumé, and I respected it too."

Gail Russo, the law firm's head of human resources, thwacked a file onto the conference table.

"Don't start, gentlemen. Mac has a great idea. Hannah Stark interviewed very well, better than any other candidate we've considered in the past six months. She's temped with all the big boys in Baltimore, has sterling academic credentials, and—are you listening?—is available."

"The best kind," James murmured.

Trent used Gail's folder to smack James on the shoulder, though James talked a better game of tomcat than he strutted.

"You weren't even here to interview her, James, and she's under consideration for your department."

"The press of business…" James waved a languid hand. "My time isn't always my own."

"You were pressing business all afternoon?" Mac asked from beyond retaliatory smacking range.

"The client needed attention," James replied. "Alas for poor, hardworking me, she likes a hands-on approach. Was this Hannah Stark young, pretty, and single, and can she bill sixty hours a week?"

"We have a decision to make," Gail said. "Do we dragoon Hannah Stark into six months in domestic relations then let her have the corporate law slot, or do we hire her for corporate when the need is greater in family law? Or do we start all over and this time advertise for a domestic relations associate?"

Domestic law was Trent's bailiwick, but because certain Child In Need of Assistance attorneys could not keep their closing arguments to less than twenty minutes per case, Trent hadn't interviewed the Stark woman either.

"Mac, you really liked her?" Trent asked.

"She won't tolerate loose ends," Mac said. "She'll work her ass off before she goes to court. The judges and opposing counsel will respect that, and anybody who can't get along with you for their boss for six months doesn't deserve to be in the profession."

"I agree with Mac." James dropped his chair forward, so the front legs hit the carpet. "I'm shorthanded, true, but not that shorthanded. Let's ask her to pitch in for six months in domestic, then let her have the first shot at corporate if we're still swamped in the spring."

"Do it, Trent," Mac said, rising. "Nobody had a bad thing to say about her, and you'll be a better mentor for her first six months in practice than Lance Romance would be. And speaking of domestic relations, shouldn't you be getting home?"

—◦◦◦—

Grace Stark bounded into the house ahead of her mother, while Hannah brought up the rear with two grocery bags and a shoulder-bag-cum-purse. Whenever possible, for the sake of the domestic tranquility and the budget, Hannah did her shopping without her daughter's company.

Hannah's little log house sat on the shoulder of a rolling western Maryland valley, snug between the cultivated fields and the wooded mountains. She took a minute to stand beside the car and appreciate the sight of her own house—hers and the bank's—and to draw in a fortifying breath of chipper air scented with wood smoke.

The Appalachians rose up around the house like benevolent geological dowagers, surrounding Hannah's home with maternal protectiveness. Farther out across the valley, subdivisions encroached on the family farms, but up here much of the land wouldn't perc, and the roads were little more than widened logging trails.

The property was quiet, unless the farm dogs across the lane took exception to the roosters, and the roosters on the next farm over took exception to the barking dogs, and so on.

Still, it was a good spot to raise a daughter who enjoyed a busy imagination and an appreciation for nature. Damson Valley had a reputation as a peaceful, friendly community, a good place to set down roots. Hannah's little house wasn't that far from the Y, the park, and the craft shops that called to her restricted budget like so many sirens.

The shoulder bag dropped down to Hannah's elbow as she wrestled the door open while juggling grocery bags.

"Hey, Mom. Would you make cheese shells again? I promise I'll eat most of mine."

"Most?" Hannah asked as she put the milk in the fridge. The amount she'd spent was appalling, considering how tight money was. Thank heavens Grace thought pasta and cheese sauce was a delicacy.

"A few might fall on the floor," Grace said, petting a sleek tuxedo cat taking its bath in the old-fashioned dry sink.

"How would they get on the floor?"

"They might fall off my plate." Grace cuddled the cat, who bore up begrudgingly for about three seconds, then vaulted to the floor. Grace took a piece of purple yarn from a drawer, trailing an end around the cat's ears.

"Cats have to eat too, you know," Grace said. "They love cheese. It says so on TV, and Henry says his mom lets him feed cheese to Ginger."

"Ginger is a dog. She'd eat kittens if she got hungry enough." The groceries put away, Hannah set out place mats and cutlery for two on the kitchen table. "You wouldn't eat kittens just because Henry let Ginger eat kittens, would you?"

Did all parents make that same dumb argument?

And did all parents put just a few cheesy pieces of pasta in the cat dish? Did all parents try to assuage guilt by buying *fancy 100 percent beef wieners* instead of hot dogs?

"Time to wash your hands, Grace," Hannah said twenty minutes later. "Hot dogs are ready, so is your cat food."

"But, Mom," Grace said, looping the string around the drawer pull on the dry sink, "all I did was pet Geeves, and she's just taken a whole bath. Why do I always have to wash my hands?"

"Because Geeves used the same tongue to wash her butt as she did to wash her paws, and because I'm telling you to."

Grace tried to frown mightily at her mother but burst out giggling. "You said butt, and you're supposed to ask."

"Butt, butt, butt," Hannah chorused. "Grace, would you please wash your hands before Geeves and I gobble up all your cheesy shells?"

They sat down to their mac and cheese, hot dogs, and salad, a time Hannah treasured—she treasured any time with her daughter—and dreaded. Grace could be stubborn when tired or when her day had gone badly.

"Grace, please don't wipe your hands on your shirt. Ketchup stains, and you like that shirt."

"When you were a kid, did you wipe your hands on your shirt?" Grace asked while chewing a bite of hot dog.

"Of course, and I got reminded not to, unless I was wearing a ketchup-colored shirt, in which case I could sneak a small smear."

Grace started to laugh with her mouth full, and Hannah was trying to concoct a *request* that would encourage the child to desist, when her cell phone rang. This far into the country, the expense of a land-line was necessary because cell reception was spotty, though tonight the signal was apparently strong enough.

"Hello, Stark's."

"Hi, this is Gail Russo from Hartman and Whitney. Is this Hannah?"

The three bites of cheesy shells Hannah had snitched while preparing dinner went on a tumbling run in her tummy. "This is Hannah."

"I hope I'm not interrupting your dinner, Hannah, but most people like to hear something as soon as possible after an interview. I have good news, I think."

"I'm listening."

Grace used her fork to draw a cat in her ketchup.

"You interviewed with two department heads and a partner," Gail said, "which is our in-house rule before a new hire, and they all liked you."

Hannah had liked the two department heads. The partner, Mr. MacKenzie Knightley, had been charm-free, to put it charitably. Still, he'd been civil, and when he'd asked if she had any questions, Hannah had the sense he'd answer with absolute honesty.

The guy had been good-looking, in a six-foot-four, dark-haired, blue-eyed way that did not matter in the least.

"I'm glad they were favorably impressed," Hannah said as Grace finished her mac and cheese.

"Unfortunately for you, we also had a little excitement in the office today. The chief associate in our domes-tic relations department came down with persistent light-headedness. She went to her obstetrician just to make sure all was well with her pregnancy and was summarily sent home and put on complete bed rest."

"I'm sorry to hear that." *Not domestic relations.* If there were a merciful God, Hannah would never again set foot in the same courtroom with a family law case. Never.

"She's seven months along, so we're looking at another two months without her, then she'll be out on maternity leave. It changed the complexion of the offer we'd like to make you."

"An offer is good." An offer would become an absolute necessity in about one-and-a-half house payments.

Grace was disappearing her hot dog with as much dispatch as she'd scarfed up her mac and cheese.

"We'd like you to start as soon as possible, but put you in the domestic relations department until Janelle can come back in the spring. We'll hire somebody for domestic in addition to her, but you're qualified, and the need, as they say, is now."

"Domestic relations?" Prisoners sentenced to life-plus-thirty probably used that same tone of voice.

"Family law. Our domestic partner is another Knightley brother, but he's willing to take any help he can get. He was in court today when Janelle packed up and went home, otherwise you might have interviewed with him."

"I see."

What Hannah saw was Grace, helping herself to her mother's unfinished pasta.

"You'd be in domestic for only a few months, Hannah, and Trent Knightley is the nicest guy you'd ever want to work for. He takes care of his people, and you might find you don't want to leave domestic in the spring, though James Knightley is also a great boss."

Gail went on to list benefits that included a signing bonus. Not a big one, but by Hannah's standards, it would clear off all the bills, allow for a few extravagances, and maybe even the start of a savings account.

God in heaven, a savings account.

"Mom, can I have another hot dog?" Grace stage-whispered her request, clearly trying to be good.

Except there wasn't another hot dog. Hannah had toted up her grocery bill as she'd filled her cart, and there wasn't another damned hot dog.

Thank God my child is safe for another day... But how safe was Grace in a household where even hot dogs were carefully rationed?

Hannah covered the phone. "You may have mine, Grace."

"Thanks!"

"Hannah? Are you there?"

A beat of silence, while Hannah weighed her daughter's need for a second hot dog against six months of practicing law in a specialty Hannah loathed, dreaded, and despised.

"I accept the job, Gail, though be warned I will transfer to corporate law as soon as I can."

"You haven't met Trent. You're going to love him."

No, Hannah would not.

Gail went on to explain details—starting day, parking sticker, county bar identification badge—and all the while, Hannah watched her hot dog disappear and knew she was making a terrible mistake.

—◦◦◦—

"Trent Knightley is a fine man, and his people love him," Gail said, passing Hannah's signing bonus check across the desk. "The only folks who don't like to see him coming are opposing counsel, and even they respect him."

"He sounds like an ideal first boss."

What kind of fine man wanted to spend his days breaking up families and needed the head of HR singing his praises at every turn?

The entire first morning was spent with Gail, filling out forms—and leaving some spaces on those forms blank. Gail took Hannah to lunch, calling it de rigueur for a new hire.

"In fact," Gail said between bites of a chicken Caesar, "you will likely be taken out to lunch by each of the three partners, though Mac tends to be less social than his brothers. You ordering dessert?"

People who could afford gym memberships ordered dessert.

"I'd like to get back to work if you don't mind, Gail. I have yet to meet the elusive Trent Knightley, and if he should appear in the office this afternoon, I don't want to be accused of stretching lunch on my first day."

Not on any day. If Hannah had learned anything temping for the Baltimore firms, it was that law firms were OCD about time sheets and billable hours.

"Hannah, you are not bagging groceries. No one, and I mean no one, will watch your time as long as your work is getting done, your time sheet is accurate, and most of your clients aren't complaining. Get over the convenience-store galley slave mentality."

Gail paid the bill with a corporate card, and no doubt the cost of lunch would have bought many packages of fancy 100 percent beef wieners.

"Don't sweat the occasional long lunch," Gail said as they drove back to the office. "Trent takes as many as anyone else, and the way he eats, he'd better."

Gail's comment had Hannah picturing Mr. Wonderful Boss, Esq., as a pudgy middle-aged fellow who put nervous clients at ease and probably used a cart and a caddy when he played golf with the judges.

From *Kiss Me Hello*

COMPARED TO MACKENZIE KNIGHTLEY, THE NEW GIRL was small, scared, and lacked both weapons and defenses. Mac held out a hand to her in a reassuring gesture, but she turned her face away.

An eloquent rejection.

"What's her name?" Mac asked the groom, who watched from across the barn aisle.

"Luna, short for Lunatic. She doesn't strike any of us as therapeutic riding material, but Adelia will have her occasional stray."

Mac suspected Adelia had had his brother James a time or two, when James had been a different kind of stray. Adelia apparently bore James no grudge for wandering away, as strays were wont to do.

"Luna." Mac said the name softly, and saw no reaction in the mare's eyes. She looked at him steadily now, her expression showing wary resignation.

Another person, another disappointment. Mac knew the sentiment firsthand. He took a step closer. Luna raised her head a couple of inches, the better to keep him in focus.

"Has she been vetted?"

"What would be the point?"

Neils Haddonfield was the head groom at the Damson County Therapeutic Riding Association's barn—the barn manager, really. He was big, blond, and quiet, gentle as a lamb with the children and the horses, and hell in a muck truck with whiny parents.

"Let's see if we can't make her more comfortable." Mac took the final step toward the mare and ran a hand down her neck. She gave no sign she felt the caress, so Mac went on a hunt for her sweet spots.

Females were females after all, and some things held true across species.

When his fingers dug into the coarse hair over her withers, she gave a little invisible shudder, one Mac understood, because his hand was listening for it. He settled in, gently, firmly, and the mare's head dropped a few inches. He added a second hand on the other side of her withers, and she braced her misshapen front feet wider.

"She likes that," Neils said, frowning.

"You give her any bute?" Mac asked as he moved his hands a few inches up her neck.

"A couple grams after breakfast."

The medication was helping her stand on the rubber brick surface of the barn aisle. Left to her own devices, she might well be lying flat out in the weak spring sunshine just to get off her neglected feet.

"We could put her in the stocks," Neils said. "Get it over with more quickly."

"And give her a horror of the stocks, me, and anybody who helped put her into them. I'm only making a start on those feet today. Getting her reliably sound will take months, if it can be accomplished at all. Can you take over on this side of her neck?"

Neils moved, taking up the slow massaging scratch Mac had started. The mare's expression registered the shift, but she didn't raise her head.

Mac pulled his wheeled toolbox over and ran a hand down one of the mare's legs. She stood for it, though she had to know what came next.

When he lifted her left foreleg, she let out a sigh, because shifting hundreds of pounds of body weight to the three hooves remaining on the ground had to be painful. The phenolbutazone would help, but it wouldn't eliminate the discomfort entirely.

Working quickly, he nipped off as much of the mare's overgrown toe as he dared, then set the foot gently back down. He stepped away, signaling to the horse she could take a moment to recover, while Neils kept up the scratching.

"Good girl," Mac said, extending his hand to her nose again. "You're a stoic, little Luna, and you have more in common with the riders here than you think. Give it time, and we'll find you someplace to call home."

He worked around the horse quickly but quietly, spending a few minutes on each hoof, rather than finishing one before moving on to another. She seemed to understand his method and appreciate it. By the time he ran his hand down her leg to file the final hoof into shape, she'd already shifted her weight in anticipation.

"She's sensible," Neils said, patting the shaggy neck. "Who would have thought? But then, they're all sensible for you, MacKenzie."

"One beast to another," Mac said, using his foot to nudge the wheeled toolbox away from the horse. "Do we know anything about this one besides that she's been badly neglected?"

"Adelia thinks she might have seen her a few years

ago on the Howard County circuit, and the arthritis in the feet suggests she might have been worked too long and hard over fences, but that's only a hunch."

"What are you feeding her?"

They went on, as only two horsemen can, over every detail of the mare's care. What she ought to be fed, with whom she might be safely turned out, how soon. Whether grass was a good idea, because spring grass could pack a nutritional wallop.

"I'd hand graze her," Mac said, eyeing the mare. "She needs every chance we can give her to associate people with good things. To horses, new grass is the mother of all good things."

Adelia Scoffield sauntered up in riding jeans, chaps, and a short-sleeved T-shirt, though the day was cool. She'd been on one horse or another since Mac had pulled up a couple of hours ago, and her exertions showed in the dark sweaty curls at her temples.

"Have you two listed all the reasons why Luna is a bad idea?" she asked.

"Shame on you, Adelia." Neils passed the lead rope to Mac. "You will catch your death, running around like that." He shrugged out of his jacket and draped it over Adelia's shoulders. Adelia gave the lapel a little sniff, something Luna would have understood, had she not been so nervous.

"We were admiring your new addition," Mac said. "I've done what I can for her feet, but it's a slow process. She was leery, but she gave me the benefit of the doubt."

"Poor thing." Adelia held out her hand to the mare, who took two steps back. Mac moved with the horse to avoid a situation where the mare hit the end of the lead rope and started making the bad decisions common to anxious horses.

"Easy," Mac crooned, his hand going to the mare's withers. "It's just the boss coming to see if Neils and I are behaving. She's good people, if you overlook her tendency to pick up hopeless cases like Neils."

"You're just jealous," Adelia said. "I came to see if Neils can go on a mission of mercy for me." When Adelia made no move to come closer, the mare relaxed marginally beside Mac.

"Neils and mercy don't strike me as the most compatible combination," Mac said, petting the horse slowly.

"We got a call from Sid Lindstrom." Adelia took another surreptitious whiff of the coat. "Sid's the foster parent of one of our new riders, and says there are two behemoth horses on their new property, horses that weren't there on the day of closing."

"Behemoth horses aren't suitable for therapeutic programs," Neils began, hands going to his hips. "You can't—"

"I wasn't going to," Adelia said gently. Something passed between the small dark-haired woman and the big blond man that suggested to Mac they were a couple, if the routine with the jacket hadn't confirmed the notion already.

He liked both of them, and respected what they were doing with the therapeutic riding program, though the idea that everybody but MacKenzie Knightley had somebody with whom they could exchange silent looks and warm jackets was tiresome.

"I *said* we could take over some pony chow, and send somebody to check on the situation," Adelia went on.

"They could be stray pensioners who broke out of the neighbor's paddock this morning, but it's spring, Neils. What if somebody's stallion got loose, and the other horse is a mare in season who's eloped with him? That's not a safe situation for greenhorns to manage, and these people know very little about horses."

"Because their foster kid rides in our program, we're going to start making house calls?" Neils tried to glower as he put the question to his boss, but the guy was whupped. He stood only a couple of inches shorter than Mac's six foot four, but Neils had become a whupped puppy the first time Adelia had turned her big brown eyes on him.

"One barn call," Adelia said. "If they can afford a four-hundred-acre farm free and clear, then they are potential sponsors for the therapeutic riding program." She reached out to the mare again, but the horse came out of the daze induced by Mac's petting and scratching, and backed up again.

"Somebody's a little shy," Adelia said, dropping her hand. "Will you go, Neils?"

"What's the address?"

She told him, and Mac's hand went still on the horse's neck.

"I'll go," Mac said. The mare shrugged, a perfectly normal horsey reminder to resume his scratching.

"You will?" Adelia's expression was curious, while Neils looked relieved.

"It's on my way home, and Luna was my last customer here this morning. It's Saturday, and I have the time."

"My thanks." When Neils reached for Luna's lead rope, the little horse did not flinch or take a step back.

Mac gathered up his tools and loaded his farrier's truck—not to be confused with his everyday truck. He took a minute to watch a therapeutic riding session getting started in the small indoor arena. A kid with no feeling below her thighs was settling onto the back of a therapy pony, her expression rapt, while the horse stood stock-still and awaited his burden.

The girl had earned this moment, learning parts of the horse, names of the tack and equipment, and doing what she could from her wheelchair to contribute to the care of the horses. Mac had watched week by week as she'd progressed toward this day.

Her name was Lindy, and Mac stood silently at a distance as she sat her mount, her expression radiant. A special moment.

Mac turned away, climbed into his truck, and drove off. Once en route, he checked his messages to see if any of his paying clients had gotten locked up Friday night—an attorney who specialized in criminal defense often racked up messages over the weekend—but, oh happy day, his mailbox was empty.

Which left him free to wonder why Luna was uncomfortable around women, or whether she'd merely been reacting to MacKenzie Knightley's own unease with the fairer sex.

He pulled up the lane of the address Adelia had given him, which was, indeed, a four-hundred-acre farm. Four hundred three and a quarter acres, to be exact.

Fences were starting to sag, and boards had warped their nails out of the posts. A spring growth of weeds had yet to be whacked down from the driveway's center, and the most recent crop of winter potholes hadn't yet been filled in with gravel. The white paint on the north side of the loafing shed was peeling, and the stone barn itself needed some pointing and parging near the foundation.

All in all, a damned depressing sight for a man who'd had as happy a childhood on a farm as a boy could.

Which was to say, very happy.

"Hello, the house!"

No response, which wasn't a good sign. Farms were busy places, full of activity. Even if humans weren't in evidence, then the dogs, cats, and chickens usually were. But this farm had no dogs, no sheep, no cows, no visible animal life of any species.

"Over here!"

The shout came from the far side of the hill, where the land rolled down to a draw that Mac would bet still sported a pond and a fine fishing stream, but the tone of voice had been tense, frightened maybe.

He didn't run. If a horse were cast against a fence, or two horses were taking a dislike to each other, then tearing onto the scene wouldn't help.

"Coming," he yelled back. "Coming over the hill." He rummaged in his truck, extracting two lead ropes and two worn leather halters, as well as a half-empty box of sugar cubes.

When he crested the hill, the sight that met his eyes was so unexpected he stopped in his tracks, and had to remind himself to resume breathing.

—⁓—

They were not horses, they were equine barges, munching grass and twitching their tails in a slow progress across the field where Sid had discovered them. They shifted along, first one foot, a pause to munch grass, then the other foot, all with the ominous inexorability of equine glaciers, leaving Sid to wonder how in the hell anybody controlled them.

If anybody could control them.

What would it feel like if one of those massive horse feet descended on a human toe? How many hours would elapse before the beast would deign to shuffle its foot off the bloody remains, to lip grass on some other blighted part of the earth?

How did animals that large mate, for God's sake? Surely the earth would shake, and the female's back would break, and giving birth to even the smallest member of the species would be excruciating.

This litany of horror was interrupted by a shout from back over the rise in the direction of the house and barn. The voice was mature male, which meant it wasn't Luis.

Help, then, from the therapeutic riding program.

"Over here!" Sid yelled back.

The animals twitched their ears, which had Sid grabbing for the only weapon the house had had to offer, useless though it likely was. Something as big as these horses could run over anything in its path and not notice an obstacle as insignificant as a human.

"You planning on sweeping them out of your pasture?"

A man stood a few feet away, a man built on the same scale as the damned horses, but leaner—meaner?

"Sidonie Lindstrom," she said, clambering down off the granite outcropping she'd been perched on. "You're from the therapeutic riding place?"

"I'm their farrier." His voice was peat smoke and island

single malt, and his eyes were sky blue beneath long, dark lashes. Which was of absolutely no moment, and neither was the arrestingly masculine cast of his features.

"What's a farrier?"

"Horseshoer." He wasn't smiling, but something in his blue eyes suggested she amused him.

"Blacksmith? Like Vulcan or Saturn?"

"Close enough. You say you didn't notice these two were on the property when you took possession?"

"I didn't say." Sid took a minute to study her guest—she supposed he was a guest of some sort—while his gaze went to the two big red horses yards away. Enormous, huge, *flatulent* horses.

"Do they do that a lot?" she asked, wincing as a sulfurous breeze came to her nose. God above, was this how the cavalry mowed down its enemies?

"When they're on good grass, yes." Absolutely deadpan. "Daisy!"

The nearest beast lifted its great head and eyed the man.

"You two are acquainted?"

"There aren't many pairs like this around anymore. Buttercup!" The second animal lifted its head, and worse, shuffled a foot in the direction of the humans.

"What are you doing, mister?" Sid scrambled up on the rocks, shamelessly using the blacksmith's meaty shoulder for leverage.

"You're afraid of them?" he asked, not budging an inch.

"Anybody in their right damned mind would be afraid of them," Sid shot back. "They could sit on you and not even notice."

"They'd notice. They notice a single fly landing on them. They'd notice even a little thing like you. Come here, ladies." He took a box of sugar cubes from his jacket pocket and shook it, which caused both animals to incrementally speed up in their approach. They were walking, but walking quickly, and Sid could swear she felt seismic vibrations.

"You're supposed to help here, you know, not provoke them." Her voice didn't shake, but her body was beginning to send out the flight-or-flight-or-*flight!* signals.

She'd gotten mighty good at the flight response.

"Calm down," Mr. Sugar Cubes said. "If you're upset, they'll pick up on it."

"Smart ladies, then, because I'm beyond upset. These are not fixtures, and they should not convey with the property. A washing machine or a dryer I could overlook, but these—crap on a croissant, they could bite you, mister."

He was holding out his hand—and a sizable paw it was too—with one sugar cube balanced on his palm. The first horse to reach him stuck out its big nose and wiggled its horsey lips over his hand, and then the sugar cube was gone.

"You too, Buttercup." He put a second sugar cube on his hand, and the other horse repeated the disappearing act. "Good girls." He moved to stand between the horses, letting one sniff his pocket while he scratched the neck of the other. "You need some good tucker, ladies, and your feet are a disgrace. But, my, it is good to see you."

Red hair was falling like a fine blizzard from where he scratched the horse's shoulders, and the mare was craning its neck as the man talked and scratched some more.

"Not to interrupt your class reunion, but what am I supposed to do with your girlfriends?"

"They aren't mine, though they might well be yours. Come meet them."

He turned, and in a lithe, one-armed move, scooped Sid from the safety of her rocky perch and set her on her feet between him and the horses.

"Mister, if you ever handle me like that again—"

"You'll do what?"

"You won't like where it hurts. How do you tell them apart?"

They were peering at her, the big, hairy pair of them, probably thinking of having a Sidonie Salad, and Sid took a step back, only to bump into a hard wall of muscular male chest.

"Look at their faces," he said. "Buttercup has a blaze, and Daisy has a snip and a star."

Sid was pressed so tightly against him she could *feel* him speak. She could also feel he wasn't in the least tense or worried, which suggested the man was in want of brains.

What he called faces were noses about a yard long, with big, pointed hairy ears at one end, nostrils and teeth at the other, and eyes high up in between. Still, those eyes were regarding Sid with something like intelligence, with a patient curiosity, like old people or small children viewed newcomers.

"How do you know them?" she asked, hands at her sides.

"Thirteen years ago, they were the state champs. They're elderly now, for their breed, and it looks to me like they wintered none too well. You going to pet them or stare them into submission?"

"*Pet…!?*"

Before she could rephrase what had come out as only a squeak, Vulcan had taken her hand in his much larger one and laid it on the neck of the nearest horse.

"Scratch. They thrive on a little special treatment, same as the rest of us."

Sid had no choice but to oblige him, because his hand covered hers as it rested on the horse's neck. Over the scent of horse and chilly spring day, Sid got a whiff of cloves and cinnamon underlaid with notes that suggested not a bakery, but a faraway meadow where the sunshine fell differently and clothes would be superfluous.

The hand that wasn't covering Sid's rested on her shoulder, preventing her from ducking and running.

"Talk to them," he said. "They're working draft animals, and they're used to people communicating with them."

"What do I say?"

"Introduce yourself. Compliment them, welcome them. The words don't matter so much as the tone of the voice." He seemed serious, and the horse was lowering its head closer to the ground the longer Sid scratched her neck.

"Like that, don't you, girl? I'm Sid, and don't get too comfortable here, because I am no kind of farmer, and neither is Luis."

The horse let loose another sibilant, odoriferous fart.

"Pleased to meet you too. There, I talked to her, and she responded. Can I call the SPCA now?"

"No, you may not. Daisy will get jealous if you neglect her."

"And bitch slap me with her tail?"

"At least."

Sid could see that happening, so she dropped her hand, then held it out to the other horse.

"You too? I'm changing your names to Subzero and Kenmore, because you're the size of industrial freezers." The horse sighed as Sid began scratching the second hairy neck, and Sid hid a smile. "Where's your dignity, horse? There's a man present, of sorts."

"You want me to leave?"

"Yes, particularly if you're going to take these two with you."

"Smaller draft horses than these won't fit in a conventional horse trailer. The halters I brought with me won't fit them either, though I'll be happy to clear out if you're—"

"No! That's not what I—" Sid fell silent. What did she expect him to do, if he wasn't going to take the horses with him? "Will the SPCA come get them, or animal control?"

"You want them put down?"

That deep voice held a chill, one that had Sid twisting around to peer at him over her shoulder. "Put down to what?"

"Euthanized, put to sleep. Killed for your convenience."

His tone was positively arctic, though he was standing so close to Sid she could feel his body heat through her clothes.

"Don't be an ass. They've wandered off from somebody's property. They're merely strays, and need to be taken home."

"I'm not so sure of that, but let's find them somewhere to put up overnight, and we can argue the details where Daisy and Buttercup can't hear us. Come along."

He took Sid by the wrist, and began leading her away from the horses.

Sid trundled along with him—beside him seemed the safest place to be—but glanced warily over her shoulder.

"We're being followed."

He dropped her wrist and turned so quickly Sid barely had time to step back.

"Scat!" He waved his hands and charged at the nearest horse, who shied and then stood her ground a few feet off. "Scram, Daisy! Shoo!"

The horse stood very tall, then lowered her head, and ponderously scampered a few feet before standing very tall again. The second horse gave a big shrug of her neck and hopped sideways.

"You get them all wound up," Sid said, edging toward the gate, "I am burying you where you fall, mister, and the grave will be shallow, because there's a lot of you to bury."

"They want to play. Head for the barn. This won't take long."

Sid did not need to be told twice. She shamelessly hustled for the gate, stopping to watch what happened in the field behind her only when she'd climbed to the highest fence board.

A two-ton version of tag-you're-it seemed to be going on, with the horses galumphing up to the man, then veering away only to stop, wheel, and charge him again. He dodged easily, and swatted at them on the neck and shoulders and rump when they went by. When they were a few steps past him, the horses would kick up their back legs or buck, and by God, the ground did shake.

The guy was grinning now, his face transformed

from forbiddingly handsome to stunningly attractive. He called to each horse, good-naturedly taunting first one then the other, until by some unspoken consent, both mares approached him with their heads down.

Sid couldn't hear what he said to them, but she saw the way he touched them, the way he fiddled with those big ears, and gave each horse one last scratch. The mares watched him walk back toward the barn, and Sid could have sworn their expressions were forlorn.

"You're old friends with them," she said as he climbed over the fence. She tried to turn on the top board, only to find herself plucked straight up into the air, then set gently on her feet. "For the love of meadow muffins, mister, are you trying to get your face slapped?"

His lips quirked, but he did not smile. "No."

"What am I supposed to do about your lady friends?"

"Nothing for right now. Who's the kid?"

"What kid?" Sid followed the blacksmith's gaze to the front porch of their new house. Their new old house.

"The kid who's going to tear me into little bitty pieces if you don't let him know I'm your new best friend."

"Never had a best friend before," Sid said, but the man had a point. Luis was looking daggers at the blacksmith, the boy's shirt luffing against his skinny body, showing tension in every bone and sinew. "Come on, I'll introduce you. Or I would if you'd told me your name."

"Everybody calls me Mac."

She eyed him up and down as they started for the house. "Like the truck? Don't they have a plant around here somewhere?"

"Hagerstown, but it's Volvo now, and no, not like the truck. Like MacKenzie."

"Pleased to meet you, Mr. MacKenzie. I'd be more pleased if you'd take those free-to-good-homes along with you."

"No, it's MacKenzie, as in MacKenzie Knightley. I'm fairly certain the horses are yours."

"You've said that twice now, and while I'm a woman slow to anger"—he snorted beside her—"it's only fair to warn you the notion of me owning those mastodons will sour my mood considerably. Luis!" Sid's voice caught the boy as he was slouching away from the porch post to duck into the house. "He's shy."

"Right."

"He is, and you'd be too if you'd been in eight foster homes in less than three years. Be nice."

"Or you'll beat me up?"

"I'll tell your horses on you, and they will be very disappointed in you."

They reached the porch, and Luis was back to holding up a porch post, his hands tucked into his armpits, because at almost sixteen, he was too macho to wear a damned jacket.

"Luis, this is Mac. He's come to tell us what to do with the horses."

"Luis." Mac surprised her by holding out one of those big hands, and Sid said a quick prayer her son would not embarrass her. "Pleased to meet you."

Her foster son, but that was splitting hairs.

Luis looked at Mac's hand, which the man continued to hold out, while his gaze held the boy's. Slowly, Luis offered his hand.

"MacKenzie Knightley, my friends call me Mac."

"Luis Martineau."

About the Author

New York Times and *USA Today* bestselling author Grace Burrowes hit the bestseller lists with her debut, *The Heir*, followed by *The Soldier*, *Lady Maggie's Secret Scandal*, *Lady Eve's Indiscretion*, *The Captive*, and *The Traitor*. All of her Regency and Victorian romances have received extensive praise, including several starred reviews from *Publishers Weekly* and *Booklist*. *The Heir* was a *Publishers Weekly* Best Book of 2010, *The Soldier* was a *Publishers Weekly* Best Spring Romance of 2011, and *Lady Sophie's Christmas Wish* won Best Historical Romance of the Year in 2011 from RT Reviewers' Choice Awards. *Lady Louisa's Christmas Knight* was a *Library Journal* Best Book of 2012, and *The Bridegroom Wore Plaid*, the first in her trilogy of Scotland-set Victorian romances, was a *Publishers Weekly* Best Book of 2012. *Darius*, the first in her groundbreaking Regency series The Lonely Lords, was named one of iBooks Store's Best Romances of 2013.

Grace is a practicing family law attorney and lives in rural Maryland. She loves to hear from her readers and can be reached through her website at graceburrowes.com.

31901055988697

"You know anything about horses, Luis?"

"Only what I've learned from Neils and Adelia," Luis said. "Horses are to be respected."

The slight emphasis on the last word had Sid's heart catching. Luis had taken to his riding lessons like nothing else she'd thrown at him, likely because of the people as much as the horses.

"They are to be respected," Mac said, "and cared for. Those two mares are in the beginning stages of neglect, and somebody will have to look after them."

Sid took up a lean on another porch post. "I wish you all the luck in the world with that, Mr. Knightley, because that somebody will not be me or Luis. Now, having settled that, may I offer you a cup of coffee?"

"I'm a tea drinker, actually."

"You're in luck," she said, heading for the door. "The only room we've unpacked is the kitchen, and the only thing we've stocked is the fridge."